# KNOWING MAX

James Long is the author of *Ferney* and four acclaimed thrillers. A former BBC correspondent, he lives with his family in Devon.

JAMES LONG

# KNOWING MAX

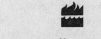

HarperCollins*Publishers*

HarperCollins*Publishers*
77–85 Fulham Palace Road,
Hammersmith, London W6 8JB

www.**fire**and**water**.com

This paperback edition 2000
1 3 5 7 9 8 6 4 2

First published in Great Britain by
HarperCollins*Publishers* 2000

ISBN 0 00 651094 9

Typeset in Minion by
Palimpsest Book Production Limited,
Polmont, Stirlingshire

Printed and bound in Great Britain by
Omnia Books Limited, Glasgow

To the memory of my father, Bill Long,
with whom I would like to have shared this book

# One

In September 1962, I fell in love. I was twelve years old and she was thirty-nine. It was the best day of my childhood and it lasted all year.

Worthing, a geriatric seaside town, was the wrong place for a confused adolescent. Two or three times that summer, I escaped from my fusty home to wander its streets and beaches, on fire with the absurd hope some passing woman might choose me for the other half of a sexual act. It was a painfully quiet place. Every bus journey took an age because at each stop the conductor would need to help three or four very old people up or down off the step.

Just down the coast was Brighton, a different place altogether – Gomorrah with a pier – but I was not allowed to go there by myself. Saturday, September 15th, 1962, was to be a special day because the Colonel was taking me to Brighton.

I had been working towards this, dropping the speed trials into what passed as our conversation in the evenings when I was sent out to the garage to help him. Talking to the Colonel was never easy, but in that heavy old house the three of us shared, my mother, him and me, the language of cars was the only language the Colonel and I had in common. He'd had his 1926 Bentley since the war and he spent two or three evenings each week tinkering with it. His relationship with it was that of a gardener to his garden, something he could potter round, doing little jobs with screwdrivers, leather food and polishing rags. I wanted it to roar and move and break out of the garage on to the open road, but that wasn't important to him. Instead, he would try in his stilted sentences to teach me about camshaft drives and how to preserve nickel plating and I would try to find a response that didn't send him back into his habitual silence. My mother, who was not a friendly person, thought these sojourns in the dark

1

garage at the back of Oakdean were 'nice'. She never came in to see how they worked in practice.

I didn't *like* the idea of spending a whole day in Brighton with him, just the two of us, but if I couldn't go alone it was a price well worth paying. That morning, however, when I got up and ate my cornflakes in the kitchen, I could hear raised voices upstairs, an unusual noise to pierce the muffling, thirst-provoking silence of woollen carpet, damask curtain, brocade pelmet and heavy oak doors. I even heard my mother laugh, but it struck me as a mocking sound. When I was washing up my cereal bowl, the Colonel came downstairs, looked past my shoulder as he always did when he addressed me, and said to the cooker, 'Your mother's under the weather. Have to catch the bus.'

He vanished again without another word. I took it that it was me, not him, who would have to catch the bus.

It was a mixed blessing. Mostly, it was great news – clear, undeniable permission to go to Brighton by myself for the very first time. It wouldn't be another of those puzzling, awkward days when I had to trail after him, trying to guess what his grunts meant and what he wanted me to do next. On the other hand, I would have to get myself to Brighton and I had never been that far by myself.

I arrived there in the late morning after a long and worrying bus journey in which I had fretted constantly about all the things that might go wrong and leave me stranded somewhere I didn't recognize with no way to get home. The sea was in sight for much of the ride, which should have been reassuring. The return bus ticket had taken up all but tuppence of my pocket money. I had an apple and six digestive biscuits in the pocket of my duffel coat, and no money left over to buy a programme for the event. Before I left the house, I thought of risking the stairs to find the Colonel and ask him for some money. I was almost sure he would have given it to me but he might just as easily have been prompted to think twice about the bus journey and changed his mind about letting me go. That was a chance I wasn't prepared to take. Anyway, whatever was happening upstairs lay inside some frightening exclusion zone for adults only, and I didn't dare infringe it.

I'd known about the speed trials since I was ten, when I had asked my mother to cancel *The Eagle* and get me *Motorsport* once a month instead. The yearly event was an inaccessible delight, right there, just down the coast, almost on my doorstep, and this year I would finally be going.

Today, twenty-six years later, I have wandered through Brighton and retraced the route I took that day. The green and cream Southdown bus with its sandpaper seats would have groaned its way off the seafront into the tiny tarmac lagoon of the Pool Valley bus station, open to the sky and surrounded by the high walls of hotels. When I was a quarter of a century younger, I would have got off and walked as fast as I could out to the pier and the sea and the start of it all. I still like to look at the sea but I think I look at it differently now. Then, I could watch the way the waves broke for hours, satisfied with the coiling, tumbling water. Now I think of practicalities, of how a boat would ride the surf, of how the groynes can stand the strain, of what time high tide will be. That's a quarter of a century of living for you.

Today, at the end of it all, my day has been full of memorials. This morning we unveiled a plaque to Natalie, who I miss so much. This afternoon I stood for maybe an hour or more in front of my father's grave and wished I had known him so that I could miss him, too. This evening, I am here where the whole thing began, and before I leave I will walk to the end of this road ahead of me, to the place by the railings which marked the end of my wonderful year.

Back, though, to the beginning.

Because I had spent all the money I had on the bus, it was a shock, as I walked towards the sound of engines, to arrive at a fence with a gate, and a man on the gate collecting half a crown from anyone who wanted to go through. The cars I had come to see were on the other side of the fence and it hadn't occurred to me for a moment that it would cost money to get to them. I could see where I wanted to be, beyond the wooden palisade. There, on the tarmac between the beach and the aquarium, the competing cars were lined up in echelon on both sides of the road, numbers newly applied, wire wheels glinting, taped headlights and bonnet

3

straps proclaiming how special they were. Half a crown stopped me getting there.

'You can go up top,' said the man on the gate, helpfully, 'it's free up there.'

He pointed up to the east, to the high railings where the seafront road climbed away up the cliff. I could see the crowds there, peering down at the lower road, the sea-level road where the cars were taking their turns against the clock. That was all very well, but it was too distant from the action. This was where I had expected to be, down here in the heart of it, peering into open bonnets, smelling the hot engines, soaking up the essence of it all.

I looked at him, eyes stinging with disappointment, hoping he'd change his mind, and then a voice spoke beside me.

'He's with me,' it said, 'pit crew. Got a badge for him somewhere.'

From above, hands came down and in a moment, around one of the duffels of my coat, a loop of string was twisted, carrying a dangling cardboard tag. I turned it round and read the printed words 'Competitor's Assistant', and stared at it in complete astonishment.

'Come on,' said the voice, 'better get to work.'

Safely the other side of the barrier, I looked up at him and stammered my thanks. All I remember is a tall, amused man looking back. If his face made any impression on me, it was about to be totally eclipsed.

'I meant it,' he said. 'Got a job for you, old boy. Come and see my motorcar.'

He led me through the crowd and I had to run to keep up, not daring to take my eyes off him though I so much wanted to look at all the cars we were hurrying past. We hadn't heard of stranger danger then, and even if we had I would still have gone with him. He dived through a gap in the crowd and there was his car. The Brighton and Hove Motor Club encourage all kinds of machines to take part in their annual sprint races. To one side of us was a vast vintage Lagonda. Its owner was using his running board as a picnic table, with a bottle of champagne and a row of glasses balanced on the bonnet. On the other side, a mechanic in RAF overalls still bearing his old unit badges was pop-riveting an aluminium sheet to the front of a skimpy Lotus, fairing in part of its air intake for more speed. Beyond that again was a Mini on fat tyres, with a huge exhaust pipe, but the car we were looking at was sitting there in the middle like a commando amongst boy scouts.

'Wriggle in under, would you, old son,' said the man who'd got me in, opening a tiny driver's door. 'Dropped my half-inch in the pedal box. Hands your size might just reach it. Head first, mind.'

I did what he asked, with the greatest pleasure imaginable, delighted to feel useful, delighted to be involved and above all delighted to be not just allowed, but actually *asked* to squirm down into a real racing car – the like of which I had only ever seen in photos. I knew it was a Lister-Jaguar, a wild two-seater concoction of lightweight aluminium around a brutally powerful Jaguar engine. It was dark blue and across the bonnet was a painted number plate, VPO 275. I was in heaven.

'Can you see it?' said the man.

'Not yet,' I said. It was difficult to see anything down there in the footwell, twisted painfully upside down under the steering wheel. I groped around with my fingers and felt something made of metal which moved as I touched it. It was hooked inside a bracket up above the steering column. 'Found it,' I said, and started trying to wiggle it out.

There was a distant announcement on the loudspeaker.

'Blast!' said the man. 'That's me they're calling. Just got to go and sort something out, old boy. Won't be two ticks.'

I didn't mind if he was two hours. There I was, being a mechanic, part of the team, helping to fix a Lister-Jaguar. I didn't care a bit that the blood was flowing to my head and my right leg was getting cramp. I mattered. The Colonel would have done it himself and told me to hold the torch. This man had just casually let me get on with it. I went on fiddling and found that by shoving my hand up as far as it would go, I could very nearly push the spanner up far enough to come out of the top of the bracket. I very much wanted to do the job properly but I couldn't quite reach.

5

Then there was a noise. The car moved slightly as someone leant on it, a hand gave my foot, sticking out into the cockpit, a shake and an unexpected female voice said, 'Who have we got here?'

I tried to pull myself out but in my haste my coat hooked itself on the brake pedal. 'Hello?' I said. 'The man asked me to get this thing, this spanner out for him. I can't push it up far enough.'

'The man did, did he? See if this helps,' the voice said, and I felt something slapped gently against my leg, out of sight up by the seat.

I reached back and found a screwdriver pressed into my hand. I used it to push the spanner up clear so that it fell on to the floor of the car and, twisting round to unhook my coat, made an undignified exit, bottom first, into the fresh air, holding it triumphantly.

'Here you are,' I said, and she smiled at me and I just stared back at her.

She had stepped out of my dreams, a woman in racing overalls with the zip half-open to show something silky below. She had red, red lipstick, huge brown eyes and a breaking wave of blonde hair. I could smell her perfume and, whatever it was, I have never smelt another one that went straight through all my senses in the same way. She was so unlike any of the few women in my life that I felt I was looking at something altogether new and entirely wonderful. My mother's skin lurked somewhere in dry folds under a camouflage of powder but hers glowed at me as if it were lit from within. She was holding a crash helmet dangling by a strap.

'Thank you,' she said. 'It's time to get this thing going.'

She obviously meant the Lister.

'It's my class next,' she said.

'You're driving this?'

'Oh, don't you start,' she said, and I didn't understand. She looked around her. 'Where's he gone?'

'They called him on the loudspeakers,' I told her breathlessly.

'You can help me, then,' she said. She jumped into the car and started it up with a loud *baroom* from the exhaust, then to my intense delight she got out again and gestured me into the seat in her place. 'Just keep giving the accelerator little prods,' she said. 'Keep it revving. Not too hard. It's the pedal on the right.'

6

'I know that,' I said eagerly.

'Don't touch anything else,' she said, then she leant into the cockpit, dropped her helmet in next to me, gripped the steering wheel and started to push the car. She was bending in over me in her effort so that her shoulder was against mine and her long hair swung against my cheek. As the car started to roll, she pulled the wheel over, brushing against me all the more. I was enveloped in a cloud of hair and scent and I was sitting holding the wood-rimmed steering wheel of a Lister. It didn't occur to me for a moment that she was only a few years short of my mother's age. My mother didn't even seem to be the same sex as this fragrant essence of womanhood. As if that wasn't enough, I was allowed, no, more than allowed, *required* to keep twitching that huge accelerator with my foot and each twitch sent that raspy, rackety, voodoo engine yelling out its horsepower at my command. Every teenage boy in that watching crowd, and probably all of the men too, would have given anything to be where I was, but I knew if I'd had to choose between the two parts of the experience, between steering the car and having her nuzzle against me, I would have chosen her every time.

'We always push it up to the line, it saves the clutch,' she said into my ear in explanation.

I didn't care what it saved.

'I can do the steering,' I said.

'All right,' she said, 'just stay behind the others. The brake is ... I suppose you know?'

I nodded.

'I wish I'd had a son like you,' she said, and bent to push again.

I don't suppose I was at the wheel of the car for more than a minute, but that minute was entirely magical. When I jumped out of the car and helped my fairy godmother on with her helmet, I was her complete slave and resolved that I would only marry a woman who drove racing cars. The loudspeaker announced the final runs in the Ladies' Class and I learnt that she was called Virginia, a perfect name. She was matched against a woman in an XK150 but I only had eyes for the Lister. When the starter gave his signal, Virginia took off in a cloud of rubber smoke and snaked away round a slight curve, accelerating hard towards the banner which marked the finishing line, a kilometre up the road.

She set the fastest time in the class and there was something extra in that, something proud and sexy, and when she drove back down the track with all the other returning cars, it was okay to return her hug, which was almost too much for me.

In the lunchbreak, I sat on the edge of their circle watching her. When she saw the digestive biscuits, she gave me strange sandwiches of thin brown bread with strong slices of orange fish inside, and because she gave them to me I liked them. Men had appeared from everywhere to join the circle and one or two other women too, but they were just wives, not drivers, and they couldn't hold a candle to her. The men got in the way though and when one of them gave me a spare programme, I decided to go off and look at the other cars in the hope that she would find she missed me.

When I came back, the racing was getting started again and she was nowhere in sight so I climbed up on to the lower promenade, making sure my tag showed prominently so everyone would know I was a Competitor's Assistant and that I belonged here in the restricted area, not up above where anyone could watch for nothing. I thought about her more than the cars until I saw the Lister coming up to the line again, but the programme told me this was not Virginia driving but a man with the same surname, who had to be her husband. I watched him as the car howled past me, feeling doubly jealous, and all I could really see was his helmet. I only forgave him the sin of being married to her because he was the one who got me in.

I found her again, by herself, before the end of the day and she asked me where I lived and whether I always came. I admitted it was the first time, and she said, 'Well, come again next year. Tell them at the gate that you're with us. Promise?' And she held both my hands in hers while she was saying it.

I promised and I thought about her all year.

Now, at the end of the whole business, on this day of memorials, I have come back here to Brighton to lay Max to rest and because I am in no hurry, I have chosen to walk this deserted tarmac road

8

away eastward from the Palace Pier to see if that helps connect me to the boy I was and all the people I have been in between. Like Max, I have lived several lives, but mine were consecutive whereas I suspect his were always concurrent.

On Brighton beach it's easy to get back in touch with the past because down here by the sea so little has changed. The low road eastward starts at the roundabout where the Palace Pier strides out into the waves, assailed by storms and rust. The poor pier has suffered reverses in its life. Built to spider out above the heaving sea, to thrill Victorians with smells and sights of air and water, it now confounds that purpose by sucking visitors inside its halls to gaudy screens. There, brain-frying machines suck their coins in exchange for electronic approximations of racing, shooting and fighting and spew them back to the shore less calm, less rich and less in tune with the world.

The road they use for the speed trials is simply Madeira Drive for the other three hundred and sixty-four days of the year, a quiet place once you've got past the aquarium, which may be called 'Sea World' these days but will always be the aquarium to me. To the right, there's just the narrow-gauge track of the Volks electric railway (opened in 1883 as its signs say) and a primitive mini-golf course between the road and the shingle banks. Each of the golf-course obstacles is outlined in moulded concrete, chipped all over as if assaulted by maddened putter-wielding losers, and the battered concrete is covered by a thick salve of gloss paint in primary red, yellow and blue. It is hard to imagine paying money for the experience of playing on it.

On the land side, the cliff is climbing and the colonnades of the long promenade are filled in underneath by angling shops, chippies, palmists and a tiled Victorian lavatory whose massive porcelain is a dense pleasure to pee on, then round a slight curve Madeira Drive aims its bumpy surface, arrow-straight, towards the east.

I stand in the road for a moment and imagine myself on a start-line. Let in the clutch here, push the throttle hard and in fifteen seconds you could be hurtling through the X which marks the spot I was heading for. Easy, you might think. In my mind, unbidden but not unexpected, a rope-trick line of smoke climbs into still, summer air – black and coiling, straight up into the sky. This side of the sea at the column's base, a furnace has come out of nowhere to consume something precious and I am pushing against the flow of a crowd running to look, pushing to get away but every few steps I have no choice but to look back and each time the column of smoke has risen higher and higher and higher.

Today I have come to do a job so I put the memory away and walk on, below the wide promenade, supported on iron tracery – each arch crowned at its apex by a cast head which alternates, arch by arch, between a bearded man who could be Neptune and a haughty woman who could be anyone but deserves a name like Minerva or Persephone or Ariadne. On my right, along the beach, they still keep wooden fishing boats, with swept-up sterns to defeat the surf, dragged up beside the rusting winches. Then, after perhaps a thousand paces we come to the railings by the Peter Pan playground – the railings I have come to see.

This place on Brighton beach, between high tide's hissing shingle and the road, has been the pivot of my life.

# Two

It was in a dark London auction room, eleven years after that magical day at Brighton, that I first saw the name 'Max Birkin Owen' in neat lettering on the lid of an old leather trunk. What has happened since then has felt like a ghost story running backwards, a dead man gradually coming back to life. I had never heard of Max when I saw the trunk, but I had heard his surnames. Indeed, the reason I paused to look at the trunk was that I had heard those names many, many times.

'Birkin Owen' was the nearest anyone ever came to a swear-word in the house where I spent my childhood. If I did anything slapdash, like jumping over a flowerbed instead of going round by the path, the Colonel would say, 'Don't be a Birkin Owen.' On the one occasion he let me tighten a mudguard stay on the Bentley and I went at the job with an adjustable wrench instead of the right five-eighths Whitworth ring spanner, he pulled it out of my hand with a savagely cross look and said, 'That's a Birkin Owen of a job. Don't ever do that again!' Anything he thought pretentious or cocky got the same response. It never struck me to ask who Birkin Owen was, I thought it was an expression perhaps everyone who'd been in the army used, just as I thought for years that 'misled' was the past tense of the verb 'to misle'. My childhood was all like that, for fear of asking.

I am quite sure he would have called me a Birkin Owen on the day in the spring of 1973, just a few months before I found the trunk, when I finally got deeply into the trouble I had been heading for. When the events of that day were over, I made my way again to the railings on Madeira Drive to find solitude. I was five years out of school, two years out of university and I leant on that same railing with the judge's words rattling through my head. An hour earlier I had been quite sure I was going to spend the rest of the year in prison.

11

What saved me, if that's the right way to put it, was the judge's view of the essential worthiness of my class. It didn't feel like that to me at the time. It felt more as if he had branded me untouchable to my Brighton friends, which was probably exactly what he intended.

'I now turn to you, Miles Drummond,' he had said, leaving the Gypsy and Joe the Wheel gaping in disbelief at the prospect of the six-month sentence they had each just been given. I was standing next to them in the dock, suddenly acutely aware that there was, after all, a system of rules that applied even to people like me. Somewhere in the back of my mind I had supposed that the law was for them. Not for me. It still all felt like a huge mistake.

'You are a foolish young man of twenty-three who has let his family down very badly indeed,' he said, peering from below his wig. 'However, I do have some hope for you. The evidence presented here suggests to me that you have fallen in with a bad lot and that a severe warning, coupled with a period of probation, may serve to bring you to your senses.'

The way the other two looked at me as he went on was what really got me. They weren't angry, they just wore identical, cynical half-smiles that said, yeah, that's right, you were always just pretending to be like us, weren't you?

I wasn't pretending, I was *being*. I was trying to be entirely different, with new people who thought and spoke differently and who in every aspect of their existence counteracted the entrenched, stifling rigidities of the world I had grown up in. It seemed to me as I listened to the judge and felt him fanning the flames of their rejection that I should not be blamed if others, for their own reasons, tried to claim me back as one of a clan I had left. It was monstrously unfair.

The other two were taken down to the cells. I got probation hung on me like the dead albatross round the Ancient Mariner's neck.

I walked out of the court that day, tearing off my tie, and there was no joy in seeing the rest of them, sitting on the pavement, waiting for me.

'Here's young Miles Drummond,' said Mugger in a take-off of the judge's voice. 'Such a good family background, don't you know. I have character references here from his Headmaster, his Housemaster and His Grace the Archbishop of Arsehole. A positively glowing academic record and as for his prowess with a bat . . . need I say more? Got into bad company, you know. Even changed his bleeding name.'

I walked straight past them.

'Come on Milo,' Lena called after me, ''s'only a joke.'

It wasn't a joke to me.

Madeira Drive seemed to me then to be the place where Miles Drummond first breathed in the seeds that germinated into Milo Malan. It was where I went that afternoon after the judge condemned me to freedom, straight down from the courts through the edge of Kemp Town to the sea. I wanted to be left alone. I wanted something to stare at. The sea seemed best. My head was full of embarrassed anger as the most demeaning moments of the trial shouted at me inside, repeating over and over. Worse than that, worse than the judge, worse than Mugger's mockery was the knife-memory of the defining moment at the beginning of it when the door of the flat crashed in and through a haze of smoke I heard a voice say, 'Police! Stay right where you are, all of you.' That was the dividing moment when the old me, the wholesome me, the timid me, screamed frightened screams inside and the outer me, the fake, streetwise, word-slurring shell fought to shut it in and only my wild eyes showed through.

I walked because I wanted to get away from everything that had just happened. My feet weren't fast enough for me. They couldn't be, because what I really wanted to get away from was myself.

The police cells were the next bad thing. The whole demeaning interchange with the cold-eyed custody sergeant, where I had to admit an identity and where I was put in a cell, a place I had never ever expected to be. I can still see that cell with absolute clarity. The light came in from high up on the right-hand wall, through rows of paler squares in two thick blocks of opaque glass. The bench, which was a bed of sorts, had a thin mattress in a stiff blue plastic cover. To the left, through an opening, was a lavatory which was no more than a hole covered with a fixed wooden seat. At first I couldn't bring myself to sit on that seat out of an odd

13

fear that something left by all those who had sat there before me might creep into me. When the black heavy door was swung shut and the cover over the inspection hole flicked down, I had only my thoughts for company and I did not want to be left alone just with me in that place.

I couldn't bear the terrible thought of prison but, almost as bad, I couldn't bear to be spared it in such a demeaning way. In a ferment of contradictory fears, caught somewhere between the restrained child Miles and the emerging free Milo, I came down to this place by the railings to get my bearings.

There are three levels to the seafront around that place. It is well to the east of the hubbub around the head of the pier. On the top level where I first stopped and gazed out to sea, the main road towards Newhaven and Hastings is backed by cream ranks of bow-fronted hotels with names borrowed from a grandiose past of empire and aristocracy. The railings along the edge of this promenade are thick cast iron, painted a pale greeny-blue, a shade I always think of as Conway Blue from childhood memories of my mother's bulgy little Austin. Details like the Austin factory's name for that colour seemed quite huge when I was seven. The hand rail is a thick cylinder of hard oak. The salt gales of the last century have turned it grey and have grooved meandering crevasses into the grain of its outer surface, but they've hardly touched it really. Those Victorians knew what they were doing.

From there, after a while, I went down the steps which run slantwise down the cliff, whose rock is here encased in grey concrete and covered in clumps of creeper. Two thirds of the way down, the stairs are interrupted by a wide promenade supported on that fancy iron framework, with its cast heads crowning each arch. Down the last flight of steps and you're underneath that promenade, where soft flutters of pigeons inhabit the high corner perches made for them by the girders. Now there's just Madeira Drive separating you from the beach but it's almost safe to close your eyes and step out across it blind. This is not a through-route to anywhere.

Beyond that again, the far side of the seaward pavement, is my particular railing which forms the inland boundary of the tawdry thirty-yard square enclosure called the Peter Pan playground though it is a long, long time since swings and rocking horses provided sufficient entertainment to seaside holiday children. Its three rails are all metal, forming a salient, poking out into the great banks of shingle which slip and slide down to the waves.

You could say that line from the top promenade down to the playground is one of the two bearings that mark the spot by the railings. It had been my line of sight the second time I went to the speed trials, in September 1963. The other bearing, the one that crosses it at right angles, is the line of Madeira Drive itself.

Right through this story, the story of the trunk and what was in it, I've had bearings in my mind. In all the time I've spent studying Max Birkin Owen, I have been trying to get his bearings, to find some crossing point of all the different opinions of him that would pin him down and tell me exactly what he was. I should have remembered the very first lessons I had on the subject. On a summer afternoon at boarding school, where I had been sent to get myself out from under the Colonel's and my mother's feet, I sat in a hot wooden hut which stank of creosote on the hill at the back of my school. Wednesday afternoon was CCF afternoon – the day when we had to dress up in the unconvincing, old, itchy uniforms of the school's Combined Cadet Force to practise for the possibility that one day we might have the honour of joining all the names on the school war memorial. I was in the naval section, and because of that I was shown how to hold a hand-bearing compass at arm's length so that the notched sight lined up with a prominent landmark, how to wait patiently while the swinging compass card steadied and how to read off the bearing, which usually continued wobbling around alarmingly to the detriment of accuracy.

When Mr Crick, the Latin master, in his absurd once-a-week naval officer's uniform, wasn't in earshot, we put down each other's efforts with the biting, destructive cleverness which serves as conversation in public schools and in all the institutions where those who have learnt it group together in later life. It was that style of talk, all speed and vicious wit, applauded by the cloistered teachers as pure intelligence, which was the first thing I sought to shed when I left school, joined a slightly wider world at university and found to my surprise that it was possible to interact with others in a less abrasive way.

Sweating in a coarse blue uniform, flapping bell-bottoms ironed, as we were forced to do with the seven horizontal creases for the seven seas, forehead rubbed by an absurd cap decorated with a Combined Cadet Force cap-band, I stood outside the hut to discover that the tall chimneys of Portslade power station, down there by the sea, bore roughly ninety degrees from me. That seemed to me to contain some element of certainty. At least it told me where I could look to find the chimneys and where they could look to find me.

As a piece of useful information, it was ridiculed by Mr Crick. A cross-bearing was what we needed, he said, some other landmark off to one side to give a second bearing. Only then, when we marked the two lines on the map and saw where they crossed, would we have any idea where we were. I knew where I was – in a shed, wasting a Wednesday afternoon.

My two lines on the map looked impressively precise. The cross where they met was a perfect definition of my position. In the search for certainty it seemed good to leave well alone. Unfortunately, there is one more thing you need to know about bearings and it is the most important thing. There is no certainty. Two bearings provide only an illusion. If you are at sea, taking a position from just two bearings will run you on to the rocks because human error, in the form of your wobbly hand, means both those lines are surely wrong. You need three bearings, not two, and what three bearings give you is definite uncertainty. The third line you draw will hardly ever pass through the point where the others meet. It will, instead, pass to one side of that point and the three lines will together form a triangle known to sailors as a cocked hat. Sailors quickly learn to take a very jaundiced view of rocks sharing the same triangle because their ship could be anywhere within it.

That's as close as you can expect to get with bearings thanks to the nature of human error and it is a metaphor which serves very well in this story. In all my efforts to find Max, to compare the different bearings, from the different viewpoints of those who knew him, I've never got a precise fix. Max subjected himself to a lot of human error, and I've always wound up with a large cocked hat.

*     *     *

16

On this day, after the trial, when I tried to get my own bearings on who I was, I seemed to be trapped back in childhood. I stood for ages, fingering the bottom railing by the playground. The uprights were caked in successive annual layers of that same blue-green municipal paint, grown so thick that it would peel off the iron knobs inside like a conker shell if you could crack it open. The paint was meant to protect the old iron from the scouring sea-salt air, slapped on over the rest, but the iron within had managed to show itself, sending its rust stains creeping to the outside world. The next coat must have been due. I kept fingering the top rail because I was amazed by what I had just found. My fingers, curled around it, had just slid into a confusion of missing metal low down on the far side where the tubing had been torn apart and welded crudely back together again. The sharp edges had been filed flat but there was an irregular chunk out of the tube, all the way through to the hollow centre. Its edges had been further softened by subsequent years of thick paint but there was no disguising the scar.

It was a vivid witness and it brought back that old column of smoke straight away, the smoke that had pushed straight up into the sky, higher and higher each time I had turned to look, all the way back to the head of the pier where the shielding buildings round the bus station had hidden it.

Later, in 1973, older, but not much wiser than I had been in 1963, I left the railing and followed the same direction back towards the pier. When I arrived there, the first thing I saw was the *Evening Argus* placard: *General's son on drugs charge*, it said.

Because of the mistake over the rank, it took five heartbeats before I realized it meant me.

# *Three*

The summer of 1973 brought a lot of changes. When my demeaning probation was over, I moved from Brighton to London because
I was no longer welcomed by the friends I'd had there. The Colonel
died during that time and an odd telegram from my mother
suggested I should not attend his funeral. She sold Oakdean very
quickly and moved to Jersey and it was three months before she
sent me her new address. Finally, in my first month in London,
Cat moved in with me, into my dark and soiled flat in North
Kensington whose walls had the property of blotting up any
daylight which found its way in.

On the Thursday when I found the trunk, the alarm punched
me from sleep at half past eight. Cat grunted, pulled the bedclothes
over her head and lashed out backwards with her feet, kicking me
hard on the knee as I rolled towards her. I looked warily at what
I could see of her shoulder and the long coil of her hair, which
was the colour of dried blood, then I inched my way out of bed.
She was older than me, she seemed to me to be a lot more real
and, being a creature of the night, she was entitled to her views
on early starts.

I can't remember the exact date, which seems odd, now. It
was undoubtedly a Thursday because the Randall's sales only
took place on Thursdays. Friday, I would have been up even
earlier, to scour the stalls of the Golbourne Road street market
looking for the sorts of thing I could buy and sell. That was what
I did. In my last term at university, most of the people I knew had
gone through the rituals of meetings with the appointments board,
job applications and interviews with the staff departments of big
corporations or city broking firms. Because I wasn't prepared
to have it all out with my mother and the Colonel, I went
through the motions and my first interview was with a firm
of brokers in the City. From the moment I got out of the tube

at Bank station I knew it wasn't for me. A pompous man in an expensive suit condescended to me, raised an eyebrow at my clothes then tripped me up with a series of questions about things I cared nothing whatsoever for – invisible exports, gross domestic product and the shape of the yield curve. Economics had definitely been the downside of my degree. The politics and philosophy had been far more to my liking but where could you earn a salary from those?

'I don't think your heart is really in this,' he said after five minutes. 'Shall we stop it here?'

I nodded.

'I'm a busy man,' he said. 'I'm sure all the other people you'll see wherever else you have interviews are just as busy. Why don't you do yourself and them a favour and decide what you want out of life before you waste their time?'

I knew what I wanted. I didn't want to be anywhere near people like him. I didn't want to have to wear a suit and I didn't want to travel in the rattling, banging, sweaty tube day in day out, sardined face to face with all the other slaves heading for the concrete canyons to spend their dark days mucking out the stables of the money-beasts.

What I liked was finding gold in a sea of dross, knowing enough to spot something rare and connect it up with the person who would recognize and value it. After a short sequence of odd jobs and even odder jobs, I decided from now on that I was a dealer and my hunting ground was the part of west London where I lived, around Portobello Road, where, under the booming, droning stilts of the raised motorway, there were streets full of old, tall terraces of houses broken up into decaying flats. I liked living there. A broad ethnic mix of people brought a dash of spice to Victorian decay. Every week, a rich flotsam of my sort of stuff would wash up in the street markets and the auctions.

It was an area where old people died alone and the landlords would let the scavengers in, getting a handful of coins and an empty room in exchange. Most of what they'd find, and what they'd sift in turn out on to the market stalls and the auction house tables was sad tat – most, but not all.

I specialized because without a specialization, those endless ranks of rubbish would drive you to distraction and reduce you to the level of the dead-eyed traders who didn't care if what they sold was a scratched record or a plastic handbag so long as it made them twenty pence. I was looking for the stuff you could buy for twenty pence and sell for twenty pounds: wartime relics, bits of planes or boats or trains, rare model cars.

Cat called me a retard when I told her what it was I bought and sold. I stressed it differently from then on. 'Combat aircraft spares' was what I said when someone asked and I kept a Hurricane altimeter and a control column spade-grip from a Mitchell bomber on the shelves to show people what I meant.

I wanted Cat to approve because Cat taking me to bed was an experience I had somehow never expected to have. She had scars on both wrists and injection pin-pricks in the veins of her arms. She had sinews and muscles and patches of pigmentation from long rough spells on the faraway primitive beaches where the seriously unfettered people went. She had a rolling, snaky way of walking and a way of holding her head back, laughing, as she stopped to talk to equally free, dangerous people, which I longed to copy. All that freedom was contained in a tough, rangy body with wide thighs and heavy, dark-tipped breasts and I was amazingly flattered to be seized on by her, to be moved in with, to be bedded and lived off. In moments of clarity I suspected that she did all these things out of sheer perversity as a challenge and as a joke to her friends so that the legend of Cat would be enhanced by this, her predation. There were not many such moments of clarity. For me, barely used to the nervous puppy nudity of nice girls still heading for their final shape, it was more thrilling than I could ever have imagined and I wanted nothing more than for Cat to take *me* as seriously as she seemed sometimes to take my body. There was no question of commitment with Cat – she was feral and dangerous and I knew that one day she might vanish in a puff of smoke. The future was not something you had to consider with Cat. As for what I did, she was wise to it.

'Piss off, Milo,' she said, 'that's not what you do, not really. Aircraft spares? You buy toys, for God's sake. I'm not even sure you sell them, you jerk. They're mostly in that box under the bed. I looked.'

'Yeah? What do you think I was doing in Greece?' I replied. 'Two Merlin engines. Still in their crates. As good as new. I cleared five grand on those two.'

'Before my time,' she said, unimpressed. 'Go out and find some more if you're so good at it. Anyway what's an engine but a fucking great toy? Fuck off and play with your engines and your toy cars and your trust fund.'

She was wide of the mark. I didn't have a trust fund as such, only a bit of monthly money from the estate of a great-aunt, but Cat didn't understand my approach to all this. I'd taken the trouble to become an expert. Die-cast toys of a certain age were proper antiques requiring expertise. She had no idea of the skill involved in telling the remains of a pre-war 24 series Dinky sports tourer from a repainted 36 series, of looking for the little differences in the wheels, the chassis and the paint that made an enormous difference to the value. Eighty quid for one, a fiver for the other if you were lucky. I made quite a bit of money that way, but sometimes I had to keep the pieces for a while before I could get the right price from the dealers with their own shops and their rich Japanese clients. That was the only reason they were in the box under the bed.

I'd never have admitted as much to her, but by itself I might have felt a bit uneasy about all that, might have suffered the occasional twinge of doubt about the manliness of toy-selling as a way of life, but the aircraft stuff made it okay. Real men flew old planes and whenever I found something to sell them, a bit of that rubbed off.

I left the house that Thursday, feeling some sort of relief that she was asleep, that I was awake and that I could spend the next two or three hours free of her scrutiny and not concerning myself with what she might think. When I unchained my motorbike, I even pushed it way down the road so I could be sure she would not hear me starting up. I didn't want her to have any fulcrum to give her leverage over my morning. The BSA was in an evil mood and backfired with a small fireball out of the carburettors on the tenth kick. I counted the kicks out of some private superstition – starting it with less than twelve meant a good day, twelve to fifteen was normal, more than that was bad news. The superstition had no basis and the results never tallied, but I still did it. This time, to be on the safe side I gave up on eleven and hauled the bike to the top of the slope down to the builders' yard where I straddled it and pushed off, but when I let in the clutch at the bottom, the back wheel locked, slewed sideways and the bike tipped me off into the road. That hurt but, having inflicted pain, the bike started perfectly on the next kick.

At the junction with Ladbroke Grove a policeman turned his head at the noise of my exhaust and showed signs of taking an interest in the state of the silencer, but a providential gap in the traffic let me blast across the road and out of his way before he could be quite sure I had realized he was trying to stop me.

I was always excited when I first walked into an auction room. When my eyes got used to the low light levels in Randall's barn-like building, they would be flicking in all directions across the ranks of tables, expecting instant results before reality set in and the sheer boring quantity of the rubbish on display began to wear me down. Keeping your concentration up was the only way to find things, but it could be quite demanding. This morning, I had an hour to view before the sale started at ten and it wasn't crowded. That should have been good news, but instead it made me worry. There had to be a better auction somewhere else or the other dealers would be here, too.

I found one possible treasure almost straight away. To get the good stuff, you had to look for the unsorted, middle-class detritus in the cardboard box job-lots that held muddled-up drawer contents and the results of the emptying out of cupboards. West London was good for the sorts of objects I was buying in those days. The officer class died more often in west London than in other parts of the city.

As a prospector can be led to gold by traces of copper ore, so I homed in on a copy of *Nice Types*, a wartime collection of RAF cartoons, on top of a big box. It wasn't worth anything much by itself but it was a signpost. Someone who had owned that might have had a lot more in his library. Sure enough, lower down in the box I found a shabby copy of pilot's notes for a Brewster Buffalo – better, and under that, best of all, an RAF-issue pilot's log-book.

I made a note of the lot number and shoved the log-book inside one of the old magazines low down in the box, hoping nobody else would find it. It looked well worth the bother, belonging to a pilot in 609, a Typhoon squadron. A snatched look at the entries for 1944 showed some dense, tiny writing which might easily turn out to be his part in the crushing of the Panzers at the battle of the Falaise Gap. That's what I mean by being a specialist. The combat details would make all the difference to its value and I knew at least two people who would pay thirty quid for that, maybe even fifty if it was what I thought. It was a high lot number, so it wouldn't be coming up before lunch.

There wasn't much else among the small lots and it was only because I had to go back past the furniture to get to the exit that I even saw the trunk. I could easily have missed it. I had to stop because a sinewy old man wearing two unmatched halves of a tracksuit was crouched down in the aisle, trying to get it open.

'Have yer got strong fingers?' he said, squinting up at me. 'I can't shift this bugger.'

He was trying to rotate the brass lever of its lock. I bent down and did my best but it wouldn't move at all.

'I think it's locked,' I said.

He said something back but I didn't notice because I was staring at the top of the trunk, where in black capital letters it said: CAPTAIN MAX BIRKIN OWEN. GRENADIER GUARDS.

That old reproof came to my ears in the Colonel's voice, which I would never hear again, and, just for a moment, I actually missed him.

The trunk was about three feet long, covered in brown leather with reinforced leather corners and bamboo strips, skids or strengtheners perhaps, right round it. It had the fragile remains of a score of luggage labels stuck to it. One said 'Furness Withy', another – very Art Deco – said 'Waldorf Asto . . .' and ended in a tear.

The old man in the tracksuit had got one of the auctioneers over, who did that authority thing of trying to open it himself instead of believing us, then scratched his head.

'It's as seen,' he said, 'take it or leave it. You could probably get it open with a pin.' He picked it up by the handle at one end but put it back down quickly. 'Comes with contents,' he said.

· 'What *are* the contents?' said the old man.

'No idea. Adds to the fun,' said the auctioneer. 'You decide. Might be the crown jewels in there.'

'Might be jack shit,' said the old man, and went off in a huff.

I looked at it. I was on a motorbike and I needed a locked trunk like a hole in the head, but the Colonel was dead and I'd never understood the Birkin Owen thing and besides there was that christian name. George Birkin Owen or David Birkin Owen might not have carried the same overtones, but Max? Max seemed to go perfectly with that sort of behaviour which had always brought the name to the Colonel's lips. There was a mystery here just crying out for solution.

It was lot seventeen, so I sat in an armchair, which was lot thirty-one, and thought about it. An old trunk shouldn't go for much, especially if the lock would need forcing and you'd have to buy the contents blind. Nagging in my mind was the fear that someone else had already seen what was inside and jammed the lock to stop anyone else finding out. That might push the price up and I wasn't flush with cash. Then I worried about what Cat would think of my dealing skills when I came back with it. I could hardly say to her that I'd bought it in a sentimental moment because of a childhood association. The thought of not buying it was worse, though.

When the auction started, it all looked good. The auctioneer rattled off the terms and conditions and only half the first few lots attracted any bids at all. I spent the time constantly changing my mind on my top limit. Ten quid? Fifteen? Twenty? At twenty there wouldn't be enough left for the week's rent, let alone food.

'Lot seventeen,' said the auctioneer. 'Leather trunk. Locked. Full of something. Could be the crown jewels.' He wasn't one to leave a tired joke to rest. 'What am I bid? Five million quid?'

My heart was pounding. It's bad, bidding when you feel like that. You get your timing all wrong and a good auctioneer can take you to the cleaners. There was a dead silence. 'A fiver?' he said. 'Four?' He lost patience then. 'Two to start me,' he said. 'Who's got two quid, then?'

I stuck my hand up and that was it. He knocked it down to me so fast I couldn't believe it, which left me no longer sure if I was pleased or not and with a transport problem.

I had to get a taxi to take it home. I put it in the hall without disturbing Cat, walked back to get the bike and found something that really pissed me off. When I'd left it outside Randall's, my helmet had been hanging from the handlebars with a lock through its buckle. Now there was just the lock and no helmet where some passing tea-leaf must have sliced through the strap. A few weeks earlier and it wouldn't have mattered that much. I would have ridden home with the wind in my hair, which was the way I liked it, but in those few weeks the helmet law had arrived and the safety of my head was now a matter of government regulation. It cost me a tenner in a second-hand shop to buy a horrible yellow one that looked as if it was made of brittle plastic and was uncomfortably tight. My morning was turning out to be expensive.

I rode back quite slowly to the flat, still thinking of what I could say to Cat. That set me thinking about her again, about the ups and downs of being with her. There was something fantastically attractive and pleasingly decadent about having an older woman. Cat was certainly thirty, could even be more – she wouldn't say. She was sexy-sleazy. In past times you would have called her a wench or maybe even a trollop. There wasn't really a word for it now. I found her, or rather she found me, at a party in Balham, rolling joints with grass over which she carefully sprinkled a few drops of hash oil out of a tiny, cut-glass bottle. I was impressed by that and by her. She'd lived a lot. There was no room for uncertainty in her and no wish or need to have dealings with anyone who didn't live life more or less her way.

There was a downside which stemmed from that. Cat had a knack of pinning my past back on me, finding my old blazer behind all the other stuff in the cupboard, holding up a cricket team photo she'd dug out of a drawer, taking off my voice if ever I let myself slip for a moment out of London-rough.

It was nearly twelve when I got back to the flat and to my surprise she was coming out of the front door with a cotton bag slung over her shoulder and my patchwork jacket on.

'Where are you going?' I said.

'Out,' she said. 'Off. Away.'

'Anywhere special?'

'Everywhere special.'

'Well, when will I see you then?'

'When I get back.'

I could hear a note in my voice which didn't sound at all the way I wanted to sound, so I just shrugged. She made a face which could have meant anything, swayed round me and was off up the pavement without a backward glance. I watched her go, then watched her stop fifty yards up where a Transit van was parked and climb into the passenger seat. The van pulled out and accelerated past me. Neither the driver nor Cat looked at me as they went by. He was big, bald and tattooed with mirror shades hiding his eyes.

He made me feel very young.

Inside, the trunk was untouched but the mail was. There was just one letter and it was clearly addressed to me. That hadn't stopped Cat opening it. I recognized the handwriting and had a sinking feeling straight away, not from what the letter might say but from what Cat would have thought of what it said. I read it through, standing in the kitchen with the paper angled to try to catch some light through the grey net curtain. The first half wasn't too bad, just a lot of inconsequential chat from Sussex, though there was an embarrassing reference to missing my mother and rather a lot about riding. The second half did the damage, particularly the way it ended:

> Well, Miles, it does feel a terribly long time since I've seen you and there's a lot I want to say that won't fit into an envelope. I think it's sad when someone special just disappears from life as you seem to have done and I do miss you. I rode up to Cissbury Ring yesterday and stopped for a while just inside the ramparts and I realized with a shock that it's two years since you and I were there and we said all those things. I don't know if you have anyone to have those sort of talks with at the moment, but I don't think I do.

How oblique, I thought, how typically oblique. She's writing

26

to someone who doesn't exist any more. There's no more Miles. Good riddance to him. She wouldn't like Milo.

There's a ball at Pickworth Park the weekend after next. Well, all right, yes it is the Hunt but there'll be loads of people we know there and they used to be fun, didn't they? It would be so good to catch up. I can get tickets if you drop me a line this week, and you don't have to sleep under a hedge. Mother says the spare room's waiting for you if you want. Do come.
Love and kisses,
Tiggy.

Cat had scrawled a message across the bottom: *Oh yes*, she'd written, *Do come. We can go in the stables and shag in the horse poo. Such fun. Kitty.*
It would have been quite exciting to think she'd gone off in a huff because of the letter, but I knew that wouldn't have crossed her mind. She'd just gone off. Full stop. She'd taken ten quid from the rent tin, *my* ten quid, and the only sign that she was ever coming back was that her hubble-bubble was still on top of the fridge. I knew she would have taken it with her if her departure had been permanent.
I looked at the trunk and started trying to pick the lock.

# *Four*

The trunk was promisingly heavy. When I'd put it in the taxi, it had been as much as I could do to lift it. Picking a lock doesn't sound all that hard, but I had no idea of the principles involved beyond sticking in a bit of wire and fiddling about. All I could find was a paperclip and it kept bending, so I got out my biggest screwdriver and, in an act that felt like vandalism, I levered underneath it until the bottom half of the lock sheared completely away from the leather. Then I just looked at it for a long moment of expectation before I opened it.

The lid was lined inside with ancient, fibrous material, striped like mattress ticking, and the stale air released around me filled my nostrils with Egyptian desiccation. I was looking at a tightly interwoven heap of papers, letters and photographs. It was what I had half expected, and wholly desired, since I tipped it up on end getting it out of the cab and felt the sliding movement in the weight of the contents slipping down inside. It was what I had most wanted it to be – a trunk full of information.

On top of the whole lot was a pair of old goggles with a brittle leather strap. Underneath them, the very first of all of Max's papers that I ever read, was a telegram – pale yellow with the printed message stuck on in strips of thin white paper.

It said: ONLY YOU. ALWAYS. WHAT ELSE MATTERS. NATALIE.

I would have said, 'Hello Natalie,' if I'd known.

The goggles might have been for flying, except that immediately under them, sinking a barbed hook into my attention, was just the sort of thing I love to find and which immediately distracted me from the telegram, pungent though it was with old passion. It was a large black-and-white photo taken during a motor-race. In the background was a grandstand packed with people, its flimsy roof held up by scaffold poles from which the giant trumpets of an old-style public-address system hung. The barrier between the grandstand and the track was draped with period advertisements which said 'Capstan', '*Autocar* – the motorists' magazine' and 'From start to finish, the *Daily Express*'. The car was a Healey Silverstone. The photo was no amateur snap, it was a large, beautifully printed professional shot and everything about it gave its date away as the fifties. The car's separate headlights had been turned back to front for steamlining, but it was the driver who really came from a different age of racing. He was tall enough to stick up into the air-stream. Instead of modern overalls, he wore a dark sweater with the collar of his shirt sticking out, and a linen helmet with goggles pushed up clear of his eyes. He was hunched up close to the big steering wheel.

This appealed both to the small boy in me, the boy who loved fast cars, and to the dealer. It held the possibility of recompense for the money I'd had to spend on crash helmet and cabs. If there was any more of this sort of stuff I could certainly sell it, if the small boy would let me. I tried to rush into it, to reach deeper into the pile, but soon realized it was going to be a long, slow job. You can get a great deal of paper into a three-foot trunk and what filled it made up a dense deposit of envelopes, bills, photos, negatives and maps in sedimentary layers, so overlapping and interwoven that you could not mine far down without ripping them.

I thought I would spend the rest of the day sorting out the good bits and see what I could make of Max Birkin Owen in the process. It already felt like a great way to pass the time – nice and casual.

With the next handful of papers I took, a ghost reached out to me from inside. It contained a folded sheaf of stiffened, yellowed air mail paper covered in spidery, blue-ink handwriting. It wasn't a letter. Each page was numbered at the top right-hand corner and the first page bore a title, written in capitals and underlined, 'A Motorcycle Mishap', so I sat on a big cushion, tilted it towards the light and read.

*Ever since I was old enough, all the money I have had, and indeed much that I haven't, has been spent on fast motor cars – the balance being devoted to skiing, and anything left over to the company of pretty women (providing they have the same qualifications as my motor cars). This has added up to a splendid way of life for a carefree* bachelor though it has occasionally earned the disapproval, based one might suspect on envy, of my more solid, married friends. Whenever I compare their approach to life with my own, I wonder which of us is missing something and I wonder also how it first started. I believe I can trace it back, through the by-passes and diversions of my life, to a busy summer's morning when I was just twelve years old.

At the age of eight, I had been sent to an austere prep school in the heart of Wales to get me and my brother out from under my parents' feet. My father was a distant and irascible man and our relationship was more that of judge and accused than father and son. It is sometimes not for children to understand the particular chemistry that may make up their parents' marriage, but my mother was an unlikely partner for a man of such Victorian qualities of distance and ready condemnation. She was a disconcerting mother, full of unexpected and sometimes inexplicable laughter, incapable of regarding us in any normal way as children. I was continually full of a sense that I had somehow disappointed her by failing to respond in the manner she had hoped. She flirted with me when she was in a good mood, ignored me when her humour was less than good and did her best to make me feel like a worm on those occasions when her mood took a sudden violent turn downwards. The only time that either my brother or I got her full attention was when we injured ourselves severely, and then only for as long as it took her to reassure herself that we were not going to die. In the end, it was inevitable that we would be sent away to school so that the old house could be run on whatever odd terms she and my father found mutually acceptable, terms which excluded us.

I put the sheaf of papers down and thought how very familiar this seemed. I had never thought I would go to boarding school until the day I heard the mirror break upstairs, with raised voices and the slam of a door. I went to the billiards room then, because one advantage of Oakdean Manor was its size and complexity. This made it possible to escape to odd corners and annexes where you might not be found and where those scaring moments of adult conflict could be pushed to the back of your mind.

Billiards was not a satisfying pastime at Oakdean. The table was full-size and had once been magnificent when Rileys had made it in some far-off time. I knew it was Rileys because of

30

the engraved plate let into its massive mahogany frame. Now its magnificence had passed away with the Empire. The felt had a badly mended tear, making a little jump for the balls to hop over, and the cushions were so dead that a ball, thudding into them, would come almost to a full stop. Only the very shortest of all the cues still had a tip on it. All the same it was a favourite place of mine because it was out next to the stables, reached by a long, part-glassed corridor which meant you could see anyone coming.

It was my mother who came.

Something about the way she entered confirmed my view that the row had been about me and what was about to follow was the price exacted by the victor. I thought that my mother often looked at me as if she would have liked to show me some form of physical affection but wasn't allowed to by the rules. In retrospect, I think I was wrong about that and she simply could never work out how I had come to be her responsibility.

'We were wondering,' she said, 'now you're nearly ten, whether you would like to go to a different school?'

I quite liked my school. No, perhaps that's an overstatement, but I was completely familiar with it and its odd mixture of old spinsters and eccentric ex-officer masters. I had a set of allies there, who were a little less than friends because they were never allowed to come home to play and therefore I was not often invited to their houses either.

'No thank you,' I said.

'It would be good practice for your big school,' she said.

'Why?'

'Well you know, boarding . . .'

I was astonished that she was thinking of sending me away to board but that was the nearest to a discussion that we came, so two months later I moved to the isolated wastes of Bidleigh Grange Boarding Preparatory School for Young Gentlemen and cried my way through most of the next term.

*Once I had become used to being at the school, which was not a place I would ever have chosen for myself, my heroes were not the headmaster, a noted tennis player, nor his deputy, a former Cambridge rowing blue, but the remainder of the teaching staff,* headed by Mr Lister – who had a racing Zenith motorcycle – down through the lesser ranks, who owned lesser motorcycles, to Mr Maxwell, who possessed a Morgan three-wheeler which looked and sounded far fiercer than it actually was. All of us there subscribed to the belief in this rigorous hierarchy and a boy's prestige depended partly on whether he had been out in Mr Lister's sidecar or what sort of vehicle his own parents possessed.

On Sports Day we gazed in awe at Dunwell, whose father had a huge Napier, or at Mapperton looking down his nose at us from the open back seat of an Alpine Eagle Rolls-Royce. I tried to persuade my mother to leave her battered Singer out of sight, the thing bearing the scars all about it of having been driven firmly into every obstruction in the neighbourhood. Fortunately she rarely came, except on occasions when some major infraction of the school rules required her presence – incidents which seemed always to centre on me rather than on my brother. He was at the time, and has always been, both far more sensible than me and also far better at avoiding being caught.

On one occasion and one only, my visitor was not my mother but a rich aunt whose bulky and unshapely form was transported to the school in an ancient horse-drawn carriage with a plume on the brow of each horse and her family crest still showing dimly through the much polished black paintwork of its doors. She had undertaken a four-hour round trip in this antique conveyance, to inspect me to see whether I might make a worthy inheritor of some small part of her family fortune. This visitation brought with it a double advantage, not only because her vehicle defied any attempt at social classification, but also because she presented me with the fabulous fortune of five pounds to mark the occasion, and in 1924 five pounds went a very long way indeed.

Now, since my very first day at school I had fantasized at the idea of becoming the secret owner of the school under-gardener's motorcycle, a belt-driven single-cylinder Royal Ajax which I knew was for sale. The under-gardener was 'a bit of a lad' and promised he would go along with the business of keeping it quiet, so I parted with four of my five pounds and fulfilled my ambition.

The news spread like wildfire on the school's bush telegraph, and from being a nobody, I was transformed into a hero.

'Have you heard? Birkin Owen Senior has bought a motorbike . . .'

This was a moment of great satisfaction. Until now there had lurked in my mind the strong possibility that the trunk might simply have been a handy receptacle for someone else's final archive. Here was the undeniable proof that the name on the lid went with the contents.

'Go on with you. I don't believe you.'

'I've seen it.'

'All right then, where is it?'

*On the under-gardener's advice, I had left my treasure in his hut, which was almost surrounded by trees just outside the French windows of my ground-floor dormitory. At first light the following day, which was Sunday morning, I led a posse of small boys out to view this wonder. I was proud and, I daresay, more than a bit poisonous about my new possession. Most were quite amazed by the undeniable reality of the oily, painted metal. Some, particularly the more senior boys, were frankly jealous and anxious to cut me down to size.*

*'Looks a bit past it to me,' said one, giving the front wheel a kick that set the bike rocking on its stand. 'I think you've wasted your money. It'll never go.'*

*'It doesn't really matter anyway,' said another. 'What difference does it make? He's far too little to ride it.'*

*With a heart fluttering with nerves and with fury, I defended myself as best I could. 'Bet I can.'*

*'Of course you can't. Go on then, I DARE YOU.'*

*Those three words made up a sacred challenge. There was no dignified way out. With all the nonchalance I could summon, I climbed on to the bike. This was not easy, as my dressing-gown got caught and in any case I was barely tall enough to straddle it.*

*'Give me a push, will you?' I said, hoping my voice sounded steady enough and hoping also that the older boys would get cold feet and decide they might get themselves into trouble as accessories before the fact.*

*No such cautionary thoughts came to their minds. Horribly willing hands immediately began to propel me forwards out of the shed and on to the drive. To my horror, the bike started immediately before I had done anything deliberate to make that happen. It seemed to hurl itself forward. I leant over desperately to bank it round the* corner of the building, straight past the window of the room where the headmaster slept, then found myself tearing up the main drive and zooming in a barely controlled left-handed curve on to the open road beyond. It had no gearbox, just a single speed, and I was little more than a passenger, doing my best to steer, clinging on as hard as I could. Terrified, I did my very best to stop the beast but nothing I could do seemed to slow its uncontrollable progress in the slightest. I had no clear idea what I was doing but there weren't very many possible levers to push and pull and all of them seemed to be floppy and disconnected from fulfilling their intended function. As curves appeared in the road ahead of me, steering commanded more and more of my attention until I gave up on all these other activities and concentrated simply on threading my way around the bends.

I sped over the bridge, sure that the motorcycle had parted company with the ground for at least two seconds as it took the crest, then on through the local village, deserted at this hour of the morning. The road took me up into the empty countryside of the surrounding hills and still I could find no way of stopping the roaring juggernaut from bucketing onwards. In the end, we came to a hill so steep that even this wilful monster was obliged to slow down. Looking down at the ground, now passing more slowly, I was wondering whether it would be safe to leap off before we reached the summit when fate intervened. As the speed dropped, the cord of my dressing-gown, which had been flying behind me, dropped down, was snatched up by the drive-belt and instantly wound tightly into the hub, stopping the motorcycle in its tracks and leaving my waist bruised and stinging where the cord had been so violently snatched from me. The Royal Ajax stopped almost in its own length, teetered for a second and fell over, propelling me off it into the long grass beyond the verge.

I had been travelling for what seemed a very long time and I was now in completely unfamiliar countryside several miles from the school and all alone – a very scared schoolboy in a dressing-gown and bedroom slippers, my toothbrush in one pocket and my sponge bag in the other. I pulled myself out of the grass and stinging nettles, sat down on the petrol tank of the fallen motorcycle and wept as if I would never stop.

After some time, a far-off squeaking noise caused me to look up and coming over the summit of the hill I saw a lone figure on a bicycle, pedalling slowly towards me. As it came gradually nearer, it crystallized into the shape of a very old and very rotund police constable. He slowed to a halt, got off with some difficulty and bent down to look at me in complete astonishment. I stared back at him, my previous thoughts of expulsion swept away by the certainty of life-long imprisonment for untold numbers of offences against the Road Traffic Act, and wept louder than ever.

The constable looked from me to the fallen motorcycle and back, then lowered himself carefully to sit down beside me, offered me a welcome handkerchief and in a deep, kind voice said, 'There, there, it can't be so bad whateffer it is, is it? But now boy, who are you and what in the name of all that's Welsh are you doing up here in this sort of a state at this hour of the morning, tell me?'

Between sobs, I told him my name was Max Birkin Owen, then, as best I could, I explained the story and told him of the fate that would befall me when he reported what had happened.

There was an odd silence and when I blinked away enough of my tears to see his face, I was surprised to find that the constable seemed to be trying his best not to laugh.

'I should haf known who you were,' he said, spluttering a little. 'Your father was Owen Birkin Owen, was he not? I knew him well. He was a wild one in his time too, though it was the horses with him. Now, what are we to do about this motorcycle?'

I was so surprised I stopped blubbing completely. The idea that he was old enough to have known my father as a young man seemed to imply that he was old enough to know Moses and Noah equally well. The accompanying idea that my father had ever been a wild one seemed incredible. On top of that, the fact that he seemed above all to be sympathetic was utterly unexpected.

'Aren't you going to arrest me?' I said in a very small voice.

This time he could not stop himself from bursting out laughing. 'Arrest you? Oh dear me, no! I'm not sure we have a cell strong enough to hold you. Anyway, us Owens have got to look after each other for if we can't get away with the odd transgression here in Wales where else can we, by damn!'

He picked up my fallen bike and looked it over, unwinding the dressing-gown cord from the hub. 'I'll have this going in just a second,' he said. 'All these cables need is a bit of tightening. The

35

clutch is stuck and that is the reason you couldn't stop it.' He kicked it and there was a twanging noise. 'That's better,' he said. 'But what are you going to do with it when we get back?'

'I don't care if I never see it again,' I said.

'Well now,' he said, 'I could do with a bit of a motorcycle myself for when the winds are strong and in my face and I have to hurry and the pedals get very heavy. What would you say to selling it to me?'

'All right,' I said.

'How much do you want for it?'

'Four pounds?' I said hopefully.

'Oh, dear me no,' he said. 'I haffent got that much to my name and it is a motorcycle with a criminal reputation you know, when it comes right down to it. Two pounds ten shillings is all I have.'

'Done,' I said.

'Righto,' he said, 'you can ride my bike back. Follow me.'

So it was that the worthy people of our village, making their way to chapel for early service that morning, were startled by the sight of a happily singing police constable riding a motorcycle, closely followed by a very serious small boy, his dressing-gown streaming out behind him, pedalling as hard as he could on a bicycle which was much too big for him. We got back to the school, early enough for the staff to be still sleeping. The motorcycle was parked in the shed for collection later and my saviour marched me back to the dormitory's French windows. Had I been escorted by the King himself it could hardly have had a more electrifying effect. White children's faces were pressed against every window in all of the dormitories. I stepped back inside, my misery completely forgotten, a true hero, feeling the whole experience was well worth the thirty bob it had cost me.

It was, however, the start and not the finish of something, because having learnt entirely the wrong lesson, namely that kind providence would always look after me, I never looked back from that day. The following year I built myself a motorcar out of an old pram, a generator and the major part of my brother's new bicycle while he was away staying with an aunt. My brother, though very forgiving by nature, was not pleased. In later years I was to go on through many, many other cars, taking lap records at Brooklands along the way and winning Britain's most prestigious rally, all fuelled by the certainty that it would always work out for me in the end.

*However, it was an act of kindness that set me on my unsteady path. If, as he then was, Police Constable Daffyd Tudor Owen of the Carmarthen Police should ever read this, I would like him to know that I shall never forget his great act of kindness to a very frightened little boy, who had no real claim to be regarded as a hero.*

I sat there for a minute or two, looking at the discoloration of the sheaf of paper, wondering from its dryness how long Birkin Owen Senior had waited after those remembered events before setting it down on paper. The little boy in the flying dressing-gown had spoken to me with intense clarity. I looked at the trunk and hoped there was more like this inside it.

I had no idea where their paths had crossed, but I was already convinced this was the same Birkin Owen whose carefree nature had made him the unacceptable model for the Colonel's swearword. I felt I knew whose side *I* was on.

# Five

Once upon a time there were only words with which memories could be easily exchanged in letters and stored in diaries. Then, with the arrival of cheap cameras, there were pictures too. They ran side by side for not much more than fifty years before the telephone took over the business of sending news and conveying emotion, so there was only that brief half-century when the record of a life could accumulate both in words and in pictures. People find it so hard to throw photographs away, as if they have some iconic significance and the act of destroying them might destroy the moment itself. Now we all have those boxes full of second-rate photos, showing us, good side and bad side, posed and unposed in the banal as well as the important moments.

Max's trunk came from that brief overlapping period, when letters and photos existed side by side *en masse* and added up to a substantial body of evidence. The trunk contained a huge record in photos ranging from sepia to black-and-white, with just one or two in startling colour, bringing them out of 'then' into 'now', and letters piled high in old, mean envelopes – such a collection as would not gather together in future years to tell its tale again. Letters are the other half of pictures: pictures usually show at least a superficial attempt at happiness; letters are often sad and sometimes deep. What happens to the piles of photos left behind may be a good measure of the happiness of the condition in which people die, of whether they left behind those who cared. Someone had simply got rid of all this stuff – the auctioneers told me it was a house clearance man who'd brought it in. Had nobody been left to care about Max?

That afternoon, I was still thinking of how I might get my money back. Period photos of old cars would sell easily and I soon built up a small mound of potentially saleable pictures – an enormous and truly exotic Bugatti Royale on a sea front somewhere with a policeman in ancient uniform bending down to peer in – could it be Brighton? A stripped Mercedes SSK on a mountain pass, a Maserati single-seater leaning hard through a corner with a Ferrari taking it on the outside ... There were already more than twenty in the pile and I had barely started.

To be honest, I had spent far more of the time on the other part of my quest, trying to piece together the scattered pages of other manuscripts into the right order in the hope of getting some further insight into Max Birkin Owen later in his life.

Spread through those few top layers which I had so far penetrated, I had found three unconnected pages of a story which seemed to be about the summer exercises of the Eton Officers Training Corps, so Birkin Owen Senior apparently progressed from his Carmarthen prep school to higher things. An Etonian who ended up with his most private possessions in a house clearance had an added poignancy about it. I wasn't really getting anywhere with what I was reading, crouched uncomfortably on the floor. There were bills and bank statements and tickets and small, square photos of groups of unidentifiable people doing unidentifiable things. After an hour or two, the difficulty of trying to trawl any definite meaning out of the mixed-up mess began to seem overpowering. Every time I pulled out another handful, ancient paper dust invaded the membranes of my nose and throat with a sharp, dry stab of old soreness, but when I opened a window to let myself breathe again, the breeze blew the paper piles I was building back into disorder. The process grew as unrewarding as fishing for hours without a bite.

One thing kept me at it. Each time I stopped and thought, enough, I would start brooding on Tiggy's letter and what Cat had scrawled on it and that was enough incentive to make me turn back to the trunk again for escape.

So far, I had been putting the letters aside unread in their envelopes. I would like to say that this was due to a natural reticence about prying but I don't think it was. Captain Birkin Owen was dead, after all. In dying he seemed to have lost his right to the niceties of privacy. I think probably my reluctance was more to do with the effort needed to decipher the handwriting and the near certainty that the result would be unrewarding.

At the point when I might have given up that part of my quest, the trunk threw out a fresh piece of bait. In the middle of one handful was an envelope with an embossed crest – a longer, lusher envelope than the rest with an official army stamp on it and a typed letter inside. The crest persuaded me to open it.

It was addressed to 'Brigadier-General GR Lane-Rivers, DSO, MVO, MC, Headquarters 203 Sub-Area, BAOR'. The date was 20th May, 1946. It read:

Dear Gerry,

I am sending this note by the driver of the ration truck to tell you that Owen duly delivered the NAAFI supplies yesterday afternoon. Both the Duchess and I appreciate the trouble you have taken to expedite the delivery of our requirements and the continuing 'loan' of Owen, who, I must say, is turning out to be a bit of a brick and did fearfully well over the matter of the wine. He is also tireless at repelling boarders on the beach when we grow sick of the pestering.

The Duchess wonders if it would be possible for her to have one dozen or, better still, two dozen more of the glass cloths as she still finds we are in short supply of this item. Otherwise we are now well stocked up for the summer.

Looking forward to seeing you on Thursday, believe me. Bring your clubs. We can have the course to ourselves if I send Owen on ahead to drive out the locals.

Sincerely yours,

It was signed simply 'Edward' and the address at the top, printed in red, was: 'La Cröe, Cap d'Antibes, AM'. The crest at the top left-hand corner of the paper, also printed in red, was the royal crest. A royal duke setting up house in the South of France after the war – a duke, what's more, with a belief that he had some sort of power over the army? It could only be the Duke of Windsor, the King who left his throne.

It's not a response I'm proud of but I have to admit that my first thought was about money. I wasn't yet entirely enmeshed in the trunk's net and suddenly my morning's outlay, even including the crash hat, seemed to be more than justified. Birkin Owen of Eton and the Grenadier Guards had some valuable stuff in his effects. There were autograph dealers who would give a lot for this. I might even take it to Christies.

The ghost in the trunk seemed to sense the direction my thoughts were taking. Like a lark distracting walkers from its nest, he reached out to lure me away, or more accurately, I suppose, to drag me more deeply in.

The very next envelope I picked up had an old blue three-peseta Spanish stamp, a 'Cordoba' postmark and the date '13 Ago 56'. It was addressed to Mrs R Sims at 75, Winslow Mansions, Cromwell Road, London W14. It was stuffed very full indeed and, suddenly alert to the potential value of the letters, I took the contents out. They were folded into two separate sections, both on pale blue paper, but one was made up of single pages and the other of double sheets folded down the middle.

The double sheets were in the same, feminine handwriting as the envelope but I read the other letter first because I already knew that handwriting and the signature at the end was 'Max'.

There was no heading address and its tone attempted to be severe:

V,

Having read your astonishing letter I am doing my best to think that you have been the victim of people seeking to do me down. I do not share the view of those who say you are a bitch and have always been a bitch. I began therefore to write you a reasoned reply, suggesting how all this twisted nonsense might have arisen and asking you to ignore it with the contempt it deserves.

I discover however, having heard all about your despicable visit to Mother yesterday, that it is too late for that.

What in the world did you think you were doing? You surely know that ever since your wedding I have made a point of telling everyone what a good friend you have been to me and what an excellent wife you have been to my dear brother Douglas. If I said a few harsh things at that time, that was only because I was worried about Douglas's future

41

happiness and I also missed his presence most dreadfully. After that, knowing you better, I was happy to let things jog along without interfering in your married life.

It is now apparent to me that there is something unsettled in your nature which seeks conflict – something I started to realize when the business of Lowndes Mews first reared its ugly head.

You know perfectly well that we were all happy with the way we divided the Trust. I chose the Mews flat. You two chose the shares. I accept that I was lucky but if it had been the other way round, I do not think I would be levelling the same rancorous accusations at you. I did not realize the hatred my fortunate choice would bring upon me.

Now, as you know perfectly well, circumstances have changed and we must do what we can to hurry the builders along so that we can sell it for the best price possible. *Of course* I have not been 'planning this all along', and it verges on the libellous for you to suggest that I have 'always intended to put Mother in a home'.

I realized some time ago that in the long term Lowndes Mews was unviable. What you describe as my 'moaning to Mother for money' was simply the kindest way to bring home to her that some action to refinance ourselves was going to be necessary. I could hardly say to her directly that we were about to lose the home we had shared for such a time. I say 'we', please note – that is Mother and I. You and Douglas do not have her living with you as I do, with all that that entails. What you choose to regard as bullying on my part was simply my tactful and kind way of preparing her for the realization that the sale of the flat was inevitable.

As for the rest of the barbs that spike your letter, I have never said that it is your fault that you and Douglas are unable to have children. This is a misunderstanding stemming probably from a conversation with Celia Carver last Christmas when she pressed me on the subject of your plans for a family and I pointed out that children were a jolly expensive business these days. This has been twisted by your malicious, gossiping friends. I never said you were barren or that Douglas couldn't keep you in the style you prefer.

You know very well that I have always been extremely fond of Douglas and I cannot imagine any circumstances, however mad or drunk, in which I would say the least thing against him. I am very grateful for the countless times he has bailed me out of trouble and for all the help he has been to me with the cars as well and I don't need to be reminded of it by you.

You say that I have never returned his kindness in any real way. I think that is you speaking, not Douglas. He would not say that to me, I am sure. Does he even know of the contents of your letter?

It would be simply too wearying to go over all the rest in detail, such as the childish accusation that I claim to be a millionaire who is forced to spend all my income on keeping you going with your expensive habits, and that I then try to borrow a couple of bob for a drink in the Castle.

You say that you know me all too well. Remember then that I too know you. I really do not believe that you will ever convince people who know me that I am a troublemaker and a retailer of malicious gossip. Quite the reverse. I wonder whether it would come as a complete surprise to you to hear that, according to several sources, you are supposed to have said that I have served time as a jailbird, that I am not in fact Douglas's brother at all, that I was given the boot by Louisa because I came back from the South of France with VD, that I am an alcoholic, that I go round to threaten Mother daily to demand money from her and thump her if I don't get it, and various other outrageous lies which are far too unpleasant to mention.

Of course I am too sensible to take more than the slightest notice of these accusations, but you should be aware that I keep hearing them from a number of sources within your circle of friends.

I have never made any secret of the fact that I talk a lot of nonsense about myself. This is partly a result of my sense of humour and the inability to resist improving a good tale, and it is partly forced upon me by circumstances too complex to explain here, but it does no harm to anyone at all, least of all to you and Douglas, so I believe that it is absolutely no concern of yours. Nevertheless you seem to have taken this as a deliberate, terrible and personal insult to yourself when it is nothing of the kind and that seems to have prompted you to start this malicious trouble in retaliation.

For two months now I have made a point of not mentioning either you or Douglas to anyone at all and I intend to carry on in the same way for the foreseeable future. Should anybody ask me about you I shall simply go on saying that I haven't seen you for ages and ages and I really don't know what you're doing.

I would be most obliged if you would please do the same for me and I take it that under the circumstances you will not be seeking to borrow the Allard for the Goodwood races after all.

One more thing which I must insist on: since, under this arrangement, you won't be able to vent your spleen on me, please do not vent it on poor Mother. She is the real victim of all of this and she is extremely upset about this rift in her family. It is not fair to try to force her to take sides and to join in your campaign of censure. Do also remember that when she appears to concur with what you may say against me, she does that only for a quiet life and you are inflicting pain on her in so doing.

Now, for heaven's sake, take a deep breath, calm down and go back to making Douglas the charming and happy wife that you were doing so well at before. Even now, having said all of the above, remember that, for his sake, I still don't dislike you. This awful background of accusation and suspicion is no way to live.

Max.

The ink looked as dry as the bloodstain on a relic, but time had not diminished the force of the situation which had squeezed it out to spider its venom across the page.

'V's' letter to 'Ma' was clearly to Max and Douglas's mother, her mother-in-law.

Dear Ma,

With some reservations I include the letter I got from Max two days ago. I suggest you go right ahead and read it now before carrying on with this one, but perhaps you should be sitting down before doing so. When Douglas and I had got our breath back after reading such a monumental mixture of fantasy and nonsense, we were not sure whether to laugh or to cry!

Max is like a guilty child caught red-handed in the classroom and saying, 'No miss, it wasn't me. It was them.' It is a very weak reply and a complete fabrication.

I would like to keep Douglas out of this as much as possible because clearly he is caught in a great conflict of loyalty, but I think it MUST be sorted out now. Anything we may have said or done has been done by us both equally. I do not come from a family background in which this type of nonsense goes on. Max may call it harmless nonsense, but I call it lying and I am not used to it. I do not mean to cause you any distress but I think we understand one another, you and I, and the Mews flat is too big an issue to let us look the other way. No wonder Max doesn't dare to face us personally with his stories!

Celia Carver was certainly not our sole source of information. I only wish she had been, but there were many, many more, ranging from Mrs Mitchell to Joe Barraclough's niece, Donald Beauchamp (and that was *before* Max bounced his cheque on him), Johnny de Zoete, Robin Aitkin and so on and so on.

In an effort to keep the effects of his fantasies within bounds we will continue to say when necessary that Max is NOT on special assignment for the Foreign Office, that he does not support us and you out of the income from a vast fortune which we repeatedly squander, that he has never been a successful racing driver excluding one cup at Brighton when his was the only car in the class, that he is not Tim Birkin's cousin, did not go to Eton, does not yet own and has not paid a single solitary penny towards the rebuilding of 4, Lowndes Mews, does not have vineyards and chateaux in the South of France or a steam yacht, was not gallantly injured in the war at Dunkirk, or at Narvik or at Arnhem – indeed, unlike Douglas, was barely in the war at all let alone doing anything remotely heroic – and is not so rich that he need never work.

This may be unpalatable to him to hear and may earn him the occasional derision of those awful hangers-on he chooses to regard as friends when they discover the truth, but we prefer the position to be clear.

As for Max's claim that I started the story that he is not Douglas's brother – this, and the rest of them, bear the unmistakable imprint of his authorship.

It is Max, not me, who is trying to put you into the firing line between us. I understand that, as a mother, you are prepared to make endless allowances for his vagaries and that is to your credit, but there sometimes comes a moment when you must choose one way of looking at the world against another. It is extraordinary that someone as balanced, sensible and honest as Douglas should have a brother as crazy as Max. I fear that if he goes on doing the sorts of things he does, he can hardly help ending up in jail! He may perhaps listen to you if you tell him that it is time he grew up.

His well-known talent for what he would choose to call exaggeration is not shared by us. One can only assume that he has told these stories for so long that he believes them to be true.

It is now quite clear that it has been Max's intention all along to manoeuvre things to the point where the Mews flat would have to be sold. Poor Douglas did not rumble this in time and still has difficulty ascribing Max's base motives to him. You do understand, I hope, that our place is simply too small to provide an alternative for you with Douglas needing his workspace at present. If you do still really want to live at Lowndes Mews and if Max will face the music and come to talk to me face to face, then maybe we can still salvage something, or at the very least make sure we get a really top price for it.

I am sure you will need the things I bought for you wherever you wind up living and as it is a little late to take them back, I shall keep them safely for you until you want them. I enclose the bill for the things I have paid for myself.

I am not sure exactly where we go from here, but at least you now know the full story. In the time I have been acquainted with Max, I have never once known him admit to being wrong, even in the tiniest thing. I suppose he will try to talk his way out of it as he always does.

As for us, we plan to make the most of our holiday and forget all about it, I hope, for a fortnight so that we will be a lot more able to cope later on!

Love, V.

That left only the third item, her handwritten copy of her reply to Max.

Max,

I suppose I should thank you for your letter, but I had been hoping you would come to meet me face to face rather than send me such a lot of specious drivel through the post.

As you know, Douglas and I are about to go away and it is probably too much to expect you to face me with such arrant nonsense. You leave me no choice but to inform you that unless you agree to a meeting during the next couple of days before we leave, I shall take your repellent letter to show to your mother.

You accuse me of creating a rift in your family. I may be an 'incomer' but I am still a member of that family, whether you like it or not, and any rift has been deliberately widened by you. It may well be directly to your advantage to foster this split because I am sure it will make it a great deal easier for you to get out with your share of

47

the Trust in money rather than in property – for obvious reasons.

Stop spouting rubbish, Max, and face up to the facts for once.

V.

My first response was to wonder how poor Mrs R Sims had responded to this hand-grenade of a letter and why she was Mrs Sims, not Mrs Birkin Owen. My second was that Birkin Owen Junior now had a christian name – Douglas. My third response was to feel an active and visceral anger with this 'V' who had vented her spleen so foully and so widely.

I found it hurt me to be asked to accept that the Max who had written that so-touching story could be the same evil Max she had pilloried in the letter. What did it say of 'V' that she was willing to place her poor mother-in-law so squarely into the nutcrackers in this spiteful war of hers? The strident tone of her accusations did not speak well of her. She said it was all a question of facts, but these were facts used like flame-throwers. She had no space in her own house for Mrs R Sims whose bills she wanted paid for the things she had bought.

I was on Max's side and I didn't want to believe the kinds of things that would have justified the Colonel's epithet.

Parts of the catalogue of misdemeanours in the letter made sense to me. I knew exactly who Tim Birkin was. Any car-mad small boy in my time had been reared on the exploits of the Bentley Boys, the playboys who took the massive green cars to successive victories at Le Mans before the war. Birkin was the most glamorous of them – the man who ran the all-conquering Mercedes into the ground, who took his huge lorry of a sports car to the front of a Grand Prix against the lightweight Bugattis, who lived his life to the full and died tragically of the after-effects of a tiny burn. He was a hero in his own right and Max stood accused of using the accident of his middle name to claim kinship.

V sounded like a vengeful woman indeed, a woman obsessed with the task of reducing Max in his mother's eyes to something unworthy whatever the pain, but something nagged at me for a moment. *We will go on saying when necessary . . . that he did not go to Eton*... Had I not just read a manuscript in which Max had been bragging of his school days in the Officer Training Corps at that very place? One small tick in V's column, but of course what I'd read might always have been meant as fiction.

I didn't want to think of the rest as fiction. I was already loath to lose the motorcycling boy with the flying dressing-gown to the realms of fantasy. Before I went out that night, I made another big leap forward because I was able, with unjustified certainty, to put faces to Max and Douglas. There were two studio photographs of young men in army uniform and to this day I believe you can tell everything there is to tell about both of them simply from those photos, though of course there is plenty of hindsight mixed in with that.

The photos were clearly taken on the same occasion and carry the stamp on the back of a photographer in Shaftesbury Avenue. The first photo is indeed, as I knew it had to be, Max. He is looking straight at you, full face but with his left shoulder twisted slightly to the camera and his head leaning just fractionally to the right. The photo, printed on that beautiful pre-war paper no longer allowed because it is rich in dangerous cadmium, has an almost oily sheen. Max stares out of it like a better-looking David Niven. He is bareheaded, his hair slicked back, up and over and gleaming with some bottled preparation for gentlemen bought no doubt in the Burlington Arcade. He is in his late twenties and at the peak of his good looks. His ears are sharply pointed, one eyebrow is slightly raised, quizzically, his pronounced lips are accented by a moustache, trimmed with narcissistic neatness. The eyes say, 'I am quite something and I know it.'

Straight away I could certainly see his vanity but I wonder if I could also see his feckless weakness, his endless capacity for untruth and his utter inability to recognize those moral limits of behaviour which circumscribe the activities of most other people? I believe I could. I also believe I could already see the charm of the boy in the dressing-gown – the charm which brought his long-suffering brother and the small, loyal core of his mostly worthless friends to his rescue time after time after time.

The other photo shows the two of them, Max and Douglas, side by side, heads turned in towards the centre, looking at each other, though Douglas seems to be looking past Max's nose rather than into his eyes. Max is on the left, wearing his cap this time. I can see why he didn't want it on in the main picture. It makes his head look small and narrow and overloaded by the size of the cap and the arresting sight of the cap badge – which at first I took for an exotic fruit until research showed me it was a stylized bomb, round like a cartoon version with flames like leaves mushrooming out of the top – the badge of the Grenadier Guards. Despite all that, Max looks immensely pleased with himself.

Where his tunic and diagonal Sam Browne belt look straight off the tailor's dummy, Douglas's already have a used patina. His cap is smaller, creased, and the pips on his epaulettes catch the light in an irregular, duller way. He wouldn't have passed muster on Max's parade ground, but he wouldn't have wanted to be there anyway.

Unlike Max, Douglas was to grow better-looking with age. At this stage, he too has a moustache though it is fainter and more blurry than the matinée idol accessory under his brother's nose. His face has not developed the muscle definition which led a friend, much much later, to describe him as the sort of Greek god you'd like to have on your side in a bar-room brawl.

Max is still looking sardonic. Douglas is simply looking kind. The option of leaving them in their trunk, to fade back into 'then' and disappear for ever from 'now' simply ceased to exist. I was already caught up in them and I suppose perhaps I even needed them to make up for something I was missing. They were coming alive before my eyes, another early step in the long development of a ghost story in reverse.

# *Six*

In October 1962, officially just turned thirteen but feeling more like ten, I ran away from school, propelled by the news I heard transmitted on the present my mother had unexpectedly bought me. This was my new grown-up public school and nothing in the loneliness I had practised in my childhood so far had prepared me for this frighteningly large dormitory, smelling of Dettol and floor polish, where I woke horribly early that first morning to wrestle miserably among the sleeping strangers with a collar stud which would not go through successive layers of cold, frighteningly unworn shirt and hostile, separate collar. I'd never had collar studs before.

My mother's surprise present was an Ultra transistor radio made of hardboard covered with padded blue leathercloth. It had an earphone socket soldered in specially by the shop so that I could listen to it without others knowing. I wonder if she felt a little guilty about sending me away, though that seems unlikely. She hadn't told the Colonel in case he banned it. She just slipped it into my trunk under the regulation piles of socks, games shorts and bed linen assembled from the school clothing list and topped by the unexplained but required 'tartan rug – one' as a treat. The fact that I felt homesick was a measure of how alien this new place felt, not how warmly I thought of home. The gift made me more homesick, not less.

What the radio brought me in the late sleepless nights amongst the coughs, whispers and embryonic snores of the dormitory was not Radio Luxembourg, as she probably intended, but the unfolding story of the missiles of October. I spent my early miserable evenings at the school listening with a child's soft ear to news programmes meant for calloused adults.

Khrushchev versus Kennedy, Cuban roulette. It was a confrontation coming to an inevitable climax as the Russian ships carrying

51

the missiles steamed towards the US blockade around the island intended as their destination. I had never been so frightened in my short life and I seemed to be the only person in the school who understood what was about to happen. In each dark night at the end of the late news, I would climb illicitly out of bed and cross to the window which I had selected because it looked north towards London. I would inspect the sky in that direction for reflections of flames, then sit on the windowsill staring towards it, expecting to see at any second some great flash which would signal the beginning of the end of everything.

I imagined it would be electric blue, zigzagging up the sky like forked lightning, and that when I saw it I would have four minutes to run away. At home, in the infinitely unreachable time before boarding school, the Colonel – I would *not* think of him as my father, however much my mother insisted – had talked of little else right through the summer. His analysis of foreign affairs centred on the repetition of phrases like, 'You have to show the Russkis who's boss, you know,' and, 'Their whizzbangs never did work properly. Johnny Russian doesn't have a clue when it comes to the clever stuff. More hammer and anvil than hammer and sickle.' He always laughed a lot at that one and he was the sort of man whose laughter seemed entirely for his own benefit.

He told me about the four-minute warning during that tense summer when 'cold' seemed entirely the wrong word for the war with Russia. He seemed to think four minutes was ample time to prepare for extinction. I would stand at the top of the kitchen garden, where the steep bank led up from the overgrown tennis court to the decaying stone wall which separated Oakdean Manor from the South Downs and the rest of the world. In past summers, whenever he wasn't around to disapprove, I would sometimes leap down that angled bank. The tennis court had been carved out of the steep slope, the earth from above being heaped below so that the slope of the hill intersected its plateau halfway, roughly at the line of the net. The geography of the court was probably terrible for tennis, not that anyone had ever played during my lifetime, because balls hit too hard to the downhill side must have bounded on down through the rose garden towards the flat lawns below, but that same geography was just great for small boys. If you got the jump just right, gravity would take you hurtling down the bank, skimming past the grass so that you felt like you were literally flying.

Its strange position and the scope for flying suited me. I could be noisy by myself up here without earning his instant disapproval. Anything exciting was discouraged. That summer I did no flying that I remember. As the Colonel hunched in his armchair inside, the armchair no one else ever used, glowering at the tiny bulging grey-green screen of our already outdated Echo television in its bulky veneered cabinet, I would time how far I could get in four minutes on the luminous sweep second hand of my watch. One way it was the main road, the other way it was the clump of trees on the brow of the hill where the rabbit warren was. Neither seemed to offer much of a refuge.

This awkward home and my new, terrifying school were part of the same geographical continuum, each sitting on the southern slope of the same rise of chalk downland, an hour's fast walk apart. Half a mile east of our house, beyond the genteel fringe of detached houses which had sprouted in Oakdean Manor's old lands, along the northern edge of Worthing stood, at the end of its own lane, the ruined remains of a burnt-out school, Charmandean, which must once have been another substantial country house. In the grounds, all overgrown with rhododendrons, was the hulk of an abandoned Austin Ruby and the place served as the perfect setting for my morbid, post-apocalyptic fantasies. This is where I would go to practise being a survivor, wondering how to snare rabbits and looking gloomily at the infested black water in the old water-tanks, thinking I would have to be quite desperate to drink it.

The television programmes I was allowed to watch were all on the BBC because our old set couldn't get ITV, but even *Dixon of Dock Green* lost its appeal that summer.

Once I arrived at my new boarding school, in a flurry of suppressed tears, cumbersome trunks and gruff farewells, this stiff home of mine was somehow transformed by the unreliable emotions of memory into a delightful haven of warmth and love. The school was too near home for my own good. I couldn't quite see our house itself from the Downs above the school but I could see the marker made by the clump of trees with the rabbit warren on the hill above it. It was no more than four or five miles away to the west. On the night of October 25th 1962, when the game of nuclear poker at the entrance to the Caribbean was at its crucial point, I became quite sure that we were all going to die and there seemed no point in sticking to the school's rules for another moment. I wanted to die with my mother even if the Colonel had to be there too, so I changed into my sports clothes, crept down the wide wooden stairs past the door of my housemaster's flat and stole through the dark to the bicycle sheds where my prim, shiny Star Rider with its three-speed Sturmey-Archer and dynamo lights was locked in its place in the racks among all the other boys' much leaner, more rakish speed machines, with their taped-up drop handlebars and wonderfully desirable greasy derailleur gears.

I arrived, exhilarated by my rush through dark roads and aghast at the amazing step I had taken, at the gates to Oakdean Manor and pushed the bike up the long gravel drive. The creeper-covered front of the house was completely dark. It was eleven o'clock and after dithering for a few heart-beats I knocked at the door. This had no effect. In the end I pulled the iron lever which rang the big bell inside, to the complete consternation of my sleepy mother when she appeared at the door.

'Miles!' she said. 'What the hell are you doing here?' And it was all downhill from there. The Colonel came down in his beige dressing-gown and started talking about 'absence without leave' and 'disciplinary measures'. I wasn't even allowed to stay the night nor, come to that, was I even given a cup of cocoa.

'Are you unhappy?' she asked when the Colonel went to phone the school. My presence there clearly troubled her greatly. I tried to explain about Cuba but she had no idea what I was trying to say and rapidly became impatient. I tried to make her understand but all she said was, 'Don't be so silly,' and then the Colonel came back into the kitchen to say that my housemaster was coming to get me.

'Feller sounded rather annoyed,' he said. 'Not surprising. Shouldn't like to be in your shoes, young man.'

In fact Mr Sherrill, my new housemaster, was the nicest of them.

I made a faltering attempt to explain on the way back but he was clearly convinced my concern over world politics was just a cover for home-sickness. Even then I knew I was being more honest than the grown-ups. They were just hiding their dark fears behind an airy dismissal of the facts. None of them seemed to have any idea how close to the brink we all were that week. We all now know that I was right and they were wrong. The world really had stood on the brink, but I found myself, for the first time in my life, in a universe of one, forced to abandon the idea that older people could see into my head and help put right what they found. I never expected it of the Colonel – to him I knew I was just the inconvenient offspring of the widow he had helped out with his offer of marriage, the baggage that came with her as part of the deal – but until that night I had thought my mother would always be able to read my thoughts.

I resented the fact that I bore the Colonel's surname and I resented the fact that my mother would relate to me only the vaguest details of my real father.

I went on listening to my radio under the sheets, feeling like a lone sentinel against the red menace, and when, on October 28th, Khrushchev backed down and turned his ships away, there wasn't even anyone to share the relief.

Now, back in London with the trunk radiating dense promises from its corner of my flat, I had an obsession once again that no one else would share. I left the flat for Zeb's party that night, walking towards Lancaster Gate, desperate to talk to someone about Max and the trunk. I was teasing away at the strands of Captain Max Birkin Owen and I wanted to discuss it, to see what else might come from that, but I knew nobody at Zeb's would have the slightest interest in it. When I arrived, no one asked where Cat was either but there was some weed going the rounds that was pure dynamite and pushed the busy stuff away to the back of my head. A girl called Bo insisted she knew me from somewhere. She was younger than Cat, much nearer my age, with yards of braided blonde hair, big eyes and sculpted cheekbones. For a little bit it felt quite good that Cat wasn't there, as if I could be me more easily. Bo did something with

55

some twisted foil over a candle flame and a little heap of powder from a plastic sachet.

I breathed in when she held it under my nose, expecting a familiar herbal smell, and instead found my head filling with sweet acrid chemicals in a whirlwind of benevolence which rushed out to my fingers and toes and simply removed anything on the way that didn't suit me.

'Is that . . . ?' I started to say through it, but stopped because it sounded so completely uncool to be asking what it was.

'It's just skag,' she said, smiling, 'nothing else.' And I nodded sagely as though I had been asking a subtle and informed question about drug cocktails. I might have been anxious if the drug hadn't already ruled that out. I knew what skag was – skag was horse, horse was H, H was heroin. This was one step further than I'd ever gone, one scary step, but we were only *smoking* it. I didn't know you could smoke it. That couldn't be too bad. It made everything else I'd tried seem mild.

Bo lay back and put her head on my lap. 'Where have I seen you, star-boy?' she said.

I didn't think I'd ever seen her before, but in the boundless brain-bliss of the moment I didn't mind colluding with her in trying to set up some sort of fiction for us both. 'Oxford?' I suggested.

'Never been. Is that where you come from?'

'I was a . . . er, I was studying there.'

She seemed to find this very funny. She was moving her head around in a comfortable way and I was stroking her hair. 'Brighton,' she said with sudden certainty, 'that's where. You knew Lena and Joe the Wheel and that lot, didn't you? You got busted.'

My skin crept but she didn't say anything else, like, 'You let them take the rap,' or, 'You got off because you were posh,' so I just agreed with her and went on stroking her hair, for once feeling magnified and not diminished by the memory. Then there was a noise in the direction of the door and she sat up quickly.

'Cat's here,' she said, and she sounded almost frightened.

I hadn't even realized she knew Cat, let alone that there was a connection between me and Cat, and anyway the stuff was really

56

hitting me strongly and there was after all just a remaining little bit of me that was scared of it.

I came down, out of a world in which nothing mattered and nothing had to make sense, quite a bit later on to find that what had seemed partly a dream was true. We were somewhere near Pease Pottage on the A23, driving south at unwise speed in a huge and ancient vehicle. Cat was at the wheel and I looked back from the cracked brown leather of the front seat to see who else was with us. All there was in the cavernous back was an ornate wooden platform with silver rails flanked by side windows of etched glass with fancy scroll-work.

The hearse had an eight-track tape player screwed at a haphazard angle on the top of the dash, playing Led Zeppelin very loudly. It was dark but it felt like it had been that way for a long time.

'Where are we going?' I said.

'Where you asked to go,' Cat said. She looked manic in profile.

'Brighton?'

She sighed. 'Where else?'

'Is this your car?' She'd never said anything about owning a hearse.

'I don't think so.'

'What time is it?'

She shrugged and pointed left. 'It's tomorrow.'

The sky was turning pink towards the sunrise.

'You want to stop?' she said.

'Why?'

'Shit, Milo. A gorgeous chick asks if you want to stop and you say why? Why do you think?'

I had thought it might be in case I needed to take a leak but it seemed inappropriate to say so. 'All right, let's stop,' I said quickly.

'No, you blew it. I demand total spontaneity. We go on.'

So we did. She was behaving very strangely. I wondered if she'd seen me with Bo's head in my lap.

'What did I say about Brighton?'

'You shouldn't be messing with that stuff. You're not old enough.' She laughed. 'You're still out of your head.'

'No, I'm not.' I was fuzzy and frightened of what I'd done but it was getting easier to sort out what was real and what was not. 'Brighton. Tell me what I said.'

'You said you had a secret place. Something like that. I thought, why not?'

If you take no other positive decision, the road leads you straight down under high bridges, through canyons of small shops into the wider grass estuary of the Steyne, where the Pavilion then looked poised for a slide into terminal decay. The road delivers you right to the head of the pier. I didn't give Cat a word of direction but she turned into the entrance to Madeira Drive, drove a hundred yards, then braked to a halt and stopped the engine, right there in the middle of the road, pointing at the dawn. We both got out. I could now see that it was a very old Humber, sagging towards the rear as if it had carried regiments of the overweight to their graves. The sea was snoring like an old man fast asleep with the heavy indrawn breath of receding water dragging shingle followed by the brief collapsing climax of the thud of breakers. Over it all high seagulls were wheeling and screaming and in the chill fresh salt air it felt like we were the only people alive.

Cat pulled her slitted silk shirt over her head so she was just wearing a patchwork skirt and stretched upward with both arms, then windmilled into a violent parody of exercises, breasts bouncing. I watched her for a minute but she stopped as suddenly as she started, jumped back in the car and revved the huge old engine violently. I got in next to her.

'Where now?' she yelled over the engine. I shrugged and pointed onwards up the Drive. She did something violent to the pedals and there was a moment when the clutch lining was burning and the back axle was winding itself round the tired old springs, then we were lurching ahead like an angry rhino round the slight curve with the sea to our right and the cliff rising above the long line of archways to our left. Madeira Drive stretched gun-barrel straight ahead and Cat kept her foot flat. Old Humbers were never fast and the hearse body didn't help, so we were nudging fifty-five by the time we reached the playground at the far end. It felt very fast all the same.

'Stop here,' I said. 'I'll tell you a story.'

'I don't want a story,' she said, doing as I asked and then putting the shirt back on. 'I want truth.'

'This is a true story.'

'There's no such thing. All stories are just one view.'

'Fine,' I said, 'this is one view.'

'I warn you, you know how easily I get bored.'

'It's not boring.'

I got out, expecting her to follow, but she stayed in her seat so I went round and leant on the door her side.

'So tell me,' she shrugged, 'but it's your risk.'

'I used to come here when I was a kid,' I said.

She started the engine and I stared at her and stopped.

'I'm bored already,' was all she said and, swinging the car round, drove off leaving me standing there alone in the Brighton dawn.

Thanks Cat, I said to myself, and walked to the railing by the playground, thinking I would lean against it for a while until she came back. I could hear the deep beat of the big engine all the way back to the pier and then it faded away.

As the first rays of the sun broke through, I was looking at the playground and with the light shining sideways across its surface, I saw the little mounds and hollows in the tarmac by the mark where the roundabout had once been and I found I didn't need an audience to hear me tell the story.

I told it to myself.

When it was over I knew that everything I had taken at the party had completely worn off, leaving me feeling old and cold and irritable. I gave up on Cat and walked back to the pier, wondering how long I would have to wait before anywhere opened for breakfast. Across the road, someone was laying tables in the dining room of the Royal Albion Hotel but it looked altogether too proper to admit me. I stopped by the inscription on a block set in its wall, a memorial.

*On this site stood Russell House, where lived from 1759 Richard Russell MD FRS. If you seek his monument, look around.*

This was a familiar landmark from all those other times later in my teenage years when they seemed only too glad for me to be out of the house during the holidays, especially during my mother's occasional, unexplained absences. I would take that slow, bare-radiatored bus, sitting on the thin seats fringed by chromed frames, which were upholstered in a dusty green and brown cloth so abrasive that you left little bits of your trousers behind on it when you got up.

The bus took you to the end of the route, that landlocked tarmac lagoon of Pool Valley bus station, just behind the Royal Albion Hotel, and the plaque was the first thing I would see on the way out between the buildings to the sea, to the pier and to the promise of adventure. I used to take the inscription quite literally and look around wondering where Russell's monument was, over and over again, never finding it and wondering if perhaps it had been taken away. In the intervening years I had grown no more knowledgeable on the subject of Richard Russell's achievements, but now at least I knew he was a medical man and could guess that his monument was to be found in the improved conditions of the living world.

I glanced at the neighbouring plaque, *William Ewart Gladstone, 1809–1898, often stayed at this hotel then known as Lion Mansions Hotel.* Another memorial. I'd already been down to look at the only memorial I really cared about, where the tarmac still showed the marks of fire. After that I explored the Lanes until I found an open café and sat in it for an hour, brooding over being Milo Malan and not Miles Drummond any more until I found myself nodding off to sleep over my fifth cup of coffee. Later, I lay on the shingle at the top of the beach and went out like a light until noon.

I woke up stiff and hacked off with Cat while at the same time admiring the complete directness of her approach to life. I shouldn't have tried to tell her anything. Conversation among people like us wasn't meant to be long and intricate and it certainly wasn't meant to be about details of past experiences in the to-be-forgotten age before we were all free spirits. The past was dull. The present was immediate. The two should never meet.

Ten minutes later, they didn't just meet, they collided.

I was walking up towards the station through the shops and I saw, walking down the pavement towards me, a dark-haired girl in a tight little top, a headband and the sort of bell-bottoms you might buy in Dorothy Perkins.

60

Nice face, boring clothes.

Tiggy.

I checked myself over. Stubble, ripped pink jeans, patchwork waistcoat. Would she recognize me? Hopefully not.

Of course she would.

She looked up, saw me and stopped in her tracks, putting both hands to her mouth. At that same moment, with complete inevitability, the Humber came down the hill, swerved straight through the oncoming cars to my side of the road through a cacophony of protesting horns and squealed to a halt next to me.

'Get in,' said Cat curtly. She was now wearing an army cap and had two men's handkerchiefs, knotted together, serving as a sort of bra. 'I've decided to be very nice to you and drive you home so you can fuck my brains out.'

I looked helplessly up the pavement to where Tiggy was now moving again, walking slowly towards me with an uncertain expression of baffled pleasure on her face. Introductions didn't seem likely to work well. 'Tiggy meet Cat. Cat, Tiggy.' It would be like introducing matter to anti-matter.

I waved hopelessly at Tiggy and got in the car.

# Seven

*I have lived a more dramatic life than most people, sometimes within and sometimes without the confines of accepted behaviour. There have been moments, I confess, when my accounts of my affairs have stretched the credulity even of my friends, perhaps because it has been easier for them to dismiss them as nonsense.*

*I was brought up amongst the respectable hills and valleys of South Wales in a family which, on my father's side, had produced a large number of vicars, canons and even bishops. Though my father, an elderly man, had, it was alleged, shown a wild side in his youth, by the time I came into his life that flame was burning low and he fought to quash any similar tendency in me. My mother, however, had a streak of eccentric rebelliousness in her which was apt to show at unexpected and sometimes inappropriate moments such as the time shortly before the Armistice in 1918 when she single-handedly captured a German spy wading ashore on Pendine Sands, cornering him with a pitchfork and attempting to interrogate him personally before handing him over to the local constable. Although it soon became clear that he was in fact a seaman from Sunderland who had narrowly escaped death by drowning, it was generally held that her intentions had been good and her bravery had been unquestionable.*

*Throughout my early life I was an enthusiast for the trappings of royalty and empire, for the pomp and circumstance of the military and in short for everything that came under the heading of King and Country. My adventures took place largely within that framework.*

*The place where, perhaps, my life was changed, stands on a strip between earth and water, between land and sea, where two elements meet, as though that was symbolic of two conflicting elements in me – the one rock solid, the other ever-changing. It is a place on the south coast of France, the Promenade de la Croisette in Cannes, where my military career reached its unlikely zenith and where, in a small garden filled with exotic plants, there stood a grand statue of King*

Edward VII now, alas, replaced by a smaller bust. The expression on his face was one of a degree of pleasure that only just allowed dignity to be retained. He reminded me of a senior croupier who has just seen a gambler lose all his winnings on the turn of the wheel which had stood to break the bank.

Beneath the statue was an inscribed plaque saying, To H M King Edward VII, benefactor of Cannes, and to that I mentally coupled the words, 'and also of Max Birkin Owen', one day many years ago on the occasion when the complex etiquette of the royal family elevated me dizzyingly to that military zenith and also perhaps taught me a new way to look at things.

Having spent the latter part of the war recovering from injuries sustained during its early months, I was posted, almost as soon as hostilities finished, as a staff captain with the British Army Command in France, and towards the end of my tour of duty a certain well-known royal personage arrived there, returning to his old haunts on the Mediterranean coast. Due to a close acquaintance with him in the pre-war years, it was decided that I should be relieved of my regular duties and attached to him as a personal aide to help ease the conditions of the exile so unfairly inflicted on himself and on the woman he had married for love. This, it soon became clear, suited both him and me quite exceptionally well.

During part of the war, the town of Cannes had been under occupation by the Italians and, while they were never as cruel as the Germans in their repression of any among the civilian population who displayed the spirit to stand up to them, they were given to drinking far too much of the local wine and going out to celebrate in a wanton and destructive manner. It was during one such spree that a band of young Fascisti decided it would be fun to throw the statue of the English king into the harbour, which they proceeded to do. They accompanied their actions by hurling after it several other pieces of French statuary, egged on apparently by the cheers with which their fellows greeted the resulting splashes.

When peace had returned and the Italians as well as the Germans had finally scurried away, the Mayor decided that they should do their best to find the missing statues and put into effect a plan to dredge that part of the harbour. If they were disappointed when they found not their own statues but that of our King, they were too polite to say so. His head had come off in the course of the plunge to the sea-bed, but this too was found and the statue was put back on its plinth where it belonged. There was, however, one change. Whereas before the war he had been gazing intently out to sea, they had now rotated him through ninety degrees so that he was staring along the length of the promenade at the beautiful women taking their leisure on the terrace of the Carlton Hotel. The French, who had known the King very well, were firmly of the opinion that this was much more realistic.

They were also of the opinion that the recommissioning of the statue should be marked by an appropriate ceremony, perhaps as recompense for the vast amount of money they had taken from the British in their casino over the years. With this in mind, I was approached by the Mayor of Cannes to see whether His Royal Highness the Duke would agree to preside over the elaborate unveiling ceremony they were devising for the statue on behalf of his late predecessor.

This was at a time, of course, when it was not immediately clear to anyone outside the most secret inner circles of Buckingham Palace and Downing Street just how they planned to deal with this former king of theirs. It is apparent now that they were most embarrassed by the question of defining the status and the extent of the freedom of activity of the man who was, since his abdication, 'merely' the Duke of Windsor. Even those of us who were close to him, and perhaps the Duke himself, believed that he was still in effect a very senior and respected member of the royal family with all the rights and obligations implied by that, and that participation in such a ceremonial event as this was perfectly right and proper.

The Duke therefore replied that he would be graciously pleased to perform the unveiling of the statue and immediately a formidable planning process for the ceremony was put into action involving the participation of the Vice-President of France, the Prefects of Var and Alpes Maritimes and a great jostling host of French admirals and generals making up for the relative indolence of their war years.

There was also to be a British naval presence because by complete chance a courtesy visit was being paid to Cannes at the time by a British destroyer flotilla from Malta under the command of Captain Sir Jeremy Dugdale. It seemed entirely appropriate for a naval guard of honour to be present at the ceremony, and this I arranged.

Although the Palace had been informed of all the arrangements at least a week in advance, they decided, for reasons best known to themselves, to leave it to the very morning of the ceremony to communicate, via the army headquarters, their decision that it would be a significant breach of protocol if the Duke was to take the salute.

The Duke himself was normally completely unflappable, the very model of a gentleman in the teeth of whatever adversity might come his way, but on this occasion he betrayed the depth of his hurt as we sat together in his dressing room looking at the signal which had just been delivered.

'Forgiveness was never their strong suit, Owen,' he said grimly. 'They are angry with me still and do you know why?'

I shook my head mutely.

'They claim I spend my time down here with unsuitable elements, you know.' His occasional stutter came out strongly as a mark of his emotion. 'They say I am friends with collaborators. All unproven of course but that is not the real reason. It is because I wish my Duchess to be accorded the dignity of the title of Royal Highness and they do not care for that.'

I thought of the fine woman for whom he had sacrificed everything and it was perhaps then that the first crack started to appear in my confidence in the judgement and humanity of those who steer our great country.

'There's nothing else for it, Owen,' he said. 'You'll have to take the salute. Get on the blower and tell the Brigadier.'

The Brigadier was startled to receive this news.

'I don't know about that, Owen,' he said. 'I don't suppose the French will give two hoots. They're not too hot on British ranks at the best of times and with all that Guards brass on your hat, you'll probably pass as a general anyway. I'm not so sure about Captain Sir Jeremy, though. Stay there and I'll get back to you.'

It was only ten minutes or so before my corporal summoned me back to the telephone.

'Look, Owen,' said the Brigadier, 'this is all most unfortunate and I've done my very best with Captain Sir Jeremy, but he would sooner take his flotilla away and scuttle it off the French coast than lead a full naval guard of honour past a damned low-ranking pongo officer. Can you do without him?'

'Not really, sir,' I said. 'His guard is the centrepiece of the entire ceremony.'

'I'd get down there myself to take it,' said the Brigadier, 'but of course there isn't time. You'll just have to do the best you can. Good luck.' And with that unhelpful instruction, he hung up.

I went back to His Royal Highness and reported what seemed to me to be a complete impasse. I had however reckoned without his ready wit.

HRH, as well as being a very great gentleman, was also possessed of an ability to think extremely fast coupled with a magnificent sense of humour, and as he pondered the matter he suddenly began to laugh. After a while, he said, 'Owen, amongst my other titles I am an admiral of the fleet, so it is within my power to command Captain Sir Jeremy to give even a "pongo" officer a salute, but I would not welcome that were it to happen to me so I suppose I must not inflict it on him. Time is running out on us and the situation calls for remarkable measures. By good fortune, it happens that I am also a field marshal and you will know that one of the privileges which accompanies that rank is the power to make promotions in the field wherever necessary. For just one day, from now until this time tomorrow, I hereby promote you to the rank of temporary acting unpaid brigadier. That should make Captain Sir Jeremy and his naval types think twice. I will have a signal sent to the War Office to that effect forthwith and if they have any objections, it will be far too late to register them in time.'

It was then a matter of assembling a suitably impressive uniform with the correct insignia to reflect my meteoric promotion in the very short time available. HRH invited me to look around his dressing room and to borrow such things as I needed from his own personal baggage. There were stars, crowns and braided epaulettes in plenty, but the only cap I could find had on it the red tabs of a field marshal and I was trying this on speculatively in front of the mirror when the Duke came back into the room and raised his eyebrows at the sight.

He said, 'I think that's a little higher than you deserve to go quite *yet but I don't suppose there's any harm in you borrowing it because I'm quite sure the navy won't know the difference.'*

*The Duke and the Duchess saw me to the door of his magnificent car and each gave me a comic opera salute which I did my best to return in best brigadier style. The driver and I carved our imperious way down into Cannes through the sunshine and I stepped out on to the red carpet at the appropriate place, facing a phalanx of press cameras, the ranks of distinguished guests and, standing rigidly at the salute, Captain Sir Jeremy who had received only the briefest of signals giving the rank, but not the name, of the substitute officer.*

*For several uneasy seconds I could not be completely sure whether he was going to explode or just burst into tears. Fortunately the press were all concentrating on me or they would have had a most unusual photograph. Naval discipline won out over his personal feelings and honour was then saved when I invited him to join me on the saluting dais, though one pace to the rear of course, leaving his guard of honour to be led by a mere commander.*

*As I pulled the cord to unveil the statute, I fancied for a moment that old Edward had a twinkle in his eye at the way in which his grandson had managed to turn the tables on the stuffy protocol-wallahs of Buckingham Palace.*

*From that moment onward, however, I was never again able to look in the same uncritical way at the decisions of those who take it upon themselves to tell the rest of us how to lead our lives.*

I was reading it for comfort, by myself in the echoes of a slammed door. It had seemed on the way back that I must have done something else to irritate Cat. I didn't know what and by that time I wasn't even sure I cared, but she was wound up like a spring when we walked into the flat. Perhaps she was reacting to the way I was, because seeing Tiggy unexpectedly had dragged me back into some sort of No Man's Land between selves. Cat read my mind.

'Who was that *Tatler* tart?'

'Who do you mean?' I knew perfectly well.

'The Sloane in the street.'

'Someone I used to know.'

'Oh I say, Miles. You have such interesting friends. I bet she plays polo just spiffingly.'

'I'm not Miles.'

'Hang about. It's not Tiggy with the horse poo, is it? She's not after your hunt balls, is she?'

I couldn't believe for a minute that Cat was jealous but she sat down, dug around in her bag and produced a bag of white powder.

'Want some?' she said.

'No thanks.'

'You smoked it with that cow Bo. What's the difference?'

So I had to – just to avoid a scene, and anyway I half wanted to because it was so good and it couldn't be as dodgy as they'd always said because if Cat hadn't happened to offer it I wouldn't even have been thinking about it. Anyway I wanted to prove that her world was my world now and I didn't belong with Tiggy and her neat, clean, new clothes. Cat started doing things with foil and a lighter as if to claim me back. There was a lot of it and it took away the need to do anything else except just lie there for a long time feeling good in a balloon-bulge of time while the evening dimmed the windows. It felt like the way I'd always imagined a mother's love might feel, like being wrapped in deep comfort. Cat broke it by getting up before I was able to and started rooting around, picking up things.

'What *is* all this crap?' she asked when I came back down to the smaller things of life. 'Been going through Granddad's attic?'

'I bought it at the auction.'

'Well, whatever that cost you it was a waste.'

'You reckon?' I dug the royal letter out of the pile. 'Look at that. Serious money, that's worth.'

She took it and looked at it. 'Who's Edward?'

'*King* Edward. Edward the Eighth, except by that time he was just the Duke of Windsor.' She looked blank. 'You know, the one who abdicated? Mrs Simpson and all that?'

'Oh, right. So who'd buy that?'

'Any autograph collector.'

'Can I have it?'

'No.'

'What about the petrol and all the stuff?' There was a shrill, slightly manic edge showing in her voice again.

'You want some money?'

'Don't be sordid. I want that.'

'Sorry.'

'It's only a bit of paper.'

'I'm selling it myself,' I said, but already I wasn't quite sure that was true.

She turned all soft then and draped herself around me, clinging where she touched like a shower curtain on a wet body. I knew she just wanted the letter but there are some things that logic and reason have little control over and I felt myself responding to her in the still, timeless evening-sealed world of that room. It was just a power game. She suddenly went stiff, broke away and sprang to her feet.

'I'll be back,' she said. 'Later. Maybe.'

I found myself not entirely sorry to see her leave, though my body was.

When she'd gone I had felt spiky and dissatisfied, but I turned to the trunk for solace and, finally putting together the pieces of the manuscript in the right order, I had read that unlikely story of the march-past for the statue on the Croisette Promenade.

It immediately brought up the essential question, what you might call the 'V versus Max question'. Could you really believe it? It was a very tall story, indeed Max himself seemed to have inserted a coded warning at the very start: *There have been moments, I confess, when my accounts of my affairs have stretched the credulity even of my friends . . .*

If I'd had to put money on it then I would have betted against it and a few minutes later I would have had to hand over my money, because that was when I saw something that looked very like the proof of the story lying face-up, staring at me from the top of the untouched mound that still more than half-filled the trunk. I inspected it carefully. Max, swagger stick in one gloved hand, stands on the left of the picture leaning inwards towards a naval officer. The other man has four rings on his sleeve and is half-turned towards Max. He also has a stick under his arm. In the background, framed between their two heads, is a saluting dais facing a plinth with a statue on it and the statue certainly has a regal look. It could be Cannes, at least it is certainly somewhere with more exotic flora than England and the thing about the picture, the really extraordinary thing, is that the peak of Max's cap is covered with a wide crescent of gold braid and his epaulettes are crawling with things that might be crowns or pips or something of the sort that the military use to emphasize high rank. It's true that Max seems a bit short of medal ribbons compared to the navy man, but his pose and his uniform certainly don't indicate deference.

Perhaps this dog really did have his day.

That was not all I found that night. I hit a rich seam of letters from lawyers and bankers relating to a wide variety of crises in Max's life – bankruptcy proceedings, allegations of fraud, involvement in divorce cases, unpaid bills – all the times he'd 'been a real Birkin Owen'. Mostly I put these to one side for the distant day when I might be able to arrange them in some sort of order and make sense of them. One or two told a simple, self-contained tale. There was the letter from the Midland Bank in Carmarthen, dated July 1952 addressed to Max at 4, Lowndes Mews:

Dear Sir,

We are in receipt of your letter of the 14th instant, the contents of which we note.

Notwithstanding the arguments you advance in that letter, we continue to be very anxious that you should reduce your overdraft in accordance with the Treasury Directive, as we are not allowed to grant accommodation for personal purposes. We therefore regretfully have to request you not to draw any further cheques.

In the matter of the two cheques mentioned by you for £250 and £55 respectively, these have now been carefully examined by us and there is no doubt that in our opinion both were drawn and signed by you. In case you have forgotten the circumstances, the former cheque was drawn on a Guards Club form and is payable to the Guards Club or bearer. There is no endorsement visible upon it. The latter was from your own cheque-book and was made payable to Mr PA Fudakowski.

You tell us in your letter to stop all cheques signed 'MB

Owen.' Does this apply when signed 'M Birkin Owen'? As both of these are after all undeniably your name, we should like definite instructions from you as to the form of signature you will use in future.

The balance of your account today is a debit of £2,348/–/10.

Yours faithfully,

WB Stone.

Manager.


Mr WB Stone contained his feelings well. You could tell that what he really wanted to say at the end of the letter was, 'Come off it. Who do you expect to believe that?' But all he'd allowed himself was the dignified censure of 'notwithstanding' and 'undeniably'. I'd had a few letters like that when I was waiting for one of my great-aunt's cheques and when nobody seemed to want to buy the stuff I was trying to sell them. I could sympathize with Max.

There was another series of letters which told an equally vivid story of what a man will do when he's sufficiently desperate. These came on headed notepaper from an office in the Ministry of Housing and they showed that in the two years after that letter from the bank Max's financial affairs had become no more straightforward. All the letters were from one Hamo McLaurin, and they related to a betting syndicate in which the two of them seemed to have a share. The tone was friendly until March 22nd, 1954. On that day McLaurin's letter started with the words, 'Private – without prejudice', heavily underlined:

My dear Max,

Since you specifically told me in your second letter, written from Switzerland, that any communications from me to you would be ignored, I have not attempted to write to you, but was obliged in my own self-defence to place your letter in the hands of my solicitors. The accusations you made against me in that letter were of such a grave character, and so completely without foundation in relation to the facts, that I could only assume that the statements about my alleged actions on which you based your letter were supplied to you by those who wished to do me a serious injury.

71

I could not, and cannot, believe that you would make them yourself if you were to hear quietly, and in the presence of witnesses if you so desire it, what I have to say about the course of events following our last personal meeting on February 13th at the Castle.

You will already have heard from my solicitors that the registered packet was opened by me on Monday 15th February, in the presence of a witness as it so happened, and that the contents (apart from your cheerful and kindly letter) were found to be sheets of newspaper.

The exact circumstances of the disappearance of the £295 in five-pound notes are being thoroughly investigated by the Central Investigation Branch of the GPO and I do not know the stage which their enquiries have reached – except that they have taken certain evidence. If in fact they discover that a post office official is responsible, you will get compensation for the loss of the money, but as far as I can gather this compensation may be limited to five pounds as no extra registration fee was paid to cover the full value of the contents.

I had looked forward to twelve months of happy and friendly partnership in this joint enterprise with you and nothing would please me better than to instruct my solicitors to burn your second letter so that I may forget you ever wrote it. With the beginning of the flat racing season, I believe we should do well.

If you are prepared to meet me, either privately or in the presence of your solicitor or another witness, I shall be most happy to meet you.

All good wishes,

Hamo McLaurin.


Another denunciation to line up with 'V', another entry on her side of the ledger, a strong support to the picture she'd drawn of the ne'er-do-well cheque-bouncer. How could he have expected to get away with it? How can a man drift from crisis to crisis supported only by a flimsy lifejacket of unlikely excuses? Or had someone really stolen Max's money? Perhaps the greatest mystery was the potentially friendly tone of the end of McLaurin's letter. After all that, he was still hoping they could sort things out. Max seemed to have a gift for that. Even 'V' had gone back to writing nice letters to him in later years, or adding her good wishes to Douglas's notes. Max seemed to have a gift for surviving the uproars he caused and coming out the other side, still in communication with the people concerned.

There were many notes – right through the 1950s – to Max from Douglas; the staunch, reliable Douglas. Usually he was the intermediary between their long-suffering lawyer and Max, prompting Max to pay bills, reply to letters, sort out affidavits, conserve his money.

'V', I found out, was Virginia, a blonde with a familiar glamour as if I had seen her on television. She had a mischievous, active, laughing face. I knew that because I found a wedding photo of her in which she was pinned to Douglas's arm in certain identification. She was holding a bouquet and wearing a hat with a veil blowing sideways, but it wasn't a church wedding. They were standing by themselves at the bottom of some very municipal-looking steps, probably a register office. Douglas was wearing a rather informal, pale tweed suit with a dark flower in his button-hole and a striped tie. It seemed odd for the early fifties, and you would have thought they'd be church-wedding people. Did someone not approve, or could it have been the second time round for Virginia?

There was also a photo of the three of them at some speed event, Douglas at the wheel of a stunning pre-war Delage wearing racing numbers and Max and Virginia standing by it. It was the late fifties now, I could tell from the newer cars in the background. She was wearing baggy trousers, and she had a large dark mark which looked like oil down one leg, so she'd probably been driving too. In the background you could just see a row of colonnaded arches and those arches had a familiar look: Brighton.

Time seemed to be suspended that night; the residue of the chemicals circulating in my blood saw to that. The trunk provided a little world for me, full of fragments which occupied my attention in passing – dusty little facets.

Odd bits came out of it that spoke briefly and loudly. A letter to Max: *You shit, I believed you. If you leave me to face the music with*

*Anthony by myself, I'll make quite sure your name is dragged through it too. You must be aware what I know about you. Evelyn.*

Another letter from an estate agent: *I enclose a further copy of the letter from the prospective purchasers which now requires your urgent attention. As a matter of fact, the tickets for the Trooping of the Colour did not arrive but no matter, thank you for trying.*

There were more and more photos of exotic cars, some with Max or Douglas at the wheel, and more and more bills for their repair and threats from garages to take action if the bills weren't soon paid.

Another letter surfaced which touched on Max's fantasy of his own life. It was addressed from the Isle of Man and dated 1947.

My dear Maxie,

I had a holiday in Cassis during August and ran into Donald Beauchamp, just back from Greece. He tells me you owe him a letter. I've got a good story to tell you about the Major, who is still very much alive and still snorts when your name is mentioned. You'll be pleased to hear he's got himself into the most frightful pickle.

I had a whale of a time but was somewhat cramped from the currency angle. Cassis is absurdly expensive these days. So much for the palms of victory passing to the winners, eh? There are all these Vichy types sitting around positively bathing in bubbly.

Actually I went with the idea of finding a plot to settle but it would take a millionaire to do that and be reasonably comfortable. I think the time has come to make some arrangements and I want you to think about the promises you made, after we managed to resolve all that unfortunate business in Pirbright, about sorting me out a cell to which I can retire.

Will you please have a squint around your vast holdings and see if you have anything you don't want for sale or rent at a reasonable price. At the outside, not over twenty acres and a vineyard would certainly suit well. The state of the house doesn't matter too much as I will have lots of spare time to get it fixed. I seem to recall you mentioned there was a small manoir or two amongst your French holdings but somewhere in Italy would do equally well. Tuscany, I think you said?

Happy Christmas and New Year and kindest regards,
Simon Marchant

What lies had Max told in the bonhomie of the wardroom? Convincing ones, certainly – convincing enough for Simon Marchant to think he could call in an old favour with no idea how little chance he stood of success. Whatever the incident in Pirbright had been, and a bouncing cheque was my guess, Simon Marchant was not going to see the long-term pay-off he had been anticipating. Poor Simon Marchant, but perhaps he had it coming.

I remembered Virginia's letter again: ... *we have been saying and will go on saying when necessary that Max ... does not have vineyards and chateaux in the South of France ...*

Virginia was still in my mind when I opened a black-edged letter from New Zealand and read in it the first intimation of her end and the first clue that the trunk was so very much more than a passing curiosity in my life.

My dear Max,

I was so extremely sorry to hear from Madge of the terrible thing that has happened to poor darling Ginny. Do give my best love to Douglas and tell him we are all thinking of him out here.

Phoebe

I crawled off to sleep after that, but sleep is an extraordinary state where parts of the brain seem to rest and other parts work a busy night shift, putting together all the little bits and pieces that the conscious mind has been unable to sort out in the daytime. In my sleep, my brain finally worked out exactly who Virginia was.

# Eight

The subconscious isn't always on your side. Why else would it hit you quite so brutally in those vulnerable moments when you first wake up? That grey morning with refuse-truck crashings outside and cold condensation trickling down the inside of my dirty windows, there was no cushioning moment between ignorant sleep and completely aware waking. I was lying alone in a pocket of warmth in that otherwise chilly bed. Cat hadn't come back and I hadn't really noticed. My brain was speeding away and my body mistook its sudden activity for fear so that I felt myself flooding with adrenaline. I had a vague sense of horrified dreams but they were shouldered aside by the immediacy of what my mind wanted to tell me after its labours of the night.

In the light of what follows it will seem, I suppose, that it took me a long time to reach this point, but consider this. The name at the forefront of my mind, the name that had, from the first, come attached to the brothers and therefore to 'V' was that not-quite-double-barrelled Birkin Owen. One part of me recognized that Max had only a dubious claim to using the 'Birkin' as part of his surname. Douglas, it seemed, had usually been content to be a mere Owen. 'V', who had just become Virginia, had been a bracket to Max and Douglas, and I had never thought of her as having a whole name. Virginia Birkin Owen would have meant nothing in particular to me before I found the trunk nor, come to that, would Virginia Owen, but shorten Virginia to Ginny and the whole story changed. Ginny Owen would have meant something to me.

I fell in love with Ginny Owen when I was twelve and it lasted a year.

I got out of bed on legs that were not nearly so awake as my head, pulled stiff cold jeans over my colder legs and lurched into the next room where the trunk's contents were arranged in their separate piles. A simple check on the postmark of the black-edged letter would tell me the complete truth, but I was sure I knew what it would say. September or October 1963 was my guess, and it was no guess, really.

I was wrong, but only by a month. Even bad news took some time to travel to New Zealand. It was 1963 certainly, but the postmark was November.

On Saturday, September 14th 1963, I finally got my lift to Brighton with the Colonel.

There are things I remember very clearly indeed about that day and there are other things which are simply great gaps. I had been planning to take the slow Southdown bus. Precedent had been set the year before and it was recognized that I was now almost thirteen, a year older, and that this was to be allowed. The Colonel's decision to take me was made suddenly that morning after another of those distant muffled, raised-voice episodes which always made me feel that time had been suspended and that I was not a free individual but a fly trapped in the house's web while two spiders argued over the division of my body.

I thought I knew what it was about. It was about names. In a moment of thoughtlessness, I had filled in a coupon for a car catalogue in the wrong name – the name which, when I was a child, I only ever used in my head. When the envelope arrived, containing its Jaguar brochure or whatever it was I'd sent for, they got to it before I did, the Colonel and my mother. Printed on the front was the clear evidence of treason, 'Miles Malan' where it should have said 'Miles Drummond'.

The Colonel was going to 'have a word' with me.

I remember very clearly what I was wearing: a thick, blue school sports shirt tucked into dark grey school trousers and, a solitary concession to style, those canvas and rubber baseball boots which preceded trainers and cost a fraction of the amount. I had packed a blue duffel bag with an anorak I didn't want to be seen wearing, a Wall's Pork Pie, a Wagon Wheel, one or two Trebor spearmint chews and a can of Fanta Orange clanking against one of those triangular-ended levers for making the two holes in the top before the days of pull-tabs. Considering that is all unimportant background detail, it is surprising that it has been etched into the same corner of my brain as the events later in the day. I feel indeed that *this* memory is more reliable because I have taken it out and looked at it and spun it round and put it away again so much less often.

I had five shillings – two weeks' saved-up pocket money – to get into the paddock and buy a programme. The Colonel appeared in the kitchen as I finished packing my lunch in the bag.

'Got to go your way,' he said to the cupboard, 'see a feller from the regiment, old sarn't major of mine. Give you a lift.'

My heart fell. 'I'll be fine on the bus.'

'In the car,' he said, 'two ticks.'

If it had been the Bentley I wouldn't have minded a bit. It was a beautiful, unspoilt three-litre tourer but it hadn't turned a wheel in all the time I'd known it, so we went in the Rover. He drove like a cavalry officer on ceremonial duty, looking stiffly in front and keeping to a steady forty regardless of whether road conditions called for seventy or twenty. Our progress, as ever, was marked by irate horns from those beyond the periphery of his vision who'd had to take avoiding action. It took him an age to start talking and we were already close to the back of Brighton when he said, abruptly, 'That letter of yours.'

'Yes?' I said much too fast.

'Name on it. Your mother's upset.'

'It was just a mistake.'

'Funny sort of mistake.'

'I wasn't thinking.'

'Not thinking? Man doesn't put the wrong name down without thinking.'

'I must have been sort of dreaming.'

'Malan,' said the Colonel. 'Funny sort of dream.'

'It *was* my name,' I said defensively.

'I've adopted you. You're a Drummond.'

'I just wanted to see what it felt like,' I said, though that was not the truth.

The Colonel drove straight past the turning to the centre of Brighton. His business with his ancient sergeant major was in Lewes, I knew, because he'd visited the man before. I realized with horror that, for the sake of this conversation, he was taking me to Lewes first while the speed trials went on their way without me. I couldn't say anything. It wasn't, I think, a vindictive act on his part. He would have thought of it in terms of the chain of command in which I was a private and he was the colonel and my needs were only to be considered as a tiny adjunct to his own.

The truth was that I used Malan as my name in my head more and more. The start of my second year at boarding school loomed only a week or so away. At school, I had the luxury of having a fantasy father, not the Colonel, who was after all only a stepfather and barely even that in terms of my relationship with him. My fantasy father was much more real to me, built up out of half-truths and hints, and Malan was a good surname for the purpose. In the early sixties, boys still read avidly about the Battle of Britain. *War Picture Library* comics were the second hottest property to trade after dog-eared issues of *Parade* magazine with its grainy, black-and-white photos of nudes sporting smooth, airbrushed crotches.

We thought that was what girls looked like.

'Sailor' Malan was one of those names, along with Johnny Johnson and Douglas Bader, which every boy of my age knew like they knew William the Conqueror. 'Sailor' Malan had been one of the few, the Battle of Britain aces, knights mounted on their Spitfire chargers who kept Jerry, Fritz, the Boche, the Hun in the sun in their evil-named Heinkels and Junkers at bay. The Germans plunged to earth trailing oily smoke with a last despairing cry of '*Achtung! Spitfeuer*,' on their black-and-white lips while 'Sailor' and his chums returned to the earth which barely seemed their proper element for a lick from their Labradors and a pint at a thatched pub. 'Sailor' Malan was much more real to me than the Colonel.

At the back of Worthing on the London road, not too far from our house for a young cyclist with a three-speed gear, was a garage on whose forecourt there stood for a few years a genuine Spitfire, a war-surplus leftover, shabby in pale-blue paint. The owner would indulge me while I wandered around it, and on one glorious occasion I was allowed to climb a stepladder and sit in the cockpit. I was heartbroken when he sold it. The rest of the fantasy was simple. I only had to explain at school that the Colonel was not my real father, which was true, and then half suggest that I was actually the son of some notable relation of the Colonel's killed tragically in an air crash, for the assumptions to be made. Being taken for 'Sailor' Malan's son had a definite cachet. True, he was South African but that was only a minor detail. I could have come to England at an early age. True also that the air crash which finally killed him would have had to have been long after the war because I wasn't born until 1949 but then the comics we read didn't say what happened to our heroes later on and none of my friends would have thought of looking it up. They would have had trouble doing so in any case in a school library whose latest reference books dated from 1936 and where two whole cabinets were full of dog-eared bound volumes of *Punch* from the last century.

I suppose I grew up thinking knowledge was a dusty museum-thing. Even our science labs were filled with ancient constructions of mahogany and brass – scales, fume cupboards, electrical cells, switches and resistors out of Jules Verne. The English teacher who startled us by handing out copies of a recent Penguin paperback for our comments soon had to find himself another job.

Recent history was therefore safe from any checking. In my day-dreams, I think I began to believe this glamorous version of my parentage might be true because it was so much better to have had a father who mattered and who might have cared than just to have the Colonel who only took notice of me on my birthday and then bought me wildly unsuitable presents. These odd objects were sometimes too dull and advanced for my age like the pewter beer tankard he gave me when I was nine. There was an equal chance that they would be so juvenile as to be deeply hurtful like the toddler's plastic fire engine I got at twelve when what I wanted was an Airfix kit of a Flying Fortress.

My fantasy had a vacuum in which to grow because my mother was always completely uninformative on the subject of my real father. Just like the Colonel, she hid any inconvenient emotion under a thick shell of formality. I already felt, in an unformed way, that it wasn't right to keep a child in deliberate ignorance of the nature of a parent. If genes begin to play their part and set you at odds with the world in which you find yourself, how are you meant to guess that this is your inheritance playing havoc with your surroundings rather than some evil of your own? Now that I know all there is to know about my parentage, I understand that, but they should have told me then.

The Colonel did his stiff best as we turned our back on Brighton where I so much wanted to be. I had been looking forward to this all year, to the moment when I would see my devil-may-care goddess and we could take up the strange, thrilling intimacy of the year before. I was taller and less of a child and she had been at the centre of my fantasies.

'Peter Malan wasn't good to your mother. Shouldn't remind her.'

'What do you mean?' I said, stung.

'You're too young. There are wrong 'uns, you know. He was a wrong 'un.'

I couldn't help myself. 'That's my father you're talking about.'

'Mm.'

There was a long silence.

'Doesn't mean he was *all* bad,' he said after three or four miles. 'Fought a hard war. Have to make allowances. Bit of a wild man. Your mother caught the thick end of it. Tough on her. Better not to talk about it. Have they changed these bloody road signs?'

Finding his way along a route he'd done many times before conveniently took up the whole of his attention until we arrived outside the sergeant major's house. I was left in the car for ten minutes which felt like an hour, then they both came out.

'In the back, Miles,' said the Colonel, 'chop chop.'

The sergeant major climbed into the seat I vacated.

'Rottingdean,' said the Colonel.

'Yessir,' said our new passenger. He was perhaps sixty, though I was at the age when you think fifty is sixty and sixty is eighty and beyond that lurk the living dead. I never found out why they were going to Rottingdean because they got straight into a routine as if the sergeant major was the Colonel's observer on some raid into enemy territory.

'Another one on the left, sir. Don't think he's seen us.'

'Thanks, sarn't major. Watch the blighter.'

In the end, I plucked up my courage to remind the Colonel to drop me in Brighton. He didn't answer but he turned the right way at the lights.

We arrived on the seafront a long way east of the pier, in fact a long way east of anything that counted as Brighton, right out of the town by Black Rock.

It was convenient for the Colonel. 'You never know,' he said, 'all that traffic,' and the sergeant major nodded his head sagely.

It was inconvenient for me. I was half a mile beyond the finishing line, the best part of a mile from the paddock where I would find Ginny.

'Got your bus fare back?' asked the Colonel.

'Yes.'

'Remember you're a Drummond,' he said, and drove sedately away across the bows of a bus.

I had been angry all the way in the car – angry that he had made me late, but most of all angry that he'd said my father was a 'wrong 'un'. I was glad he'd fought a hard war, glad he was a bit wild, but who was that man, that shut-off, stuck-up man who was *not* my father, who was he to pass judgement?

They'd been running the speed trials since the days of Edward the Seventh, he of the statue on the Croisette. Ahead of his visit in 1905 the Brighton Corporation laid new-fangled tarmac on the dusty surface of what had been called the Madeira Road and were so impressed by the result that they decided to entertain the King with a speed trial. No less than four hundred cars raced. The highest speed was recorded by Clifford Earp in a huge Napier, who reached a headlong ninety-three miles per hour. That makes it the oldest motor sport event in Britain. At one extreme are the amateurs in the fierce cars of yesteryear who just want a quick gallop up the standing start kilometre. It only gets spectacular in the later classes, where you see the quick, modern jobs – the pensioned-off Formula One cars and the nitromethane-burning sprint motorbikes ridden by brave souls who cling to them like jockeys on a rocket. These are the machines which compete for the holy grail of the event, Fastest Time of Day. It's known as FTD because if you're in the speed business you haven't got time for all those syllables.

The road is now called Madeira Drive.

I could already see as I got nearer the finishing line that the top promenade was even more crowded than usual. Today, there was a big attraction. Two American dragsters had crossed the Atlantic to show us what acceleration really meant; huge-engined, purpose-built slingshots. Patriotism was an issue here. Up against them on the British side was a motorized Don Quixote, a bulky old man blinking through pebble glasses – Sydney Allard, a hero of the British back-street sports car business. Never mind his car, even his *name* didn't sound fast enough against the American star, Dante Duce. Sydney's car was a crude blacksmith's cartoon of theirs. Did he stand any chance at all? Patriotic spectators were hoping for a miracle to avoid his humiliation, racked up there above the colonnades waiting to see all that horsepower unleashed down a track which had been dangerous enough at the speeds of seventy years earlier.

That was meant to be coming later.

Every driver is at their limit when they cross that finishing line a thousand yards from the start. Each has spent the past few seconds – twenty if they're quick, thirty if they're slow – wrestling their car straight over the bumps and correcting the squirming of each frantic gear-change. At the finish there's the biggest bump of all and then, from flat out, it's hard on the brakes. Each driver is intent on pushing their particular limit back by just that extra hundredth of a second, which would give them a new personal best.

It is at the limit that small errors are magnified into big mistakes.

I would have walked straight past the finish and on towards the start and the paddock, which was where I wanted to be, but as I passed it, the man on the Tannoy said, 'Now we come to Class Eight, the Ladies' Class, and the first two runners are Virginia Owen in the Lister and Penny Kingslake in her Aston.' So of course, I stopped to watch the run.

But for Ginny, the Ladies' Class would not have seemed a big deal. Pat Coundley, the star woman driver, took her serious runs in her 'D' type Jaguar with the men in the 'Unlimited Sports Cars'. She was every bit as quick as they were. This Class Eight, back in unreformed 1963, was the lesser class where the 'gels' could have a bit of a go in the chaps' cars and be hailed as plucky for their fine efforts – so long as they didn't run the men too close. During the year since I had seen her, I had followed Ginny's progress at hill-climbs and sprints in the pages of my magazines. I knew from her results that she liked to run her man close. In my frequent fantasies of her, I was that man. We would wear matching racing overalls, she and I, and at the end of a thrilling day's dicing, in which I would just but only just beat her, I would drive that snarling car to some evening cliff-top. There, overlooking the sea, we would turn to each other and kiss, because kissing was still so much more understandable, thrilling and manageable than all the other biological stuff I was just starting to glimpse.

Craning past the other watchers, I saw her start, my perfect woman whose hair I hoped to smell again before the day was over. The Lister was darting around on the track and really going for it, leaving the much quieter Aston floundering behind. It was past a hundred miles an hour in the first fifteen seconds, getting larger and louder as it rocketed towards us, taking up the middle of the road. Ginny was pushing hard and I was thrilled to my core. The Lister, that old war-horse, was rushing towards the point where her bearing and my bearing intersected, when the things you expect to happen stopped happening and a new, impossible sequence took their place.

There was a moment of frozen denial when the front of the car started to shake violently and the back wheels, losing their adhesion to the tarmac, skipped a little sideways. She was no more than fifty yards from the finish, travelling with huge speed, and I saw her look over her shoulder as if puzzled by the way the steering felt. The car started to wander lazily towards the sea in a gentle arc and I could see her trying to correct the steering, unaware the steering wheel no longer had anything to do with it. An odd anger rose in me as time slowed down and I wanted to shout that this wasn't right. This must be stopped *now*.

The car's gentle swing became abruptly sharper as something metal that should have been holding things together came apart and then the whole car was dancing, bouncing, veering in a terrible, uncontrollable curve towards the kerb. I already knew that once it hit that kerb then the forces of momentum, tyre grip and stability which had kept it stuck to the road would be thrown into the air to land as they may. Once it hit that kerb, there was no hope of a safe outcome.

Try hitting an oil can hard with a hammer. The noise you get is tremendous. Now think of something with a thousand times the mass of the hammer, all fabricated, forged, bolted and riveted in intricate shapes, travelling at getting on for a hundred and fifty miles an hour. The noise that structure makes as metal tears, tubes compress and castings crack is simply unbelievable and its echoes stay in the head, playing over and over, for a long time.

There was a moment when the violent, vile noise was over and just that echo remained, when the holiday crowd, which had not come here to see this, was holding its breath; when young eyes were staring at the flailed, useless wreckage which had vaulted the torn railings to land, of all the unsuitable places, on a cast iron children's roundabout in the closed playground. There was that daft moment when silence returned and it was all sinking in, when I thought maybe, just maybe, that rag doll squashed down sideways below the steering wheel would get up, smile and take a bow to relieved applause. It was not to be. That was the closest I got to Ginny then or ever again. The moment was perhaps a second long, no more, then the cruel nature of things asserted itself and the powerful, thin liquid spilling out all round the torn metal achieved ignition where the battery, hanging from its straps, was spilling its acid and shorting out against the chassis in a shower of sparks.

The next noise we heard from the railings was a dull concussion that sounded like 'whomp', teamed up with a blast of heat, and then I broke the cross-bearing. I took my eyes away because I could not bear it any longer. I looked at the sea because that still looked just the same, then I turned to run away, down the promenade back towards the start where Ginny would be there to comfort me, to let me sit in her car again, to lean over me in the place where such things do not happen.

Many other people, quite unaccountably, were running the other way, eager to see, and I wanted to tell them not to. I'd seen and I didn't want to see again, but despite that there was a temptation to disbelieve and a need to know the worst, so that every few yards I slowed and turned and looked back to where a finger of black smoke was climbing higher and higher into the still and uncaring summer sky. It was the vertical marker of that fatal cross-bearing and at its base, X marked the spot – dust in the air suspended – that marked the place were the story ended.

That was where I had last seen Virginia Owen.

# Nine

The trunk had sprung its trap on me and an addiction was ignited. It had built up in easy stages. I had bought it on a whim, the coincidence of 'Birkin Owen' and the chance of learning why that seemed to be the worst personal term of abuse in the Colonel's vocabulary – a summation of all that made up an unreliable, slapdash character. I had gone on delving inside because I soon had the sense that I was uncovering the shape of a person moulded in the dust of this paper Pompeii. Now, abruptly, it closed its grip on me and this was no longer easy in any way. There was a moment of giddy merger as I stood by the trunk, weak-legged – a moment when my slain, burnt Ginny stepped out of her petrol pyre to become one with 'V' the letter-writer, 'V' Max's critic, Virginia Douglas's wife. Separate binocular images moved together to join and unbalanced me as they did so. This was *her*, my Ginny – and if it was Ginny who had said all those things about Max, not just some unknown spiteful 'V', then how could they be wrong?

There was a far more important question to be solved here than the reason for the Colonel's epithet. Ever since that second day in Brighton, I had wanted to know *why* Ginny died. Over and over again in the days after the crash, my brain tirelessly replayed the scene and sometimes filled in for me what I hadn't stayed to see as the fire burnt out. I couldn't stop it and a series of fantasies and 'what ifs' teemed along with it. What if she had crashed because she saw my face in the crowd watching? What if the Colonel hadn't made me late and I'd met her in the paddock? Wouldn't everything have been just that bit different? The second at which she came to the starting line, the way she held the wheel, the force of her foot on the accelerator? Then might not those tiny changes have brought her and her wayward car to a different and less dangerous crossing of the bearings? I even thought later, as the newspaper talked of a breakage, that perhaps I could have saved her, that I could have arrived just in time to spot the failing suspension or the missing bolt or whatever else it was that had sent her there to melt the tarmac in the Peter Pan playground.

It may have been a long time ago, but finding the answer to *why* it happened still mattered because I still thought that was a question that could be answered. I needed to hold someone responsible because if Ginny's savage death was just a random event, how could I ever trust the world again? If people you loved could be obliterated by a whim of fate then you should never risk loving anyone.

Although the horrid thing I saw in my head these days was a fraud of memory, copied, recopied and probably changed in the process, I still saw it clearly, whatever it was.

That September day in 1963 was a turning point for me in several ways. Looking back with the detachment of years I might say that I needed to transfer my emotions to fantasy figures, to the imagined hero who was my father and to Ginny who was lover and ideal mother rolled into one. That makes it sound silly, but I have to stick up for the thirteen-year-old and say it was nothing of the sort.

Ginny's death saved old Sydney Allard from defeat. After they cleared up, they let the racing go on but the dragsters' demonstrations were much reduced for safety. Beyond the pier, sitting on the beach the far side, I had to walk myself out of hearing range when the engines started again because the noise made me feel ill. I sat on a bench and stared at the sea. Two hours passed by in which the car crashed and burnt over and over and over again. The worst of it was imagining that she had time to know what was coming, three, four, five long seconds of knowing it was going to hurt, like the time I'd swerved my bike off the garden path down the steep bramble slope into the cucumber frames.

It didn't end my enthusiasm, that crash. Ginny had cared about fast cars and if she was prepared to give her life to them then I thought she would have wanted me to go on too, but for years afterwards I preferred them on paper, in the safe pages of books and magazines, rather than in unpredictable reality. On that September day though, I needed to get right away so I caught the bus home to the reality of the Colonel and my mother who had not understood me the year before when the missiles seemed set to fly. I could only hope that they would see my distress and be the people I needed them to be to fill the hole Ginny had left.

The Colonel was back. The Rover was parked in the drive and I walked past it, carrying with me my burden of grief, shock and disgust flimsily wrapped up inside me. I walked past the old gardener, Mr Hoskins, who was in on a Saturday earning overtime because as the Colonel had put it, 'Got to get the flowerbeds dug in before Johnny winter tests our defences.' He surveyed them as if they were slit trenches. Mr Hoskins said something to me in vague greeting but I don't think I responded. I cut across the grass to the gap in the hollyhocks which led to the side lawn, and from there threaded my way through the rosebeds to the back door. I was meant to take the long way round on the path but, that day, I granted myself an exemption. The back door had a brass thermometer next to it with a marker for the lowest temperature and another for the highest. A horseshoe magnet hung from a string next to it. Only the Colonel was allowed to use the magnet to reset the markers. Below the thermometer was a red plastic gadget with a dial to tell the milkman how many pints to leave which, even to me, looked out of place in the old brick grandeur of Oakdean's stableyard. My mother liked red plastic. The kitchen clock, made by Smiths, was also red plastic. I hated it. The milkman always left two pints whatever the dial said.

The Colonel and my mother were standing in the kitchen. I had interrupted them in the course of something. Thinking back, I wonder whether it might have been something to do with affection, but it wasn't an option that seemed likely at the time. My mother's standard demeanour was that of adjutant to the Colonel, one who ministered dutifully to his needs, and it never occurred to me at that age that the needs might range beyond being fed, provided with clean clothes and reminded of doctors' appointments. I had no understanding then of what it was he did for her either.

'Miles, dear,' my mother said, 'you're back early. Wasn't it fun?'

The Colonel stood there tall and stooped, looking at me with his oyster eyes, inspecting my clothes.

'There was a crash,' I said, and it was odd that having been starkly dry-eyed and grim all the way back on that slow, slow bus, my voice began to twist in my throat the moment I spoke.

'Oh, dear,' said my mother vaguely. 'Did they have to stop?'

'No.' I needed them to know I was suffering but I couldn't just say it all. In the Colonel's house, you didn't do that. I took a few breaths. 'It was in front of me.'

'What's this?' said the Colonel. 'Did you have a good view?'

'Yes. It was right there.'

'What was?' He hadn't been listening.

'The crash. The woman was killed.'

'Oh, dear. How horrid,' said my mother.

'Killed?' said the Colonel. 'Who was?'

'The woman who was driving the car.'

He snorted. He didn't believe in women driving cars except in wartime.

'Did they stop the race?' my mother asked.

'It wasn't a *race*. It was a speed trial. I don't know. I left.'

'How disappointing. You were so looking forward to it, too.'

I so badly wanted to say, look, I have just seen a woman, a friend, more than a friend, someone I don't know the right word for, crushed and torn and burnt in front of me – a woman who had laughed with me and leant against me – and I didn't know that happened to live, laughing, pretty people. I didn't know that happened casually, so you could see it without some sort of warning, some sort of age certificate to protect the young, like in the cinema. I didn't know the waves just rolled on when things like that happened and I didn't know that people would rush towards it, not away from it. I so badly wanted them to say, 'Oh, Miles, poor Miles,' and sit me down and ask me all about it and listen to me and make it better. I wanted to describe it inch by inch and how I felt about it because that would help to make it go away. Above all, I wanted them to explain it so that it made sense, so that I would understand *why* it had happened.

'What sort of car was it?' said the Colonel, and for a moment I blessed him for asking.

'A Lister-Jaguar,' I said.

'Oh. Modern thing,' he said, losing interest and turning away.

I said, 'I'm going upstairs,' and my mother said, 'Have you had lunch?' in a bright, 'Oh, isn't this fun?' tone of voice.

I shook my head.

'Anyway, I expect you've still got your picnic to eat, haven't you?' she said.

I couldn't imagine a more disgusting thought than the idea of eating that picnic which had been through it with me, soaking in the grief. It was a witness, it wasn't food.

Later on, coming down the stairs after lying on my bed for an hour, staring at the plastic models twisting on the threads that hung from my ceiling, I found their attitude slightly changed. The accident had made it on to the radio news and that had transformed it. If the Home Service said it mattered, then it must. My mother had gone silent and baffled but her eyes followed me when I sat down in an armchair with a book. The Colonel decided to debrief me for the sake of unit morale.

'This crash thing of yours. Heard it on the wireless,' he said.

'Oh.'

'Said this woman bought it. Mrs Owen. Bad show.'

I was silent. It was too late to talk and it wasn't him I would have wanted to talk to. It wasn't even my mother. The memory of my mother when I was small enough to cuddle would have done, if that was a true memory. 'Sailor' Malan would have been better. He wouldn't have just been gruff. He would have gone to the heart of it and explained the flames and the noise and the smell and the sudden transition from all right to all wrong that had me so completely baffled.

'These things happen you know,' said the Colonel, and that was as close to it as he came.

Natalie said later that it would all have happened anyway, that however kind and understanding they had been on that occasion, I would have rebelled at some point. The unfolding of the 1960s and my growth into my teens would have set me at odds with that closed, claustrophobic, silent, musty world of the two of them. Probably that's right. Just then I wanted to be surrounded by fundamentally different people who could laugh or cry or anything like that. Ginny had known how to laugh and to take her life to the edge and say exactly what she felt, not what she thought she ought to.

Khrushchev and Kennedy had started it for me. Brighton had simply confirmed that the Colonel and my mother weren't there when I needed them. These people who had always been the warders of my life had nothing to offer me in the way of rules by which to lead that life. Milo Malan was conceived that day, inside sad little Miles Drummond.

I stood there on that shocked London morning, staring at the trunk as if I could see people clambering out of it. There was still so much to explore in it and there was now so much more reason to explore. Also, I sensed my relationship with it change in another way – for the first time I felt that I really owned it. Before, all that had happened to justify its presence was a commercial ritual of purchase. I knew it had never been meant for the auction when those hands, on whatever authority, had lugged it out of Max's last house to dump it, and everything that marked his passing, in the street. It had been meant for obliteration, for a quick passage to the incinerator, not for resurrection by the totters and dismemberment through the dung-beetle trade.

It wasn't a question of the law of possession. It was mine by law, but what really made it mine was this revelation that my own past was intricately bound up with its dusty documents. I'd paid my subscription at Brighton and now, by virtue of that violent event, I felt all at once that I had a perfect right to read anything I might choose from inside it, to ask any question I wanted to ask, to chase down these lives and to fill in the blanks, to try to fill in the blank I still felt within myself.

I wanted to read some more but I also had to earn a living, or at least to earn the balance between the dribbling monthly cheque from my great-aunt's trust, the Miss AT Roberts (Deceased) Will Trust, and what I needed to get by on with London prices. That morning, despite the weight of the discovery, business came first or I was going to have trouble making up the missing rent money which Cat had taken with her.

On a snowy December night in 1944, a Bristol Beaufighter two-seater ran into trouble in the skies over Yorkshire. I don't know what happened but the crew bailed out and the plane did one of those mysterious things that planes sometimes do, sorting itself out without any help from its departed crew and gliding down to what would have been a survivable crash landing in the middle of Wheeldale Moor. It was much too far away from roads to be retrieved and there were no helicopters then to pluck it out of the bog in which it had fallen. Thirty years on, a crash-site fanatic called Lenny Osborne found what was left buried in the peat and the heather and brought me down a few battered bits and pieces to test the market for the rest. Most people would have dismissed them as broken rubbish, barely worth the attention of the scrap-man, but to an enthusiast they were altogether special. Anyone who knew their stuff would have recognized them as a throttle quadrant, a trim wheel and a gunsight, and there were also some weathered fuselage panels to make up the first haul. Collectors love each other and hate each other. The others who share their interests are the only ones who fully understand their obsessions, the only conversational partners who won't be bored stiff by the end of the first sentence. They are also the most direct threat – the ones who might outbid you or cast aspersions on the authenticity of your favourite pieces.

I was on a fifty-fifty split but the sale was proving a little difficult. Jerry Fratton, a stockbroker, who was usually first in line for stuff like that, wasn't in a trusting mood after an unfortunate episode when I sold him in good faith something supposed to be a Spitfire Mk IX rudder pedal which turned out to be from a Chipmunk trainer.

I knew there was a man called Peel somewhere in Chiswick who liked Beaufighter bits, so I started calling all the people in the phone book who might be him and failed and, sort of naturally, because O comes just before P, switched to looking through the Owen list just in case something jumped out at me, but nothing did. There were one or two 'M Owens' and even more 'D Owens' but that didn't help and I wasn't really expecting much. When, rather aimlessly, I turned to 'Birkin Owen' wondering whether Douglas might have turned pompous in later life or whether Max's last address might be listed, I was astonished to see there was an entry and it was 'Birkin Owen, Mrs L' with an expensive-looking address near Harrods.

'Mrs L' didn't seem to fit at all.

Dialling the number was easy. Deciding what to say if anyone answered was hard.

'Hello?'

'Oh, I'm sorry to trouble you. Is that Mrs Birkin Owen?'

'Mrs Birkin Owen. Yes, that's right.' The voice was upper crust, perhaps slightly Scottish and very guarded.

'My name is Miles Malan. We haven't met, but I wonder whether you're related to Max Birkin Owen?'

'Why do you ask?'

I should have known that anyone who'd had any connection with Max might be reluctant to admit it.

'It's just that by a rather odd coincidence I happen to have found some photographs which belonged to him.' That sounded safer than saying 'papers' or 'documents', but I was uncomfortably aware that she might still think it was some sort of blackmail.

'Yes?'

'Well, if you were related to him, I wondered if you'd like to . . .' I almost said, 'have them back,' but I couldn't bring myself to do that '. . . to see them?'

'No, I don't think so, thank you.'

That left me stuck. I risked everything.

'It's just . . . Well, you see, I'm trying to find out more about him.'

'Why would anybody want to do that?'

'It's a personal thing. I was there when his sister-in-law died and I . . .'

'Virginia?' she said with a note of surprise. 'You were there when Virginia was killed?'

I let out a deep, silent breath. 'Yes.'

'So what is your interest, Mr Malan?'

'Something quite important to me. Not just curiosity. I want to know a bit more.'

'And you want to talk to me about it?'

'That would be very kind of you.'

'I'm rarely kind,' she said. She seemed to be thinking. 'I would judge you to be quite young by your voice.'

'I'm twenty-three,' I said.

'And you want nothing else, just to talk to me?' she said.

'Yes, that's right.'

'Well, Mr Malan. I am going abroad very soon but you can have half an hour of my time tomorrow afternoon if you agree to take absolutely not a minute more than that. Come at four o'clock and we shall have a cup of tea together. If you've found my number, I expect you have my address?'

'I do.'

'The porter will be expecting you. He is a fierce man so be to sure to explain who you are.'

The porter might have been fierce once, but extreme age had taken the edge off him so I guessed that had just been a warning shot in case I was after all a thief of some sort. The door on the tiled, second-floor landing of the Victorian block was opened not by Mrs Birkin Owen but by an elderly and immaculate man in a kilt with a sporran, and he *did* look fierce. I was wearing the most suitable clothes I could find – a Tootals shirt Tiggy had given me two years earlier, a pair of jeans which were respectable solely because I had only worn them once, and an old school jacket which had come in one of the boxes from home and which I had never unpacked. It probably looked extraordinarily scruffy – the laird or whatever he was certainly thought so – but at least it was conventional. He raised an eyebrow pointedly as he stood back for me to come in.

'Hello,' I said, 'I'm Miles Malan.'

He ignored my hand and nodded through the hall at an open door without saying a word. I walked through into a large sitting room crowded with delicate furniture. A woman in her sixties got up from an armchair and looked me up and down. I was acutely aware of the man in the kilt who had followed me in and was now standing at the door, alert to my every move.

'Mr Malan,' the woman said, and the Scottish accent was less noticeable than it had been on the phone. 'I don't like mysteries. Sit down and tell me what this business of yours is all about.' She made no effort to introduce the laird.

I did my best to explain, though not completely, about the trunk. I made it sound as if perhaps it was just a small bundle of stuff I had found and that I had by chance recognized a photo of Ginny. She was nodding and when I came to the end she looked round at the laird and said, 'I think it will be fine now, Ian, thank you so much.'

'I'll be just across the hall, Laura,' he said, with a meaningful look at me and went out. Insurance. That implied I was now trusted, at least by Laura.

'What sort of tea would you like?' she said.

'Oh, anything,' I said.

'Lapsang Souchong?'

I was more used to PG Tips. 'Yes, thank you,' I said.

'Stay there,' she said, 'I'll only be a minute or two. I would be obliged if you didn't move.'

Oh, God. She still thought I might be out to steal the silver. I looked round as much as I could, rooted to the spot, like someone who's missed the ball at French cricket.

The walls were hung with a great many large paintings, taking up all the available space with the implication that there would once have been a much bigger house for them. The furniture was fine, spindly, fussy stuff which would have mostly benefited from the attentions of a good polisher. The side-table was piled with letters. Laura Birkin Owen came back, bringing with her an atmosphere that was slightly warmer following the laird's departure, but only in the sense that a fridge is slightly warmer than a freezer. She was a proud and rather fine-looking woman, in an old-fashioned way. A sister? No, and anyway she'd been 'Mrs' in the phone book.

'Now who was it you really wanted to know about?' she asked. 'And why? Was it poor Virginia or was it Max? You mentioned Max first of all.'

'I'm terribly sorry,' I said, 'I don't even know where you come in all this.' It wasn't perhaps an elegant way to express the question but I couldn't think of a better one.

'Me?' she said, surprised, and now it was my turn for surprise. 'Oh, I was Max's wife.'

I had been completely and utterly sure that Max had never had a wife. There was no sign of a wife in anything I had seen. The trunk was not the trunk of a man who had a wife. I must have looked at her in disbelief because she frowned slightly and said, 'I'm sorry. You didn't *know* Max, did you? You're not a relation or something?'

'No, no. I just hadn't realized he was married.'

'Well, I expect there's a great deal else that you hadn't realized.'

'Were you, um, together for long?'

She looked as if I had asked something very impolite. 'We were only together, under the same roof, you might say, for a short time, but that is more my business than yours, I would have thought.'

But you kept his name, was what I wanted to say, so presumably you stayed married, why was that? I couldn't say it, though.

'I was wondering how the photos ended up where I found them, in an auction,' I said.

'I don't know at all,' she said. 'Max died a little while ago. He had three strokes, one after the other. I think his brother probably cleared out his flat. It was the cars you were interested in, was it?'

'I've always been mad about cars,' I said. 'I told you, didn't I, I was there at Brighton when Virginia was killed. It had quite an effect on me.'

'You can't have been very old,' she said, but her implication was that I couldn't have been old enough to care, not that my youth must have made it worse.

'It was terrible for Max, of course. She looked over her shoulder, you know. That was why she lost control. It really wasn't Max's fault. He shouldn't have let her drive, but she so wanted to.'

I couldn't imagine why she should say that so vehemently. What right did Max have to tell his sister-in-law what she could and couldn't do? She saw my frown.

'Oh, didn't you know? That's what some of them said afterwards. They said Max didn't look after the car properly.'

'The Lister was *Max's* car?'

'Oh, yes.'

'I thought it belonged to Douglas. I thought that's why Virginia was driving it.'

'No, Max didn't drive his cars in races, you see – only on the road, poor dear.'

'Why?'

'He was never fit after the war. He was wounded you know, at Narvik. Have you heard of Narvik?'

Yes, I'd heard of Narvik. I'd heard of it in several ways. There was Ginny's letter ... *was not gallantly injured in the war at Dunkirk, or at Narvik or at Arnhem – indeed unlike Douglas was barely in the war at all let alone doing anything remotely heroic ...* Without that I would have heard of Narvik anyway, from *War Picture Library* and from all the other accounts of the action in the Arctic circle when Warburton-Lee's destroyer, HMS *Hardy*, led its four sister ships up a Norwegian fjord in a near-suicidal attack on the German ships moored there. I'd even built a model of the *Cossack* which took part in the second attack. That probably put me rather closer to the action than Max had ever been, but Laura clearly believed he'd been a hero.

'What happened to him there?'

'He never really talked about it. Men who've killed other men in wartime often won't, you know. But I do know he came within an inch of drowning. It all caught up with him later on, his chest was never the same.'

I sought to switch the conversation. 'Was Virginia a good driver?'

'I couldn't say.'

'What was she like?'

'I don't know. I never met her.' She said it as if it should be obvious.

'You never met her?'

'Max and I were married after she died, you see.'

After 1963? They were both getting on a bit.

'What about Douglas? Do you still see him?'

'I haven't seen anything of him for years now. Just the phone call to tell me when Max died.'

She withdrew a little then and we both sipped our tea. It tasted utterly unlike tea and was not at all what I wanted. I didn't know where to go with the conversation.

'So she looked over her shoulder,' I repeated dully.

'That's what Max always said. Then she hit the kerb, you see.'

That was certainly true.

'He knew about these things. He used to drive there himself, you see. Soon after the war, when he was stronger.' She turned, pulled a drawer open and brought out two old photographs. I recognized the one on top straight away, a policeman peering curiously into a huge Bugatti. I had a larger print of it in the trunk.

'That was one of Max's,' she said. 'A king owned that car originally, you know.'

My attention was fixed on the other photo. It was clearly at Brighton. A vintage sports car was just leaving the starting line and all you could see of the driver was eyes staring through goggles and a comically ill-fitting pudding basin crash helmet balanced on the top of his head. It had huge headlights and swept wings and it looked like an Alfa 1750 with a Zagato body except the radiator was far more massive. I have always been proud of my detailed knowledge of obscure cars and I had no idea what this was.

'That's him driving,' she said, 'soon after the war, I think, when he still could.'

'Do you know what the car is?'

'I wouldn't have any idea at all.'

She was getting fidgety and though the promised half hour was nowhere near its expiry, I had clearly outstayed my welcome.

'Now, I wonder would you mind terribly if we drew this to a close? I'm going to Spain tomorrow and I have to collect my tickets at Harrods, you see.'

We shook hands.

'It is all quite some time ago, you know,' she continued holding on to my hand for a moment longer than necessary. 'I don't really feel that I quite understand what it is that you want, but some things are best left to rest.'

I walked to the tube thinking about it, aware that in some ways I knew more of Max than she did, this brief unrecorded wife of his who still kept his name. I wondered what had split them up, though almost everything I knew of him amounted to an explanation several times over. I could see her as a pillar of the local community, an upholder of standards. She made an unlikely partner for the Max I was starting to know. As the provider of a cross-bearing, Laura had me all at sea.

Swaying and rattling along in the tube, I suddenly thought of the man who'd got me through the barrier at Brighton. I had taken so little notice of him once I had met Ginny and, since I'd found the trunk, I had assumed he was Douglas, who drove the car later that first day. What had he said, though? Something like, 'Come and see *my* car.' The Lister was Max's car. Could it be that I had met Max? I wanted to go straight back to study his photo, to see if I could resurrect any of that memory.

I knew Cat was back as soon as I got home. The door was wide open. There was a strong smell of dope coming through it and loud, unfamiliar music was playing.

I walked in to find Cat sprawled in a beanbag, smoking. She started laughing as soon as she saw me and couldn't stop.

'What the fucking hell . . . Why are you . . . ? What *are* you dressed up as?'

I pulled the jacket off.

'Nice to see you too,' I said.

'Cool it. Come and have some of this.'

I sat down on the floor next to her and took a drag. It was very strong. 'Where have you been?' I said.

'Morocco.'

'What? Just for two days?'

'There's a lot you can do in Morocco in two days.'

She went to score dope, that was clear. Knowing Cat she would have just walked straight through customs, carrying it without a second thought.

'Did you miss me?' I said foolishly, wondering whether she'd been by herself.

'Fuck, no. Course I haven't. I've been in Morocco for Chris'sake. I didn't go to bloody Morocco to *miss* you. I went for a good time.'

'And you had one.'

'Oh, yes. Oh yes indeed.'

The floor was covered in the stuff, not so much unpacked as tipped evenly all over it. It consisted of two or three shirts and a lot of packets that looked like they'd lead to a quick jail sentence if any policeman followed his nose up the steps and through the hall.

I looked at it morosely, then I realized there was an absence of the other things that had been on the floor before this lot.

'Where's all the stuff?'

'What stuff?'

'The things I was sorting out on the floor. The photos and that?'

'All that waste paper? I binned it.'

# *Ten*

In the time it took me to get out to the dustbins, I imagined finding them empty, chasing the truck through the streets, begging the bin-men to let me search it or even ending up wandering the rubbish mountains of some lunar landscape dump where crows fought with starving scarecrows for every scrap. None of that was necessary; the bin hadn't been emptied and it hadn't rained since Cat had dumped it all. This was just as well because the dull fluted sides of my galvanized bin had been on the receiving end of much violence and the lid no longer fitted on top. We didn't use binbags then – everything just went straight in – so the photos and the letters which almost filled it had been tipped in on top of a layer of festering vegetables, used teabags and plate scrapings which had already covered the bottom. It only took me five minutes to get them all out again but it took two hours to wipe the crap off them, and I was so annoyed with Cat that I could hardly speak to her. To start with, I was sure that she must have done it on purpose. She showed not the slightest interest in my anger or in what I was doing and went to sleep on the cushions. It didn't take long for the annoyance to turn to admiration, despite myself. She looked great, curled up there, feral, sensual and only predictable while she was asleep. That was why I had her there, to challenge what I did. I knew really that the only reason she'd chucked them out was that they meant nothing to her and they were in her way, that was all.

The good thing about having to clean all the stuff was that I found Laura in there.

I wiped a thin slice of potato peel off a large photo and her face came out from underneath it, smiling oddly. I put that picture to one side and it was joined after a while by a second, though I almost missed her in that one. When I finished and had time to look at them, it soon began to seem to me that just in those two photos you could read the story of how their marriage must have been. They were big enlargements, both taken at nearly but not quite the same time, and it is very hard to make complete sense of the occasion. The first one is of three people, sitting close together and smiling at the camera. In the middle is Max, slightly hunched down and looking almost bashful, his mouth open in a rather juvenile grin. He is wearing a blazer and a striped tie. The arrogance of youth has gone and so have much of the film-star good looks. This, I realized, had been within the last ten years because Max and Laura had come together and separated again in that time. It must have been nearer the beginning than the end of that time, so from what I knew he must have been in his mid-fifties. It's starkly different from the pre-war David Niven version. His hair is receding, the flesh of his face has been blurred and softened by years of bad living, his moustache is mottled and a little ragged and his smile, which is strangely bashful, shows teeth which are no longer white and even.

Was this the man who got me through the barrier and took me to 'his' car and to Ginny? I thought perhaps it was, indeed I wanted it to be him, but I could not be sure.

Immediately to the left, with her arm spread along the top of the seat behind him, is Laura, her face smiling in a slightly fixed way. She looks altogether too substantial, too proper, to be in the same picture as Max. Her hair has been recently permed. She is wearing a dark, short-sleeved dress with lace trimmings around the neck and a string of pearls.

The odd thing about the picture is the other woman. There, flanking Max on the other side, indeed leaning into the shot so that she is all over him, is a girl who must be half his age and she's *really* enjoying herself. She has short bobbed hair, very shiny lipstick and a round face for which pretty is the only possible word, with all the limitations that can sometimes imply.

The place looks sleazy, a club, perhaps, with part of a dirty-looking sunburst effect on the wall, made up of radiating strips of glittery cloth. On the table is a half-full glass of beer – all rather downmarket for Laura and maybe even for Max.

The other and even odder thing is that Max and the girl are wearing identical white carnations, which seem to tie them together as a couple into this event, whatever it is. It is possible that Laura may have a carnation, too, but Max's shoulder is in the way of that half of her chest and Laura doesn't look like one of the carnation club. The girl and Max seem to be sharing something to which Laura is a spectator, going along with it despite herself.

It is the second picture which should help supply a cross-bearing but instead adds layers of intrigue to the situation. In this one, we are clearly abroad so that perhaps takes the first picture there with us. It could be an Alpine lodge or a *bierstube*. There is a carved wooden fireplace in the background and the photo is taken from the end of a table littered with bottles, a St Raphael ashtray and a packet of Camels. There are several people sitting round the table, and this time the clothes suggest a skiing trip. The same girl is there, third down on the left, and she is the focus of almost everyone's attention. She is laughing with her eyes shut, dressed in a sweater with such an extravagant rollneck that it looks almost like a clown's ruff. There's another of these pretty girls opposite – a girl rather like her, though this one is chubbier and has bulging eyes. She's waving her hands about in front of her. Among the others there's a good-looking, slightly older woman in profile with a rictus grin and between her and this interloping girl of ours is a handsome young blade in a striped sweater and a cravat – very Cresta Run. Then, of course, there is Max. He is back left, just beyond the girl, and he is *so* posed. An elbow leans elegantly on the table, wrist curled in towards his head which leans in so that he is almost full face. He too is in a rollneck and it makes him look much younger and fitter than he does in the other picture.

He is gazing at the girl with complete and somewhat lascivious adoration.

At first sight there is no sign of Laura but then you suddenly spot her. In the background, mostly obscured, are other tables, and in the far right corner three women are sitting together. Two of them can only just be seen but the third is straining up to look over the intervening heads towards Max. She has a grim expression on her face.

That's Laura.

It's difficult, this business of getting cross-bearings on strangers. You would think that sequence told the story – the girl coming in to join the couple, then Laura being pushed out into the wilderness. But then I turned the prints over and there were serial numbers on the back. The big group came first, number 11618, and the threesome followed at 11889. Does that reverse the chronology or were they just printed out of order? Who knows. It seemed to matter but nothing much that was in the trunk ever added up to complete certainty.

At this point, with my head full of Max's mysteries and Cat asleep, stoned out of her mind on the beanbag, partly dressed in a ripped shirt with one of her nipples showing, Tiggy pressed my front doorbell. I knew it was her because I looked out of the window and saw a red Hillman Imp parked directly outside. A red Hillman Imp was Tiggy's sort of car. Her father bought it for her twenty-first to make up for the fact that he was in Antigua with his new wife and sadly couldn't be there for the party. Wife number one, Averil Scott-Morrison, a sad, graceful lady, had been left with, I guessed, a fairly substantial settlement to run Sompting Grange and provide Tiggy and her brother Jeremy with the tail end of their education.

I met Tiggy at a dance at Roedean in my last year at public school. It was regarded as an 'away match' at my school and discussed by some as though the girls were objects of sexual fantasy and by others as if they were a hostile team we had to face. Girls were, after all, a novel concept to us. They lurked somewhere in the future along with the job in the city and the certainty of great wealth, but in the present single-sex world, most of my contemporaries were more concerned with the charms of the latest batch of third-formers. I wasn't. The day before I left home for the start of my first term, the Colonel had called me into his study, a room he used solely for reading the papers and writing occasional choleric letters to them, urging them to take a tougher stand on foreign policy or disputing the finer points of some military obituary. My mother had clearly put him up to this conversation as stand-in father figure and he was as ill at ease as it was possible to be.

'Um, Miles,' he said, swivelling part of the way round in his chair so that he was looking at the bookcase. 'New experience, for you, boarding school.'

It didn't seem to be a question so I kept quiet.

'Eh?' he said, so I agreed.

'Funny things happen. All men together. Best steer clear of all that.'

I genuinely had no idea what he was talking about. 'All what, sir?' I knew he liked me to call him 'sir' though he never said so. It put us on a safer footing.

There was a short silence during which he produced a lot of saliva and turned a dull purple.

'Sex things,' he said eventually. 'You know. Men. Man and man.' There was a silence while I looked at him curiously. 'Boys, that is,' he added. 'That's it, then. Not good in a regiment. Greeks thought so. We don't. Good lad. Off you trot. Left, right, left, right.'

So I steered clear as directed. After a short period in which I continued to be puzzled, I soon realized what he meant when I got to school and found most of the older boys and some of the masters engaged in a life in which sodomy was combined with religion, eating and sport in roughly equal proportions. By the time I reached the sixth form and was eligible for the Roedean dance, I was no wiser in the ways of girls than my fellows but I knew a lot less about the ways of boys, too.

The Roedean dance was patrolled as heavily as the Dover Straits in World War Two. There were strict rules on where you could go and where you couldn't, what you could do and what you couldn't. Space had to be observable at all times between any pair of bodies. Grim-faced mistresses with torches stalked relentlessly while the masters who had accompanied us mostly sat and talked to each other. Doors had been sealed off, promising gaps in the hedges had been blocked with wire. Only in the closing moments when the mass exodus to our coaches took place was there a chance to evade the observers. I had danced with Tiggy for most of the evening and there, right by the snorting exhaust of an elderly AEC, I kissed her for at least ten seconds and went on my way with her address in my pocket and my blood fizzing all the way back to school.

She could have lived anywhere at all, from Scotland to Sarawak, but blessedly she lived in Sussex and only a few miles from me. This made it easy for us to see a lot of each other and it sort of lasted through most of university in an on-and-off way, though we were heading in opposite directions by then. Her mother didn't want her to be too brainy. That sort of thing puts boys off, you know dear, so for her there was no university though she could easily have done it. Instead life consisted of being a Muribird, running ski chalets in winter and various long trips to Italy or Greece doing easy jobs for friends of the family in the summer, with the occasional spell of helping schoolfriends with their cordon bleu catering ventures in London or rushing home to Sompting when life crowded too closely in on Averil and she needed reinforcements. She remained unchanged by all of it, and when I graduated badly and went to live in Brighton she was still the same easy-going, funny person that she had been when I first met her. I was harder work by that time, though. I couldn't fit her in to that Brighton life, so I would go to see her and find reason after reason why she should not come to me. London was no easier.

She had never been to my flat and this was not a good time to start, not with a semi-naked Cat on the cushions and the thick, herbal smell of dope filling the whole flat. I was fairly sure Tiggy would never have smoked a joint but I was not so sure she wouldn't recognize the smell. The bell rang again, Cat stirred slightly and, shoving the Owen documents back in the trunk for safety, I decided on a strategy. I took a handful of the papers at random and opened the door as if unaware that anyone was there, heading purposefully for the outside world so that I was suitably amazed to see Tiggy, standing on the step looking a bit nervous.

'Tig! Wow! What a surprise! Didn't know you were here. I was just going for a coffee. Come and have one with me. Let's go in your car.'

I got her into it without giving her a chance to argue, wanting to get out of range of Cat. There was the Purple Haze in Bramley Road where I usually went, but it was full of people who knew me so I steered her straight past it and we went to the old coffee bar on St Ann's Road, where nobody I knew would ever be seen dead.

'How nice to see you. What are you doing here?'

She looked round doubtfully at the grey Formica and the

Vapona flystrips hanging from the naked lightbulbs in the ceiling. A brown sauce bottle was stuck to the table by the gummy deposit of an old overflow. She put a hand out to move it further away, then thought better of it. She seemed ill at ease.

'I just wanted to see how you are. I brought Mummy up shopping for the day and I was at a loose end.'

'I'm fine.'

'You didn't look very fine when I saw you in Brighton.' Trust Tiggy to go straight to the point.

'Oh, then. Well, I hadn't had much sleep.'

'The girl you were with. Is she your girlfriend now?'

'Cat?' The word girlfriend didn't seem to go with Cat. 'Um, well, you know . . . she's around at the moment.'

'She looked very, well – you know, druggy.'

She was, oh, she was.

'Maybe. I don't really know her very well. She gave me a lift to Brighton that day. I needed to go to Brighton.'

Then, out of the need to turn this conversation aside, it occurred to me that here was the one person who would completely understand about the trunk. Here in fact was the only person I had ever really told about the crash. More than that, I had even taken her there, right to the spot one day in our first, intense, children-in-love summer – taken her to the place where you could see the traces in the railings and the tarmac and the kerbstone and told her why it mattered so much.

In that final year of school, Tiggy had brought to me the warmth that the fantasy of Ginny had briefly offered. For that first year together, before the sudden freedom of university began to warp my view of her, she was all I had ever wanted. You might have thought she would have been welcomed into the world of Oakdean Manor, having the right sort of background, the right address, the right accent, but it wasn't that simple. The Colonel and my mother found it hard to be as free and easy with her as she tried to be with them. On the one occasion Tiggy's mother was asked to dinner, I was horribly aware that Averil, used to her gins and tonics, as they were to their pots of tea, found the teetotal austerity of our house just as unnerving as the stiff, sporadic conversation.

That was all a while ago, but whatever we'd had together had not entirely gone away even if I was now aware of feeling some embarrassment at Tiggy's wholesome, out-of-place, uncool, county air. She still understood who I had until recently been, so there, in the horrible café over several horrible cups of coffee made from liquid coffee syrup and warm, sweet milk, I told her the story so far and she was utterly fascinated by it and understood it and wanted to know everything there was to know. I told her of Ginny's accusations and of the likelihood that some of them at least were true. I told her of Max's constant legal problems, of Douglas riding tirelessly to the rescue, and she took it all in.

'How much of it have you looked at?'

'Less than half so far. Maybe only a third. It's incredible how much you can get into a trunk.'

'Is that some of it?'

The stuff I'd grabbed before I left was unsorted – just a bunch of letters with a few photos in amongst them. We started looking at them.

Some of the photos came from long foreign trips, of which I had already seen evidence. Max and Douglas in a rakish Lagonda Rapide, a phalanx of exhaust pipes snaking out of the side of the bonnet like a battery of heavy artillery, somewhere up in the snowy Alps before the war, then the two of them with a bunch of young friends round a Mediterranean-looking café table, Douglas sporting a very art-student moustache.

'Can I open this?' said Tiggy, holding up a long, luxurious envelope in rich cream.

'Go ahead.'

Was it blind luck or was it instinct? I don't know. It was a vital moment, this second glimpse of Natalie. Without Tiggy, I might have overlooked the important bits. Second glimpse? Yes, second because there had been that brief telegram which had formed the opening ceremony to the entire thing: *Only you. Always. What else matters. Natalie.*

It was written on both sides of notepaper headed 'UNITED NATIONS' at the top left and 'NATIONS UNIES' at the top right. The date was June 23rd but no year was given and the postmark was too faint to be sure, though it could have been '46'. She read it well, going slowly through the words, discovering them as she went.

My dearest Max,

I haven't heard from you since you left Geneva on your bold endeavour and I am sure that you must be back in London by now with or without the spoils of war. What of Douglas, I wonder? Was his trip to Rome equally successful? If I read that either of you have been rumbled, I shall either disown all knowledge of you or come and saw through your prison bars one dark night – knowing me, you may decide which I am, St Peter or the Scarlet Pimpernel.

Now for my news. I have decided to leave the UN at the end of the summer. I can see the fun going out of the job as the ramshackle days are coming to an end. I am not made to be an organized bureaucrat. Yesterday they tried to give me a secretary, a ferocious-looking woman with a beard, unless it was a man with a bosom – I could not be sure.

Europe will not be the same without you 'down the road' at Antibes and I don't think Wallis welcomes me with quite the vigour she used to. She can be quite difficult at times to say the least as you have, I think, begun to find out. To be charitable, you might say the burden of not being proper royalty lies ever heavier upon her. I may go to Massachusetts to practise being American again for a few weeks or months or years. I suppose there is no point at all in trying to come through London on the way, so perhaps you will save up to come and see me in the hills.

All my love,
Natalie

'Wait,' said Tiggy, 'there's more. There's another letter with it.' She looked at it. 'It's dated the next day.'

Dearest Max,

I was about to post the letter when I read it through again and knew I was being a coward and skipping all the things I had decided to say to you. I fell off my bicycle today because I

110

caught the wheel in a tramline and the people who picked me up took me to a pharmacy where I made an idiot of myself by passing out. It's only cuts and bruises, and they taped me back together again and painted me yellow and violet. You would not approve of the colour scheme because it clashes with pink but I had to come home to bed and that brought me face to face with the fact that this may be my one and only chance to say what I want to say.

Max, you and I have a strange life, don't we? I see you in all the places that are not your home, at Davos, or at La Cröe or here in stolid old Swisstown. I see you when we're having fun, when life is just a party, when the best way out of trouble is just to put our skis together and schuss flat out for the bright lights. That is how I know you but I don't think that should be all there is. There is more to us than that. Now, and this is the difficult part and it isn't at all the sort of thing that a woman should say to a man unless she covets a reputation for extremely forward behaviour, I want you to know one thing. I do understand that your various English estates are full of cuckoos in your nests and that current circumstances oblige you to adopt a simpler lifestyle than you would like. None of that means anything to me at all. I don't even want to see your rotten old stately homes. I would prefer to be with you in a shoebox somewhere so if you like, we could pretend that we were very poor and see how we got on.

Now if all this embarrasses you terribly just put it down to the fact that I may well have concussed myself on a Geneva tramline and then we can laugh about it whenever or wherever we next meet. Just remember, for me, you come plain and unadorned and no clouds of glory are necessary and I believe I would like the Max who stood thus revealed before me.

Tell me what you think,
Natalie.

'He wouldn't have liked that,' I said.
'Why?'

111

As I opened my mouth to answer I discovered an odd certainty that I knew more about Max than seemed to be justified by the fragments of his life I had so far inspected. I knew that Ginny was both right and wrong in her accusations, right in the substance but wrong in the spirit, that Max's entire tragedy was that he was a *nice* liar, that his dishonesties were just fantasies, not meant to hurt others but simply to fill in some gaping holes inside himself. If it were otherwise it could not have lasted. That Max continued to lead his life in that way was made possible by the fact that he had friends who forgave him. I knew I was leaping too far ahead but I also knew I was fundamentally right. Even if such deceits can often turn sour, that may not have been their intention.

'He would have been ducking and weaving for all he was worth. You can see what's happened, can't you? She's an American, isn't she, and he's spun her a whole load of old British moonshine about the family estates and the vineyards and I don't know what and he *daren't* have her come back home with him because he knows all there is to show is some poky little mews flat.'

Then Tiggy, with enormous intuition, spotted what I had missed and began to open up the whole enormous tragedy of Max and Natalie.

'She knows that,' said Tiggy, shaking her head. 'Can't you see? It's blindingly obvious. That's what she's telling him – that she knows it's all rubbish and *it doesn't matter* – that she'll come anyway if he gives her half a chance. She's giving him a safe way of letting her in by going along with the pretence. I think she sounds brilliant. Do you think they ever got together?'

'No,' I said, 'I'm afraid not, at least not for long. She doesn't really appear later on. Look, she's talking about Antibes and Wallis. You know who that is, don't you?'

I just wanted to spin out the drama of the revelation. Tiggy shook her head.

'That's Wallis Simpson. Natalie must have been involved with the Duke and Wallis as well as Max.' I thought for a moment about Wallis, who so wanted to be called Her Royal Highness, but in the world's eyes was destined always to be Wallis Simpson even once she'd become Wallis Windsor.

'There's a lot of stuff you said you hadn't looked at yet,' Tiggy said defiantly, and I realized she wanted the trunk's history to show that Natalie's honesty had worked, that there had been a happy ending of some sort.

'He married someone else in the end and not for long at that.'

'So he died alone?'

'Yes, I'm sure he did. That was the final price of it all.' It was a rash assumption but I knew no better then.

Tiggy fanned through the rest of the stuff I'd brought. Max with blonde girls, Max with dark girls, Max with Douglas and a pair of girls. A girl on her own.

'That's Natalie,' she said.

'Come on. You can't know that.'

'I do. Would you like a bet?'

'How? By instinct?'

'No, by simple observation. It's written on the back.'

Natalie it was, unless there had been two Natalies in Max's life. This Natalie certainly looked capable of writing such a letter. She had an interesting face of great character, and also great but unconventional attraction. The photo certainly didn't date from after the war. I was getting to know Max at all his ages and this, I was sure, was Max in his tousle-haired, fresh-faced pre-war, pre-military days before the rather self-conscious veneer came over him at the sight of a camera, so Natalie must have been around, one way or another, for quite some time.

Natalie had an oval face with eyes set slightly too close for conventional beauty but a full mouth, a delicate, tip-tilted nose and a mane of dark hair in large ringlets framing her face in irregular whirls. It could have been a jacket photo of a rather good female novelist and you'd just know the book would be well worth reading. They're sitting on a seaside bench, both wearing coats – Max's looking like First World War officers' garb and hers black and stylish. She had legs to die for – very Marlene Dietrich.

'Can I come back and see the rest?' Tiggy said, and I felt she was watching me extra closely.

The thought of taking her to the flat with Cat there was too awful to contemplate.

113

I looked at my watch. 'I'm running a bit late,' I said, 'would you mind if we did it another time?'

'I don't get up here very often,' she said, with a touch of sadness as if I had just confirmed something. 'I could give you a lift if you've got to go somewhere.'

So I got a completely unnecessary lift to a randomly chosen corner of Notting Hill, still clutching the letters, and to make my conscience feel better I had to agree that yes, I would come down to the Hunt Ball.

As I walked back to the flat, I was struck by a horrible thought. Cat had thrown all this stuff in the bin. I had rescued it, but was it all there? She had seen the Duke of Windsor's letter, she had known it was valuable and she had wanted it. It hadn't been in the bin. Was it still safely there, inside, untouched? I didn't think so. I knew Cat's way with money and with anything of value. I started to run.

# Eleven

I sometimes thought Cat only moved in with me because she had nowhere to sleep that week and she decided it might be interesting to see how quickly she could deprave me, if deprave can be used as an active verb. Depravity was her special subject. After our first night, she said I knew less about screwing than anyone she'd ever met. To make the point more firmly, she said that included a monk she'd spent a night with in Goa. She said she'd give me lessons and it was implicit that the use of my flat, my money and anything else that took her fancy came as part of the deal. She introduced me to a lot of other things besides unfettered sex, but when I looked at her and the ever-changing band of her friends who would come and disconcertingly change the whole centre of gravity of the flat, I was always uneasy. These arrivals meant my space was not my space and I would have to become a forgiving chameleon spectator for as long as they wanted to be there, and when they were I knew I did not yet fully, convincingly, pass as one of them. I was constantly expecting Cat to denounce me as a hopeless sham and walk out and I knew, at the moment, that I would not be able to welcome her departure whatever measure of relief might be in it. Cat was a crash course in moving away from what I had been and I still needed her.

When I walked back into the flat, out of breath, she was doing yoga. I went straight to the trunk and started searching. She watched me.

'Cool it, Milo. I haven't been near it.'

'Yes, you have.'

'Okay, so I threw out some stuff. What does it matter? It's not your Granny's ashes.'

The Duke's letter wasn't there.

'You took something, didn't you?'

'No, I didn't.'

'Cat, I know you did. That letter I showed you from the Duke. It's gone.'

I must have sounded as angry as I felt and I was standing over her and all at once she looked a little scared. She's been hit, I thought, hit many times and she's not as tough as she thinks she is. For a moment, before I felt ashamed, it gave me a sense of dominant power.

'I know you've taken it. I need it back.'

'Don't make a big deal about it.'

'Where is it?'

'I sold it.'

'*Shit*! Why?'

'To buy stuff.'

'What stuff?'

'Grass, skag.'

'You sold my letter for *that*?'

'Don't get so high and mighty, Milo. You used it too.'

'What did you get for it?'

'Ten quid.'

'Jesus. Who's got it?'

'Maria thing. You know. Down in the Arcade. The fat one.'

'Have you got any of the money left?'

'No.'

'I've got to get it back.'

Cat never had a high opinion of my ability to make deals and it was true that things had been a bit slow since she arrived, maybe because of the amount of gear that got smoked and otherwise ingested. It took time and energy to make deals, to find the appropriate things, then to track down the right person in the right mood at the right time to pay the right price. Cash was very tight even before she had walked off with the rest of the rent money and it was two weeks until the next cheque from the trust was due. The cheques weren't even enough to get through a month, let alone to cover a deficit.

I went straight down to Portobello and found Fat Maria.

'You bought a letter,' I said, 'signed by the Duke of Windsor.'

'Yeah?'

'It's mine. It was nicked.'

'Tell that to the fairies, sonny. You got proof.'

'I want it back.'

'No problem.'

'You've still got it?'

'Yeah.'

'Let's have it, then.'

She shrugged and her cheeks wobbled. 'Sixty quid and it's yours.'

'Sixty?' I didn't have sixty. 'You only gave her a tenner for it.'

'That what she told you? Lying cow. I gave her twenty-five.'

'I'll give you fifty.'

'Seventy.'

'Hang on, you said sixty.'

'Yeah, and you said fifty, college boy. If you can go down I can fucking well go up.'

I felt hopelessly out-gunned. 'All right, sixty. Look, Maria. I'll put a fiver down to hold it. I'll get the rest, okay?'

'Two days.'

Cat was in the bathroom when I got back, which was just as well because she would have recovered her screw-it composure by now and I wasn't sure I could have held on to the higher ground. There was an urgency driving me so I took up where I had left off on the phone, trying to find someone to buy the Beaufighter bits, and this time I eventually got smart and found Peel, because he wasn't Peel, he was Peal and he sounded like he might be interested.

'I've got to go to Chiswick,' I said to Cat, through the door. 'Got some pieces to shift, thanks to you.'

'Sod off and play aeroplanes,' she said. I heard an explosion of bubbles in the bath and she laughed.

I picked up the heavy bag with the smaller bits in. If he wanted the panels, he'd have to come and pick them up from where they were stacked in under the basement stairs. Before I went, I opened the trunk and took out a handful of fresh papers to read on the bus. It was probably safe to leave the rest here now, I couldn't see Cat bothering to search it for any more plunder. Anyway I had no choice.

I sat on top at the front, as I had always tried to do when

I was a kid. It used to be because that felt a bit like flying, swooping along, face pressed to the glass as new, soft growth of tree branches swished past you, thumping the window before rattling along the roof. This time I did it because I could get a little privacy with the papers that way. Two of the letters were from Max's lawyer – long, detailed discussions of some property deal which, from a fairly rapid read, seemed to have gone as sour as everyone except Max would have expected. I decided to look at those another time. They needed concentration.

The bus was the other side of Hammersmith when I turned to an envelope which was unused and was only there to protect its contents. It was with a degree of excitement that I recognized the bunch of lined paper, covered in Max's crawling script, which meant another of his stories was waiting to be read. His need to chronicle his life was the fuel that drove me on through these old papers. This one was called 'The Spoils of War'.

*For a young man in his early thirties, Europe in the immediate aftermath of the latest bout of unpleasantness was a garden of opportunity in which I was able to wander with pleasant abandon. It happened that, following an injury incurred in the early part of the war during the Norwegian campaign – an injury I would not wish to dwell upon except to say that it taught me always to check the odds against me before leaping on to the deck of an enemy ship – I had spent a great deal of time recuperating in a series of hospitals. At the close of hostilities, in one of those rare postings by which the army occasionally and loftily rewards such endeavours, I was serving as a staff captain to the commander of British troops in Southern France. In the course of this, I was attached as personal aide to a certain royal personage who was then in a form of unwarranted exile at Antibes and had also, by coincidence, brought me into the ambit of his social circle during the period when he had been the Prince of Wales.*

*I had known the remarkable lady who had become his wife in such difficult circumstances before the war in conditions which had been much more pleasant. I had met her for the first time and the Prince for the second time towards the end of 1934, when I was asked to join their skiing party at Kitzbühl in the Austrian Alps. I was overwhelmed by her immensely attractive features and extraordinary personal magnetism. It was impossible not to fall under her spell and I could fully understand why the Prince considered her worthy of any sacrifice.*

*I first met the Prince many years before that, when I was only nine. It was a summer day in South Wales when he arrived with Prime Minister Lloyd George to visit this part of his domain and I had been singled out to make a special greeting to the Prince from the boys at my preparatory school. I failed to deliver the greeting in quite the expected manner, being so overcome by the sight of the terrifying mane of white hair on Lloyd George's head that I stumbled appallingly through my short speech, unable to take my eyes off it throughout in case it should pounce on me. This, I was to discover much later, earned me both the attention and the sympathy of the Prince, who was himself possessed of a stammer.*

*At Kitzbühl, the Prince and the beautiful American had done their best to appear no more than friends. To one as callow as I was, there was no sign of the great and blooming passion that they were keeping so tightly confined and it was not until the following year, he was to confess to me later in Antibes, that he had allowed himself to recognize that he was in love and to confront all the problems that was to bring.*

*As he had pondered that decision and eventually, as he had to do, realized that he must marry the woman he loved, storm clouds had gathered over him in London, presaging the thunderclap that would echo around the world. Out of that electric crackle of talk, threat and counter-threat, there had sprung sudden support for the young king in a movement which called itself 'The King's Party', and I was proud to be a founder member of that movement. We covered our cars with slogans and toured the capital in those tense days spreading our message with banners and with loudhailers to the effect that he should be permitted to marry the woman he loved.*

*We dreamt of a surging tide of popular support which would force the hands of those in power, but we were destined to be disappointed. In the false name of Duty, the public, led by a mean-spirited government, sought to deny him his happiness for their own base motives. It is, I sometimes think, a sad reflection on the constrained and stultifying nature of this impassive island race of ours that true romantic passion comes so far down the list of acceptable motivations. The movement came to nothing and* whatever hopes the King might have had for support, his case died with it.

Despite that, my name was still lodged in his memory, it seemed, and thus it came about that my assistance was requested in the immediate aftermath of the war in helping the Windsors to set up house in the chateau near Antibes that they had occupied before the war. Foreseeing that my country was doomed to a dull decline into middle class tedium, the posting carried with it the promise of helping to prolong a more splendid age and a more thrilling set of values. It was a task made doubly pleasant by the fact that amongst the Duchess's entourage, for an all too short time, was a young American friend of hers whose beauty was as great as her discernment and whom I had also met and been greatly taken by in those halcyon days at Kitzbühl. The Duke and I shared this in common, that we had, in those far off days, both formed a deep attachment, though in my case the war had separated us for eight long years.

Now it so happened that one of my functions in those days, apart from acting as gorgon at the gate to drive away those sightseers who would invade our driveway or bring their motorboats close to our beach, was to assist the Duke and his Duchess in acquiring the necessities of life to transform the war-ravaged villa back into the gracious house it had once been, a copy of the plantation mansions peculiar to the southern states of America, admirably suited to a sunny climate. This entailed not only the hiring and supervision of painters and decorators but also the procurement of many house-hold necessities and it was this that brought me into contact with 'Alphonse', or so I shall call him, and also with the black market.

I met Alphonse over the most banal matter, when the Duchess urgently required some more glass-cloths. She had discovered that the most regrettable deficiencies of food and decoration at dinner could be covered up by the use of candlelight and its reflection in first-class, lead-crystal wine glasses. The glasses themselves were not an impediment to this plan. At the last possible moment in 1940, when the Duke had gallantly rescued the Duchess from the chateau only hours ahead of a bombing raid intended to kill both of them and had taken her, pursued by agents of the Gestapo, to the safety of Barcelona, the house's silver and glass had been carefully hidden

120

*in a place where the occupying powers were never able to find them. All that it required to bring her plans to fruition was a copious supply of clean glass-cloths to impart the necessary sparkle to the revived glasses and some half-decent wine with which to fill them.*

*I was able to supply sufficient glass-cloths without too much trouble from army stores, but the wine was another matter. Viniculture had suffered during the long period of hostilities and the thin red liquid we were drinking in the Mess was not to be confused in any way with the fine vintages to which the Duke and Duchess were accustomed, and this was where Alphonse came in.*

*I was introduced to Alphonse one afternoon in Cannes when my enquiries had otherwise drawn a blank. He was reputed to be a former hero of the Maquis and he turned out to be a mysterious fellow indeed. Alphonse arrived in an ancient Citroën camionnette smelling strongly of pig, and insisted on whispering into my ear at very close range, a habit which demonstrated that he too smelt of pig and which drew far more attention to us in the middle of the street than if he had simply stood at a distance and bellowed at me. Although I speak fluent French, the conversation was not easy.*

*'You want wine?'*

*'I want good wine.'*

*'Do you know what good wine is, monsieur?'*

*'I believe I do.'*

*'You are English. How can you? It will be wasted on you. Come with me, we will see.'*

*From the back of the Citroën he produced a bottle, half-full, which he uncorked with his teeth and passed to me. The bouquet was overwhelmed by the odour of pig, but I put the neck of the bottle to my mouth, swilled it round and spat it out thoughtfully. He was watching me.*

*'What wine is that, monsieur?'*

*It was good and my knowledge of wine is sound but, masked by the porcine aroma, this was hardly a fair test. I could not be entirely certain which of the Bordeaux vineyards had created it.*

*'It is from the chateau that costs ten dollars a bottle and for which I have enough dollars for five cases,' I said.*

*He considered the matter and the immediate future of the Duke and Duchess's cellar hung visibly in the balance. He scratched his* nose, looked at me, looked at the bottle, then made a 'moue' of discontent or perhaps fatal acceptance.

'That is almost the correct answer, monsieur. It is from the neighbouring chateau that costs twelve dollars a bottle, and you may have your five cases.'

He led me in my army Austin Utility, with its distinctive headquarters markings, up out of the town towards the foothills behind. After a fifteen-mile drive along smaller and smaller roads, we turned in through the ruined gate of a fine old estate and drew up in the courtyard behind a large, ancient house almost obscured by the creepers that clung to it in profusion. Here he stopped the engine of the Citroën by simply driving it slowly into the nearest wall so that the little truck bounced sharply backwards, stalling in the process, then he got out, turned to me and beckoned. I followed him past the end of the buildings and through thick undergrowth until we stopped by what appeared to be a very solid hedge. Pushing through it, he heaved and grunted and a door slid sideways so that I could see this was an even more overgrown building, possibly a stable or an equipment shed, long forgotten as nature had invaded the estate. The sliding mechanism for the door, however, was well-greased.

It was hard to see inside, but near the door cases of wine were stacked and these, helpfully, had labels. They claimed an excellent premier cru pedigree, and on opening one I was forced to agree that they were indeed from that chateau that costs twelve dollars. I was sure the Duchess would be well pleased.

This however was merely the start of the day's surprising events because as my eyes became slowly accustomed to the depth of the gloom inside this building, a building which the occupying Nazis had clearly overlooked, I was slowly able to put a name to the extraordinary shape which revealed itself in all its overwhelming size before me.

It was a car, but not just a car. It was a huge car, an immense car, a car built for a king. I had known of this car for a long time but I had never expected to see it, nor indeed to come face to face with it in a Provençale shed. Now, I am a self-confessed lover of the motorcar, and in the course of my life I have owned some of the finest and fastest ever made, from the unique and ferocious 'dodici-cylindri' Moretti, and various Allards and Facel-Vegas, to the fastest of all

*the racing Lister-Jaguars, a dark blue demon which now lurks in
my garage awaiting its next call to battle, like Drake listening for
the beating of his drum . . .*

My hands started to tremble and I put the papers down on
my lap and stared sightlessly out of the window as those words
brought Ginny's tragedy abruptly close. I felt my heart beat faster,
but when I looked down there was no more on the Lister – that
had been just an aside.

*I do not expect others to be so moved by anything made of metal,
wood and rubber but this car, I believe, was an exception to every
rule and even to those who do not share my passion; its story is
remarkable.*

*You do not have to be interested in cars to be interested in Ettore
Bugatti, who was an artist in metal. He built machines of a fine
construction and a delicate beauty, which achieved extraordinary
success in motor racing throughout the twenties. In the turmoil
of those frontier parts of Europe between the wars, he was an
Italian-Frenchman living in the Franco-German mongrel borderland
of Alsace. You might say, therefore, that he brought to his art the flair
of the Italian, the precision of the German and the Frenchman's
culinary skill at blending ingredients correctly. His creations were
usually known simply by their type numbers. All the way up to
his type forty, he designed them as a ballet dancer would design,
creating svelte, slender machines. Perhaps something happened to
the Alsatian wizard when he reached number forty-one. Perhaps
he reached a moment in his life when he started to think about
posterity, but some worm turned in his brain and he created the
Golden Bug.*

I very nearly missed my stop, but I looked up again just at the
right time and realized we were already almost at the Chiswick
roundabout, so I ran down the stairs and swung off, to much
tutting from the conductor, as the bus braked for the turn. Peal
was waiting for me impatiently, a wiry little man who clearly
thought attack was the best form of everything.

'Let's see it then,' he barked, and I took the contents of the bag
out carefully and showed him the throttle quadrant. He took it
so eagerly that he almost pulled it from my hands.

'Mk VI, is it?'

'I expect so.'

'Where's it from?'

'I'm not telling you that.'

'What else?'

'Trim wheel. That's here, too.' I rummaged for it and he pounced. 'Plus two panels, one off the wing, one off the rear fuselage, I'd say. They're back at my place.'

'Any legible markings?'

'Part of a letter.'

'Well here's how it is, Mr Malan. You tell me where the site is and I'll make it a hundred and twenty quid for you. I have to know the site 'cos that way I can get the full low-down from the records. Otherwise it's sixty quid top whack, take it or leave it. I do need to know the provenance, you see.'

My friendly Yorkshire wreck-site expert wasn't going to be happy but I needed at least sixty quid and we were going halves.

'A hundred and forty and it's yours.'

'I said a hundred and twenty and I meant it. I don't bargain, right?'

Another one of those. It wasn't my day for making deals. I thought a bit. 'When you say you can get the full low-down from the records, um, how do you do that?'

He looked mysterious. 'I've got a mate, has access to that sort of thing.'

'Can he get at army records too?'

'Maybe. Depends what.'

'Army personal file on a wartime Grenadier Guards officer.'

'I reckon he could. What's in it for him?'

'It's more of a question of what's in it for you. I know where the engines from that wreck are. Two Hercules XVIs, impact-damaged but complete. You get me the info and I could see about doing something.'

He licked his lips. He actually licked his lips. 'What's the deal with your bloke then? Any comeback?'

'No. He's dead. Just interest.'

We exchanged information and money.

'It might take a while,' he said, 'but you will hear from me. Yes, you'll definitely hear from me.' And I left him to do whatever he was going to do with his ancient wreckage. I couldn't wait to get back on the bus and go on reading Max's story.

I read the rest of it at the bus-stop because there was no sign of anything like a bus for ages. Max seemed obsessed by the statistics of the Golden Bug, its huge engine, carved out of a solid block of aluminium to propel this three-ton behemoth, which stretched twenty feet from bumper to bumper, at unheard-of speed. Then there was its exclusivity, just six made, and its pure luxury, for this was no racer, this was the ultimate rich man's carriage.

*The car was properly known as the Bugatti Royale and I knew as soon as I saw it which of the six cars this was – the Royale built in 1927 for a royal, for King Carol of Rumania – the car later rebodied with a superb Coupe de Ville body by the coachmaker, Binder, and lost from sight as the war clouds rolled over Europe. It was extraordinarily intact, lacking only the silver elephant mascot which should have graced its radiator cap. When at last I was able to get it out into the light, I found that it was still nearly perfect. Even the Jaeger chronometer was still in place in the centre of the steering wheel. As soon as I saw it, I knew I had to own it.*

*Alphonse was amazed by my interest.*

*'Think of the essence, monsieur. Who could afford to drive it now? It is no use – a chicken shed, maybe.'*

*'Is it yours?' I asked.*

*'It is mine and it is not mine. The owners, God rest their souls, have no more use for it where they are now. This is a sad and empty house since the Fascists had their way with it.'*

*The story of all that happened next and how the Bugatti was eventually secured is a long one, and one perhaps that should not be told for many years to come until all those who played a part in its mysterious journey home to England have safely passed over to a realm where they can no longer be cross-examined. Suffice it to say that there came a day some considerable time later when a tank transporter carrying a heavily sheeted load, disguised under the tarpaulins with cleverly arranged lengths of timber so that in profile it somewhat resembled a Sherman tank, turned off its designated route from Southampton docks to an army depot near the New Forest and dropped its load instead at a garage owned by an old friend under cover of darkness. That it was dark was fortunate as some of the nails* had come loose and in the final miles of its long journey the wooden gun barrel had developed an unconvincing bend half way down it.

The Bugatti was not alone. My brother was also on the loose in Europe, attached in a roving way to sundry commands which gave him a certain freedom to explore. In fighting his way up through Italy, he had discovered and earmarked several delectable sports cars. Once he told me about them it seemed only right that this rich harvest should be gathered in to protect it for posterity, though he was far more concerned than I about the propriety of such actions and was usually able to pay money to someone possessing some claim to ownership. Several fewer tanks arrived back at their depots than the paperwork suggested thanks to my efforts.

There was however a postscript to this story. When my royal friend had moved on from Antibes and time had released me from army service, I undertook a wager from an old friend that I could not pass myself off as an Indian nabob in Paris. Aided by the impressive sight of the Royale and dressed in an absurd variety of silks and satins, we stormed the city, ran up absurd credit at all the best eating places with the Royale parked ostentatiously outside, and even had two nights at the Hotel George V without ever seeing a whisper of a bill. Near the Tuileries in the early hours of our final day, we walked somewhat unsteadily back to the vast car to discover that someone was inside it. On investigation we found that a gaunt, elderly and unattractive woman had somehow gained access to the passenger compartment and was seated in the rear.

Thinking her to be some poor creature of the night, understandably lacking custom, because no man, however desperate, would have availed himself of anything she might offer, we remonstrated with her and sought to eject her from the car, but she proved resistant to our efforts.

She was extraordinarily insistent that the Royale was her car, so, now thinking her deluded and reason having failed, we resorted to the most mild force to extract her from the seat. She held on tightly to the door but then seemed to change her mind and voluntarily made her exit.

'It was *my car*,' she said, 'our car – my husband's and mine in the old life that is no more in Provence.'

*The reference to Provence startled me, but I was still sure she was making it up.*

*'You must ask your husband, madame,' I said politely. 'There were other cars of this type.'*

*She shook her head and began to walk away. 'This was the one. You may try asking him, if you please monsieur, but to do so you must go to Sobibor. My husband has remained there.'*

*She wanted nothing more to do with us or the car and at that time the name of Sobibor meant nothing to me. Recently I have learnt more of it and now that I know what fate befell those who were sent to that merciless place, I have thought of trying to find her again and I confess that I have wondered whether all is really fair in love and war.*

# *Twelve*

On the way back I stopped off at a stationery shop and used a bit of Mr Peal's cash to buy myself a whole mass of files. Knowing Max properly seemed to demand a more organized approach than I usually took and, knowing Max, that was bound to throw up all manner of unseen complications. After that I went straight to Fat Maria's and used half the cash to get the Duke's letter out of hock. Lenny wouldn't mind waiting a little while for his share of Peal's money – not if I told him I might do him a deal on the engines. Quite how he was going to get things that size out of a bog in the middle of nowhere was another matter, but that wasn't my problem.

The first thing I did when I got back home, apart from wondering why it felt such a relief that Cat wasn't there, was to take the photo of the Bugatti Royale out of the pile of pictures I had put aside to sell. I stared at it for a long time before putting it safely away in a file with the manuscript story, a connection made, two pieces of the jigsaw fitted together. It was definitely for keeping now.

In the photo, which was another big enlargement, the car still wore its French numberplates and the mascot, an elephant rearing up on its back legs, was now in its proper place on the radiator so perhaps Alphonse had been keeping it safely somewhere all the time. The car looked glossy, immaculate and immense with only a large windscreen to shield an open driver's seat in front of a short enclosed passenger compartment, the style known as a *Coupé de Ville*. The sun was glinting off the inverted horseshoe-shaped radiator and off the two huge headlights. The car towered over the Ford Prefect next to it, both of them parked rear end on to seaside railings. The pier which cut across the background from the right of the picture was, I now saw clearly, Brighton's Palace Pier yet again, so I wondered if the occasion was a much earlier speed trial, sometime in the late 1940s perhaps, when Max had taken his new behemoth down to show it off.

Facets of the pier's landward pavilion caught the sun, the ribs of the dome that projected from the whale-back curve of its roof. The round windows, like a row of huge portholes, glinted in the same sun. The pier's iron and glass looked well kept, despite the recent war, still magnificently frilly and Victorian. The days when it would be diminished by decay and tawdry electronic amusements were still to come, though perhaps distance was being kind to it.

The policeman makes the photo much more than just another car picture. He is in profile beside the car, a dark diagonal, leaning in to peer at some detail of the cockpit with his hands clasped behind his back in perfect old-fashioned bobby style. His helmet has more of a curve to its base than I remember, a true coal-scuttle dipping down over the back of his neck, and there's a little shiny knob on top in the shape of a pawn. His profile is gaunt, his tunic is buttoned up to a tight collar and he just epitomizes the way you think of policemen back then. You can imagine him in those austere days of the late forties when wartime discipline still held sway over most of the population, being utterly impressed by this huge extravagance of the ruling class – stopping the traffic to let it out into the road before going back to the station to regale his colleagues over his packed lunch of dripping sandwiches and sweet tea with a description of this extraordinary vehicle.

Then I did one of those flip-flops which can easily happen when you've been reading far too much into something and realized I'd been misled by the perspective of that long bonnet. He's not looking into the cockpit, he's looking at the base of the windscreen where you might expect to find a tax disc and where there is instead some fancy badge or shield. He's looking to see if it's taxed and of course it's not taxed. It belongs to Max and it's still registered in France, for heaven's sake. That must have been bending the rules, so of course he won't have done anything straightforward like taxing it and isn't he going to have to do some quick explaining when he comes back to the car? Who knows, perhaps he'll be a nabob for the occasion, or perhaps a Free French war hero colonel. He'll get out of it. Fast talking is his special subject. Unless, of course, he was already there. Someone had to have taken the photo but a quick glance at the back showed it wasn't him. There was a stamp there: 'Copyright Photograph. Sam Bishop. Serial Number 6/820. 4 Sep. 1948'.

I went on sorting the stuff for another hour or so. A plastic bag was stuffed with old brown film wallets full of negatives, sandy-coloured 'PC Service' wallets with a green printed segment of a magnifying glass showing an enlargement of a very fifties woman suffering from large teeth, tight hair and ugly earrings. The price list in the back flap showed it cost three old pence to develop a film and tuppence for each postcard print.

I put it all away as soon as I heard the front door go.

'Milo,' Cat called from the hall. She sounded husky and hurried which usually meant she wanted something from me and was going to take an interest in me until she got it.

'In here.'

'All right, then?' she said as she came in. She was wearing my old flying jacket and the shoulder seam was starting to go. 'Have you got any bread? There's some people coming round. I need to go and score a bit of this and that.'

She had a nerve.

By three o'clock the next morning I was considerably poorer, a bit deafer and a lot more bombed than I had ever been in my entire life. The tinfoil had nothing on what Cat was doing that night with little glowing piles of powder stuck round brown gummy lumps. You could taste the power when you breathed it in. It took everything scratchy out of my head, poured cream around it and left me silent and dreamy. That was the best way to be with Cat's friends. It was that or tell them to leave, or – more realistically – leave myself, and know I'd failed the test.

It wasn't clear to me how these people exchanged any useful information and I don't mean that sarcastically – I really wanted to learn the secret. As far as I could hear, conversation was made up entirely of slurry street banalities and joshing repetitions. There had to be more to it because they seemed to know things about each other and about how the system worked but I never heard them talking about things like what you do when you're busted or how you tell what dope's good and what isn't. They must

130

have talked like that sometimes because how else could they have reached that level of enviable self-assurance? Wisdom and information had to come into it somewhere. Conversation was not their strong point, nor was diction, and I didn't yet seem to have the knack of how they did it. It was what I wanted to learn so that I could submerge into it. I could look like them with no trouble, the outside was all right, but the inside still gave me away as soon as I opened my mouth.

'How's it with yer, Mi?' Georgie said when he came in. His skin was very pale with a clammy look.

'Yeah, it's er . . . you know,' but I'd already lost him. He'd glazed over, moved on and was squeezing Cat's bum and laughing into her face. By the time there were a dozen people there I felt this was not my flat, it was suddenly completely theirs, and I had no business opening my mouth because all that would come out would be absurd and artificial, coded completely wrongly so I would be labelled alien with every word of it. I turned up the music and whenever I was offered something I took it straight away.

It took the next two days for the party to disperse. There were still three guys and a girl slumped against walls, giggling, smoking or snoring when I woke up at lunchtime on what I decided was probably Thursday. The phone was ringing, my head was pulsing in time to it and my skin was itching with invisible spider tracks. This was not good.

'Milo?' There was a buzz on the line.

'Er, yeah.'

'God's sake, Milo, you sound, I would say, bloody terrible.'

Cat wasn't in the bed but most of her shoes were.

'Go on, I'm all right.'

'It's Ephraim here.'

He pronounced it 'Ee-fry-eem' in his deep voice.

'I know it is.'

Ephraim Bar-Lev sounded a long way away because he was a long way away. All I knew about him was that he lived near Jericho in Israel and he was a useful person to know. The thing about Israel is that the Israeli air force flew Spitfires and other piston-engined aircraft quite far on into the fifties. They didn't have much respect for old machinery so Ephraim kept his ears open for bits and pieces left behind, unwanted, in store sheds. It was a dry climate so metal usually stayed the way it was meant to be and didn't crumble into rust. Ephraim was good at getting in ahead of the scrap man and I was one of the people he rang when he had something to sell.

'Got a good one. Whole crate of Vokes tropical filters for the Mark 8 Spit.'

I hated him then for waking me up.

'Come off it. You know I can't sell those, mate. No use for the warbird flyers here, are they? You only needed them for dusty deserts. What would anyone want filters for here?'

He chuckled. 'Just seeing if you're too sleepy-headed. You awake really? It's better than what I said. I need you awake. You want to hear what I really have?'

I did.

'I have a pair of Spitfire wings and I am sitting here looking at them. A beautiful sight, you would think too. Brand new, "C" wings.'

This was good. No, this was great. It was one thing flogging souvenirs of bust-up wrecks to collectors but this was one of those things I could take to the real fliers and, because of what I had to offer, they would want to talk to me. They were the people I wanted to take me seriously – the men who still flew the old planes. If I had stuff like that to sell, I would be dealing with them on the level, I'd be a serious person, a proper warbird person.

'Are they good?'

'Good? Totally unused. Still got factory tags. Not marked, not used, not screwed, not bent. Wait for it, Milo. Better still is to come because that is not all – four pairs of cylinder heads from the Merlin 64. This is not four heads, this is four *pairs*, I tell you.'

The Rolls-Royce Merlin was the Spitfire's power unit. Stuff like that was worth real money. I was wide awake now. 'What am I on?'

'Ten per cent if you do it in a week. Twenty if you do it today. I need you to be quick. Get someone with good credit and I ship them over tomorrow.'

'That's a bit tight.'

'Too tight for you? I can ring my old friend Peter if you are too busy for me.'

I didn't want him to deal through Poser Pete and I wanted twenty per cent, not ten.

'I'm on my way. How much are you asking?'

The price he quoted wasn't an unreasonable price and twenty per cent of it was well worth having, but it didn't give me much time. There was only one place nearby where I could quickly reach people with the need and the cash. I found my flying jacket lying with one cuff in a puddle of what I hoped was beer. It smelt of Cat, which meant smoke. I didn't like leaving the trunk in an unlocked flat full of her friends but there didn't seem much choice so I did the best I could by looping the chain I normally used to lock up the bike right round the trunk and through its handles and then padlocking it tightly. The BSA's tank was down to reserve and I reached into my jeans back pocket for the rest of Peal's roll to find there was nothing left there at all except for a ball of paper squashed right down in the corner which turned out to be a fiver when I uncrumpled it. Cat must have overlooked it. I did vaguely remember her, or maybe it was someone else, saying they had to go and score some more at some point during the party but I hadn't realized they were taking what must have been my money to do it. Nice. I was getting a bit tired of this. It certainly looked like I needed some quick income.

Between the flat and Booker Aerodrome I had to shed one identity and put on another. Milo the drug-crazed hippy would not be welcome at Booker. Mechanical Miles, the spare parts man, would be. Booker was just off the old A40 Oxford road on the far side of High Wycombe and it was one of the places where people who really knew their aircraft kept old warbirds flying. In the hangars at Booker you could always find a Spitfire or two, and if they weren't actively rebuilding one at the moment they'd certainly know who was. It wasn't necessarily the first place I'd go if I had bits to sell because there were others who'd offer more money, but if time was of the essence, then Booker was only half an hour away.

The motorbike seemed to feel like I did and popped and banged its way unevenly down the road with only half its engine on duty. It would have been sensible to stop and try to sort it out, but my head simply wasn't up to the job of fixing it so I kept the twist grip open and carried on, hoping it would clear up all by itself. I had a ferocious thirst and the itching was getting worse plus there was something unspeakably black in my head, a feeling of despair as real and physical as a small, hard ball in the top of my skull.

I made three resolutions. First, I mustn't let Cat get her hands on any more of my money. Second, I was going to stick to grass from now on. I hadn't done anything really bad. I'd only been smoking the other stuff, not sticking it in me, but it might be a slippery slope and if it left me feeling like this it definitely wasn't a good idea. Third, Cat's friends should hold their parties somewhere else.

The cool rushing air of the ride helped a bit. Even in this sorry state the bike could hold sixty-five to seventy, and by the time I trickled it round to the front of the Booker hangars, put it up on the stand and switched off I felt more alert, even if the doom-ball was still pressing on my thoughts. I had come to see Dicky Dixon, owner of a nice Spitfire himself but more importantly founder and sole proprietor of the English Warplane Company, and always on the look out for parts to speed the rebuild of his customers' projects.

One of his mechanics walked out of the hangar and squinted at me.

'Can I help you?'

'Miles Malan,' I said. 'Is Dicky around?'

'Mr Dixon? Yeah. He'll be back in a tick. Your bike sounds sick.'

'Yes. I'll have to give it a going over.'

He glanced down at the engine. 'One of your plug lead's dropped off,' he said, and he gave me a look that made me feel two feet tall before he turned and went back inside.

I looked down and, sure enough, the lead was hanging down in mid-air. It didn't take a moment to push it back on but it hurt. He'd seen through me just like that – a prat in a flying jacket riding a big bike who didn't know enough to fix the simplest problem imaginable. Well, he didn't have a head like mine. He'd change his mind when he heard what I had for sale.

I looked into the hangar and there was a Spitfire Mk V up on trestles while they worked on the undercarriage legs. When I was little and my room began to fill up with badly painted plastic models of fighters, the Colonel tried to get me interested in tanks instead.

'Damn fine thing, tank warfare,' he declared. 'Strategy. Tactics. Teamwork. One lot of chaps depending on another lot of chaps. That's what won the war, you know, not these Johnny-head-in-airs of yours.'

I asked my mother whether he had actually fought in tanks, but all she ever said was, 'I think he prefers to keep his stories to himself, dear. Better not to ask,' as if it might be hush-hush. My head was full of Sailor Malan. The glory of single combat represented by the Spitfires seemed far preferable to the earthy world of tank manoeuvres. The symbiosis of man and that slender-winged machine seemed to me then to be the most noble thing imaginable, and that belief had never left me as I grew up.

I spent fifteen minutes looking round the hangar at the bits of planes and the work in progress, then a jovial shout announced the return of Dicky Dixon and his handlebar moustache.

'Jesus wept, it's the hippie again. What can I do for you this time, flower child?' he said. I felt hurt. I'd sold him some instruments six weeks earlier and I'd thought I was on the way to being accepted. It must have been the length of my hair because my clothes were all right. I wanted to be one of the boys, not 'the hippie again'.

'Can I talk to you?'

'I've got two minutes. Make it snappy.'

'I might have some bits for you,' I said, 'good bits from a hot, dry country, the sort of bits you like best.'

'Spit bits?'

'Just so.'

'Okay, that's different. Come to the office.'

I told him what I had and he was delighted. We did the deal on the spot, subject to the bits arriving in the state Ephraim claimed they were in. I prayed he had been describing them accurately.

Some parts look fine but the reason they've been left in store is because they were defective straight from the factory and they still weren't any better twenty-five years later. I couldn't afford to lose Dicky as a customer. Dicky rooted around in his desk drawer and found me a hundred quid in cash to put the seal on it.

While he was doing that, I looked around the room and remembered, prompted by the pictures and the models, that Dicky was a Jaguar racer as well as a flyer.

'Quick question, Dick. Do you remember a pair of brothers who raced cars? Owen? Max and Douglas Owen, sometimes called themselves Birkin Owen.'

He squinted and frowned. 'No. Don't think so.'

'They had a Lister-Jag they used to run at Brighton. Ginny Owen was killed in it.'

'Christ. That one. The Horror. I certainly do.'

'Any idea where I might find out a bit more?'

He turned round in his swivel chair and looked up at the shelves. 'I've got the Maurice Nelson book somewhere. Yup, here it is. Have a look. I'll be in the hangar when you're done.'

Maurice Nelson's book was a history of the Lister-Jaguar marque and fifteen minutes later, when I'd read the full detailed story of VPO 275, I knew exactly why Dicky called the car 'the Horror'. It was the first evidence that there was something extra about the tragedy of Ginny Owen, that her death sprang as surely from a toxic cocktail of personalities as from a chance combination of circumstances. I'd been believing there had to be a reason for ten years and now perhaps I was on the track of it.

There's a guru for every rare make of car. I wanted to find a Lister expert to answer some questions.

I went back into the hangar and found Dicky.

'Still here?' he said.

'Yes. Thanks for the book. It helped. Who do I ask if I want to know more about Listers?'

'Jim Tucker. He knows everything there is to know. He spanners for John Harbold when he goes racing. Harbold's got one.'

'Where do I find Jim Tucker?'

'Shut your eyes, turn round, take three steps and open them.'

'He's here?'

'He's right behind you. Does Spits, too. I pay his wages.'

Jim was huge and gruff with a messy beard spreading over his chest like someone vomiting sofa stuffing.

He looked a bit doubtful when I accosted him and glanced questioningly at Dicky, who was a harsh master when it came to talking on the firm's time.

'Tell him what he wants and get him out of here so we can get some work done,' said Dicky.

'Listers, eh? What do you want to know?'

'I want to know what happened to the Horror.'

'VPO 275,' he said. 'There's a funny thing. Ex-Ecurie Ecosse team car. I was just talking about that one the other day. You could go and see it.'

He didn't know much after all. He was supposed to know everything. 'I can't. It was wrecked.'

He did know everything. A twinkle came into his eye as of someone who knew he was about to surprise me. 'Ah, but things don't necessarily stay wrecked. Not these days, when they're getting to be worth a few bob.' He lowered his voice. 'It's not all that far from here. Just outside Oxford. The only thing is the bloke who's got it, Chinnery, he's a bit, well, I suppose difficult would cover it. Some would say bloody-minded. I don't mind telling you where it is, but for Christ's sake don't say I told you.'

With money in my pocket, the day ahead of me and a bike that sounded like new again there was no reason not to go straight there. It took only half an hour, but it led me into a whole new phase of the affair.

The farm was near Cumnor, beyond Oxford, and the gates leading to a long drive promised a lot more than the ugly stone building and the scattering of ramshackle tin sheds which greeted me at the far end of it. The noise of the bike set a dog barking and rushing at me on the end of a long chain. Sputtering bright blue flashes from inside the open half of a pair of double doors showed someone was welding in there but I couldn't get to the door because it was within the arc of the dog's chain so I revved up the bike to attract his attention and that seemed to work.

The flashes stopped, the dog got a curse for its trouble and a small man in blue overalls stepped into sight from inside the shed. He was carrying a welding mask and he didn't look happy to see a visitor.

'I don't do bikes,' he said, shifting from foot to foot as if he couldn't wait to get back inside.

'I haven't come about the bike.'

'Then it's no thanks.'

'To what?'

'To whatever you're offering.'

'I was hoping to talk to you about a Lister.'

That got a reaction. His face was furrowed and the furrows were accented with grease like stage-paint. Now they deepened as he squinted at me. He had grey hair and I realized he was older than I'd thought.

'Go on,' he said.

'I heard you had VPO here, or what's left of her.'

'Did you?'

This wasn't promising. I remembered what turned the trick with Laura and decided to try it again. 'I saw the crash. At Brighton? I've been trying to find out a bit more, you know, about the Owens and about the car.'

He made a derisive noise. 'Bloody Max Owen. You anything to do with him?'

'No. Anyway he's dead.'

'About time too. He should have been strung up.'

'Could I see the car?'

He looked at me doubtfully and the dog suddenly rushed at his leg. He swore at it and it retreated, walking backwards so the chain got tangled with its legs and it fell over in the mud.

'Well,' he said, 'I like to keep my business to myself. You come in here, you stay *stumm*, right? Not a word to anyone. I don't want those Hooray Henrys from the poncy Jaguar Driver's Club coming in here and putting their sticky fingers all over it and telling me what I should and shouldn't be doing. Is that a deal?'

'It's a deal,' I said, and checking that he was holding the dog's collar, I stepped inside and found myself face to face with what seemed to be all that was now left of VPO 275.

# Thirteen

I went into the barn with all the slow, careful dread of a relative waiting for the sheet to be lifted for the awful moment of recognition because what I was expecting to see inside was the corpse of a car. What I saw under the neon tube lighting, propped on trestles, sitting squarely on the concrete floor, was not a corpse at all. It was something new – not yet a car but the frame of a car, a chassis made of shining, straight tubes with suspension parts hanging off its four corners.

'This is it?' I said in amazement.

He nodded. I knew his name was Chinnery but that was all I knew about him. In the lights he was even older than I'd thought. Late sixties but wiry, grizzled. The barn had two beaten-up tractors in the back of it and all the bits of heavy iron and hydraulic pipe that went with them but it didn't look like anyone had been doing any farming here for a long time.

'It all looks, well . . . new.'

'Hey,' he said angrily, 'less of that. It's legit. I've saved everything that could be saved. It's a repair job, not a copy. This is the real thing.'

I'd touched something very sensitive indeed. He jabbed a finger at the chassis. 'Original cross-tubes, there, there and there. See that bracket? Original. Instrument panel, body fixing points, all original.'

If you looked closely, you could see a difference between the virgin, unsullied tube that made up most of the stiff spaghetti of the chassis and the duller, stained stuff he was pointing out, but the old tubes were really little more than isolated islands, overwhelmed by the surrounding seas of new metal. Still if that was the way he wanted to think . . .

'Yes, quite,' I said. 'It's just that last time I saw this, I would never have thought . . .' I was about to say, '. . . that it could ever be rebuilt,' but I realized he would react badly to that, so I changed it to, '. . . that anyone would ever have the skill to put it straight again.'

He nodded as he considered that. 'You saw the crash?' he said abruptly.

'Yes.'

'Come and sing for your supper then. I wanna hear about that. Got some stuff you can look at.'

I followed him across to a corner of the barn where there was a partitioned-off section like an office in a warehouse. Next to it was an interesting shape under a tarpaulin. Something big, with pre-war flowing wings and the bottom of a large, rusty wire wheel of massive proportions just showing like an ankle under a Victorian skirt.

'Keep your nose out of that,' he said, seeing where I was looking.

The office was where he kept his drawings and his photos – the guide-lines for his resurrection business.

'He should have been shot, you know, our Max. He caused it.' Chinnery pulled a plastic folder from the shelf and put it in front of me. 'Go on. Read that.'

I stared at him and then down at the folder. Black plastic, unlabelled. It looked unimportant but if what he'd just said was right, it held the answer to that old, old question of mine.

'What is it?'

'Coroner's file.'

'How did you get that?'

'Friend of mine let me have it.'

He watched me all the time I was reading it and I didn't feel happy with the nature of his scrutiny and whatever lay behind it. The inquest was held on the 23rd of September 1963. The papers gave Ginny's essential details, age forty, address in Buckinghamshire, 'wife of Douglas Owen, an advertising executive'. She had driven in competitions from 1954 onwards and competed at Brighton on seven occasions, having won the Ladies' Class the previous year. I knew that. The car's owner was Max Owen, at an unfamiliar address in Ranelagh Close, London W4, who 'had driven it on the road frequently'.

On September 13th Douglas had driven the car down to Brighton with Ginny following in another car, reaching 120 mph at times on the way. It had seemed normal and the newly rebuilt engine had been working perfectly. At seven-thirty a.m. on Saturday the 14th, Ginny had taken it for a trial run on the A23 for half an hour and practised some starts. After breakfast at the hotel, they drove it the short distance down to the paddock. Douglas's verbatim account then followed and the hairs stood on end on the back of my neck.

I badly wanted to be reading this by myself, somewhere quiet, not here in this barn with this odd man who seemed to have his own peculiar agenda staring hard at me, watching my every response. I had no choice.

*I pushed the car to the line as it was likely to overheat if it was driven too slowly and the clutch was difficult . . .*

That was *me* the year before. I'd done that with her. Douglas hadn't been there to help. Was it Max who'd been called away to the organizers' office or was it Douglas? Maybe it was Douglas because why else wasn't he there? I smelt her and felt her hair all over again.

*. . . I exchanged a few words of encouragement with my wife. She was looking forward to her run. At the signal to go everything seemed perfectly normal. She went off well around the slight bend and then accelerated hard. I turned to a friend and remarked that she'd got the hang of the clutch, then I followed the track of the car with my eyes until it went out of sight around the bend. I could hear the engine note rising and falling as she changed gear, until it cut off. I assumed she had reached the end of the course and I heard a loud bang, but as the engine was prone to backfire on the overrun, I thought little more of it until some seconds later I saw a plume of smoke rising from the end of the course . . .*

A black column of smoke boiled up in my mind, rising higher and higher in the still air. Again I heard the thud of the fire's ignition and the sound of my feet.

'Go on,' said Chinnery. 'There's a lot more.'

*. . . At that point I realized that an accident must have occurred involving either my wife or the other competitor who started with her. The fire engine and the ambulance moved off from the paddock.*

I saw the doctor getting into his car and ran to join him. I urged him to drive faster and he took me to the eastern end of the Peter Pan playground. There I saw the trail made by a car through the iron railings. Inside the playground I saw that the car was VPO 275 and that it was blazing fiercely. My wife was nowhere to be seen and I was told that she had not been found.

I was restrained from going closer to the car and after some time had passed I was taken back to the start. Later I was taken by car to the police station where an officer showed me a ring. I identified this as an engagement ring belonging to my wife which she had been wearing when she started off.

'Poor sod,' said Chinnery, when he saw I'd got to the end of that one. 'He didn't know the half of it, did he? Now read this.' He reached across and flicked the sheets over.

*Witness statement of PC159 Donald Roger Steadman.*

I was stationed near the finish of the speed trial course to prevent any incursion into the danger area by the public. As the cars approached the finish, the Lister-Jaguar VPO 275 was well in front of the other car and had moved across the road to take up a position approximately in the centre of the carriageway. It was travelling at very high speed, I would estimate approximately 150 mph, and I noticed that its front wheels suddenly began to patter from side to side. The tyres appeared to be bouncing off the road surface. The front of the car started to turn towards the sea, drifting towards the kerb, and I could see that the driver was making violent attempts to get it back under control. In this fashion, it mounted the pavement approximately fifty yards short of me. As it hit the kerb, immediately parts of the car started coming off, including the bonnet, the complete front suspension as well as the radiator and part of the chassis broke away and hurtled towards me. I jumped forward in time so that these parts passed immediately behind me and collided with a heavy sand bin. The rest of the car finished up on the easternmost children's roundabout and exploded into flames which at once rose to about ten or twelve feet. I ran towards the car immediately but no sign of the driver was visible above the sides of the cockpit area and the heat made it impossible to get at the car. There was no way through the flames. After I had been there for a short time, a track marshal arrived with a very small fire extinguisher which proved to *be ineffective at controlling the flames, so, fearing a further explosion, I forced him to go to a place of safety. A man who identified himself as the driver's husband then arrived with a doctor and I prevented him with some difficulty from attempting to approach the car. The fire engine arrived from the starting area at the same time and it quickly got the blaze under control with foam. The foam was washed off when the fire was out. The deceased was lying in the car . . .*

I looked up.

'Squeamish?' said Chinnery. He knew just where I'd got to.

It was a moment of choice. If I wanted to know more I could just look down again. If I didn't I could close the file.

'Why do you say Max Owen should have been strung up?' I said.

'You read it. You'll see.'

So I didn't really have that choice and I seemed to have become part of some game he was playing. He wanted me to read this, wanted me to go through the full ugliness of it.

*. . . She was clearly dead and her body was very severely burnt, beyond recognition. The body was lying sideways, with the head on the nearside of the car and the lower limbs twisted to the offside. The feet were trapped beneath the offside of the chassis. There was no . . .*

I skipped the next bit when I began to realize how detailed the description was. This was what I had run away from so that I would not have to know how much of Ginny had been destroyed, how great an obscenity had been created by fire and impact. Chinnery was still doing his odd thing, gazing at me as if he wanted to rub my nose in it, so I cheated. I kept my eyes moving just below the typing so that he wouldn't see, trying to concentrate on the small gap between the lines, not the words just above, absorbing them despite myself but doing my best not to. I reached safer ground beyond the description.

*. . . The deceased was taken to the borough mortuary. I returned to the police station and there I saw the deceased's husband again, Mr Douglas Owen. He was most anxious to visit the mortuary to see his wife but bearing in mind the condition of her body, he was deterred from doing so.*

The next statement came from a consulting engineer who said

the front part of the chassis and the front suspension had broken away from the rest of the car at two places where the chassis tubes had rusted through over half their circumference. It was his opinion that this had taken place while the car was at maximum speed, possibly as it hit a bump in the road surface and that the failure was the result of imperfectly repaired prior damage.

Max's own version came next:

*I purchased the car, a 3.8 litre racing Lister-Jaguar, during 1959 and used it from time to time on the road. I was in America at frequent intervals that year and the next, and I allowed my brother and his wife to use the car in various speed events because at that time they had no suitable car of their own, though both of them had often competed in the past in a variety of powerful vehicles. I had the Lister maintained carefully at Farley Heath garage, of which I was then co-proprietor. I had no knowledge of any previous uncorrected accident damage to the car which might have resulted in any weakening of the chassis.*

There were a few other bits and pieces. One witness said the driver looked over her right shoulder. The pathologist who performed the postmortem said that she died from brain injuries and burns. With it was the report from the local newspaper, which described it as an appalling and tragic disaster in front of thousands of holidaymakers, caused apparently by front suspension failure, and gave details of a long exchange during the inquest in which Max apparently cross-examined the consulting engineer.

*Asked repeatedly by the owner of the car, Mr Max Owen, as to whether there was any definite evidence that neglect in the preparation of the car was the cause of the accident, Mr Alexander Rawson, the consulting engineer, said he could only repeat his view that the accident was caused by rust in the chassis tubes resulting from previous repairs. On being asked by Mr Owen whether there was any evidence that he, as the car's owner, should have known of this, Mr Rawson said that was a question for Mr Owen himself to answer. He was then pressed to answer and said that he himself had no evidence on the matter.*

'That's why you think Max was to blame, then?' I asked. 'Because his own garage had been looking after the car?'

'Oh, not just that,' said Chinnery. 'Lying sod, wasn't he? Bloke like him knew exactly what that car had been through.'

'What had it been through?' I asked, though from my researches in Dicky's office I knew at least some of the answers.

'Half the walls in Europe,' said Chinnery, and laughed. I hated him for the laugh. He ticked off each point on his fingers. His list echoed some of what I had just been reading in Dicky's book, but it went even further.

'Ninian Sanderson bent it straight off the truck first time they tested it at Charterhall. Suspension upright broke and he hit the pit wall so hard the whole bloody wall moved three feet. Ivor Bueb shunted it in Germany – the Nurburgring 1,000 kilometres, that was. He flew straight off into the forest at a bend they call *Schwalbenkreuz*. Did the front of it no end of harm. Bill Wrigley turned it over in some hill climb, Prescott maybe, I forget now – and finally, best of all, five million people saw it get stuffed into a rock face on the Llanberis pass.'

'Five million people?'

'Well, I don't know. Lots, anyway. Anybody who saw the film at the pictures.'

I must have looked blank.

'It was in a film,' he said. 'Didn't you ever see it? 'It was called *Win or Lose*. Crap plot, but lots of racing stuff in it. They used the car for filming some of it. You know, there was a hero and a villain and the Lister was the villain's car. All right, maybe Max didn't do his homework on the rest of the car's history, but he definitely knew about that one.'

'You don't know for certain he saw the film. Even if he did, there's no reason why he should know it was the same car.' I felt oddly moved to protect Max.

'You think he didn't know about it?'

'I just don't see why you should jump to that conclusion.'

'He was *driving* it, for God's sake. For the film. I think he probably knew about it.' He could see I didn't believe him. 'I was there, too. I was unit mechanic for the film unit. It was bloody Snowdonia, pretending to be the Italian Alps. Cheapskates. They couldn't afford a proper car and driver so they put the word round and they got Max bloody Birkin Owen and the Horror. My fault, really. He owed me money so I gave him a buzz when I knew how desperate they were to hire something. I thought that way I'd get the money back.' He gave a short derisive laugh. 'He'd only just bought it and he couldn't drive it to save his life. He wasn't meant to crash it just then. He was only meant to slide it round a bend, but he lost it. Wallop, straight into the cliff – took the front right off it. Lucky the cameras got it. They had to rewrite the script to make it fit the plot.'

So Max lied to the inquest. What did he say to Douglas? Did Douglas know about the car? Presumably not, or he wouldn't have let Ginny drive it. Had he ever seen the film? Who knows.

'Anyway,' Chinnery said, 'time for you to tell *me* a few things. I want to know what *you* saw. You were there when it happened, were you? Did you get close?'

'I saw her look over her shoulder, then it was just the way the policeman said.'

It wasn't enough for him. I knew what he wanted. He wanted another eye witness account of the death, not the crash. This man was fascinated by the death more than by the car. The car was maybe just a means to an end – a way to turn a good profit by putting together a plausible replica with a few straight bits, the executioner's axe that had twelve new heads and eight new handles but was still the same axe. That was not the reason he had this file in here. I didn't like it and I didn't want to associate it in any way with my own interest.

'Did you look at it afterwards?'

No of course I bloody didn't. I was trying not to.

'No.'

'I've got the pictures,' he said. 'The pictures the fire brigade took – you know, for evidence.'

He had put them where he could go straight to them and I looked at them, then quickly looked away. They weren't just of the car. Ginny was in them too.

He sneered a bit when I got up from the table. Whatever the test was, I seemed to have failed it. Later on, when I understood more about the whole thing, I realized just how Max had tried to involve him in shifting the blame. Chinnery wasn't a nice man, but he wasn't a bad man either and I'd scratched the scab of an old sore for him. Maybe he was haunted by what happened to Ginny and when I came asking, he saw a chance to give the ghosts a new home.

'Thanks for your time,' I said.

'Show yourself out,' he said. 'I got a weld to finish.'

'Do you mind calling off your dog, then?'

He started to move towards the door but then he smiled and stopped again. 'I haven't got time,' he said. 'Go out the back and round. He won't get you there.'

We left the office and I stood and watched while he picked up his welding mask and struck an arc. As the bright flashes started I looked at the chassis there and it seemed to have nothing to do with Ginny and Max and Douglas. There were sections of a brand-new unpainted aluminium body shell on the ground beyond it. Someone was going to be buying what was almost entirely a new car.

He was taking no more notice of me. I'd failed his final nasty test after all. I went to the back of the barn where he'd pointed and through a doorway into another lean-to section and got the shock of my life, which was probably just what he'd intended because lying there under the lean-to, unheeded, was the real car.

What was back there on the trestles being put together had never been through the mill of history and tragedy. This had. This, the real Lister, lay there on the ground, a blackened, twisted heap of tubing with the melted, charred shell of its body carelessly heaped up behind. You could see where his hacksaw had been at work on the bits of tubing that were still relatively straight – the bits that had been transplanted to give the copy out on the trestles its slender claim to reality. Bright, cut edges showed through the carbon, rust and grime. The engine had gone and the entire, separate, front section of the chassis was shoved into one side. That was the bit that had broken off and gone careering past poor PC Steadman and caused the crash. The tubes which snapped that Saturday had now rusted evenly right round their twisted ends.

The remains of a steering wheel and a charred seat frame showed where I had sat with Ginny's scent around me and where she had died and I didn't want that awful place where she had mixed with the burning metal to be left here, unsanctified. If ever a machine needed a grave it was this one. It should have been lowered into a deep hole to dissolve away into the acid ground. It should not be here, being picked apart to give life and value to a metal impostor.

I was glad to leave.

# Fourteen

I came back from Chinnery's place through the middle of Oxford and stopped the bike to sit on a wall near Magdalen Bridge, thinking how well I used to feel when I was a student and how bloody awful I felt now. The statements I'd read and the photos I'd glimpsed had brought back all the black despair I had felt on the way down that morning. I'd been on the noisy, vibrating bike for too long. My joints ached, my muscles had uncomfortable cramps and when I took my crash helmet off, the headache it had caused refused to go away. I could buy a new one when Ephraim's money came through.

What I felt most of all at that moment was that I wanted to start again but I didn't have the slightest clue how to do it. This was a familiar wall. I'd often sat on it when I was a student, watching the world go by, thinking I was learning to see the true beauty of the world and to find peace in the middle of hubbub when all the time I was just a bit stoned. I'd come to this place as one person, left it as another, and now I seemed to be a third. It didn't feel like third time lucky. I thought, sitting here, that if Chinnery's account was to be believed, maybe I could blame Max for the state I was in. If he really caused Ginny's death by his sloppiness and his evasions, because Ginny's death helped propel me to where I was now, then that was his fault, too. A real Birkin Owen indeed. It only struck me then that I'd lost sight completely of the original reason which had prompted me to buy the trunk. The Max I had got to know was the perfect prototype for the Colonel's expression but I had no idea whether they really had known each other. Max and his peculiar way with his cars was an enigma.

A bicycle with a very squeaky pedal crank went past me and triggered a memory of the summer days of my degree when I started to walk the mild wild-side of soft drugs, stone quadrangles and rising overdrafts and when, for the first time, there was no one to tell me to get my hair cut. I had a tutor with a high, cracked voice who lived entirely inside his head, in his room and on the routes between the libraries which he pedalled constantly on his own squeaky bicycle. He had a bee in his bonnet about speed and class distinctions.

'Young men such as you,' he said, in the soporific stupor of his room, where glinting dust particles took the place of air and blocked the passage of knowledge, 'young men such as you have a built-in love of speed. It is in your genes, put there as a survival mechanism so that the fittest amongst you can flaunt your fleetness of foot as a card in the mating game and thus perpetuate it into the next generation.'

He fixed me with a gaze magnified by his thick glasses into something aquarian. 'You, Miles. You are, I'm sure, interested in perpetuating yourself?'

There was a dutiful titter of laughter from all three of us, which he joined in with his own galvanic snort and he looked at the other two benignly. He was not a man who seemed likely ever to have taken any of the steps necessary for his own self-perpetuation.

'Before there were horses to ride,' he said, 'speed on foot was the only speed there was and running was the only way to compete. When horses came along they brought in a new kind of speed. Young men now raced each other on horseback but some worthwhile genetic prowess still held sway. They needed balance, bravery, mental empathy and physical control to get the best out of their horses. There was still, you might say young Miles, a point to it all. Do any of you ride?' he added abruptly, mostly to see if we were listening.

Geoff Coulter shook his head. Abbas looked startled, caught in mid day-dream. To get him off the hook I admitted I had been known to.

'You, Miles? You are the last one I would have suspected of latent equestrianism, but then I suppose your family are probably possessed of sufficient resources to waste some of them on a skill you are never likely to use again. The trouble is, you see, a horse is a physical possession and a good horse has a high value, so very soon the pursuit of pussy . . .' He said that to shock us and show us that he was an unpredictable and fascinating man, which he was not. '. . . became inextricably intertwined with the pursuit and possession of wealth and status. Soon the youth higher up the social tree had an automatic advantage in this mating game over the less fortunate.'

Abbas, seeking to show he was back with us, interrupted. 'But surely,' he said, 'that is a valid genetic survival strategy? Those who are rich are more likely to be well-fed and strong.'

The professor gave him a long, silent look intended to convey disapproval. 'The Arabs were, one might say, the heart of the problem,' and Abbas flinched visibly. 'The whole thing moved up another notch when the Arabs were first imported to Britain and bloodstock breeding began. Human bloodstock was being bred at the same time. Now you needed pots of money to win the speed game.'

The professor was not a man who liked cars. His bicycle had a three-speed gear and a bent chainguard that clanked on every turn of the pedals.

'The arrival of the motorcar merely switched the game from the horse to the internal combustion engine,' he said, 'and that muddied the rules a little. It dulled the fine skills needed to get the best out of your steed. You, Saifee . . .' Abbas flinched again. 'You, I believe, are responsible for that loud red thing which booms up and down New College Lane.'

'You can't boom up and down it,' said Geoff, 'it's one way.' He enjoyed playing a bluff stage northerner.

'It should be no way at all,' said the professor, who had perhaps suffered on his bicycle from Abbas's erratic driving. 'In the past you rich young blades would have raced your hunters from church steeple to church steeple for high stakes, or for the regard of the squire's daughter. Now you race your MGs and your . . .' The professor was casting around for the name of another sports car and failed to come up with anything plausible. '. . . your Brabhams to public houses outside the city for exactly the same purposes.'

It was engagingly dotty stuff, exactly what universities are all about, and it was only unusual in that the subject we were meant to be studying was French.

I wondered what the professor would have made of a man like Max, who had the fast cars but let others do the racing and

151

earn the adulation. He probably would have decided that Max was not interested in displaying his genetic advantage in public and he wouldn't perhaps have been surprised that there should be no sign that Max had procreated himself.

Laura's story didn't wash. There had been no war wound at Narvik to justify his non-participation, of that I was quite sure, so where did that leave Max? A coward, perhaps? That was possible. There was a self-pitying quality running through all the copious letters he had written to his mother during the war from his various safe barracks in the Home Counties. The tone was always the same. There was Max, chafing at the bit to get at the enemy, and there was lucky old Douglas having all the fun out there in the desert. His mother must have kept those letters and they'd come back to him during the time when they lived together in London, the time when Ginny accused him of plotting to sell the flat. Did his mother write back sympathetically from her wartime hideaway in the country? I didn't know. I hadn't found any of the letters which might have flowed back in that direction.

There was a 'Major D' and a 'Colonel L' who featured in some of them as bad guys. Max seemed to have trouble with his senior officers on many occasions. If it had been 'Colonel D', I would have thought I had found the answer to the 'Birkin Owen' question.

Deep down, I still wanted to think the best of Max. I preferred to think that even if there was no war wound, there was some other disability that had clipped his wings.

When I got back to London, my flat had emptied completely. Even Cat had gone, and two days later she was still gone. I went to bed feeling ill and stayed there. After Ephraim got the money draft from Dicky, he somehow got my commission to me in cash, eight hundred pounds in tenners delivered by a man in a small white van. It was exactly what he'd promised and I immediately went looking for a hiding place for it in case Cat came back and had another party. While I was doing that, I found her stash, which was hidden in the top of the cupboard where I had been going to put the money. There was something tempting about the powder. I'd tried aspirin and paracetamol and various cold cures, but none of them had taken away the ache and itches.

She wouldn't miss just a little for a good cause and it worked much better than any of the medicine. It even pushed back the blackness and filled in most of a day.

A little turned into a bit more.

Cat didn't come back for several more nights.

I wasted a lot of my time in the days in between them, low on energy in the wake of whatever virus had hit me. For an hour or two every day, when I felt up to it, I rooted through the trunk, piling anything to do with the cars straight into my box files unread for another day. I wanted to know more about life not death, about the people not the cars. I wanted nothing more to do with Max's cars for the time being. In particular, I didn't want to think about petrol and power and the fusion of what is left of metal and flesh when things go wrong. I wanted to know more about the Duke and his Duchess but, above all, I wanted to learn whatever there was to learn about Natalie.

One of the film wallets had identification pencilled on the back: 'MBO, France 46–47'. The pictures were washed out, a little over-exposed in shades of grey. They showed a large, square house with a Deep South balcony over shaded arcades of pillars. There were shots taken from that balcony too, and by putting them together side by side I found you could make up an approximate panorama of the view as though that was what the photographer had intended, taking the pictures in turn as he swung round. Despite the distancing effect of the black-and-white, that turned it abruptly into a real place. There's a winding rough drive to the left among trees, a vista of sea and islands ahead and the roofs of a small town off to the right. This must be La Cröe. It fits the description.

Most of the photos are sterile, just the house and the view. There are one or two interiors, a sweeping staircase and a small sitting room but there's nothing on the walls, a few sticks of uncomfortable furniture and a single small bunch of flowers in a vase. Perhaps it is early days in the Windsors' attempt to make the place habitable. It is clear that someone, very possibly Max, is exaggerating wildly by calling it a chateau. It is a large villa at best.

Only two of the photos have people in them. One is Max

himself, sitting in a hard chair on the balcony, wearing just a pair of shorts. He never looks quite relaxed in any photo, he is always uneasy, as if he doesn't want to be identified quite so firmly. Beyond him another, older officer has his shirt on too, as well as knee-length socks. There is a cup of tea beside his chair and a copy of *Life* magazine. They have the look of men who are just sitting and waiting for the next of their not very arduous duties.

The other photo is the same balcony but it's not a tired picture like the first one. It is full of life thanks to the powerful presence of a woman in a swimsuit who is sitting on the balcony, dragging the attention of the camera, the photographer and the viewer entirely to her. She has one leg drawn up in a model girl pose and she is laughing so that you want to laugh too. The hair is a little less wild and the face has tightened over its cheekbones since the pre-war photo of the two of them in their coats, but it is certainly Natalie. So Natalie *was* there at La Cröe with Max and she was, it seems, able to spend time on that side of the social divide with the military staff, rather than paying court to the Duchess.

I found several more scattered bits of Max's manuscripts as I delved, and one of them, folded and looking complete, was headed 'Antibes Antics'. It was written on different paper, whiter and less brittle so that it seemed decidedly more recent than the others, written when he was older. Certainly the handwriting was harder to read, flattened out so much that you had to search for the peaks as clues to help in the process of decoding it.

*During that period in which I was privileged to serve the Duke of Windsor as, in effect, his aide-de-camp at his splendid house at Antibes, I was on several occasions required to exhibit considerable dexterity of wit to preserve the dignity of the royal personage, none more so than when the Duke decided to indulge in the sport of underwater spear-fishing. The Chateau La Cröe was possessed of its own private plage and after a short time in residence there, the Duke and Duchess established a daily routine from which they rarely departed. In the morning the Duchess would reply to her latest correspondence and deal with tradesmen while the Duke would work on his memoirs. These, I am pleased to say, I had prevailed upon him* to write after many fascinating evenings in which, with his equerry, I would be invited into his study after supper to hear him reminisce. This was always a most interesting experience.

In the afternoon, the Duke would invariably go to the Biot golf course close by, where, by virtue of his neat and accurate game, he would equally invariably beat those more powerful hitters who took him on. On his return he would change and then join the Duchess and her friends at the bathing plage. Any other guests who arrived while the royal party were on the beach were expected to change and then join us there, where it was my duty to announce them to the Duke and Duchess. This was always a strange scene as the men in their swimming trunks would give formal, stiff bows and the women would have to make deep curtsies, which never looked quite right without the rustle of a wide dress to cover the scissoring of their legs.

There was a moment at which a certain dispute was to arise through the offices of those in the household who, it seems, may have served more than one master. These spies in our camp reported back to the unsympathetic ears of the Palace that the Duke may have been inviting to the house some who were supposedly unsuitable for his circle of acquaintances. 'Collaborator' is an ugly word and such charges were unproven. I am inclined to think such allegations were the sour outpourings of those who were too timid to put the overriding priority of a great affair of the heart in front of the sterile list of obligations they termed 'duty'. To such people, their notion of 'duty' is all too often simply a barricade for them to shelter behind, justifying their abstinence from a plunge into the joyful and dangerous whirlpools of life. In this case, they sought to further blacken the reputation of the Duke and to curtail the social life with which, against the odds, he was endeavouring to make his exile more bearable.

The Duke, being the remarkable man he was, did his best to resist the Palace's long-distance interference and would often refer to the Duchess, against their specific wishes, as 'Her Royal Highness' – a splendid personal declaration, it seemed to me, transcending mere protocol. It was a declaration of how things should have been had the heart and not sour 'duty' been allowed to reign.

On these beach occasions, the Duke would take his spring gun in search of the fish which thronged the rocks at the fringes of the beach. This can be a dangerous sport and it was my duty, in safeguarding the former king's person, to be constantly on the look-out. In the shadowy depths below the rocks of Antibes, there live great fishes which may attack without the slightest warning and there can be nothing so terrifying as the sudden grip of an octopus tentacle wrapping itself around your ankle to pull you down into the shadows. In these days before proper diving masks were freely available, we were obliged to use modified versions of army gas-masks which, being made partly of canvas, would often slowly fill with water and attempt to drown us, so the perils were indeed manifold.

On one such day, my attention had been distracted in the most charming way imaginable by a member of the Duchess's party, a Miss Vanderberg from New York, who was later to become a cellist of some renown and had been a friend, or perhaps I should say a protegée, of the Duchess's for many years. We had met on a previous occasion in the thirties, whilst we were both members of the Duke's skiing party at the Austrian resort of Kitzbühl.

I stiffened and stared at the manuscript with the certainty that 'Miss Vanderberg' and Natalie were the same person.

That had been an extremely romantic occasion, being the time at which it had become quite clear to those few of us who were taken into his confidence that the Duke had fallen deeply in love with the beguiling and gracious Wallis. It was perhaps the infectious magic of the time which cast its spell over myself and Miss Vanderberg, so that we too walked with our feet an inch or two above the snow for the rest of those magical, pre-war weeks.

Now she was here for a long holiday before taking up a position with the United Nations in Geneva and I was discovering that those same sensations were making themselves once again painfully apparent in both our breasts. She was an unusual and engrossing person, full of vivacity and charmingly unimpressed, in that republican way the Americans have, by the glamour of the court-in-exile that surrounded us. Although I was myself possessed of a significant estate in England and a number of holdings in the better parts of the world which most would envy, I found that she had no interest in that aspect of life so that I was obliged to play it down in my conversation with her at all times. Although our lives had touched only briefly before the terrible interruption of the war, we seemed to have known each other for all that intervening time when the rigours of the battlefield had kept me wholly occupied and when I had been unable to communicate with her at all. I was therefore deeply engrossed in conversation with her when I was suddenly appalled to hear a cry from the Duchess to the effect that the Duke had disappeared. She had last seen him swimming by the rocks and now there was no trace of him at all.

I plunged into the water and was at the scene in no time.

Here he had crossed something out. It started with 'despite' and I thought I could see the words 'war wound' in the middle.

. . . and when I reached the rocks I was extremely relieved to hear the Duke's voice coming at me from the shadowy cave behind them. 'Owen,' he hissed, 'I'm glad it's you. I have suffered an unfortunate accident.'

It soon transpired that he had been swimming along in pursuit of a large fish which had darted into a hole in the rocks. Taking a deep breath and attempting to follow it in, the Duke had felt something catch hold of his leg and then slide up to take a firm grip around the fabric of his swimming trunks. It was one of our old friends, the octopus. The Duke had to swim furiously to regain the surface and in doing so, the octopus – with no respect for the royal personage – had dragged his trunks entirely off. There was now no sign of the creature which had, doubtless, withdrawn into its hole and was doing its best to eat the garment.

'This is a pretty pickle,' the Duke opined. 'I can hardly go back to the beach like this.'

'You must borrow my trunks, sire,' I said at once.

'Good show, Owen,' he said. 'That's just the ticket. I'll get a pair brought out to you right away.'

Whether any of the guests noticed that the Duke had gone into the sea wearing white trunks and had come out of it wearing black ones was never clear. They were far too polite to say anything if they did. I would like to put it down to the many weighty matters on the royal mind rather than to any deliberate playfulness that the Duke, on returning to his guests, omitted to fulfil his half of the bargain. He left the plage soon afterwards to take, I subsequently discovered, an important telephone call at the chateau which doubtless, and understandably, displaced this other matter in the royal mind.

*I pondered my situation for some time, treading water in the concealment of the rocks, but then duty once more called, this time in a most irritating way. It had become an all-too-common occurrence for boat loads of French trippers to sail close in to the private beach in the hope of seeing the Duke and Duchess, whose presence at Antibes had regrettably become widely known. This was eventually one of the main reasons for the couple's decision to leave the chateau, but at this time it fell to me to do the best I could to drive such sensation-seekers away. One of these boats now appeared, its occupants with their binoculars trained on the beach, so I was obliged to swim out towards it, bellowing in French for it to go away. The man at the helm took no notice of me and I swam closer, giving vent to my very best French swearwords at the top of my voice. He now cut the engine and glided to a halt quite near me. It seemed I had partly succeeded in my objective because the trippers had now switched their attention from the Duchess and were devoting it entirely to me.*

*I trod water and told him in more polite French that this was a private beach and that if he persisted in infringing our privacy I would bring the full weight of the French law to bear on him.*

*He considered this, then replied in perfect English, 'My friend, the water here is very clear. I would advise you to find some suitable clothing before you attempt to address the* gendarmes *in the way you have just addressed me for you run the risk of being arrested under certain articles of the penal code relating to modesty in public places.'*

*I looked down and saw immediately what he meant, which put me at something of a disadvantage and also explained why I had become the target of the trippers' binoculars and cameras. I could hardly explain the circumstances of my involuntary state, so I turned and swam away, doing my best to keep my dignity submerged.*

*My adventure was not entirely over, however. Miss Vanderberg alone of the party had noticed the incident with the boat and my subsequent disappearance back into the cover of the rocks and she swam out to find me. In an age where chivalrous behaviour was still . . .*

I came to the end of the page and realized that was it. There was no more. The rest of the manuscript was not there. I very badly wanted to know what happened when Natalie met Max behind the rocks. I rooted through the trunk hoping to find another sheet of the white handwritten variety, but there was nothing near it in the sedimentary layer which had produced the rest of it. I filed it carefully away for another time in the hope that the end of that story was somewhere in the remaining papers.

Looking again at the photos of Natalie it seemed to me that it would be a tragedy if, as I believed, the two of them had not got together. Natalie would have been good for him, of that I was quite sure.

If any of this was true.

That was the problem. The story was quite far-fetched. What could I be certain of? The photos put Max in a house that looked right for the part of La Cröe. The letter from the Duke showed that Max had been some sort of dogsbody to him. The manuscripts really proved nothing.

Two hours in Kensington Reference Library confirmed a few incidental bits for me the next day. The Kitzbühl holiday was famous or perhaps infamous as the occasion on which long-suffering Mr Ernest Simpson stepped back and absented himself, knowing full well his wife had designs on the young king-to-be. No, perhaps the manuscripts did prove something after all, if I still needed it to be proved. They proved that Max could not be counted a reliable source. After Eton and Narvik, I now had the disparity between his two accounts of that skiing holiday – the 'extremely romantic occasion' in which 'those few of us that knew him well' spotted immediately that Edward and Mrs Simpson were falling in love, and the earlier version in which nobody suspected anything until his confession much later.

None of the writers who had had a go at chronicling the Windsors' odd story seemed to know much about what happened during that holiday. The universe of history is an empty place full of black holes. The recorded segments are tiny asteroids in that vastness.

If Max wrote his stories to make his own life significant, as well as to change his own history when it suited him, then they needed to be handled with care. Some events rise to stand head and shoulders above their fellows, attracting the deserved attention of historians. Some deserve that same attention but fail to get it because, deliberately or not, they go unrecorded. Was Max's story one of these or was he pushing it further than it deserved to go? I couldn't even tell whether he'd written it for a readership any wider than himself and that took me no further.

I got somewhere with La Cröe, however. A couple of shots in the books proved it to be the same place. Whatever else had happened, Max and Natalie had certainly sat sunning themselves on the balcony there. The Duke and Duchess had leased it before the war, gone back to it in 1946 as a summer retreat, then grown disenchanted with the insistent tourists and switched to Paris instead.

What I really wanted to see was some shadowy trace of Max, maybe lurking in the background of one of the book illustrations, but he wasn't to be found however hard I studied the small, grainy photos. I did find the other man though, the older man who had sat next to him on the balcony. He was getting out of some sort of army staff car in the background of a picture of the Duke escorting Wallis up some steps in Cannes.

Best of all, I found Natalie.

No credit was due to me for that. It was pure accident. The man at the table next to me had a stack of books on music sprawled across his section and overlapping on to mine. He was a heavy breather with a balding head, a string vest under a fraying blazer and a distinctly sour smell about him. I was about to be annoyed when a book on Yehudi Menuhin slid off his stack and knocked over my own pile, then I took another look at what had finished up under my nose and there was Natalie, laughing with Menuhin. I went to pick up the book and he snatched it back aggressively.

'Could I have a quick look at that?' I said.

'When I've finished with it,' he said.

'You're not reading it at the moment.'

He started ruffling through the pages.

'I am.'

'Well, can I borrow it when you've finished?'

'It's from the stacks. You have to do it properly.'

'What do you mean?'

'I'll have to give it back in at the desk and they'll put it back and then you have to request it to get it out again.'

'For God's sake, I only want to look at it for ten seconds.'

'That's not my fault.'

I settled the matter by grabbing it out of his hands. He snatched one of my books in retaliation and sat there holding on to it, glowering at me. I took no notice.

The caption to the photo said, *Menuhin congratulating Natalie Vanderberg after the Boston concert. 1964.*

She must have been in her forties but she was still the same woman, attractive, quirky, lively-looking. She was holding something I thought was probably a cello. I gave the book back to the man who cowered away, still clutching mine.

'Thank you so much for your help,' I said.

Now that I knew where to look, Natalie Vanderberg was all too easy to track down. *Who's Who in Music* had the fullest entry. From it I discovered that she was born in 1919, that she studied music in London and Paris, that she served in the United Nations immediately after the war, that she had been (m) in 1966 to a German-sounding count with a complicated name but (div) in 1968. There was a great deal about her career as a soloist, absolutely no mention of any children and a line to the effect that she was alive and well and living in America.

I could go and see her. If I had the money. If I was brave enough. If there was any point.

I had no trouble at all in reading between the lines of her biography. An unsuccessful marriage late in life fitted in with my idea that she'd had a soulmate she had never quite managed to recognize. At least, that was the way it seemed to me.

# Fifteen

There were two letters on the mat late the following morning, when I got up with my head full of squirming evil, having slept through the phone call which could have changed my day. I didn't want to open either of them. One was from the bank – not just a statement in a window envelope though that would have been bad enough, but a *letter*. A letter meant something personal and intrusive, a demand for action, something which set a clock ticking. It was quite inconceivable that it could be anything good. I had my stash of Ephraim's cash as protection but the very existence of the letter implied some of that was going to be tugged straight out of my hands.

When the Colonel died it became clear for the first time that he had amassed a great deal of money in his quiet way, spending his time in his study with a copy of the *Investor's Chronicle*. It all went to my mother, of course, and by that time she had decided not to talk to me any more. The only thing that hurt was what happened to the old Bentley. At the back of my mind, because it had been our one real point of contact, I had thought he would leave that to me. Sotheby's sold it and I only knew because I saw the photo in the auction report in *Classic Car*.

It was absurd to mind, because where on earth would I have kept it and what could I have done with it except sell it myself? I would have liked to have had that problem. More realistically, what had I ever done for the Colonel, except puzzle him for years and then put him on the newspaper placards? When my mother found herself to be a rich widow, she couldn't wait to move to the Channel Islands; it was as though she needed to put a stretch of defensive water between us.

Even looking at the outside of the bank's letter was bad enough. I had to hide it end on between the cereal packets in the kitchen before I felt safe enough to get on with the rest of the day. The other letter looked almost as threatening. It was from Tiggy and it was bound to be about the Hunt Ball, so that went in between the cereal packets as well.

It didn't work.

I found I couldn't even go past the kitchen with them there, so in the end I took a deep breath and opened the bank's letter before I could get cold feet again. Words like 'need to reduce overdraft limit' and 'as per our agreement' jumped out at me. I was two hundred pounds worse off than I thought I was, which was a real puzzle. Dark thoughts of Cat and my cheque book came into my mind. That had triggered a revenge raid by the bank on the size of my overdraft and the bottom line was that I needed to pay in five hundred pounds from Ephraim's nest-egg straight away just to get back to square one.

It was a bummer of a start to the day, because I had gone to sleep the night before bathed in the cosy glow that came from knowing I had a big fat wodge of cash to fend off the sharp edges of life. I hadn't slept for long because at two in the morning I was treated to a graphic demonstration of those sharp edges, waking up with a jerk to an insistent, squeaking, scraping sound. Someone was doing their best to saw through the chain which attached my motorbike to the railings outside the flat. I switched the light on and that didn't stop the sawing noise for a moment but it did show me, when I peered cautiously between the curtains, that there were two of them at it, their backs bent over the bike. They didn't seem to give a damn about the light and in those days in my early twenties, before I filled out, I was not someone to reckon with physically, being thin to the point of emaciation, so the idea of going out there to confront them wasn't appealing. In the end I had tried screaming at them to go away, the fright showing through the falsetto in my voice, and they went, in their own time, with a glance at my face showing between the curtains and a laugh that indicated they would probably be back to finish the job at some other time when I was sleeping more soundly.

When they'd gone, I went outside and did the best I could, locking the padlock through an undamaged section of the chain, while I kept a wary eye on the road in case they hadn't gone far. The bike (a BSA Lightning) was my main material possession. I'd gone into debt to get it and I wouldn't finish paying for it for another two years. I wasn't about to lose it that way. There was an instant therapy it could provide whenever I was most unsure, simply by getting on and directing its thundering dynamics. As Thom Gunn said in what was then my favourite poem, you're always nearer by being on the move.

When I'd secured it, I walked up and down in the room, badly rattled, feeling completely unlike going back to sleep and scratching my itching forearms in the bright light of the unshielded bulb until I thought of Cat's stash and decided she wouldn't begrudge me a little medicinal dose under the circumstances.

So it was that I didn't hear the phone ring at nine thirty in the morning and it took a little longer for everything, absolutely everything, to change. The phone was a pipe, pressured with potential news bursting to flow just as soon as I lifted the handset, but I had gone on sleeping instead.

When I did get up, to the letters and my sick head, I promised myself I would stay away from the stuff regardless of what or who tried to persuade me otherwise. Going out was unthinkable: out meant effort and planning and maybe conversation, all of which seemed as unappealing as breakfast.

I tried to look on the bright side. There would still be money left, just not nearly as much. The trunk, that other opiate, was there to make the hours pass until I felt better able to cope.

I was nowhere near the bottom of its contents but I was finding more and more reasons to go back through the piles of baffling paper I had already put aside. The more I knew, the more I was able to glean from documents that had previously had no meaning, like a miner with a better sieve going back through his old spoil heaps. A Cunard ticket from 1958, for example – New York return for M Birkin Owen – now carried romance in it, a visit to Natalie, surely. Ditto BOAC, 1959. *I was in America at frequent intervals that year and the next,* Max had said in his statement to the coroner. What would he have flown in, a Comet? The folder containing the stub of this ticket also had a handwritten note tucked into it, a note from Douglas to Max.

Bro – here's the ticket. I put it on my account. You can pay me back when this business is settled. Don't go mad in Manhattan but I suppose it might be best if you stay away until I sort out Harrison and this lot blows over. Hope N doesn't mind keeping you, D.

Max was fleeing the country, helped by sheepdog Douglas. 'N' had to be Natalie and I'd seen Harrison's name before. My new filing system meant it took only a bit of scrabbling to turn up the complicated legal documents I'd put aside concerning Max's little property problem. As soon as I leafed through them, Harrison's name leapt out at me from the first line of a long legal statement, neatly typed out. With it was Max's original hand-written version of the same. I sat down and kept the devil in my veins at bay by reading the bizarre details of the Calvary Street affair. The typed document told a story so entirely typical of Max that you could only laugh or cry, or both. It was good for me. It wasn't only me who could be brought back down to poverty just at the moment when riches seemed within my grasp. Compared to Max, my own difficulties with my bank suddenly seemed the merest trifle.

*I, Max Birkin Owen of 4, Lowndes Mews, London SW1 will say:-*

*I am the plaintiff in this action. I live at the above address with my mother. I first met Mr Harrison when I was skiing in Switzerland during February and March 1956. Up to the year 1953, I was a Captain in the Grenadier Guards. Between 1946 and 1952, I lost a lot of money due to the fraudulent activity of a colleague in an unfortunate investment in the motor business. I was obliged to leave the army in 1953 because I had very little capital left and could not afford to stay in. When I left the army I had no regular employment to enter into, no training or professional background to fall back on and I have never earned a sum in excess of ten pounds per week from that time to this. I am at present employed by the Belgrave Garage for whom I perform irregular services as a chauffeur, courier and foreign agent. My average earnings are ten pounds per week.*

*I purchased the properties in Calvary Street and Westminster Bridge Road in 1946 for the sum of eleven thousand pounds at a time when I had inherited some money . . .*

There followed a convoluted explanation of how he had bought this enormous bomb site – because that was all it was, acres of rubble – helped by a loan from a friend, how the friend had then killed himself, how his executors had demanded repayment then issued a bankruptcy notice and so on. It was full of details of compensation payments due under the War Damage Act, options granted, remortgages, letters that never arrived and all the typical paraphernalia of Max under pressure, ducking and weaving away. This was Max portraying himself as broke, a pitiful victim of circumstance. The inconsistency of the detail amused me. *Never earned more than ten pounds a week* in one line, then, *average earnings of ten pounds a week* almost in the next sentence. I could imagine some pompous barrister picking that one to bits: 'Mr Birkin Owen, would you not agree that for average earnings to be ten pounds a week, that requires that earnings in some weeks should be less than ten pounds and in others should be more than ten pounds and yet in your statement you say . . .'

What on earth did a foreign agent for the Belgrave Garage do? Chauffeur and courier clearly lacked glamour, but 'foreign agent' sounded rather good. I couldn't imagine that a West End garage would run a private spy network. It probably meant he would drive their customers to France if they asked him to.

Reading on, I realized Max was staring into a deep hole, a hole he had managed to dig mostly by himself. At first, the statement was an account of a masterly piece of evasion in which Max had staved off ruin, and with the help of the long-suffering family solicitor, Pritchard (and dauntless Douglas in the background), had arranged to sell his terrible property investment off piecemeal for enough money to come out with a reasonable profit. Then there was this:

*I first met Mr Harrison's friend, Mr de Sanctis, in 1959 while discussing the sale of a Jaguar motorcar. At that time I mentioned, as an aside, that I still owned part of the Calvary Street property and would be prepared to sell it if he or any of his associates were interested. It is clear that they subsequently went to see the property because in the early part of November they contacted me on several occasions to press me to give them an option to buy the land and I told them any negotiations would have to take place through my solicitor.*

Just before Christmas, we met at the Warleigh Arms in Morrow Street, where I told them quite clearly that I had now signed a contract to sell the land to a third party. I did tell them that they might be able to negotiate a firm contract which could be exchanged before the present one. Thereafter they still continued to press me on many occasions to grant them an option and they contacted me constantly by telephone, by letter and on two occasions by telegram.

As a result of my excesses over the course of the New Year holiday, I was not at all well and I was at home at Lowndes Mews on the 3rd and 4th of January 1959. In the course of one or other of those days they telephoned to invite me to have lunch with them at the Hussars Club and I agreed to do so.

I met them in the bar of the club between twelve thirty and one o'clock on the 4th January, and there, for the first time, I met Mr Tolliver who, I believe, has interests in the field of building speculation.

We had a great deal to drink at the Hussars Club, but we decided that we would not have lunch there but would go to a club in Soho called the Ace of Hearts. There we had a very boisterous meal and they pressed a great many more drinks upon me. I had to become a member of that club and I now have a membership card in my possession dated the 4th January. It is clear on inspection of that card that my signature is extremely impaired and is almost unrecognizable. During the course of lunch I became very drunk indeed and my recollection thereafter is far from clear. I know that Mr Tolliver left us after lunch and when we went to get into Harrison's car we discovered it had been towed away by the police and it was at the depot near the gas works in Vauxhall Bridge Road. We thereupon took a taxi to the depot to collect the car. The officers at the desk in the depot will certainly remember the condition in which I found myself as I understand I attempted to dance with one of them.

Immediately after this, my companions suggested that we should all go and look at the Calvary Street site and by this time I was in no state of mind to take any active part in the proceedings and I do know that when we got to Calvary Street I was repeatedly sick. I was left to sit in the car while they carried out their inspection.

From Calvary Street we returned to the Hussars Club, ostensibly for me to be revived, and I understand that Harrison and de Sanctis had to help me in. When we got inside they gave me two large brandies which they said would help to 'bring me round'.

I have no recollection of anything that went on in the Hussars Club after that point except overhearing somebody say, 'You have got him too drunk to sign anything,' and someone else saying, 'Leave the poor bastard alone, can't you see he isn't well.' My next recollection was being helped into a taxi by a friend who took me home and put me to bed where I stayed for a further five days.

That was not the end of it. Max, recovered from his excesses, went ahead with his original deal to sell the land to the Marquis of Callingford and went off skiing and then straight on to New York, clearly to see Natalie, and didn't come back until the end of February.

When I came back, I went through the letters that had arrived in my absence and among them I came across the document I now know to be the option agreement I am supposed to have signed at the Hussars Club dated the 4th January. I was at first misled by all the stamps into believing it to be some sort of receipt and I therefore put it aside, but some time afterwards when I chanced to look at it again, I was very surprised to see what it contained. As soon as I realized the importance of the document, I telephoned to Harrison but got no reply, so I wrote a letter asking what it was all about. Thereafter there were telephone calls reassuring me that they would not enforce the agreement as they did not wish to put me in any difficulty. When I wrote a further letter asking for the return of the option agreement I received evasive replies by telephone and since that time they have appeared to be avoiding me as it has proved most difficult to get in touch with them.

On the 28th March I was at the offices of Welham, Smith and Bogle in connection with another matter and I mentioned this agreement to my solicitor Mr Pritchard, but told him that I did not attach any real importance to it. He asked me to let him have it immediately and I duly posted it to him on Sunday the 3rd April.

I could imagine the scene in the solicitor's office as the realization that his feckless client had sold the same piece of land to two different people began to dawn on patient Mr Pritchard. I couldn't resist looking through Max's original handwritten version to spot the points where he had tried perhaps to stray from the truth and the firm hand of Mr Pritchard had brought him back on track. In that first version, the cause of Max's peculiar state of health was not 'over-indulgence' but 'a recurrence of jaundice'. He was not brought home by a friend but by, 'My brother, who was visiting my mother at teatime to say goodbye before going abroad.' Mr Pritchard's response is rather more vivid in this version:

*I managed to see Harrison before I went abroad and suggested he go to see my solicitor, which he did. My solicitor went through the roof and told Harrison he had better go and consult his own solicitor.*

Poor Mr Pritchard. I felt I knew him a little bit and I sympathized with him a whole lot more. Max's statement was so entirely Max-like. How entirely typical of him to claim that when he got back to the Hussars Club he could remember nothing more except, by happy chance, the two snatches of conversation which would exonerate him, and which he seemed to remember word for word. I certainly wouldn't have believed him if it had been down to me, and in any case the papers showed this was not the first court battle over Calvary Street. There were bits and pieces hinting at a whole lot more beforehand – disputes with owners of neighbouring properties, with moneylenders, with a neighbouring company who had an option over part of the land. Calvary Street had had a bad war and then a bad peace as drunken Max and his entourage of opportunist spivs rampaged through the rubble the Luftwaffe had left behind. It had clearly represented the rich, sunlit uplands of future affluence to him as he dreamt of planning permission, war damages, redevelopment and huge profits, but it was so absolutely in his nature to trip himself up at the slightest opportunity that Pritchard's final surviving letter on the subject, written at the end of that same April, came as no surprise:

Dear Max,
      *re: Mr Simon Harrison and Others.*
I refer to our telephone conversation of Wednesday last, when you informed me that you had been able to meet Mr Harrison and his associates and believed that they would be prepared to release you from your option agreement so as

to enable you to complete the binding agreement with the Marquis of Callingford.

Consequent upon your further instructions I today visited Messrs JL and T Wilcocks, where I had a long interview with Mr Stirbold, the solicitor who is acting in this matter. I left him in no doubt about the very difficult position in which you are placed together with the absolute certainty of the gravest possible difficulty if his clients persisted in their claim to have a valid option upon the site. Mr Stirbold gave me the impression that his clients would be prepared to release you though only at a very serious price.

I explained that you were under contract to sell the land and that the significant sum which would be left after the clearance of your costs and mortgage was most important to your personal finances.

Mr Stirbold stated that his clients had spent a great deal of time and money relating to the site and had negotiated a sub-sale at a substantial profit to themselves and it was now quite obvious that this could not proceed if they were to release you. I formed the view that they will require the whole or a substantial majority of the profits arising from your sale to the Marquis.

To put it plainly, I do not believe you can now look to receive any financial advantage from this transaction except a very small one indeed, and needless to say I am extremely sorry about this unfortunate turn in your affairs.

It was signed, 'Yours sincerely, John Pritchard'. How different letters were in those days. Before electric typewriters, let alone word processors and the possibility of perfection, the manual typewriter produced ugly, irregular lines, in this case much altered by someone who was clearly not a good typist.

At least then Max had Natalie to balance against his financial crucifixion. He had gone straight from skiing to New York. He must surely have been skiing with Natalie and then been unable to leave her, so unable that though everything pointed otherwise, he was still willing to spend the money on a plane ticket. There seemed to be some hope for him in that.

I was in the kitchen, believing I should eat but with no appetite for any of the tired, wilted odds and ends in the broken fridge when the phone rang.

'Mr Malan?'

'Yes.'

'Glad I got you at last. It's Brian Peal here.'

The name meant nothing to me.

'Brian who?'

'Brian Peal,' he repeated, sounding exasperated. 'From Chiswick. You sold me those Beaufighter bits.'

'Oh right, yes. Sorry.'

I knew what was going to happen. He was going to say they weren't from a Beaufighter at all and demand his money back and that would be the end of my dwindling nest-egg, but that wasn't it at all. I had forgotten the rest of our deal.

'You told me you'd point me towards a pair of engines if I got you the army records.'

Max's army records. In his voice, I could hear that he was a man who had something to trade. Suddenly the phone had my full attention.

'That's right. I did.'

'Well, I can't get them.'

Shit. 'Why not?'

'That's the thing, see? It's not my bloke's fault. He would have got them. He never normally has any bother, but you didn't give me the full story, did you? You told me a porky. Could have got him into a lot of trouble, that could.'

What was he on about? Had Max used a different version of his name? Had I got the regiment wrong? I didn't think so.

'I didn't mean to. What's the problem?'

Peal sounded pissed off, as if he could see his precious engines slipping away.

'I've got an address for you,' he said. 'That's worth the info. Tell me where the engines are and you can have that.'

I quite wanted to know where Max had spent his last days. It would be good to go and look at the place the trunk had come from. There might even be a landlord who was prepared to tell me what the man had been like, though really, what do landlords know? But I'd been expecting meat – papers, folders even, copies of files, the sort of stuff I could plough on through when the trunk had given up everything within it. This didn't sound to me like a fair exchange.

'That's not much use,' I said. 'His last address. I could probably get that myself. What's the problem with the records?'

'It's not his last address, that's the whole point,' Peal said sourly. 'It's his *present* address. That's why we can't get the bloody records. You didn't tell me he's still alive.'

# Sixteen

I took the easy option and chose to disbelieve Brian Peal because it was far too complicated to believe him. Max simply could not be alive. Alive, he was a moving target, who could not be reduced into a formula of words in the way I wanted him to be. Alive, he had the right to privacy and I had already breached that right. He had no business being alive. The most precious secrets of his life's archive had been thrown, uncaring, out on the street. That should not happen to living people in whose veins fear, pride and jealousy still seethe. His wife, who surely ought to know, had said that he was dead without any hint of the interest or emotion which are the fuel for lies. I needed him to be dead. If he wasn't dead, what possible right had I to go on chasing his fuzzy trail?

That worked for an hour, then I had to go and check, which was absurdly easy. Dead people don't have addresses. In particular, dead people don't have addresses two hundred yards away from my own – addresses which, when you ring the doorbell with some lame excuse about having a badly addressed parcel and ask for Max Owen, produce a woman in a nurse's uniform who says brightly, 'Maxie? Oh yes, he lives here. Just drop it in and I'll make sure it gets to him,' and who when you say, just to be certain, 'That is Max *Birkin* Owen, isn't it?' reply, 'Yes, that's him. He does love his middle name.'

All the time a big part of me was hoping she would say, 'No, no. Sorry, that must be somebody else.'

So there he was, in a home, only a front door away from a conversation and known as 'Maxie' to the staff, with all that that implied. A lack of dignity, certainly. Senility perhaps, or maybe it is what you call a jolly old rascal who is loved by all. I could find out. I could just go back to that door, press the bell marked 'Visitors', ask to see him and I would be in the presence of the living, breathing essence of Max, the ghost of this story of mine suddenly made flesh.

I couldn't imagine what I would say.

'Hello, Mr Owen, Mr Birkin Owen, Captain Owen? I've been looking forward to meeting you.'

Then what? 'I've read a lot about you.' Hardly.

'I've come to hear your life story.' Why?

'I've come to fill in the gaps, to tidy up the mess you've left, to rewrite the story with a bit of truth in it for a change, and by the way, you can't fool me. I know too much.' He'd like that, wouldn't he? That would be a kind thing to do to an old man.

Wouldn't he be entitled to know why I was there? I wasn't sure I could give a convincing answer. Max's life had overpowered and infected me. I could only marvel at his weaknesses and their consequences and perhaps I really could see somewhere amidst them a survival lesson for myself. There must be something at the heart of Max which had kept him afloat. Seeing him, seeing the real thing, would surely take me nearer to understanding that than not seeing him.

That begged the question, what did I really know about him? I knew who Max liked other people to think he was. I knew who he was to his lawyer, to those who had suffered at his casual hands. I knew who he was at the starkest moments to Ginny. I had been on his side, then I had been on Ginny's side and now I was seeing it all ways and trying not to be on anyone's side. Did I know who he was to Douglas, who had pulled him out of so many of his holes? Could I possibly know how it was between brothers when loyalty is stretched constantly to tearing point? What I still did not fully understand was what Max had, apart from superficial charm, which led people to forgive him his trespasses again and again so that his continuing survival was possible. That was what I most wanted to know. That was the glue which held his life together and tore Ginny apart. If he had been as unreliable as he looked in black and white then no one in their right minds would have ever driven his cars, lent him money, joined in his deals or, in Natalie's case, offered him their love.

We do not have secure institutions for the congenitally incorrigible when their misdemeanours add up, not to a crime, but merely to the constantly unforgivable. If we did, Max would surely have been in one rather than the old folks' home because that was what it was, despite the imprecise sign on the door which only said 'Weston House'. At the bottom of it all, I knew I was getting very fond of Max despite himself. Whatever it was, he had something.

I now knew what *should* have happened with Natalie. In the stunned, silent afternoon when I came back from knocking on Max's door, I found and read the letter she sent him, the huge, central letter which echoed and then amplified the earlier letters from Geneva so that there was no longer any ambiguity. Then I read, because they were clipped together, the first draft of the letter he should have sent her and finally her reply to the far less honest one that it seemed he must have sent instead. In sending that other letter, it seemed to me he blew away his one lasting chance of happiness and it raised a scream of frustration in my head that I could not turn the clock back to give him a second chance. It was as if the trunk had offered them to me on purpose, as if it had risen to the occasion by shuffling up out of its remaining depths a set of documents to match the moment.

Max, my curious and uncertain love,

The cab driver who took me back home from LaGuardia turned and handed me a Kleenex as we passed over the bridge and said, 'You sure he's worth crying that much for, kid?'

I could only say, 'I don't know,' which is a scary thing to have to say to a cab driver when you're going on forty-three years old and you've known someone on and off for more than half that time.

He didn't say anything else until we got to Third Avenue, then when I paid him, he held on to my hand for a minute. He was what Ethan calls a Brooklyn grizzly, one of those nice, chunky, lined old cabbies who still know how to get to Canal Street without going through Times Square more than twice. He said something about how he did the airport trip a hundred times a year and how he'd seen all the ways of crying there were and then he said his wife had died this year and it had made him think tears shouldn't go with partings in life, only with partings in death, because we can change life. That made me sit back down. Then he just looked at me and he said, 'If it's worth it, go and get it. If there's something in the way, knock it over. If it ain't worth it, forget it, and walk away with a laugh.' Then he wouldn't let me give him a tip because he said if he took a tip I'd think he'd only said it all to get one. How about that? A Manhattan cabby who wouldn't take a tip? That's got to be something.

So I went in and I dried my tears and I found the flowers where you had put them and your funny card which wasn't so funny right then and I thought, well, what exactly is it that is in the way? I thought why do we only see each other when we manage to fix up to ski at the same time or when you come over here? The Alps are just great in their own cold, high, white way but I've had enough of sharing you with twenty people, a mountain and a case of wine or trying to stay with you on the piste for long enough to shout the odd tender confidence through my muffler at your woollen hat as you whizz by. In the evenings, no one says anything sensible, do they? I like your friends in the right place but I sometimes think the right place is an intensive care ward for the liver-damaged. As for your trips here, we're watching the calendar all the time, aren't we? When I met you off the plane I was already living the next time we'd be at that same spot in the airport, when I'd be saying goodbye not hello, and all the time you were here I felt our days dwindling so fast and so hard that I couldn't take full pleasure in each one as it went for the dreadful knowledge of what it was doing to the little stack of what was left. So, Mr Max, maybe it's just my old grizzly cabby talking and then again maybe it's not, but I've decided it's time to look at what's in the way and see if we can't knock it over.

Now, before you read any more I know just what a panic this will be kicking up inside your tweed jacket so I want you to sit down and pour yourself a large glass of Noilly Prat and maybe put something like Gershwin on the gramophone –

something soothing, anyway. Have you done that? Okay, down to business and I have to try to say this plainly or I guess there's no real point in saying it at all.

I have always felt there was something very particular going between you and me, from the very first time I saw you at KB before the war, holding Wallis's ski sticks for her while she looked at you like she wasn't sure whether to buy you a bag of sweets or take you round behind the lift shed and roger you until your hair fell out. I felt like shouting, 'Leave him alone, he's my age,' but I 'spose you have to make allowances for Wallis, though I feel sometimes I've been doing that all my life and that maybe I've had enough of that game because I don't think she has ever really deserved it. This will shock your romantic royalist soul, but I believe she is and has always been a grasping, calculating woman.

That, I think, was in general a bad assembly of people and of their values for us to first encounter each other in. Power and money and taking things for granted was what those people were all about. I know you were only there by accident and I was only there because ... Well, why was I there? I never really knew. I think it was really because Wallis borrowed me to be some kind of cheap American version of a lady-in-waiting, though she never said so. She just told my parents I really ought to learn to ski and she'd pay half my fare. Half, eh? That's Wallis.

I do understand that you had to hold your end up in that company but I guess maybe it set some kind of pattern for us so that the castles in the air got to be part of our joint story.

Now, what I want to say to you as plain as I can is this. I don't care about castles in the air or on the ground and I don't care about yachts and I don't care about cars and I don't care about all the rest of that status stuff. I don't believe in any of it. I care about people or to be precise I care about two people, you and me. I don't want you to have to explain ever again that you're 'still at' Lowndes Mews because you just can't get the tenants out of the Manor or the Hall or whatever. I like the sound of Lowndes Mews. What the hell is a mews, anyway? Come to that, what is a Lownde and why would anyone need more than one? Mews makes me hear cats and seagulls. If it's cosy, all the better. I want small, I need small. I have to live in New York all week so I want something different, something low and tiny that you have to bend your head to get into and I would not mind if it was in London, not Massachusetts. I know I told you I was going to build the house of my dreams there, but maybe that house already exists and you're living in it. I'll tell you something else. I want poor, too, as well as small. I don't want to go on living a life in which everyone has loads of money though never quite enough. If all there was in the cupboard was a packet of biscuits and an egg I want to have to find a new way of cooking that makes that egg and those biscuits turn out just great, then I want to curl up and stay home and talk and talk and talk because talk isn't just free, it's also BEST. Get it?

So this is what I want, Max, my hopeless darling. I want you to write me a list. It will be a list of the things we agree neither of us ever has to mention again and I do mean ever. It will be some kind of inventory of all the rich hopeless things, the castles in the air which might exist or might not exist but surely have come to clutter up the simple space between you and me. I won't tell you what to include but it might be your castle in Wales and your vineyards and your Hall, unless it's a Manor. Then when I've got your list, if you want, I will jump on the first Stratocruiser heading east and then you can show me round what's left and if it's just Lowndes Mews I will be completely happy and if it's more then that's fine but I don't need it, and then we can try spending some simple, clean time together just in that little world.

This may be a lot to ask, I can't tell, but if it's not too much then please, please sit down and start listing because time is running out and it shouldn't have taken a cab driver to tell me that.

You are everything I need,
Natalie.

On a double piece of lined paper, pulled from an exercise book, with staple holes rimmed in rust like the bullet wounds of a tiny, dry murder, Max had groped for a reply amidst a welter of changes and crossings out.

My dearest Natalie,

I bless your Brooklyn grizzly cabby and his philosophy of life and I have taken very much to heart every word of what you have said in your letter though, as you will guess, knowing so very much more about me than I know myself, that has not come easily to me.

Do you really, really hanker after the simple life? Life at Lowndes Mews can be very simple, you know. There's usually more than egg and biscuits in the cupboard but not so very much more.

Yes, we got off on the wrong foot at Kitzbühl, didn't we? I was trying to remember what it was like because your remark about the way Wallis was looking at me came as a great surprise and set me thinking, because I do not remember that aspect of it at all. I think the trouble was that the rest of the party, not just the Prince but Ogilvy and Lyall as well, put their skiing first and after Wallis found she didn't like doing that much the only other man left to escort her around was that James Dugdale. Well, of course, he was too glamorous by half. Now, I don't know if you ever knew this but the whole reason I stayed on with you all after I first helped Wallis out of the snowdrift was that Ogilvy begged me to so that I could be chief coat-carrier to Wallis and not the dangerous Dugdale. That being so, I suppose you could say I was chosen because I was less likely to appeal to Wallis. Poor Dugdale developed a furtive look and hid in his room for the rest of the holidays which makes me think that whatever she did to her men to turn them into slaves was probably quite painful. If you hadn't been there I don't think I would have enjoyed myself at all, especially when Wallis started all that business about making sure nobody tipped too much. She's always been a bit of a miser, hasn't she?

The next section had all been lightly scored through but it was still easy to read. It said:

Anyway, what I wanted to say was that there I was, twenty-three years old, a callow youth from South Wales with a shallow veneer of provincial money and very little expertise at anything outside parties and a spot of storytelling, thrust into this so, so glamorous party, with nothing but one suitable set of evening clothes and my wits to support me. If I opted for a touch of romance, you cannot blame me entirely. Massingham started the ball rolling by getting me confused with my cousins, the Birkins, who in those days seemed to own about half of England, and asking me loads of questions about what I was going to do when I inherited the castle. The rest followed from there and has dogged me to this day. I can't, I suppose, just blame circumstances. There is a heady excitement in reinventing one's self, though there is the danger too that by inhabiting a castle in the air, no one but another air dweller will be able to reach the front door. You, my dearest, with your admirable common sense, have offered to build me a bridge. So, here is my list, as you request.

All of this had lines scored through it and, as if it had come too close to the central issue to be bearable, what replaced it was no more than a horrible shadow of it, words that I hated as, one by one, they curved further and further away from the escape route she had offered him.

I suppose what the Kitzbühl time brought to light was that our family affairs have always been tangled and the precise question of who owns what between the Birkin and the Owen side of the family has always been extremely confusing and, in recent years I regret to say, the subject of considerable litigation.

I wanted to scream, 'No!' at him. No, don't scratch out that sweet honesty. Don't you dare write your pompous evasions to her. Don't use words like 'considerable litigation'. Not now, not when a generous and forgiving hand is being stretched out to save you.

It is certainly true, as you surmise, that I have been caught on the hook of my own optimism and perhaps of my continual under-estimation of the darker side of human nature. I have trusted people too much and that is why my affairs are so tangled. If that is too much for you, I quite understand and it would certainly be simpler by far to turn my back on all those of my interests and holdings which are in dispute and lead a quieter life around the solid core of what remains. Would that suit you? If you want to and you really prefer the simple life, I will abandon all else except for Lowndes Mews and the small income from my trust which sustains me. Could you be happy with that? As you know, I keep myself active in ways which are perhaps a shade uncommon for someone of my background, but it amuses me to see the reaction of your compatriots in particular when their 'chauffeur' turns out to be something of an aesthete and I love to make new acquaintances in this way, being limited as you know in what I am able to do by certain discomforts incurred during the war. I will now do as you suggest and list all those disputed claims and entitlements which are best left to pass into history and I agree that, if you want to come and live that smaller life together which sounds so very, very attractive then we need never look back to them again.

No list was attached. No further evidence existed of which version of himself Max had eventually committed to paper except that Natalie's reply spoke volumes.

Oh Max,
I can hardly believe that you have done what you have done and shrunk back into the twilight. It is as if you have not understood a single word of what I was saying to you. Can you not see that time is flying by and the wind

is changing? I was very drunk once . . . Well, of course, you were there so I hardly need to tell you. It was in Geneva when you came through with those cars all sheeted away on their trailer, pretending to be something else. Not the Bug, which still makes me laugh when I think of your efforts to disguise the poor old thing as a tank. It was the next two cars after that, wasn't it, and Douglas was there and the poor bar tender at the Delphine misunderstood your instructions about how to mix some lethal cocktail.

I don't know why I should remember some of the things that make me laugh when what I most want to do right now is cry, but I do remember that I was very, very ill and the room went round and round and the only thing for it was to be horribly, horribly sick, but I've never liked being sick and I somehow forced myself not to be which was the very worst thing I could have done.

I think it must be the same for you now. I know it will be better if you can bring yourself to do it – to get rid once and for all of all that rubbish inside you, so I am going to forget the letter you sent and urge you to start again. We have one last chance to be ourselves, together, Max. Please hear me.

Yours in love and despair.

N

I had to assume from what I knew of the rest of his life that whatever it was he had written back, it hadn't been anything like that first disarming, crossed-out confession. At that moment, Max's actions seemed to me to be the saddest thing I knew. Then I surfaced out of that thought into the renewed and shocking knowledge that this story was not yet over, that it was the unfinished story of a man still living.

# Seventeen

I went to the Hunt Ball simply because I had left Tiggy's letter hidden by the cereal packets too long to make an excuse not to go. She and I used to go to them from time to time and it was an opportunity to talk to her away from Cat and London and all the other things that measured the changes in my life. That was what I thought, anyway. I took a train down to Sussex and then a taxi from the station to Pickworth Park. However much the currents of life have washed you away from the whinnying classes, you still can't arrive at a hunt ball on a motorbike, especially if, in the grand tradition of British bikes, it throws a steady spray of oil sideways over your legs.

I didn't begrudge the train journey because I could go on reading and the light was better in a train than it was in my flat. I had picked out some bits and pieces from the trunk to take, and the last of a series of birth, marriage and death certificates which had arrived in the post that morning. I used the journey to inspect them.

If you have been born, married or died in England and Wales since proper records started being kept in 1837, there is a large ledger on a rack of shelves in a room in central London which has you listed, marshalled and constrained by the alphabet and by date as if that is all it comes down to in the end. It is a compulsive, disturbing business, this procuring of certificates, because those lines of ledgers force you to look at the frantic pace of life and death in another way. It's as if someone somewhere believes that only impeccable bureaucracy can keep the tide of life at bay. As well as straightforward births, marriages and deaths, there are the obscure sub-divisions, the lists of those who died at sea, the consular records for those who perished in a foreign land, then 'Armed Forces died abroad' divided up into separate ledgers for officers and other ranks as if they did not belong between the same covers.

This is no hushed library, this is a noisy, working place. The people who crowd through it, fighting more or less politely for space on the sloping reading desks and glowering if you get the volume they wanted just ahead of them, fall into one of several categories. There are always a few puzzled old folk with a new interest in death, devoting their dwindling, quiet days to checking out the genealogy of those who went before them as they prepare to enter the next ledger themselves. They usually need help from the staff, those old folk. Mostly, though, there are brash young men, the blue-collar workers of the legal business, doing the donkey work behind the lines of the paternity cases and the disputed wills. They wallop the heavy ledgers down on the desks, flick straight to the right part of the alphabet, then slam them back on the shelf again to reach for the next one in something more like weight-training than research. Finally there are always a few who are out of place, two Sloaney girls when I was there, giggling rather loudly as they read out an extract in the births register, speculating on the word 'unmarried' in a way that suggested it was not their own entry they were looking up.

It's all right if you have the right name and the right date. If all you have is the name, then after a couple of hours your wrists will be aching from the effort of heaving book after heavy book in and out of their places in the shelves. 'Birkin Owen' would make life simpler, but the authorities had clearly decided that Birkin had no official right to be considered part of a surname and there are an awful lot of Owens. All the time you're combing through the entries, you're praying no clerk made a tiny error which put your quarry in the wrong column where you will never find them.

The thrill of the chase is there to sustain you and the shocking impact of the neat, indisputable, defining entry, when you eventually find it, is enormous.

You can't do it all at once. If you want to track down a marriage partner or a parent then you need the certificate in your hand, with all its extra information, not just the bald entry in the book. They'll only send you that through the post after you've paid the fee, so the whole search process becomes a series of fits and starts, broken up by waiting for the envelopes to arrive before you can grope back another stage.

After three visits spanning a week and a half, during which Cat had wandered in and out and more of my money had gone up in various sorts of smoke, I now had enough to get my teeth into and as the train rattled down towards the Sussex Downs, I unfolded the one headed 'Certified Copy of an Entry of Death'. It contained its emotion in neat, small, unpunctuated typing. Under 'When and where died' it said, '14th of September 1963 Peter Pan's Playground Madeira Drive Brighton.' Name and surname were listed as 'Virginia Marianne Owen.' No sign here of an interloping 'Birkin'. The 'Occupation' column was a muddle. It said, 'Of Darnley House Chalfont St Giles Wife of Douglas Owen Architect.' Funny to think of Douglas suddenly as an architect. In the coroner's report he was an advertising executive. Before that he was just a person. Under 'Cause of death', it said: 'Burns Contusion of Brain. Crashed while driving motorcar which burst into flames. Accident.' Ginny's age was given as thirty-nine.

Next I looked at Max and Laura's marriage certificate. Their wedding was on the 1st of October 1965 at the Kensington and Chelsea Register Office. She, forty-five years old, previous marriage dissolved, with a good address in Chelsea, was the daughter of a colonel. He, fifty-three years old and masquerading as a 'civil engineer', a bizarre claim for a profession, was son of Owen Wyn Owen, deceased, landowner. Laura's maiden name was Dalziel-McAlister, which explained the burr in her voice and perhaps the guarding presence of the man in the kilt. Other certificates cast little scatters of illuminating rays. Perhaps that's a bit of an exaggeration but it felt that way to me because these were guaranteed, copper-bottomed official facts in a sea of speculation. Douglas and Ginny's marriage certificate from 1953 showed that she was nine years younger than him with an address near Eaton Square, right in the heart of desirable SW1. I knew that had become Douglas's address from the evidence of envelopes. Lucky Douglas. That explained how he came to move out of their shared mews.

Another character began to emerge from the shadows through these documents, Mrs Rebecca Alice Sims, previously Rebecca Alice Owen, born Rebecca Alice Aston. She was Max and Douglas's mother. In 1911 when she married Owen Wyn Owen at Carmarthen she was only twenty-seven years old, but all it said for him was 'full age'. He was a widower, she was a spinster. His age was not so full that he couldn't procreate. Max was born in 1912, just over a year later, and Douglas only fifteen months after that, both in the South Wales interior, at Llangunnor just outside Carmarthen. Their father's occupation here was not 'landowner' but the less grand 'solicitor'.

There was so much room for creative guesswork here in these official answers. In particular Rebecca's own birth certificate, issued in Southampton and showing that she was born in 1884, also revealed that her place of birth was a lunatic hospital on the Solent. I thought at first this could have been because her father was listed as 'Sergeant in the Medical Staff Corps' rather than because her mother was an inmate, but by the time Rebecca married old Owen Wyn Owen some strange things had happened to her certificated life. Her father's occupation was now given as 'Clerk in Holy Orders' but he didn't seem to be the same father. On her birth certificate he was 'William John Jarvis' whereas here he was 'Steven Alfred Jarvis'.

Speculation on that one took me a good ten miles further down the track. Had Rebecca's birth been a tragedy after all, a squalid incident inside a Victorian bedlam after which a good-hearted relative had stepped in to save the little girl who was the result?

The last thing I had in my collection of envelopes was Old Owen Wyn Owen's will, written out longhand in extremely tidy legal copperplate by some punctilious and probably underpaid clerk. It passed through probate in January 1921, so they had less than ten years of married life. When Owen came to the end of his 'full age' his two sons were eight and six respectively. It certainly looked as if old Owen created fertile ground for the growth of a feckless son. The disposal of the estate was described exhaustively down to the 'carriages, horses, harness, stable furniture, motorcars, motor accessories, garden stock, wines, liquors and consumable stores'. His shares were not to be sold yet, 'due to the heavy depreciation which has taken place in the value of securities by reason of the Great War'. The funeral was to be paid for by the sale of war stock and the money was to be left in trust for his wife to enjoy the income for the rest of her life.

On her death, it was to be divided equally between Max and Douglas.

Rebecca, who was later to marry again, to a Captain Ronald Sims, was destined to live another forty-two years before dying in her late seventies. Imagine those forty-two years for Max. Did the knowledge that a substantial pot of gold was waiting for him disable him? Is that why he never seemed to have made any attempt at a serious job, why his life consisted of absurd speculations, gambling and borrowing against his securities when it all went wrong? I could imagine him watching glumly as the years passed and his mother lived on, sometimes, as far as I could see, in his various flats with him after Captain Sims died – watching as that pot shrank and shrank, eroded by inflation and by the raids he seemed occasionally to be able to make on it. There had clearly been a time when, though his mother was still alive, they had been able to split up the trust or there wouldn't have been that reference to taking the mews flat as his share. Did old Owen, with his gloomy Victorian Welsh solicitor's conservatism, accidentally design his son's destruction by the supposedly cautious terms of his will? It was a bit hard to blame him for that. There seemed to be a wilful strain of gene in Max that had no plausible connection with what could be discerned of old Owen, whatever the old story of the policeman and the motorcycle had claimed. Perhaps Rebecca had brought with her some wild streak from her origin among the lunatics.

But then what did I know? This process of deduction involved reading a very great deal into a bunch of dry, old certificates and a stilted will. The evidence could equally point in either direction. There was old Owen, married at least once before, taking a young bride when he should have been in his dotage and fathering two sons on her. Perhaps it was after all Owen who was the wild one and young Rebecca had no idea what she was getting into. Perhaps the kindly policeman really did remember the father as a wild young man. It seemed unlikely. If old Owen Owen was really 'of full age', the policeman would have had to be way past retirement. Another black cross against Max's version of autobiography.

I already knew what Rebecca looked like from cross-referencing the photos. There was a wedding picture that just had to be her second time round, marrying Captain Ronald Sims who looked a glum chap. He was much given to complaining about the heat and his poor health in Second World War letters sent home to her from a posting he clearly hated in India. I'd read several of these but it took me a long time to realize who they were to, because Rebecca wasn't Rebecca at all. To Captain Sims, she was Alice, her second name on the certificates. Perhaps she always had been. This evasive, patchy, pieced-together world of people reduced to words was so very confusing. A Rebecca felt quite different to an Alice even when I could look at the same photograph of both of them. She was a gaunt woman with large protruding teeth which meant she smiled very carefully and as a Rebecca it seemed to me that the part of her which underlay the picture had a touch of sorrow and soulfulness about it whereas, being Alice, I suddenly imagined instead a touch of childish fun within her. If so, Captain Sims's gloomy view on life must have strained her funny side. I had read his letters from an unhappy wartime posting to India.

My Dearest Alice,

I have arrived in this benighted spot, which is not very far from the last place and rather worse. Naturally I have had no letters this week and it will take time for them to be redirected so I am left hoping for news of you. I had hoped to be up in the hills by now where it is cooler, but was sent on a course instead to become expert in the repair of tracked vehicles, a skill I am quite confident I will never be called upon to use. I must say I am very fed up at being moved which was to my mind quite unnecessary. I am moderately well in myself but the leg is still bothering me as it won't clear up and this heat does not help . . .

They were all a bit like that. There was one that touched on the captain's stepsons:

I have written to Douglas for Xmas. He must keep you guessing from one day to another who will eventually be your future daughter-in-law. I am sorry to hear that Max's health still restricts his activities so much. He must envy Douglas all the excitement he has been getting but I am glad for your sake that Max's safety is assured. It would be nice if he were allowed to have a little experience of what it has been like for the rest of us before the whole show is over.

Your very affectionate,

Ronnie.

Dull, dutiful 'Ronnie', stuck away in his prickly backwater of Empire, was fully aware that one of his stepsons was hero material and the other a lead-swinger. I knew what he meant about Douglas because I'd been going back through some of the formerly meaningless documents I had put to one side. I was learning that it was dangerous to discard *anything*. Even the most obscure letter or photo might later prove to fit into the jigsaw. The very idea of selling *any* of the material had started to feel like sacrilege and now there was the added, scary possibility that Max might one day help me unscramble it all. Among it there was a letter from Douglas to 'Ma', who was now Alice rather than Rebecca.

It was written at a quiet moment in his busy war, some time at the end of 1943, from somewhere which sounded North African from his description of the mosquitoes and the weather. Douglas's style was always hectic. He was describing the visit of a concert party to entertain the officers:

Unfortunately we had a very funny football match with blacked-up faces, wearing full uniform and gas capes against a side dressed in captured Jerry gear, during which someone bit a piece out of my ear. This rather cramped my style with the local ENSA damsels for a while, though I think I escaped lightly because the ref decided to lob a grenade at the goal to end the match before I bled to death. ENSA is a godsend, not so much because of the entertainment quality of their shows, but because of the much-needed glamour that comes with them. I think I told you about the fair Annette with the husky voice, mile-long legs and terrific

189

blondeness, but since then another company has arrived in the area who gave us a fantastic show. They came round to the Mess afterwards (all six being blondes!) and the party was such a success that hardly an officer has been seen in the evenings since. I had a date with one of them and when I went round to the hotel where they live, found a military policeman on guard outside who said, 'You can't go in there sir, but I can get her for you, otherwise HOUT YER GOES,' with that sort of gap before a final SIR that only MPs seem able to do. This rather flummoxed me as I only had a vague idea that her first name was Jean and no idea at all about her surname, so I said, 'Get Jean for me,' with great confidence, which he did, only a completely different but much prettier Jean came down so I gratefully accepted the twists of fate and took her out to dinner instead. Sylvie and Margot, my love twins, are still writing and if they're both around when I get back then young Owen is in a SPOT. Do tell them I'm dead or something if you should see either of them. I'm sure you can embellish that somehow. Just make sure it was a gallant death, won't you old thing.

I'd been saving the best for last. It was always a moment of delight when one of Max's manuscripts surfaced, but I hadn't found any more whole ones recently. What I had found was one which started at page two and its contents looked promising, so I read it with a keen sense of anticipation.

*. . . departure was delayed by the after-effects of a night spent well but not wisely. This saw us emerge, blinking, on the streets of Geneva, to get our unlikely convoy under way again. The tank transporters had been too large to bring into the centre of the town so we had left them in the yard of a friendly garage on the outskirts and it was to there that we now repaired in the Jeep and the Humber, collecting our two tame squaddies from the house of ill repute where we had left them. They both had happy smiles on their faces when they emerged into the dawn though in Private Archer's case I have to add the word 'probably' as his physiognomy had been so battered by his way of life that it was difficult to be certain about any of his expressions. His*

happiness was however confirmed by his suggestion that this should be the model for all such convoys from here on.

With no further attractions to lure us away from our official route, we made good time over the next forty-eight hours and arrived at Dieppe at the prescribed time for the crossing. I could see that my brother's heart was in his mouth, though I was now starting to feel like a seasoned smuggler. We had stopped and carefully adjusted the framework of timber covering the Delage and the Mercedes and I was moderately sanguine that it would pass anything but a close inspection. I told Douglas that, as his papers were all in order, he should accompany the other transporter, which was, after all, carrying a real tank on it. I pointed out that I might as well be hung for a sheep as for a lamb as I was meant to be on detached duties in Luxembourg rather than anywhere near the Channel, so I would stay with our less-than-legal load. He staunchly disputed this division of responsibility but I insisted so he gave way and I made sure the vehicles arrived at the docks with a decent gap in between them.

Loading was the usual chaos as there was still a great deal to be done to set the place back to rights from the conflicts of the year before and it was during the loading that the unfortunate event occurred which threatened to overturn all our best-laid plans.

Private Archer, who understood every detail of what had to be done and was entirely willing to follow my somewhat questionable instructions in return for the deal we had made, decided to spend the two hours in which we were to wait in the loading area in pursuit of alcoholic oblivion in a nearby bar. With other things on my mind, I had no idea that this was his intention until just before our time came for loading, when I was informed by an intimidating member of the military police that they had my transport driver under lock and key for a variety of offences ranging from inebriation to a violent attempt to make the closer acquaintance of the bartender's disapproving wife.

'It's all right, sir,' the aforesaid policeman told me. 'We've been able to find you a replacement driver and he needs to go back to Pirbright so I think you'll find him just the ticket.'

Quite so, but for the fact that I had absolutely no intention of taking what was under the tarpaulin anywhere near Pirbright. A

191

whole week's work on Private Archer had just gone down the drain and when they delivered Private Brooks to me in his place, I shuddered at the sight. Private Brooks was young, impeccably turned out and as keen as mustard. In short he was chalk to Private Archer's cheese and the task of corrupting him totally in the short time available to us seemed quite impossible.

I did my best on the boat. 'Private Brooks,' I said, 'due to circumstances I am unable to explain to you in detail, we are to deliver the load on your transporter to a secret address on the way back to Pirbright.'

He stiffened. In the remaining duration of the journey across he gave me to understand that while orders from an officer were of course orders, he had been trained to regard the transport document as the Holy Bible, the Koran and the Torah all rolled into one and, of course, he would do exactly as I said just as soon as he had the requisite replacement order in his hand in written form.

I found Douglas out on deck and told him what was going on. He came up with the simple and elegant solution that Brooks should drive the other transporter and Morris, who like Archer was already in it up to his neck, would take the one carrying the cars. Returning to Brooks, I discovered that he was now well into the fine print of military regulations and he pointed out that his order required him to drive the transporter carrying that particular serial number, and no other, to Pirbright.

All seemed lost until, arriving at Southampton under cover of darkness, Douglas had the brilliant wheeze that we would find some suitable transport café where the drivers could gorge themselves, and while they were doing that we would swap the trailers over so that the one with Brooks's number on it would now be pulling the trailer which actually carried a tank on it.

This was achieved quite quickly and we went in to have our share of the food, passing Morris on the way out who gave us a great wink, signifying, it seemed, that he had guessed what we were up to. 'Don't worry, sir,' he said. 'Leave it to me.' When he rejoined us five minutes later he suggested that Brooks should get on his way smartish on the grounds that his lorry wasn't as fast as the other one.

We watched Brooks drive out of the car park in the dark with some satisfaction, which was somewhat blighted when Morris confided that he had just switched the number plates on the two vehicles. It took a second for it to dawn on us that, as we had already swapped over the trailers, two wrongs had just made a right. The sanctimonious Brooks was now heading for Pirbright, towing the two cars behind him, and we were going to be in terrible trouble when he arrived.

We set out in the Jeep and the Humber to stop him in any way we could but fate had taken a further hand and he had decided, we subsequently discovered, to follow some eccentric by-route of his own in the belief that it was faster. In the end, we gave up all hope and I could see my army career coming to an ignominious end.

That seemed the most likely outcome when Brooks arrived at Pirbright and a curious sergeant-major, wondering what dawn had just revealed to him in the form of our non-standard, tarpaulin-covered framework, lifted the corner of it and was astonished to find a blue racing car and a white sports car where there should have been a brown Sherman tank.

I was immediately hauled up in front of a man I had better call Major Sharp in the light of what subsequently happened. The Major and I were not on good terms. He had a low opinion of me in every way and this was an opinion he had frequently shared with Colonel Ladd. It was quite clear from the look in his eyes that he saw this as my final downfall and to say he was gloating was an understatement. He was a man I had first crossed one night in the Mess when I had referred to him, as I was wont to do, as 'the hip flask hero' without realizing he was standing directly behind me until the hush that instantly fell tipped me off that something was terribly wrong.

The Major had come to us accompanied by many stories of bravery, but bitterness had overcome him after an injury prevented him from taking a further active part in the war. Alcohol and anger provided the outlet for his feelings. I could sympathize with the injury and the enforced rest it had earned him, having suffered the same myself, but I could not sympathize with the rest of it and we were destined not to get on.

On this occasion the Major informed me with great satisfaction that as soon as Colonel Ladd returned on the morrow, I would be on the carpet in front of him. That is undoubtedly what would have happened but for the extraordinary events of that night.

It happened that the Major's accommodation was almost next

to mine and it also happened that for some weeks he had been conducting an illicit liaison with the most dangerous woman within miles of the barracks. Melanie Chester, as I shall call her because that has a certain relevance to her physique, was already married to a fellow officer whose credentials as a true hero of several theatres of war were undeniable. It was often said that he was mad rather than just suicidally brave and he and his wife were both very, very fond of a strong drink. In his case, it was the fuel which propelled him to his absurd acts. In her case it was probably the only way she could have any contact with him that made sense.

Somehow the Major had stepped into the middle of this dangerous pair as a third element while Chester was away on active service. The first clear evidence of this arrived fortuitously on my doorstep that very night, when, alerted by the breaking of glass and someone trying to stifle a drunken giggle, I went outside to find Melanie, in the magnificence of totally inebriated nudity, having climbed out of the Major's window while the Major inside was doing his best to haul her back in.

I rose to the occasion, seeing lights coming on elsewhere and also seeing an opportunity to sort out my own little problem. Melanie was hidden in my room with a gag in her mouth and then spirited away to safety by a route that I had used for not dissimilar purposes on many occasions.

Strangely, the entire affair of the tank transporters was forgotten in the cold light of dawn and the Major was himself seen driving a sheeted load out of the camp, following a map I had drawn for him.

There was, oddly enough, a postscript to this story. Some years later, walking up the Strand with a friend who had also served with me, I saw the Major, a shadow of his former confident self, walking down the opposite pavement wearing a face that would have curdled milk.

'Good heavens,' I said, 'who would have believed it?' And learnt from my friend that, after a highly dubious confrontation in which Chester the gallant hero had managed to shoot himself rather than the Major, probably by mistake, the Major had wound up marrying 'Melanie' out of some misplaced sense of decency and was dedicating his life to the almost impossible task of keeping her off the booze and on the straight and narrow. There was a certain satisfaction in hearing

*this and reflecting that out of all the tight spots I have ever been in,
providence has rarely come to my rescue quite so dramatically.*

Arriving at the station made me think a little harder about the
evening ahead and the tight spot I could well be in myself before
the night was out. Suddenly I knew I shouldn't have come. There
would be many people I knew there tonight – people who knew
me, Miles Drummond, the Colonel's stepson, not people who
knew Milo Malan. I wasn't sure I could be Miles any more. The
conversation would be about jobs and promotion and holidays
and other things I didn't do.

I hadn't told Cat where I was going – hadn't and couldn't. I
said it was work and I'd be back and I hoped she hadn't bothered
with the fine details of the letter she'd read from Tiggy. My being
mysterious about my movements to her didn't seem nearly as
convincing as her being mysterious to me because she didn't
really seem to care. In the afternoon, I wasn't feeling all that
great, black and scratchy again, but she seemed to guess what
was wrong so we helped it away with a little hit with the tinfoil
and then a bit more when that didn't quite seem to do it. It was
Cat's stuff because I never bought it, but then I suppose it *was*
my money. What I did have with me, just to round off the sharp
edges if the 'huntin'' set proved too unbearable, was a large lump
of best red Lebanese hashish in my pocket in a pouch with the
Clan tobacco and the Rizlas.

Clan was the business as a disguise for the pungency of the hash
because it was an aromatic tobacco. Its smell would never fool
an expert, but in those innocent days it could certainly confuse
anyone who wasn't quite sure of their ground. Anyway, it had
this great slogan in the French market, which went, '*Encore, un
homme qui fume Clong*', or that was the way it sounded, which
always seemed hysterically funny when you were stoned.

I put on a bow tie in the train just before we got to the little
station between Worthing and Littlehampton and did my best to
brush the ash off my jacket after a quick smoke in the train loo. It
left grey streaks on the satin lapels, which would not have stood up
to forensic analysis, then I went into the station yard and climbed
into the slippery plastic rear seat of an old Ford Zephyr taxi.

195

The drive up to Pickworth Park was busy with Rovers and Jaguars. There were marquees in the garden and the Master of Foxhounds in full kit was standing at the top of the steps doing a one-man receiving line. He had brown, veined cheeks and bright eyes swimming in a film of gin. I had to hand my ticket to a man at a table at the bottom of the steps and I was hoping not to have to go past the MFH but traffic was channelled that way so I had to wait a few moments while he barked, smiled and slavered at a beefy couple in front of me, from whom prosperity exuded like a special form of sweat to coat them in a polished sheen of affluence.

'Terrifically good to see you, Binkie. Good show,' he bellowed between them, so that I had a brief moment to wonder which of them was Binkie before he inclined his head a fraction towards the woman and gave the game away rather perplexingly by adding in another genteel shout directed straight at her, 'And you too, Jumbo. Looking very fine, very fine.' Then he turned to me, looked me up and down, snorted and said, 'Are you sure you've come to the right place?'

# *Eighteen*

At the far end of the ballroom, a time-warp band of grinning middle-aged men was playing a bouncy orchestral version of 'Lily the Pink' from five years earlier, smoothed into something like a waltz rhythm so that the older people wouldn't be too frightened by it. The senior landed gentry and the newer branches of their family trees were there in force, dancing separately, stiffly and unsuccessfully opposite each other. Even the younger ones were moving disconcertingly out of time with the music in a way that proved they would be much, much happier doing the Gay Gordons.

Noel Campbell had once been the nearest thing I had to a best friend. He was allowed into our house occasionally and under sufferance because he was the latest of several generations of Campbells to live in Higher Findon Grange and his father had been a wartime rear admiral. My stepfather disapproved of many of the ways in which people accumulated their money. He looked down his nose at fortunes made in trade, the City, music (unless it was strictly classical) and art (which he considered to be a confidence trick unless the artist had been dead for over a century). That didn't leave much except 'old money' and a curiously pragmatic decision he had made to exempt from criticism any high-ranking ex-officer who subsequently went into business or finance. This, he said, was 'bringing their know-how to bear on setting the country straight,' as if familiarity with flanking fire, dead ground and other elements of battlefield strategy was the perfect training for managing the paper minefields of balance sheets and take-over bids. Noel's father, who was chairman of Wayland Felton Insurance, benefited from this exemption. My stepfather, who, I suspected, had never had to exercise any great military skill in his entire career, apart from telling junior officers to 'carry on' with what they were already doing, would not have lasted five minutes in that wider world.

This all came to mind because, while looking unsuccessfully around the crowded ballroom for Tiggy, I saw Noel for the first time in a couple of years. He was talking to Julian Trotter, someone I had particularly disliked as a boy, and before I could duck out of sight he had waved me over so that I could not decently ignore the summons.

'Hello, Miles,' said Noel. 'You know Jules, don't you?'

'Mmm.'

'Well, well, Miles,' said Julian in his high-pitched voice, 'surprise seeing you here. Heard you'd gone native, turned into a bit of a hippie or something.' He brayed.

'Tiggy said you were coming,' said Noel, raising an eyebrow. 'Have you seen her?'

'She's somewhere around.'

'Gather you had a spot of bother,' said Julian Trotter. 'Police and all that.' He seemed delighted to have the chance to mention it.

'No bother,' I said as dismissively as I could. 'Just another day on the street, Julian. I don't suppose you'd know what it's like out in the real world.'

'I don't call *drugs* the real world.'

'Sorry, Jules,' said Noel quickly, 'must just have a private natter with Miles. Back in a sec.'

He steered me out on to the terrace through the French windows.

'I'll clock that little shit if he goes on like that,' I said.

'I know. I could see it on your face. That's why I brought you out here.'

'I can't think why I came.'

'Because Tiggy asked you?'

'I suppose so.'

'She still talks about you all the time.'

'Oh yeah? What does she say?'

'She's worried about you.'

I laughed. 'Why?'

'Some – girl she saw you with in Brighton.'

198

It was easy to tell from the hesitation that she hadn't used the word 'girl' when she had spoken to Noel.

'Who is she?' he asked.

'Cat? She's just someone who's around at the moment.'

'What's she like?'

'She's been around.'

An expression that might have been envy came over his face and he looked down and dragged his toe in the gravel.

'Was that what you wanted to talk about?'

'Um. No, there's something else.' He looked quite uncomfortable.

'What's bothering you, Noel?'

'I just thought I'd better tip you off. There's a bit of, well, a *thing* about you here. Tiggy's mum told her friends you were coming and the news has sort of got round.'

'A *thing*? What sort of a *thing*?'

'Um. Well, you know, a hostile sort of thing, I suppose.'

'Ah.' I shouldn't really have cared but this hit me quite hard. I didn't know I was a social leper.

'What exactly are people saying?' I asked.

'About your . . . well, about the Colonel,' he said. He knew I didn't like the word 'father' for him.

'What about him?'

'You know, Miles. Because of what happened. They're making a connection.'

'A connection?' I couldn't think what he meant.

'There's a few people out for trouble.'

'Why? What have I done, for God's sake?'

'They think you've let the side down. You know, joined the druggies, broken the rules. They're frightened of what life's like out there. You're a threat.'

'Pathetic.'

'Well, it might be but don't be surprised if they take it out on you.'

'Me? Why?'

'Because you've changed sides,' said Noel, 'Look, here's Tiggy, I'll see you later.' He dived back into the room.

Tiggy looked pretty and wholesome, like some illustration from

*Ideal Country Girlfriend* magazine. It had the effect of making me feel I would leave dirty marks on her if I touched her.

'Hello Miles,' she said, with a warmth that crossed the barrier, 'where did Noel go?'

'Away as fast as he could. He's just delivered the bad news. I'm a social outcast, apparently.'

'Oh, really. He's exaggerating.'

'I'm not sure he is. The word seems to have got round.'

'What word?'

'Brighton. The case and the rest. You know.' I didn't want to say that it was her mother who had put it round.

She took my arm without looking to see if anyone was watching, and by that she seemed to be declaring to anyone who saw that I was not contagious.

'Do we care?' she said.

'Of course we don't.' But I did.

She led me down to the lake and we sat on a seat in a bower next to the boathouse watching men in overalls set out the fireworks for later.

'Tell me what you've been doing,' she said. 'Have you got any further with Max?'

'Max? Oh yes, certainly.' This was safe ground for both of us. 'I know who Natalie was. I've even found the car, or what's left of it.' She was much more interested in Natalie than the car so I told her all about that first, but when I got round to Chinnery's shed and the remains of the Lister, she held my arm tightly. As I told her about it, a nagging thought resurfaced and turned into a certainty.

'He *wanted* me to see the wreck. He made me go out of the barn that way on purpose. I think he meant it to come as a shock.'

'He sounds horrible.'

'It's more than that. It's as if he despised Max. He wanted me to know he didn't give a toss about Ginny's dignity. I think he broods on it. He's got all that information stored up.'

'Did he know Max?'

I told her about the film but that didn't seem to cover it. 'Maybe it goes back further.'

'Is there anyone you can ask?'

'Well, there's Max, I suppose.'

She swung round and stared at me speechlessly and I realized I had left out the most important bit of news of all, left it out because in some odd way I had told her in my head at the time, but only in my head.

'Max isn't dead,' I said. 'He's living in a home. It's just round the corner from me.'

She put both hands up to cover her mouth and stared at me wide-eyed.

'What do you make of that, then?' I asked.

'It's incredible,' she said, and meant it, and the fact that another human being *cared* about it was the single best thing that had happened to me in weeks.

'I'm quite sure Laura thinks he's dead. You know, his wife. The woman I went to see.'

'What are you going to do?'

'I don't know.'

She understood the problem. 'You can't just crash in on him, can you? Heaven knows what state he's in. Can you imagine what it would be like for him? All that stuff that you know and nobody else does.' She stared at the men as they hammered rocket tubes into the ground.

'So Max is alive and Natalie's alive too,' she said in the end.

'I think so. I found some more of their letters. I wish I'd brought them with me. They're really sad. It was just like you said.'

I told her as best I could about Natalie's attempt at reaching Max, at getting him to drop the pretences. The letters' power had carved some of the phrases into my memory so I made a good job of it.

'She did it as kindly as it could be done. She made it *so* easy for him. All he had to do was play along with her. He could have just buried all the lies and he would never even have had to admit to her that it was all nonsense, but when it came to it, he couldn't do it.'

'It's not surprising,' Tiggy said. 'He'd got so used to covering up, hadn't he? He would have had to admit it all to himself. That might have been harder than admitting it to her.'

'He drank a lot, too.'

She looked round sharply at that. 'So?'

'So he had a lot to escape from.'

'Is that why people drink?' she said, and there was something a little bit sharp in her voice.

'I suppose so. I wouldn't know.'

'Is there a difference between using alcohol and using drugs?'

'Oh yes.'

'What?'

'Well, alcohol's about escaping from things, isn't it? But drugs are about exploration. They're about finding new ways of looking at the –'

'Come off it, Miles.'

'Come off it yourself, Tigs. Is this about me or Max?'

The sharpness disappeared. 'It's only about you if you want it to be. You're trying to understand Max, aren't you? It might help, that's all.'

I wasn't convinced. 'Are you sure you're not on a mission? Save Miles from those dreadful drugs or something?'

There was a silence while she frowned and looked at the lake. 'Maybe. If I am then I don't see why that should be so bad. That's not what I *think* I'm doing, though. I think I'm just trying to help you get inside Max's head.'

'There's a load of difference. He was into that whole world of drinking clubs and old school ties and shady deals and wanting to make money. It's the exact opposite.'

She looked at me in a way that indicated she still didn't believe me, but in the end all she said was, 'It sounds to me like he was trying to run away from something.'

'What something?'

'Himself, probably.' She looked at me again and I knew, I just *knew* that she was wondering whether to go on, to say, 'Like you are,' but she stopped short of it. 'Do you feel like facing the firing squad?' she said instead. 'I'd like to dance.'

The band was playing 'Delilah' in a galumphing one-two-three beat and some of the thirty-year-olds, faces flushed from a crowded drinking schedule, were starting to sing along. Tiggy danced well despite the music and we had found a corner of the dance floor where the flailing arms of the prematurely drunken didn't pose too much of a danger. 'Delilah' came to a merciful end and the band switched into 'Homeward Bound', played so slowly that couples were forced to move in and hold each other. This came as a surprise to some who, at this early hour of the evening, were getting their duty dances out of the way and now found themselves stuck with partners whom they had no wish to hold quite so closely. At this moment, just as I was enjoying the forgotten feeling of holding Tiggy in my arms and comparing it with holding Cat, which was never a gentle experience, Julian appeared at her shoulder and, ignoring me, said, 'Hi, Tigs. How about one, eh?'

She smiled politely and said, 'Thanks, Julian. Later perhaps. I'm dancing with Miles.'

'Takes all sorts,' he said, and went off. I watched him go, feeling my blood pressure rise, and at the side of the dance floor I saw him join his brother Philip and a little group of his friends. They'd never been friends of mine and they were standing there eyeing the girls, looking like what they were, a group of rugger players confronted by an alien race.

Julian was pointing at me as he talked to them so I turned my back on them and put my energy into dancing an ostentatious blend of waltz and tango. Tiggy laughed and joined in, matching my movements until she looked past me and stopped laughing abruptly. A hand fell on my shoulder. Philip. He had a very large hand.

'This dance is a gentleman's excuse me,' he said. 'So excuse me.'

He tried to push in between me and Tiggy.

'No it's not,' I said.

'It is now.'

I did my best to stand my ground but it was like trying to stop a tank and I found myself pushed out of the way by a broad back. Tiggy ducked under his arm, and somewhere in the confusion their ankles got caught up so that he pitched sideways to the ground with her on top of him.

There was nervous laughter around us and a few calls of, 'Steady on,' and, 'Don't frighten the horses.' I'd had nothing to do with it.

Philip got up and turned on me. 'Why don't you just piss off?' he said threateningly.

'Stop it,' Tiggy sounded anxious.

'You're a lot better off dancing with me,' he said.

'Hang about,' I said. 'What right have you got to –'

A loud voice cut in on me. 'Drummond,' it said, 'a word with you, please.'

I turned to find myself surrounded by a phalanx of the Master of Foxhounds and two other serious-looking, older men. 'Committee' was stamped all over them.

'Do excuse us,' said the MFH to Tiggy. 'I think your mother wishes to see you by the buffet, Miss Scott-Morrison. Right now, please.' He sounded like a schoolteacher.

'Just wait a minute,' Tiggy said. 'Miles was doing nothing wrong, nothing at all, until this rude –'

'Would you take Miss Scott-Morrison to her mother, George?' said the MFH to the nearest committee member.

'Wilco, Hugh,' said the man, a dapper little fellow with a receding chin. He marched Tiggy off with almost but not quite unacceptable force.

'Leave it to us, Philip,' said the MFH. 'We'll go out on the terrace, shall we, Drummond?'

I didn't have a lot of choice, but when we got outside I decided it was time to take the initiative.

'For a start, my name is Malan. Not Drummond,' I said. 'And I'm not having this. That oaf came barging in. I didn't even trip him up. It's not my fault he's got two left feet.'

'We've had our eye on you, Drummond,' said the MFH, whose cheeks were getting darker and darker under the rich ochre of fox-hunting fresh air and port-swollen veins.

'Malan,' I said again. 'You must have done. You were over here in three seconds flat.'

He ignored me. 'There are standards to be kept up,' he said, 'and we are not at all sure that your presence here is a good idea. Your recent background is well known. You've embarrassed your friends and your family and I have a good mind to ask you to leave immediately.'

'I haven't done anything. Why should I? What would you have

done if someone had cut in on you as rudely as that and tripped up your partner?'

This seemed to get through to him, as though cutting in during a dance not intended for that purpose was almost as serious an offence as smoking dope.

'You mark my words,' he said. 'We shall be keeping a close eye on you for the rest of the ball. Any monkey business at all and out you go.'

I shrugged because there was nothing else I could say or do. He turned to go, taking with him the remaining committee member who had been frowning censoriously throughout, then turned back for a moment.

'Your father wouldn't have stood for all this,' he said. 'Fine man. You should be proud to carry his name. I used to know him well.'

'No you didn't,' I said. 'That was just my stepfather.' But I said it to myself.

I couldn't bear to go inside for the time being so I walked down to the bower by the boathouse again and sat morosely staring at the lake. Tiggy would come back here, I thought – if she was allowed to. I rolled myself a strong joint, crumbling the soft resin into the tobacco, and let it take me off to a different place where the insults still hit their target but their target was cushioned, laughable and somewhere off to one side of me. I had just lit a second one when I heard footsteps and a voice and I looked round the corner of the bushes behind the seat, hoping it was Tiggy but it wasn't. It was a tall man, arm-in-arm with Tiggy's mother Averil, who looked at me in surprise and walked on, talking to him in an urgent whisper and looking back at me over her shoulder.

I very nearly left at that point. I hadn't come to be the butt of everyone's prejudices and suspicions. All I had really come for was to spend a bit of time with Tiggy for old times' sake. You grow away from people but there's a part of you left – a part that remembers lying on the grass together on the old ramparts of a downland hill-fort while the horses grazed a few feet away and thinking that was almost all you needed from life, lips sore from kissing, jeans tight from unreleased pleasure. A kept boy and a kept girl still provided for in the safe, constricted home harbour, still moored to a set of values they were only just starting to question. So safe, so thoughtless and when the world suddenly unwrapped a dazzling set of unsuspected urban complexities, so dull. There was a bit of me that still wanted to be back there on the grass, making absurd promises about the future made possible by complete ignorance about the alternatives. There had been a romantic, eighteen-year-old time when I thought I might spend the rest of my life in Tiggy's sweet arms, before I found the wider world and knew that I would have died of boredom in their embrace.

I started to wonder if it had been that way for Max, coming from South Wales into the glamorous Guards and a London life which overthrew his framework of values. That's if he ever had a framework of values.

This chain of thoughts probably took quite a time, it was hard to tell – then I heard running feet and looked round the bushes again to see a girl, holding up her gown, racing across the grass. It was Tiggy, breathless and horrified.

'Miles,' she said, 'get going! You've got to go. Now.'

'Why? I'm not bothering them.'

'They smelt the ... the stuff. You know. What you were smoking.'

'Who did?'

'My mother and the chief constable.'

'Chief constable?'

'They walked past you. He was with her. They've called the police.'

I was stoned enough to find that funny. 'He is the police. Why did he have to call them? He could have just rung himself up.'

'Stop talking. Just *go*!' She was almost crying.

I took the bag out of my pocket and looked at it. There was still a good big lump of it left. Then I heard more footsteps, a lot more footsteps, and looked up. There were posses of people coming, the MFH, what looked like his entire committee, Tiggy's mother, the chief constable, Philip and his friends with Julian in tow. There must have been thirty or more and they'd done a flanking move-ment so that groups of them were coming from all directions.

'Oh bugger,' I said, and pulled the lump of resin out of the bag.

Tiggy grabbed it. 'I'll get rid of it. Go and meet them.'

They surrounded me as I walked towards them like Red Indians swooping on a covered wagon, swarming round as if to cut off my escape. The MFH waded through his henchmen and fronted up to me, standing uncomfortably close, blowing a wash of wine fumes over me, fumes turned by his body chemistry into something sickeningly sweet. I noticed with fascination that his eyes were on slightly different levels. Philip and his friends grabbed my arms with unnecessary roughness.

'Right, Drummond,' said the MFH, 'you'd better come along with us.'

The chief constable forced his way through. 'There's no need for that,' he said mildly. 'Let's keep calm. You can let go of him.'

The rugger players let go reluctantly though Philip gave my right arm a deliberate and uncomfortable wrench in the process.

'Mr Drummond,' said the chief constable hesitantly, as if it were a long time since he'd had to remember the fine detail of practical police procedure. 'An allegation has been made about you which I'm sure you'd like to help us clear up. Would you mind coming inside with me? Entirely voluntarily, of course.' He turned to the MFH. 'Is there a private room we can use?'

It took ten minutes for them to get the key to the office on the first floor and another ten minutes to make quite sure that there was nothing more harmful in my pockets than rolling tobacco and cigarette papers, though the chief constable leafed through the collection of death certificates with puzzled interest.

'It's just the smell of the tobacco,' I said hopefully, 'it's aromatic.' But the chief constable was no fool. He had already looked closely into my eyes.

'Dilated pupils,' he said. 'Anyway, I know what I was smelling. What have you done with the stuff?'

'What stuff?'

There was a tap at the door and the MFH came in, glaring at me with undisguised hatred. He whispered in the chief constable's ear and I heard him start with the words, 'The girl . . .' The rest was lost to me.

The chief constable seemed to move immediately into a different and far more frightening gear. He frowned at me and said, 'Mr Drummond, you'd better tell me what it was and you'd better tell me right now. It would seem that whatever you gave to her, Miss Scott-Morrison is very much the worse for it.'

'My name is Malan,' I said again wearily. 'I don't use the name Drummond any more and as far as I know she hasn't had anything that could hurt her.'

As I was saying it, I was thinking, Tiggy? Tiggy hadn't had any. Tiggy had probably just thrown it in the lake. Unless, unless she was afraid it would float, unless she'd eaten it . . . I hoped she hadn't. It wasn't going to do her any harm but you get a hell of a long high by eating it and to someone like Tiggy, who I was quite sure had never smoked any in her life, that would be a disturbing experience. Particularly if she was surrounded by this lot.

The chief constable said, 'Would you mind staying here with him?' to the MFH, and left the room.

The MFH sat down heavily and stared at me belligerently.

'If any harm comes to that gel, I'll have your guts for garters,' he said. 'You did this on purpose.'

'Of course I didn't,' I said.

'I'm sure you did,' he said. 'After all, you killed your father.'

# Nineteen

That was the night that I had a vision in a shop window. It was not a comfortable night. A loose-fitting dinner jacket over a thin dress-shirt lets in the chill all round the chest and neck. At sixteen, when my mother bought it for me, I must have been heavier than I was now. I had slept or perhaps just passed into a shivering trance, on and off in a seafront shelter until a policeman moved me on. After that, a doorway sheltered me from the rain which fell from five past four in the morning until nearly five thirty and I had nothing better to do than time the rain.

I hadn't deliberately gone back to Brighton, that magnet of mine, but the bright headlights of a caterer's truck came down the drive behind me as I was trudging out of Pickworth. It was going that way and there seemed no reason not to go with it. The young guy driving it had no time for the nobs so he was highly sympathetic when I told him what had happened.

'Go on,' he said. 'They didn't find anything on you and they still gave you the boot. You should do them for that. Take them to court. I mean, you bought a ticket, didn't you? What right have they got to do that?'

In fact Tiggy had bought the ticket. I thought of her being carried off dramatically and quite unnecessarily to hospital and decided that taking them to court wasn't really an option.

'I tell you what,' he said, 'are you hungry? I've got enough left in the back to feed an army.'

That was how we wound up at midnight, in a lay-by off the A27, eating canapés by the mouthful and washing them down with champagne from the case he had managed to tuck out of sight along the way. It was a small victory to think that all those stuffy hunters were subsidizing our feast.

He was going on through to Uckfield so I asked him to drop me off on the Upper Brighton Road and wandered slowly down through the sleeping town towards the sea. I seemed to be making a habit of spending nights out and about in Brighton and perhaps it was the symmetry of it that made me turn down his friendly offer of a sofa in his downstairs room for the night. More likely, it was the thought of waking up in the morning to be polite to strangers and having to extricate myself from that and from Uckfield, where I did not wish to be. I was nursing a head which was throbbing from a monstrous accusation, and a few quiet hours before the complicated world woke up again might help me to work it all out. Looking back now, from all these years later, it would be very easy to say something else was at work here, that the trunk was driving its story on in its own way, anxious for me to uncover the next stage. You can believe in coincidence or you can believe in some sort of predestination in this story but, whichever it was, there were key moments when there seemed to be a powerful force at work and this was one of them.

If this, if that. If I hadn't turned down the driver's offer, if the policeman hadn't bothered to crunch down the shingle just for the pleasure of moving me on, if the rain hadn't pushed me into a doorway, if . . . The doorway was in the Lanes, the maze of small streets where the antique shops clustered together. It was the way into a small gallery between two such shops and the door itself was set back three feet or so from the pavement, making a short, covered passageway which kept me completely out of the way of the chill drizzle. I could hear footsteps from a long way off, so I would be forewarned of the approach of any more policemen.

I sat in a state of immense, jittery agitation as the champagne and the rest wore off, thinking of the MFH and his furious purple face. I could not believe he had said that. How dare he? The Colonel had been seventy-four, for God's sake. He could have had a heart attack at any time. It wasn't anything I did. Trying to put it to the back of my mind, I stared instead at the gathering puddles of water on the pavement, watching the separate pools bulge towards each other, then link and rush into a new shape. At five twenty-eight it stopped raining and by five thirty, when I woke from a brief doze with my feet freezing, the sky was beginning to grow a little lighter. It was enough to turn the gallery's side window, the small, three-foot window which formed one side of my passageway, from a black slab into a silver transparency through which its grey contents could now be seen, and when I looked at them I shivered in the dawn chill because in the middle of the window, right in the middle, was a large, framed, black-and-white photograph and it was the big Bugatti, the Golden Bug, on the seafront, right here, with that same antique policeman leaning over to check its tax disc. It wasn't just a similar photo, it was the same one.

It was not alone.

There was a vertical row of five pictures, all of them big blow-ups in black-and-white and all of them framed identically. A neatly lettered sign underneath said, 'Prints by Sam Bishop. £20', and of course I knew that name. It was the same name which was printed on the back of my own much older and more dog-eared copy of that identical Bugatti print. Sam Bishop had taken the photo long ago and this must surely mean that Sam Bishop was a local photographer, local and still alive.

I got up and went to look in the front window, but there was no more of his work. The gallery sold nothing but photographs and the main window was full of modern, trick, colourful stuff. Sam Bishop was a sideline in a side window, nostalgia for visitors, not the cutting-edge for the smart set.

I went straight back to that side window though, because what drew me there was another encounter with unlikely odds. It was possible to accept the Bugatti picture as a wonderful fluke, a piece of period Brightonia entirely likely to have cropped up in a shop like this for the sake of the tourists, but it was not possible to accept the other photos in that vertical row of five in the same way. They were all taken in Brighton certainly, but it was well against the odds that two of the other four should have been pictures of Douglas Owen.

Both those pictures were taken at the speed trials, probably within seconds of each other. In one of them, Douglas sat waiting at the wheel of his pre-war Delage, which had to be the same pre-war Delage that Max had smuggled in for him on the transporter – some sort of post-war booty. He was wearing a linen helmet, with Ginny leaning against the tail and both of them looking ahead towards the start. The other was taken from exactly behind the car, just as he let the clutch in with smoke coming from the exhaust and the back tyres and the tarmac tapering away into the distance beyond the car.

The other two pictures in the row were also cars, but they were of no interest to me, unknown faces at different times, but that didn't matter because three out of five, whichever way I looked at it, seemed to be conclusively beyond the realm of coincidence. I filled the next lump of cold morning time before the gallery opened as best I could, taking a fast walk up and down the seafront to try to chase the bad stuff out of my blood. Breakfast helped a bit and I spun it out as long as possible, getting some curious looks for the bedraggled state of my evening clothes. I hoped I looked glamorous and mysterious, but I wasn't at all sure.

At nine thirty, as a man in his early thirties walked up to the gallery door, I was there waiting.

'Won't be a minute,' he said, fiddling with the locks.

'Don't hurry, I'm not really a customer, I'm afraid.'

'What are you, then?' He looked me up and down, puzzled.

'I'm just curious about these Sam Bishop photos.'

'Yeah?'

What could I ask? 'Have you been stocking them for long?'

'Put them in last week as a try-out. We've only got them there to see if they sell, to tell you the truth.'

'But you know Sam Bishop?'

'Oh, yeah. Comes in now and then.'

'I wanted to get in touch, you see. I don't have a number. There's something about the photos I'm interested in.'

'I don't know about that. Sam is a bit of a . . . well, not exactly a recluse, but, you know.'

He wasn't going to tell me, so I told a white lie. 'It's all right, I used to know him. I just lost touch.'

'Oh, right. You used to know him?'

'Yeah.'

'That was before the operation, was it?' he said.

'I didn't know he'd had an operation.'

'Oh yes, a very successful one,' he said sarcastically. 'He's been a she ever since I've known her.'

'Sam Bishop is a she?'

'Sam as in Samantha. Funny you not spotting that. Somehow I get the feeling she wouldn't want you to have her number.'

Great. A completely unnecessary lie and I'd blown my chance just like that.

'Look, I'm sorry. Okay. I don't know her but it's really important that I get in touch with her. Would you ring her for me?'

'Yeah? And say what exactly?'

'Say . . .' Say the obvious, stick to the truth. 'Say my name's Miles Malan. Tell her it's about Max and Douglas Owen.'

He phoned her, which was quite nice of him under the circumstances, though he went to the back of the shop to do it so he could say quiet, warning things to her and keep an eye on me at the same time.

'She wants to talk to you,' he said after a while, and waved the receiver at me.

The earpiece had his warmth in it. My hand was damp with sudden, unexpected sweat.

'What's this all about then?' said a gravelly voice in my ear.

'I'm researching the lives of the Owen brothers and –'

'Why?'

'What?' I said, startled.

'I asked why? Why would anyone want to do that? They are not famous. People do not "research" the lives of such as them. Are you maybe a debt collector or something?'

'No, I've got a perfectly normal and healthy interest in them and I'm not a debt collector. I just happened to see your pictures, that's all. I really need to talk to you.'

'Charlie says you look like a concert party violinist who's been left out in the rain.'

'Look, I've been up all night,' I said, irritated despite myself, 'I got thrown out of a hunt ball and I slept on the beach.'

She laughed then. You never can tell what will put people on your side.

On the way to her flat, I stopped at a phone box and rang Tiggy's home number, but whoever picked up the phone put it down again as soon as they heard my voice. I was walking because Samantha Bishop had asked for an hour to get herself straight.

Being far too early, I sat on a bench and began to unravel as the night before came up and hit me like a sandbag full of guilt.

My court case hadn't been a big deal outside Brighton. My mother, when she consented to speak to me again, for precisely five minutes, said one reporter had rung the Colonel afterwards, that was all, and he'd refused to talk anyway. It was a whole month later that he had his heart attack. Until last night no one had ever said there was any connection, well never to me, anyway. I'd had no idea that was what they thought.

Samantha Bishop lived on the top floor of an old block of flats where Brighton turns into Hove, looking out over the sea. Her flat was hung not with photographs but with what seemed to me to be good paintings, small, dark oils in heavy gilt frames, some graceful nudes in sepia ink and, dominating the sitting room, a large Italian-looking picture mostly in sepia tones of a marble swimming pool shaded by a roof held up on graceful columns, with a group of brightly dressed, slender girls standing talking next to it in a brilliant splash of colour.

Samantha Bishop herself was a riveting sight. Her trousers and shirt were made of extremely soft black leather, boldly accenting her white hair, and she had an air that implied she'd been a very sexy woman thirty years earlier.

She looked me up and down for a long time, then laughed rather scornfully as though she thought I might have been dangerous and was disappointed by the reality.

'A ball, you said? What are you, Cinderella?'

I was envious of her voice. Her vocal cords had been glamorously corroded by years of abuse.

'Would you like a drink?' she asked. 'Or just coffee? I suggest coffee in your case, perhaps.'

We sat down on tall stools at a bar in her kitchen. A stuffed seagull in a glass case dominated the room and she saw me looking at it.

'I shot it,' she said, 'here in this room. With a revolver.'

I wasn't sure I believed her.

'Now, what do you come to me for?'

It occurred to me that at some faraway time she had come from middle Europe, Hungary maybe. Samantha seemed an unlikely name for her but perhaps Sam was an approximation of some difficult, polysyllabic Magyar name.

'The Owen brothers,' I said. 'You must have known them.'

'Why must I?'

'They're in three of your five photos down in the town. That's over the odds.'

'Two of the photos only, and they are both Douglas.'

'The other one, the Bugatti – that was Max's.'

She considered this. 'You have certainly done your research. It is true that I knew them both for very many years. That does not mean that I want to talk to you about them. You had better explain yourself.'

'I bought a trunk. It had loads of photos and stuff from Max's flat in it.'

'The hell you did. What was it like, this trunk?'

'Brown leather, with Max's name on it. Captain Max Birkin Owen, Grenadier Guards.'

'Oh damn it,' she said, 'that was a mistake. My mistake. It was meant to be thrown away. You bought it? Where? Why? Did you need a trunk?'

'No. It was in an auction. Locked up. I was just curious.' It seemed too difficult to explain the Birkin Owen connection.

'You are a nosy person, then. Have you been looking at all that old stuff?'

'Some of it.'

'Then I have to say I think you had no right. He is dead now, old Max.' Her face had started to stiffen but it was in for a penny, in for a pound. If she helped clear out the flat, she must know that wasn't true.

'You can't say that. I know he's not dead. I've been to Weston House.'

That really shocked her. 'You have *seen* him? That is not good at all.'

'Well, no, I haven't seen him, not yet, but I know he's not dead. Why does everyone keep saying he's dead?'

'Look, whatever your name is, when it comes down to it, what business is it of yours?'

'My name's Miles. It's my business because I was there when Ginny Owen was killed.'

'You were?' She brooded on that, twisting a cigarette into a holder and lighting it. She didn't offer me one. 'So was I. So were many people. So what?'

'It's been with me all my life.'

'What are you, a cry-baby or something?'

'No. Just someone trying to understand why it happened.'

'Why the crash happened? There is no "why". It happened because it happened, because some people like speed and like to play with their fast cars.'

'Yes, but . . .'

'What is this question of yours? Can't you hear what I say?'

'I knew Ginny a bit and . . .'

'You were a kid. How did you *know* Ginny? What does all this matter now?'

She was so dismissive that I felt quite cross and forgot the usual rules that cover politeness and the soliciting of information.

'Look, it matters to me. It matters a lot. I've stumbled into all this stuff about Max and now I find he let Ginny drive a death-trap.'

'Oh so *Max* killed her, did he? I see.' Her voice was immensely sarcastic. 'All this time Douglas thought *he* killed her and I thought it was just a car crash and now *Max* killed her.'

'How do you mean Douglas thought he killed her?'

'Look, little Miles. Let us get some things straight. I am not going to trade tittle-tattle with you about my old friends because I don't know if I can trust you, and anyway I don't see why you have any right to know anything at all about this old dusty business which ought to be allowed to slip back into history where nobody will bother with it ever again. Max prefers to be dead. Douglas prefers him to be dead and so do I. As a dead man, nobody bothers him any more. That is best. He leads his quiet life and he is safe from all the men with bills and threats and writs. Why do you know any better, eh?'

'All right,' I said. 'I know what you mean but I haven't come here to do anyone any harm.'

'So what *do* you want to know?'

'All I ever wanted to know is what they were really like.'

'Ah. You are a clever boy, because that is a good question – perhaps the one question I do not mind answering.' She considered. 'I can see that you will not stop asking, so I will offer you a deal. The price will be high.'

'What is it?'

'That you leave them both alone.'

'Both? Douglas is alive too?'

'Of course Douglas is alive. Did you not know that? He is very much more alive than poor Max. He is living quietly back in Wales where he came from, with another wife who is a peaceful person and not at all like poor Ginny. So what do you say to my deal?'

'It's not a deal yet. You've only told me half of it.'

'Ah, yes. That was my half. Now you want to know your half. Well, perhaps I will tell you some things about them. Things I choose to tell you. I have an hour or so now and that is all you get.'

'That *is* a high price.' But it wasn't really. I had already found out for myself how hard it would be to walk in on Max's world. I couldn't imagine it would be any easier to do the same to Douglas. It was a coward's deal because it let me off that hook. By agreeing to it, I would no longer have any choice in the matter. I could say to myself that it was honour which stopped me from having to go and knock on their doors, and at that moment it was an option which quite suited me.

'Do we have a deal, then?' she said.

'Yes.'

'Can I trust you? Look at me.' And I did, noticing that her eyes were almost green and were still girl's eyes. 'I think I can,' she said, as if that had come as a surprise to her. 'I think I can. All right, we should sit somewhere more comfortable, and no notes. Do not take notes. This is for you to understand, not to put down anywhere.'

We sat in armchairs either side of her fireplace.

'The only reason,' she said, 'the *only* reason you ever found Max's trunk is that I was careless. We cleared out his flat. Three of us. Douglas, me and another old friend because Max was so very, very ill. He had a stroke, then another stroke, so he could not talk for a while and he had to go into a home.' She said the word 'home' after a slight pause, which seemed to indicate great distaste or perhaps even fear of her own future.

'He wanted everything with him, absolutely everything from that terrible place he lived, but it was not possible. It was an awful mess. He had been abandoned there by some mad woman he lived with. No one had been to see him for two months and it was like animals lived there.' She shuddered. 'We persuaded him he had to leave it behind in the end. He was distressed, poor fellow. We took the trunk outside and I would have tipped it in the dustbins but they were full so I left it there next to them hoping the bin-men would take it. Now, I suppose someone else got there first and took it off to sell. Imagine, people thinking they could sell *that*, but then of course they were right because you came along and bought it.' She stared at me. 'Unless you took it. Perhaps you are someone who goes searching round dustbins.'

'No.'

'You have to understand that we were trying to do the best thing we could. Poor Max had such a complicated life and there were always people blaming him and wanting money from him for this or that. It was so much easier you see, once he was in the home, to say he was dead to anyone who was not his good friend or who still wanted money from him. It was a good trick. All the bad things just went away then.'

'You said that even to his wife?' I wasn't sure how she would take the interruption, but she just nodded.

'To Laura? Yes, even to Laura, not that she had been a wife for many years and hardly even then. That was an accident, really. We had forgotten about her. She hadn't been in touch for years but someone told her he had died and she told someone else and by the time we found out it was a little late to go to her and say, surprise, he's still alive. Do you understand?'

'Yes, I suppose I do.'

There was a silence and she seemed to want a question so I took a risk.

'The accident. Can you tell me what you remember?'

She frowned and was silent for a long time and I wasn't sure at first that she was going to answer. 'If I must. It was the one time of the year I knew I would always see them, every September. In the old days when we did mad things I would see them all the time, but later they had their lives and my life was here. I knew they would be here in September. They called and I had breakfast with them at their hotel. They were always in good spirits, like two children, Douglas and Virginia. He was such a lovely man, so good-looking. He got better and better as the years went by, you know. Like a Greek god, the sort of Greek god you would like to have on your side in a bar-room brawl, I think. Virginia was . . .' She seemed to search for a word. 'Very alive, I would say. Life was never quiet when she was around. She was all bubble and froth.'

'She didn't like Max.'

'Why do you say that?'

'They had some terrible rows.'

'Not in front of me. They were very English.' She stopped talking and frowned again and I knew I had to be very careful.

'But let me tell you what you wanted to know about,' she said. 'I was standing with Douglas as we watched her go off in the car . . .' *This* was what I wanted to hear. I hung on her every word. 'I remember exactly what he said. "She's got the hang of it. She loves to try to beat me," he said, "and I love her trying." We stood side by side and watched her go up the track. The car went very well, very fast indeed. Then right up there, far away, it went into a blur and something flew off and I felt Douglas go very stiff next to me. We heard the noise and we saw the smoke and he just turned to me and said, "There's nothing to say, Sam, don't worry." He was very brave.'

That is the nature of the cocked hat again. You have two bearings on something and everything's looking fine, then along comes a third bearing and bang goes your certainty. I'd read the coroner's statements in Chinnery's office, the statement from Douglas.

*. . . I followed the track of the car with my eyes until it went out of sight around the bend. I could hear the engine note rising and falling as she changed gear, until it cut off. I assumed she had reached the end of the course and I heard a loud bang, but as the engine was prone to backfire on the overrun, I thought little more of it until some seconds*

219

*later I saw a plume of smoke rising from the end of the course. At that point I realized that an accident must have occurred involving either my wife or the other competitor who started with her.*

Two people standing side by side remember such similar and yet such different things. Years later, is it possible to tell which one is right? Is it even possible to tell whether there is one right version of events? Does the account given at the time count for more than the memory now? It should, but perhaps Douglas needed to deny the evidence of his own eyes, to go on hoping he hadn't seen it happen and that another explanation was possible. Or was it that Sam had put together a mental composite of what she saw and what she soon knew? How could I tell?

'Did you see him later?'

'He was taken off by the doctor and the police. I think Max took him home.'

'Max was there?' Of course he was. Odd that I hadn't remembered that. He seemed to have little emotional connection with the event. Perhaps that was because the coroner's records showed how keen he had been to distance himself from any blame. It felt cold, his part in it – poor recompense for all that support Douglas had given him over the years.

She pursed her lips and nodded.

'Can you tell me what Max was like?'

'He was like the song, he was a nowhere man.'

'What does that mean?'

'Have you not met people like that? He was the most charming man it was possible to meet but he was like the weather, never quite what you hoped. I think there was a big emptiness at the centre of him or perhaps it was something he did not want you to see. Those two brothers, they were both *fun*, always fun, but with Douglas there was so much more and I came to think with Max, that is mostly *all* there was. Oh, of course, being with Max was marvellous, like the most romantic thing you can imagine. He only had eyes for you. He would listen to every word you said as if it was the wisest thing that had ever been said by anyone. Then maybe he would borrow five pounds from you because he had left his wallet behind or because he had forgotten to go to the bank and you wouldn't begrudge him it for a single second, not until you thought about it afterwards, but that was it – that was all there was, nothing more. There was no part of his heart for anyone else, at least not for more than a few days. Douglas is so completely different, so good and brave.' She stopped abruptly. 'But Douglas is alive and it is no part of this deal of ours that I should talk of Douglas.'

I wondered whether she had slept with either or both of the brothers, whether Max had let her down and whether perhaps she had envied Ginny.

'How did you meet Max?'

'He wanted a picture taken. Well, you have seen it of course. It was that huge Bugatti of his.'

'What was the policeman doing? Did he just happen to come along?'

She smiled and shook her head. 'It was for the composition. He was standing there and I asked him to go closer, then maybe he saw something which interested him because he suddenly bent over like that and I knew I had my picture in that moment.'

'Why did Max want the picture?'

'He had to sell the car because, like always, he had no money and he wanted something to remember it by when it had gone. It had some special meaning for him, that car. I think he got five hundred pounds for it. Do you know what it would be worth now?'

'A thousand times that.'

'More. Much more. He wanted a good picture to send to some American he thought might want to buy it. I used to think that old car was so like him, so fantastic to look at, a wonderful dream, but somehow struggling through life underneath, leaking water and oil at every one of its joints.'

She would only come at him obliquely, I thought.

'But he got away with it, didn't he?'

'Got away with it?' She gave a short laugh. 'He peaked too soon, our Max. His best days were his young days. He burnt up all his life's credit and all his friends' patience so that his life afterwards was always a struggle.'

'His friends went on supporting him.'

'His true friends, but fewer and fewer. The things he got up to, they sometimes made it hard to be his friend.'

221

'He was married though.'

'Oh, yes, and such a wife. Poor woman. She should not have married him. She could have been good for him if he had not been so bad for her. She hated his friends. She blamed us all for leading him astray. Us! It was not us. She saw through him in four weeks I think, no more than that, but she stayed with him for a whole year and I think, maybe, for that she deserved a medal.'

'Was there nobody else?' I asked.

'Nobody else?' She arched her eyebrows which tightened the skin on her face and took years off her. 'There were *thousands*,' she said, and I was quite sure then that she had been one of them. 'Moths to the flame, delighting in being burnt up. After the drinks and the meal and the bed and perhaps the skiing or the stories or the driving, they would gradually discover the awful truth.'

'What truth was that?'

'That they could never have any part of Max completely for themselves.'

'Did you know an American woman, Natalie Vanderberg?'

She looked blank. 'Natalie? I don't remember any Natalie.'

'She was a cellist. He knew her through the Duke of Windsor.'

'Oh, the Windsors. You would think Max was their best friend. Does that not tell you something, that he made so much of those shabby people?'

'But you never heard of Natalie?'

'Where did she live?'

'Geneva, then America.'

She laughed. 'It was hard enough to keep track of Max if he was in a different room, never mind a different country. Perhaps she was one of his secrets.'

'When you said Douglas thought *he* killed Ginny, what did you mean?'

She snorted impatiently. 'He had the car hotted up. Some special work on the engine to make it go faster. It was the sort of thing people blamed themselves for afterwards.'

'But it was Max's fault. He knew the chassis was botched up. He knew about the crashes.'

Mistake. I had pushed my luck too far. 'You are very young and you do not know that we all live in a patchwork of imperfect guesses. Life is not a well-oiled machine. People are people and life is made up of people so it is a creaking, tearing, flimsy thing. Now I think that is enough questions. What are you going to do with all these answers?'

I hadn't been there for anything like an hour but it seemed unwise to argue. 'I don't know.'

'Leave this old stuff alone. Let it crawl back under its stone. The old, who have done all the good and bad things that people do, should be allowed to let time cover up their mistakes. Imagine how you would feel.'

I nodded.

'You must not go to see them,' she said, staring at me.

'I promised.'

She relented slightly then.

'Max gave me a story he wrote,' she said. 'It is about the car in the picture, the Bugatti. It will tell you a bit about the way things were in those days. Would you like to take it with you?'

I already had one of his Bugatti stories. Could this one be different?

'Yes, I would. I'll be sure to send it back to you.'

'No you won't. That is the sort of thing people say and think they mean and never do. At my age you learn not to take risks like that. For this reason and others, I have a photocopier.'

She went away and came back with the story and I put it in my pocket and then she said, 'Read it and think about it but remember, there was less to Max than met the eye.'

# Twenty

Sompting Grange was a soft, crumbling house where flakes from the nineteenth-century brickwork were turning back to mud around the roots of gnarled creepers and where a mossy horsebox with a flat tyre had been partly blocking the drive ever since I could remember. I had always liked walking up that drive but this time it felt like a sortie into enemy territory, full of the possibility of ambush and denunciation. I was in a mood to see threats everywhere. All the coffee I had drunk to counteract my sleepless night had filled me with huge, twitchy unease and a dreadful, breathless sense of foreboding. At the gates it got too much and I turned back, but all that black overhang still followed me and any slight sense of relief was overpowered by guilt after a few yards. I couldn't leave Sussex without trying to find out how Tiggy had fared, but I had no wish to encounter her mother or any of her supporters who might be lying in wait.

Many times in past years I had sat politely in the kitchen, drinking tea from fine, cracked cups while Averil, her secateurs always on the verge of falling from the pocket of her scruffy old gardening jacket, twittered brightly on about films and books and her own peculiar take on items of news: 'Oh, don't you think they really should insist Mr Heath gets *married*. How *is* he going to make all those decisions a Prime Minister has to make with nobody to *talk* to? I know what it's like. Believe me, I know.'

These conversations were to be suffered until the magic moment when Tiggy and I could slip away to her room in the long hot summer silence, or failing that, escape on to the downs on horses that were just a means of getting away to some quiet dip where they could graze their way through the afternoon.

Since Tiggy's father left there had never been quite enough money to cope with the rate at which the Grange was decaying. Where other country houses were by now on their next generation of kitchens – fitted, wooden and extremely expensive – the Grange had fifties-style pastel cabinets of metal-edged flecked plastic sheet. The conservatory was a leaky old Victorian affair of softening wood, cracked panes and crevassed, crusted putty. Inside it, two dishevelled Lloyd Loom chairs and a split leather pouffe were the only furniture and rows of flowerpots held things which were not quite dead yet. No one sat there for long because its air was unbreathable, full of the warm exhalations of its decay.

The main drive curved round so that you couldn't see the house until you were almost at the front door. The last ten yards across noisy gravel held no possibilities for concealment from Averil if she were inside, so I edged down the path past the kitchen garden which ended in what had once been a stableyard, going very carefully indeed now to check for signs of life. I didn't want to be there. I wanted to be somewhere where I didn't have to have my body or my head with me.

The back garden opened up as I turned the corner of the stables, the lawns curving away through a screen of high trees and in the middle of the grass was a swinging seat, its back to me, all cushions and canopies. I thought it was empty until a foot appeared, kicked the ground and the seat started to sway backwards and forwards, creaking. I stood absolutely still and looked carefully into the yard. The garage doors were open, Averil's little Renault was nowhere to be seen and there was no sign of life anywhere inside. For all that, I kept to the trees, trying to tread quietly until I could get an oblique view of the occupant of the swinging seat. It was Tiggy and she was giggling.

'Never join the SAS,' she said, 'you sound like the Ents marching on Isengard. I knew it was you.'

'Is there anybody else here?'

'I rather hoped your first question might be, "Are you all right?"'

'Sorry. Are you?'

'It was an interesting experience,' she said. 'But you'd know all about that, wouldn't you?'

I shook my head carefully. 'I've never eaten a lump that size, I haven't a clue.'

A pigeon clattered out of a tree. I jumped.

'Calm down,' Tiggy said, raising her eyebrows, 'Mummy's gone to Worthing to see her shrink. She had an attack of the heebie-jeebies this morning after we talked. She said it was because I was so ungrateful. I ask you! She only went fifteen minutes ago so she won't be back before lunch.'

It had taken me nearly fifteen minutes to walk up the lane from the bus-stop so I can't have missed her by much. That was lucky because even short-sighted Averil wouldn't have missed *me*, not in a dinner jacket. I shivered.

'We'll hear her from miles away,' said Tiggy reassuringly. 'Her car's got a hole in its exhaust pipe. You can always hide in the bushes.'

I sat down on the grass by her feet. 'What happened to you?' I said.

'Nothing much to start with. They were terribly polite and kind. You'd have thought I was a hostage and they'd just rescued me. They asked me lots of questions about what you'd been doing. Some of them were searching the grass and the bushes. I lied like a trooper, said I hadn't seen you smoking anything funny at all.'

'Thank you.'

'It would have been all right but then I started giggling. All those angry men with red faces and bossy women. The MFH kept saying, "Patricia, you must tell us what that young scoundrel has been doing. What was it he was smoking?" I was doing my best not to laugh but I couldn't help it because he started to look exactly like a bulldog and I kept imagining him cocking his leg against the wall. I think I started copying his voice and that was when the chief constable realized what was happening, so they took me off to hospital.' She made a face. 'It really wasn't the most relaxing way to try it for the first time.'

'What happened at the hospital?'

'Nothing much. They spent ages checking me over and doing this and that, then they decided I wasn't in any particular danger so Mummy brought me back here. That was the worst bit. Her driving's terrifying at the best of times but when you're well . . . what's the word?'

'Stoned?'

'Stoned.' She tried it for size and said it again with a touch of wonder in her voice. 'When you're *stoned*, it's dreadful. Terrifying. All those things coming at me. It made me feel dizzy.'

'What things?'

'Oh, lamp-posts and bollards and stuff.'

'You weren't hallucinating?'

'Hard to say, really. Of course she's gone on and on at me this morning. Says I've got to have absolutely nothing to do with you ever again.'

I looked up at her and she was staring at me.

'Are *you* all right?' she said.

'Yes. Why?'

'You don't look all right. Are you . . . *stoned* now?'

'No, I'm not.'

'Don't get cross,' she said, mildly.

'I'm not.'

She said nothing.

'Anyway,' I added, 'I've got nothing to get stoned on. I just spent a night in a shop doorway.'

'That doesn't sound like fun.'

'It had its moments.' She looked ready to give me a lecture so I told her all about my meeting with Sam Bishop to head her off and she listened without interrupting. 'She gave me a copy of another of Max's stories,' I said at the end.

'You can't go anywhere without stumbling over Max, can you?' she said.

'It does feel a bit like that. It's just luck.'

'No, it's not. You've always kept your eyes more open than other people do. If it's there to be seen, you see it.'

'Maybe.'

'You can read me the story if you like.'

So I did, sitting there on the grass in front of her, under a cedar tree with one ear cocked for the return of the avenging Averil while Tiggy, still prone to giggle at unexpected and slightly unsuitable moments, sprawled out across the swinging seat as if she would never have the motivation to move again.

It wasn't easy to read because the photocopied handwriting came from what I was learning to recognize as the later part of Max's life, and was spidery and elongated.

*In that period immediately following the cessation of hostilities, when Europe was in the grip of lawlessness and entire populations were finding their way back to the homes from which they had been so brutally ejected, I found myself detached from normal service to perform special duties of a private nature for a certain royal personage in the South of France. It was a time when much that had not already been plundered and pillaged from the surviving grand houses by the retreating Nazis was falling into the hands of opportunist looters, but it was my good fortune to be in a position to save one such artefact from an ignominious fate while at the same time restoring its owner, who had suffered much, to something approaching fortune himself.*

*It happened that my duties had taken me, one sunny day, into the foothills of Provence, west of Grasse, on a sensitive errand vital to the welfare of my royal charge. Circumstances dictated that I should use a half-ton truck for this errand rather than my more usual staff car and that I should drive it myself, for this was far too sensitive a mission to allow the presence of the driver who would normally have chauffeured me. I was driving up a winding country road in the truck when I was alarmed to see a thin man stagger from the undergrowth beside the road and fall headlong into my path. In the ensuing skid, I avoided him by no more than inches but on jumping out of my truck to give him a piece of my mind, I was astonished to see, as he picked himself up, that he was barely more than a skeleton, covered in a patchwork of thin cotton rags.*

*'Monsieur,' he gasped in French with an accent that said he was no Provençale peasant, 'I see you are a British officer and I pray that you will help me in this, my hour of need.'*

*'Tell me,' I said, 'are you ill? Do you need a doctor?'*

*'Alas, monsieur, you see me in this state not because of illness but because of long cruel hunger and ill treatment. I have just returned from a place close to Hell, a place named Sobibor.'*

*The name struck me like a hammer blow. Being privy to the latest military intelligence, I was aware as others were not of its significance. As those of us close to the heart of the command structure learnt of the death camps built in the shelter of the Polish forests, we finally understood the full evil of Hitler's programme of extermination. Of these camps, Sobibor was amongst the worst – a production line of death, whose name should be ranked with*

228

*Treblinka and the rest in the darker annals of the barbaric history of that time.*

I stopped and muttered something to myself, remembering reading that name before in Max's earlier story of the old woman in the Bugatti in Paris. This wasn't going to fill in any gaps. He'd changed the story. It seemed far more likely to add to the puzzle.

'What is it?' Tiggy asked.

'Doesn't matter,' I said. 'I'll tell you later,' and I went on.

*Those of us who carried the burden of this knowledge were inclined to be less forgiving of any German prisoners we encountered and more determined in our attempts to track down collaborators who played their part in sending innocent people to that grim end. I was therefore fully aware that to have returned with his life from that vile place made this man a rare survivor indeed.*

*'Are you alone?' I asked, as I helped him into the passenger seat of my truck and gave him the lunch I had taken with me.*

*'My wife remained at Sobibor,' he said simply, and I knew enough to understand what that must mean and did not question him any further. He ate my sandwiches as if they were the finest food he had ever seen, not ravenously like the starving man he clearly was, but almost fastidiously, and when he had finished I asked him how I could be of service.*

*'In the old days of the other age before the war,' he said, 'I was a wealthy man and I lived in a great house here in these hills, a house with a large estate and a wall around it and there I lived happily with my wife, attending to the needs of the estate and keeping a careful eye on my investments. In the year 1943, due to the jealousy of a business partner whom I had regarded also as a friend, over the matter of a motorcar of all things, I was falsely denounced to the occupying powers and my wife and I were arrested as Jews.'*

*'And are you a Jew?' I asked, because there was little about him to suggest that might be the case.*

*'No, monsieur, I am not,' he replied, 'but my ancestry is complicated and most of my family came from certain parts of Armenia where there was much about the people which might be mistaken for the features of that unhappy race, so I was not able to prove my accusers wrong.' He sat up a little straighter in the seat, though I could see that the effort caused him pain, and held out a hand to me in a formal manner.*

'I have not introduced myself,' he said. 'I am Paul Tajirian, at your service.'

'And I am Captain Max Birkin Owen of the Grenadier Guards at yours,' I replied.

'Regardless of anything I could say, we were sent away, my wife and I, shipped off like cattle first to a labour camp where we suffered for many months and then when our strength was exhausted, to the final meeting with our fate at Sobibor.'

'But you survived,' I said.

'Only through chance,' he answered. 'At the very moment in which we were herded from the transport into that grim place, the moment when we knew we had crossed the Rubicon and there was no hope left, a word passed amongst our guards and though we did not then know what it was, it was possible to see a change take place in them. It was the word that told them their plan had finally failed and their leader was dead.'

'They let you go?'

'No. They did their best to kill us all so there would be no witnesses to what had happened in that place but for some of them, the younger ones, their heart was no longer in it and they were thinking perhaps of a future world in which such orders would no longer be given. I lay there under the hopeless cover of undergrowth into which I had crawled and one such guard came to me, raised his gun and fired a shot which missed my head by an inch so that the pain of the blast of hot gas from the barrel of his gun made me cry out. Then he lowered his gun, speaking in German that I understood clearly: "You are dead. Dead men lie still." And he went on his way.'

'And after that?'

'After that I crawled deeper into hiding until all had gone, then I went to search for my wife and I found her and I buried her with the last of the strength and the words which were left to me. Then the Russians came and after very many more difficulties and a series of fortunate happenings I made my way back here.'

He fell silent for a short time, then spoke in a low voice, staring out ahead of him through the windscreen of the little truck.

'Now that I have come back, I wish I had stayed there,' he said in the end with some vehemence, 'so my bones could have mingled with my wife's in the Polish earth.'

I remembered what he had said when I stopped the truck for him. 'You spoke of your need, monsieur, and asked me to help you. What is that need?'

'I returned to my house this morning,' he said. 'I approached it aware that I was using the last of my reserve, hoping to find that my old servant Alphonse was still there, that he might have kept the house safe for me against my return.'

'And you did not?'

He made a despairing noise. 'Alphonse was not there. Instead, I found the last person on earth I wished to see. Jacques Sommer, the man who denounced me.'

'He was living there?'

The man nodded. 'From the moment we had been taken away, I would guess.'

'Did he see you?'

'Oh yes. I was filled with so great an anger when I saw him through the windows that I hammered on the door and shouted in the greatest voice I could find for him to come out and face me. He came out, monsieur, and he laughed at me and said I was a walking dead man. I tried to hit him. I could not help myself, but my strength failed me utterly and when he pushed me, I fell over. Then he cursed and kicked me and I feared for my life.'

'How did you escape?'

'He ran at me to kick me again and all my suffering, all my pain and all my anger came together in my hands to give me power and I clutched at his foot and caught it and pulled him so he fell backwards and hit his head on the step. He lay there, stunned, and I crawled away from him and got myself to my feet and walked off as quickly as I could until I came to the back gate and from there I pushed on through the woods until I came to this bank and fell into your path.'

'Your house is near here, then?'

'No more than one kilometre.'

I looked at my watch. There was time. My duty to the Duke would wait for a little while and he, great soul that he was, would surely approve.

'Come with me, then,' I said. 'We will go there now and deal with this collaborator.'

'Monsieur,' said the man, 'I appreciate it greatly but you are alone. Would it not be wiser to summon your men?'

'There is no need for that,' I said, because I too felt infused with a righteous anger at the story. 'He will not argue with an officer in the Grenadier Guards and if he does, it will not be for long.' I did not even bother to ask if Sommer was alone in the house.

Under his direction, we turned in through the ruined gate of a fine old estate and drove down a long drive to draw up in front of a large, ancient house almost obscured by the creepers that clung to it in profusion. At my insistence, he crawled into the back of the truck to be out of sight. I sounded the horn of the truck in a peremptory way and after a few blasts a man appeared at the door, a man I disliked on sight, a fat man with a bald head and small eyes who squinted down at me and waited, saying nothing. He was holding a pad of cloth to the back of his head.

I got out of the truck and he still said nothing, so I said, 'Monsieur Sommer?' in French.

'And what if I was?' he replied in a boorish manner.

'Then I would have to inform you that the Headquarters of Allied Forces are considering investigating allegations against you concerning charges of collaboration.'

I put on my best staff officer's voice and it seemed to get through to him. His jaw dropped open. 'But monsieur,' he said in a smaller and more polite voice.

'There are no buts,' I said. 'You are also required to leave this house immediately and not return.'

'It is my house,' he blustered.

'You know that is not true. Failure to obey will lead to the most serious consequences.'

I unbuttoned my holster to show I was serious and he blanched.

'I need time to gather my possessions,' he said.

'Five minutes is all the time you deserve,' I said sternly.

He disappeared into the house and I stood there considering. After two or three minutes had passed, I followed him in and found him standing in a scene of indescribable squalor. It had once been a fine dining room but now it was littered with filthy glasses and empty bottles of wine, and in a clear space in the middle of the table the man was shovelling wads of banknotes into a leather Gladstone bag.

It was clear that he was a black marketeer. No other trade in that lawless and famished time could have earned him so much hard currency. The evidence was stacked against the walls, crates and crates of wine bearing the emblem of an excellent Bordeaux vineyard.

'Stop,' I said. 'Put that bag down. I am confiscating that money on suspicion that it is the product of illegal activities.'

'Why are you doing this?' he said. 'It is nothing to you.'

'I am doing this for Paul Tajirian and for Sobibor,' I replied.

He frowned uncomprehendingly but he was not inclined to obey me until I pulled my service revolver from my holster and then he took my point. I escorted him to the door but his eyes kept straying backwards towards the bag of money and at the door he decided to make his stand. He lunged at my gun but I stepped back, raised it and fired a shot over his head. He took to his heels then, running for his life down the drive, and I encouraged him on his way with a couple of well-aimed shots into the gravel behind him.

When he had gone, I opened the back of the truck.

'You may come out now, Monsieur Tajirian,' I said. 'The house is yours again.'

He climbed slowly and painfully out and looked at it mournfully.

'You are kind,' he said, 'but I cannot stay here. This is a house that eats money and I have none. My days here are past.'

I led him inside and showed him the contents of the Gladstone bag. 'You can feed your house and yourself.'

He sat down at the table and stared at the money in amazement, shaking his head, then he looked at the cases of wine. 'But this is my wine. Why is it not in the cellar?'

'I think Sommer has been selling it. Good wine is rare now. That is perhaps where the money has come from. Be assured the money belongs to you. It is the very least that can be done to make up for things.'

There were tears in his eyes and he nodded. We pulled two chairs up to the table.

'What did you mean, monsieur,' I asked, 'when you told me that his jealousy started over the matter of a motorcar?'

So he told me the story of the great car he had bought before the war, the remarkable Bugatti Royale, the Golden Bug, and how Sommer had been consumed with jealousy over it. It was, he said, a machine of vast *size, luxury and colossal speed and I knew he was not exaggerating because I knew of the famous car myself.*

'Sommer wanted it so badly,' he said, 'so badly that I considered letting him have it but then I suppose I already knew his wanting would not end there. There was the house and my wife as well, and I believe he wanted both of those.'

'What became of the car?' I asked.

He shrugged. 'I expect the Nazis found it,' he said, 'but perhaps not. At the start of the war Alphonse and I concealed it well. Perhaps even Sommer has failed to find it.'

It took a great deal of work, hacking through the concealing vegetation at the back of the stableyard to his instructions and then painfully forcing open the rusted hinges of the door that was finally revealed, but it was all worthwhile when at last the sunlight penetrated the hidden shed for the first time in many years and revealed the sleeping monster within.

At the sight of it, he began to cry.

'Close the door,' he said, 'I do not wish to see it again. For that car, my poor wife gave her life. I wish it gone. I shall burn it.'

I gave a cry of alarm. 'That would be a crime, monsieur.'

He looked at me. 'You like it? Then you shall have it. That is the very least I can do for the officer who has restored to me my house and my fortunes.'

It was at that moment that another man came into the courtyard, a small man with grey hair and a big moustache who looked hard at us then ran with cries of pleasure towards Paul Tajirian. It was Alphonse and I knew then that his master would have a good and devoted friend to nurse him back to health.

Nothing I could say would sway him from his determination that I should have the car and in the weeks to come I was able to arrange the transportation of the great machine back to England where I ran it for several extraordinary years but always, whenever I drove it, my mind was carried back to that terrible place in the Polish forest and, in the end, I was glad when it passed to another owner.

Not all, it seems to me, is really fair in love or in war.

I stopped and noticed that Tiggy was dabbing her eyes.

'Don't waste your tears,' I said.

'Don't say that,' she said, affronted. 'I thought it was a wonderful story.'

'It was, but that's all it was – just a story.'

'Why do you say that?' She sounded indignant.

'Because I've read the real version of how he got that car. The original version he wrote before he decided to change it all.'

'There's a different version?'

'Completely.'

'What's different about it?'

So I told her about Max's black market dealings, about Alphonse selling him the wine and the car and, at the end, about his dismissive treatment of the old woman, the Sobibor survivor who confronted him in Paris.

'How do you know that's the real version, not this one?' said Tiggy, who clearly didn't want to accept my verdict.

'I'm getting to know Max pretty well, that's how. I think he saw the car and he wanted it and he didn't ask too many questions.'

'But he did, didn't he? You said he mentioned Sobibor at the end of the first story and he said something about wondering if all was fair in war.'

'Hindsight,' I said. 'I think the word just stuck in his mind and he found out later.'

'So he felt guilty?'

'Yes, I suppose so, and so what does he do? He rewrites his own history to let himself off the hook.'

'You don't know that for certain. You don't even know if the first one you read *was* the first version.'

That had a disturbing truth to it.

'Who do you think these stories were *for*, Miles?'

'I don't know. Not for his children. He didn't have any. For publication?'

'I don't think so. How could they be? If they were lies, all his friends would know, wouldn't they?'

'Maybe he told them the same lies,' I said. I wasn't up to an argument.

'Not if he kept changing it.'

'All right then, what's *your* theory?'

'I think he wrote them completely for himself,' she said. 'Maybe

235

as a sort of apology, because they tell it the way he *wishes* it had been.'

'I don't know. I think it's very sad. It makes him so unreliable.'

'Oh, right,' she said, 'that's a bit rich coming from Mr Reliable here. Maybe you shouldn't be so judgemental. I think Sob – whatever it's called, must have stuck in Max's mind and one day he found out and then he was horrified.'

'What would that prove?'

'It would prove he had a conscience.'

'So he rewrote the story and that's meant to make everything *better*?'

'I think it's a magic diary,' she said. 'If he couldn't bear the facts, he could rub them out and start again.'

'Oh I see, so I could just write a story saying the Colonel was still alive and everyone would stop blaming me?'

She looked at me, shocked, then reached out a hand and touched my cheek. 'Oh, poor Miles,' she said.

I wished I hadn't said it and I didn't want to go on with that.

'I don't know if all this is right. He could have written the story for this woman I've just seen, Sam. I think they had something going once. Why did he give it to her if not?'

'Perhaps. There's this brother of his, isn't there? What's he called?'

'Douglas.'

'Didn't you say Douglas was a *real* hero?'

'Yes, I think he was. He seems to have been right in the thick of it all through the war while Max was stuck in training camps back here.'

'And didn't you say this woman Sam reckoned he was the more attractive of the two?'

'Definitely. She said there was something empty about Max.'

'So this was Max's attempt to prove he was a hero too.'

'It's a bit over the top, isn't it? All this pompous stuff about the Grenadier Guards. He's just boosting his ego all the time, pretending he's John Wayne, shooting his revolver at the villain's feet as he runs away.'

'So he's a child. Can't you see the need in him?'

'I'm not sure I can be quite that easy on him,' I said, turning my head to listen as a car drove up the lane then droned on by. 'For another thing, he's a terrible racist.'

'Yes, I spotted that,' Tiggy said. 'He didn't want the man to actually *be* a Jew.'

'So what *can* you tell about Max?'

'Only that he was capable of feeling guilt and that some people mattered enough to make him want them to think well of him.'

'Isn't that true of everybody?'

'No, I don't think so,' said Tiggy. 'It's true of you though, isn't it? You've got a conscience about things that aren't even your fault, really.'

'Meaning?'

'Don't sound so aggressive. You know what I mean.'

I was still sitting on the grass and my eyes blurred a little and then she got down from the seat, sat beside me and put an arm round me, tugging my head down on to her shoulder. 'Come on,' she said, 'I know it must have been horrible last night. I shouldn't have invited you.'

'Why did you?'

'I wasn't sure if you were all right. It was hopeless trying to see you in London with . . . well, with other people around.'

I knew she meant Cat.

'I think you're having a hard time at the moment, aren't you?' She moved away from me and looked at me. 'You're taking too many . . . risks.'

She'd been going to say something else and I felt she had no right to go sticking her nose in.

'Don't look at me like that,' she said.

I got to my feet. I didn't need a lecture. She sighed. 'Oh dear, now you're going away. Well, if you need to talk, just ring me. I'm going to be here for a while.'

'Ring here? What happens if your mother answers the phone?'

'Use a different name. Disguise your voice. Say it's Max. Remember, if you find out any more about him, make sure you let me know.'

'I will.'

'Same thing goes if you find out any more about yourself.'

I thought about that one all the way back.

237

# Twenty-one

All that happened around the Hunt Ball tipped me off balance and set the scene for an unsettling week, in which I did things that might have been better left undone and went somewhere I didn't expect to go. When I left Sussex, accelerating from foot to bus to train as if breaking free from its gravitational grasp, I thought I couldn't wait to be back in town and it would make me feel better in every way. It didn't. When I reached London, slowing down through those same stages, I found I didn't want to be there either and it all began to fall apart. I brought it on my own head from the moment I walked into the flat still wearing my worse-for-wear dinner jacket to find Cat waiting like a trap for me, in scornful mood. The jacket told a clear story of where I'd been, so in pre-emptive self-defence I gave her an edited version of my run-in with the police, doing my best to make it sound dramatic. Cat showed no sign of being impressed and, as I told the story, that undermining enemy part of me which always sits in judgement began to hear it through her ears – an incompetent encounter which had come to nothing and, to someone like her, would have been just laughable. I left out what Tiggy had done to help me because I knew Cat would use it for ridicule, indeed I left Tiggy out completely and she didn't spot the gaps in the plot.

Cat rolled a joint and offered me some as an afterthought and the day slowed down. She got horny as she often did when she was a little bit stoned, and because I happened to be there we performed athletic sex, her body with its skin that felt like tight brown rubber arching above me, hair flailing. She looked everywhere but at me and there was no love in it but we stayed lying with each other for a long time. In that addled silence, we smoked some more of the harder stuff, the stuff I didn't like to think of by its right name, its frightening name, but preferred to call smack or skag like she did.

She had a lot of it and I didn't realize until afterwards that she'd found my cash and late that evening, when she told me that I had no idea what it was *really* like, she produced a syringe and challenged me to turn the offer down. Warnings came to me too faintly, dull knockings on a far-off door, and in the end I lay back and let her do it to me and wished I hadn't and was blissfully glad I had all at the same time. For the first time, in that extraordinarily peaceful place it takes you to where all the knots of life are ironed out, she seemed to be treating me as an equal, not as some specimen on whom she was performing a perverse and intricate experiment.

When I came down, I felt an overwhelming and rather childish relief that nothing significant had changed and that I did not immediately crave for another hit, but perhaps something changed after all because when Cat offered me some more of the same the next day, I didn't feel anything like the same reluctance, feeling now that I knew I could handle the stuff. We lived like that for a few days, cruising along until there was no more left. I got nothing done because in that frame of mind all the pressure that drives you to do anything simply vanishes.

It took a lot to get through that haze but Cat managed to spur me out of it when she had tipped the last of the powder out of the cellophane packet because then she got up and pulled my old travelling bag out of the cupboard. It was only then, as I watched her from the cushions, that I realized that she shouldn't be unzipping the little pocket inside the bag because she shouldn't know that was where I had stashed what was left of Ephraim's money.

'What are you doing?' I said drowsily.

'We need some more.'

'Yeah, but why . . . Have you been taking my money?'

I got up unsteadily and she turned away to try to keep the bag from me. I pulled it out of her hands and reached into the pocket. What I took out was a much smaller roll of notes, which left a cold, sick feeling inside me. There was only a hundred and fifty pounds of it left and I realized that what we'd been sticking into us that week represented the rest of it.

'How did you find that?'

'I just looked.'

'In *my* bag?'

'Serves you right for hiding it. If you don't trust people that's what happens.'

239

'If I *did* trust you it would still have happened only faster, right?'

'Call it my fee if you like.'

'Your fee? Fee for what?'

'Turning you into a real person.'

'Oh, really? From what?'

'From a stuck-up, scared little Lord Fauntleroy, public school, bull-shitting toss-pot.'

I couldn't think of a quick reply.

'You've had half of it anyway,' she said, which was true.

'No more,' I said. 'I need that cash.' Though I had a pang of regret at the thought of life without the little sting and its delicious wave of ecstasy.

'You can get some more.'

'How?'

'Your friend from Israel, he seems to give you lots.'

I couldn't think who she meant for a minute. 'Ephraim? You're talking about Ephraim? He pays me when I sell things for him. That's all. What's he got to do with it?'

'He rang you, didn't he?'

'When?'

'Don't bloody shout like that! When you were away poncing around at your ball.'

'Christ almighty and you didn't tell me? What day is it?'

'Thursday.'

'Oh, Jesus.' I hadn't called him back. He wasn't a patient man. If it was more business, the chances were he would have put it Pete's way by now.

Cat left, as she always did when she knew she was in the wrong. I dialled Israel as soon as the door closed behind her.

'Miles. You take your bloody time,' he said in his growly voice.

'Ephraim. I only just got the message.'

'That was your secretary I spoke with?'

'No, no. No way. Just a girl. Not the most reliable person in the world.'

'She has other points, I bet.'

I wasn't sure. 'Anyway, can I help?'

'Maybe. Maybe not. You didn't call so I rang Peter.'

Damn. 'I'm sorry. I didn't know. I would have rung you straight away if she'd told me.'

He chuckled. 'Peter is away. He does not answer either.' Great. He'd been winding me up.

'Okay,' I said slowly, 'what exactly is it you want?'

'I want you to do some travelling for me. You don't mind travelling? First you must come here.'

'To Israel?'

'Yes, yes, of course. Can you not hear what I am saying? Why do you ask these questions? Just come. Go buy a one-way ticket.'

'Aren't I coming back?'

'Of course you are but I have other ticket for you here. You must go somewhere else after here. I will fix all that. Buy your ticket and come as soon as you can. Bring clothes for one week or two. I will give you back the ticket money when you arrive. I meet you at the airport, at Lod.'

I had never done anything like that before.

'It's a bit difficult.'

'Then I phone Peter again. Is never difficult for Peter.'

'No. I'm coming. Just a day or two, that's all.'

The problem, as I knew all too clearly once I'd put the phone down, was that Ephraim thought I was a big-time trader. Though we had now talked twenty or thirty times on the phone, we had never actually met. I'd bought some parts he'd advertised in one of the aeroplane rags and sold them off again pretty quickly, then he'd started ringing me when he had other stuff to sell. I'd done pretty well for him so far but from things he'd said from time to time on the phone, I knew perfectly well he had an inflated idea of what sort of operation I ran. He sounded as though he'd been in the game for a long time. I could imagine him – about forty, pretty tough, a desert fighter to match the gravel voice. The Miles he was expecting would have the ready money for a ticket and all the right clothes for whatever occasion. The Miles he was expecting would have a creased passport full of entry stamps, not my pristine example with a teenage photo from a school exchange trip to Heidelberg.

I had exactly a hundred and fifty pounds and I didn't think that was going to cover me for all eventualities on a mystery tour of the Middle East.

Booking the ticket took most of it and the earliest I could get on a flight was Monday so in desperation I got out all the bits and pieces I'd put aside for a rainy day and went selling. My favourite Dinky toy dealer operated out of a stall in Alfie's Market in Church Street and he blinked when I opened my bag and started bringing out valuable toy cars by the handful.

'What's this then?' he asked. 'Is this a closing down sale or have you robbed a museum?'

I got five hundred pounds for a bunch of stuff that should have raised half as much again, but everyone's cash was tight and cash was what I needed so it would just have to do. I spent nearly a hundred of it on a jacket, jeans, shirts and shoes which I hoped, by being at least new if not especially smart, would get me by. I got some sunglasses as well because my eyes seemed suddenly very sensitive to bright light and I suspected there would be a lot of that in Israel.

That left Sunday and on Sunday I felt like I was coming down with something. I had a terrible headache and I couldn't get comfortable in the flat, where the chairs seemed hard and hostile. My joints ached like the worst flu I'd ever had. Aspirin didn't get anywhere near it. The thought of travelling far outside the previous boundaries of my life was extremely frightening, as if bad things were lying in wait.

The trunk produced two letters to distract me, two letters from opposite ends of Max's spectrum. Richard P Curtis typed a neat letter on headed notepaper to him in November 1960 from Oakland, California.

Dear Max,

At this time of year I expect you'll be working on some dodge to take a bunch of good-looking popsies as paying guests to one of your winter flesh-pots like St Moritz or Davos. Marcie and I just came back from a hunting trip in Montana where we were up above 7,000 feet much of the time and turning blue with cold every night.

Back in June, we brought Marcie's Jaguar out here with us on the Queen Elizabeth then drove right the way across. Easy stuff in that car, it held 110 mph all day.

Towards the end of our sojourn in Europe, I was becoming decidedly nervous about the political situation. Those Frogs know how to make problems. Now, the damn Russkies and all their Warsaw Pact pals are stirring up so much trouble I suppose the best thing we can do is stay right here. As you say, even merry old England is crawling with people who just don't belong there these days. On the other hand, it is a sight more amusing over your side. The laughs we've had, eh old boy? Remember that pub near Silverstone where we filled my room with all the fixings for Pimms and the old trout who ran it tried to throw us out and you said you were the Duke of Nottingham? It was worth the bill.

If we do decide to make another trip, I would plan to arrive in your neck of the woods in April maybe, so we could do the Aintree race as well as the Grand Prix. The Mercedes is still garaged in Geneva so we might go get it on the way and bring it over in that funny ferry plane from Le Touquet, taking your advice of course.

On the subject of Geneva and times past, we saw a piece in our local newspaper about the lovely Natalie. She was performing something or other in 'Frisco. Lauren Dawnay's sister Jo met her in New York at some event or other. Says she's living quietly out in the Berkshires and couldn't stop asking after you. The old flame still burns, I guess.

Say hello to all the auto racing and boozing fraternity for me. Try something different and ANSWER this note for a change!

All our best and keep that natty chauffeur's suit well pressed.

Rick and Marcie.


The second letter was from a year earlier, on a smaller, scruffier piece of lined paper, a prison letter form. An off-centre red stamp filled in the prison name as WORMWOOD SCRUBS. There were initials and numbers scrawled on it in various places as if it had been passed by censors. The writer's name was 'Boxhall' and his pen hadn't been working at all well because the letters varied wildly from thick and blotchy to almost illegibly faint.

Dear Max,

I have received permission for you to visit me so that we can sort out the business we have on hand. Could you also ring Josh Miller, or find him at the Coachmaker's and ask him if he has yet received the money from R James and if he hasn't, please go ahead with a county court summons. Please excuse writing but nib is not good and no others available. Have you been able to fix that bill for fifty bob? It is most important. I am sure you will not mind doing these things as you will know very well that I would not be here at all if I had not taken your advice. Please reply by return as it is horrible in here. My best to your girlfriend.

Alfred.

Another sad little mystery. I wondered what Max had advised Alfred to do and how long a sentence that had earned him. I lost the appetite for reading then and was finding it hard to breathe in the flat so I went out on to the September streets with no deliberate intention except that of walking aimlessly through the leaf-falls to clear my head, and immediately found my traitorous feet taking me deliberately and directly to Weston House. I walked past, then felt myself drawn back, so I sat down on a low wall opposite and stared at the windows of the old folks' home.

Inside was the certain reality of Max Birkin Owen. Outside was me, guessing, with my suppositions and concoctions about him. The wall was an impregnable barrier put there by my choice just as much as by my forced promise to Sam Bishop. I could probably concoct an excuse to get in. Perhaps I could say I wanted a place for my father and ask to look round, just for the chance of catching a glimpse of him, of knowing the living presence of Max. Supposing I could sit down and talk to him, what then? It takes ages to get to know someone that way, to really get to know them, especially if you're young and they're old. The trunk had given me a shortcut, a much faster way of knowing the real Max and, apart from curiosity, no purpose could be served by going in.

I could see the tops of white-haired heads through the downstairs window, the inmates sitting in their chairs in some day-room where the seats were too low and the windows too high for them to see out. The occasional nurse walked amongst them. Sitting there on my wall, I almost persuaded myself I could see which one was him, a forehead which was browner than most with a thin covering of curly hair, leaning diagonally against the wing of a maroon armchair. The whole time I watched, that forehead never moved once. Did Natalie know that Max was here, that this was where his inability to give up his fictions had brought him instead of to a full old age with her? Did he bring it all on himself? Had his strokes only come to cripple him because of the self-inflicted stresses of that life?

I looked at that still forehead and thought after all that it might not be much of a living presence in there and that perhaps it was best to preserve Max as I knew him. I was glad my promise to Sam Bishop gave me such a good excuse.

Back at the flat, I filled a file to take with me, putting in some of the papers I wanted to read again and a few more promising possibilities pulled out of the unread pile. After that, I found I hated the idea of leaving the trunk so vulnerable to anything Cat might decide to do, so I stowed all the rest of its contents back in it, lashed it up with a length of clothes-line and took it upstairs. Old Mr Pascal on the second floor, who'd been very grateful when I found his cat for him, said he'd look after it for me while I was away. When he closed his door on me, I felt I was leaving Max behind, flying away from him. I had no idea then how much closer to the reality of Max my trip would bring me.

I tried to have a nap but I had to keep rubbing my legs and arms to stop the cramps and later on as I was packing my bag, still feeling dreadful, Cat's friend Jago knocked, thinking Cat was in. He couldn't wait to get away when he found it was just me, but I knew Cat bought some of her stuff from him and before he went I managed to score a little bag of it. I tried smoking some but it seemed to be weak stuff so I found Cat's needle and did for the first time what she had done for me before, overcoming my distaste at sticking it in me. It was more effective than any medicine for whatever I had and it made me feel much better straight away.

Cat came back at some point. She looked at my bag and asked me where I was going. 'Israel,' I said.

'Oh, right,' was all she answered.

Monday was the 1st of October. I was very nervous on the flight and all the more so when there was nobody to meet me as agreed at Lod airport and no answer from Ephraim's number when I had got my hands on some change and discovered the right way to dial on an Israeli phone. It was a low point. The El Al flight had already been quite an experience, starting at the check-in desk. I didn't know airline security could be so strict and I was extremely glad I had abandoned my first mad idea of taking what was left of the powder in the bag with me. I also had no real idea what Israel would be like except some mistaken inkling that it would be a sterile, ultra-modern place. This half-Arab, half-European terminal in the hot desert air was far more unsettling than I had expected. London had been in the middle of a cool autumn spell when I left. The heat came as a shock.

I was not the only one waiting for somebody else to turn up. The crowds from my plane had gone and there was a lull. In front of the terminal, there was a young man sitting on the bonnet of a tatty old Peugeot, looking at his watch. I decided he was probably an Arab but I'd wondered at first if he might be a driver from Ephraim, sent to pick me up, so I'd loitered around near him looking hopeful but he hadn't given me a second glance. Then another car pulled in just behind him, a new Opel, and the man in it matched my image of Ephraim perfectly – aviator shades with leather side-guards and a medallion round his neck. I walked across to it and the driver wound down the window, looking at me questioningly.

'Ephraim?' I said. 'I'm Miles.'

He just frowned crossly and shook his head, then the young Arab who wasn't an Arab after all uncoiled himself from the bonnet of his old car and astonished me by saying in Ephraim's familiar, growly old voice, as if by ventriloquism, 'Miles? You're Miles? Oh boy, did I have you figured wrong.'

'Me too,' I said, looking him up and down. He looked younger than I was and he also looked like he didn't have two beans to rub together.

'I thought you were much older,' he said, and we both laughed.

'Oh shit,' he said. 'Babes in the wood together. We better go hide before the wicked witch comes.'

'Where are we going?'

'Somewhere for a beer then another place to show you something.'

Over a beer in a bar with fans everywhere, we talked about old aeroplanes which helped make me feel less far away, cut off and vulnerable, and about the bits and pieces I had sold for him. That made us feel like a team, almost like friends. Then Ephraim started to talk about new aeroplanes instead of old ones and undid the whole process.

'I like to fly best in the early morning,' he said, 'before the heat starts, when you can see the rocks of Sinai, sharp like through a telescope.'

Until that moment, I hadn't realized he was a pilot. I'd assumed he was just another one like me, on the edges of flying, fingering the old bits and dreaming of their history.

'What do you fly?' I asked, expecting him to say one of the usual things, like maybe Piper or Cessna. I'd flown a Cessna myself. Twice. That is I'd taken the controls for a few minutes, safely up in the air.

'Kaffeer,' he said, or that was what it sounded like. I'd never heard of it.

'How's that again?' I said. 'Don't know it.'

'Spelt K-F-I-R,' he replied. 'Kfir. Israeli plane. We make them here. I am, what do you say? Converting to it.'

He then utterly destroyed my new-found confidence by explaining quietly and without a hint of boasting that the Kfir was a fighter aircraft based on the French Mirage 5, with an enormous jet engine out of a Phantom somehow stuffed into it, good for more than twice the speed of sound.

As I listened, this bar we were in, which had become almost comfortable, rediscovered an alien edge. For a few minutes I had thought we were equals, Ephraim and I, but now as I looked at him, it became clear to me that I was nowhere near him. The sinews of his body were controlled by skills and a quality of determination which I could not for a moment aspire to. He knew what the cutting-edge of life was like, I could only read the accounts of others.

'You're in the air force?'

'Of course. Maybe what you would call the reserve. This is Israel. It is only six years since we were last at war.'

'You flew in the Six Day War?'

'I was too young. How 'bout you? You fly modern stuff or just the old-timers?'

The whole thing had suddenly turned inside out on me. This kid of my age was the real thing. I didn't dare ask him what rank he was in case he turned out to be a colonel. I felt like a complete sham confronted by this defining question of his, which was why I shook my head and looked at him and said, 'Just the old-timers,' and suddenly the picture of bullshit Max and truthful Douglas came into my head, and I knew which of us was which and wished I hadn't said it.

'What types, Spits?' asked Ephraim with interest. 'You ever fly the Mark Nine?'

It seemed as though this might lead into a discussion of flying characteristics which would expose me as a fraud, so I borrowed inspiration from Max.

'I've not done much lately. Medical problem, had a bit of a crunch,' and managed to look sufficiently brave and sad that he changed the subject.

'You did well for me with those wings and stuff,' he said, and I felt that I had successfully crossed a minefield.

We finished our beers and got back in his car in the sudden darkness to start a long, slow drive. I was trying to see what we were passing, foreign smells flooding in from the open windows, but I had no idea where we were or which direction we were going in and in the end, after passing little enclaves of activity, shops, flaring gas lights and sounds of exotic music, we thudded off the road, through a ditch and up on to a long, long, twisty track. I caught a glimpse of a black hulk beside the road with a gun barrel drooping beside it.

'What's that?'

'Tank.'

'What's it doing there?'

'From the Six Day War. A dead one.'

He was concentrating on the track and he braked hard as a camel wandered into the headlights, swearing at it as it dipped and scrambled off into the dark.

'Like butterflies,' he said, 'they like the headlamps.'

'Moths,' I corrected.

We stopped after a long, uncomfortable time and he got out, taking a big flashlight with him.

'Come on,' he said. 'Not far.'

Over a sand bank beside the road was a flat, hard surface and some way across that, through a maze of twisted metal, lumps of concrete and the shells of roofless huts, was what looked like a junk pile except that when he shone his flashlight to one side you could see it was all heaped up against the wall of a wide, low building, hangar-sized but not like any hangar I had ever seen. He ducked through a gap and I followed and what I saw when I was inside made the whole journey worthwhile.

'P51,' said Ephraim. 'Mine.' He didn't like wasting words.

The P51 Mustang was America's equivalent of the Spitfire and the huge, dark, dusty machine took my breath away, standing there on its wide-set undercarriage, the tyres flat, but who cared about that? It was filthy, scarred and dented, but from the four-bladed propeller backwards it looked all there. A flyer's dream, the ultimate warbird.

'How did you find it?' I asked.

'I ask and I search.'

'How did it get here?'

'World War Two. P51H. Long-range job for the Far East. You know it?'

'By repute. Fastest one they ever built.'

'Yeah. Finished up here. Don't know how.'

'Markings?' I said, taking the flashlight from him and playing it over the wings and fuselage, looking for US Air Force stars or unit letters.

'None. Painted over. Maybe the Hagana hid it.'

'The Hagana?'

'Yeah. You know, our army before we were a state. They bought what they could here and there. Maybe they bought this. Maybe they stole it. My guess is someone hid it here, then . . .' He shrugged and made a throat-cutting gesture.

'You own it now? You bought it?'

'I got it. The man who owns the land, he got something for it in exchange.'

'You brought me all the way here to see this? Why? Do you want to sell it?'

'What you think I am? A travel agent? You think I decide to give you a holiday, Miles? Huh.'

'I'll need a good set of photos, and some sort of survey report on its condition.'

'Done. Full set. Inside and out. Back at my place.'

'What sort of state is it in?'

'Rebuild job. Not total though. Dry air here so no corrosion. Structure looks okay. Engine turns. Someone did a proper job. Pushed it full of oil and grease.'

'It'll take a while to do it properly. Mustangs are a bit rare in England.'

'Who said England? Did I say England? You don't sell this in England. Are you crazy? You sell this in America. Maybe I call Peter. He wouldn't say crazy things like that.'

'Just testing,' I said.

'You go to America tomorrow. Sell it quick.'

'America? Tomorrow?'

'Your ears okay? Yeah, sure, America tomorrow. I book your seat. Economy class.'

I didn't have a clue where to start except for a vague idea that there was something called the Confederate Airforce down in Nevada or somewhere like that, but I didn't want to admit it.

'Why don't *you* go?' I said.

'Can't. Duty.'

It took more than a day because he'd forgotten I had to get a visa and the American Embassy took its time to satisfy itself that I really deserved one. I wasn't feeling great again, maybe because of the heat, but on Thursday, after a lot of hanging around, I was on my way by Pan-Am to New York with a ticket on to London in my pocket plus seven hundred dollars which Ephraim insisted was easily enough to cover my expenses. I wasn't so sure. My head ached badly on the plane and I was desperately uncomfortable, cramped and scratchy in the seat. There wasn't nearly enough leg room for someone my size and the plane was full so I couldn't spread out. It hurt. Balanced against that was the knowledge that if I could get Ephraim's

250

price I was going to be better off to the tune of ten thousand quid.

Going to America for the first time would have been a scary, amazing experience if I hadn't just dulled the parts of me that could feel such things in the exotic overdose of Israel. I spent a lot of unnecessary time on the flight wondering how on earth I was going to start finding a buyer for the Mustang, but I needn't have worried. The first bookstall I saw when I arrived at JFK offered me three different aviation magazines. I tried to be a hard-nosed businessman on the ride into Manhattan and read through them for useful contacts, but the fairy-tale towers ahead got me instead and I gawped out of the cab window in wonder. I'd been hoping for a helpful cabbie, one of Natalie's Brooklyn grizzlies maybe, but it seemed they were an extinct breed. My driver spoke little English and had trouble finding the mid-town hotel Ephraim had booked for me through his uncle, who he said was something big in catering in New Jersey.

I woke early the next morning, Friday, jet-lag laying an extra layer of discomfort over my dehydrated, aching head and, unable to get back to sleep, read the aircraft magazines. After breakfast, when their offices opened, I rang one of the editors and told him I had an unknown Mustang for sale and he could have the story and the pictures for his magazine if he helped me out. Within half an hour I was getting phone calls. By the end of the day there were a dozen possible buyers lined up, all wanting to see the pictures and discuss price. We fixed on Monday for a series of meetings at the hotel and that left me the weekend.

That was when my thoughts turned to Natalie.

# Twenty-two

I have never been very good at being left to myself with nothing to do so it was a form of cowardice that made me decide to track down Natalie. On the plane from Tel Aviv, an unexpected weekend in New York with no commitments had seemed exciting, until the weekend began to arrive. Now, looking diagonally down at the noisy Manhattan street from my hotel bedroom brought home to me that it was likely to be horrible. Two days of lonely sightseeing and solitary eating with only an internal dialogue to sustain me when I didn't know where to go or what to do was the worst thing I could think of, especially in the rain that had just started to sweep past my window. Two days of sitting in this weary, stained room watching inane television with only my aches and pains to keep me company was an even worse prospect. I thought maybe that I needed something to smoke.

As soon as I hatched the project of locating Natalie, I became desperate to do it. I needed information and by English standards it was very late on Friday afternoon to be starting the job. The first step was to find out where she lived, and after that everything else would have to wait and see. I did have a vague starting point in Rick and Marcie's letter from thirteen years earlier which said someone had met Natalie in New York and she'd been living 'out in the Berkshires'. That seemed to imply that the Berkshires, whatever they were, might be close to New York, or might they just as easily have said, 'out in Alaska'? Anyway, it didn't mean she still lived there. A lot could have happened since 1960, indeed a lot *had* happened. She'd been married in 1966 and divorced in 1968. That was only five years ago.

Phones in English offices would have rung and rung to weekend emptiness at six o' clock on a Friday but this wasn't England. Encouraged by my success with the aircraft magazines, I rang *Classical Music Monthly* at its address in the Rockefeller Centre and was put straight through to someone who sounded like he was in a huge hurry.

'I'm sorry to trouble you,' I said.

'You're not troubling me yet, pal,' he said, 'but feel free to go on trying. You from England?'

'Yes. My name's Milo Malan. I'm trying to get in touch with a cellist, I think she's pretty well known. Natalie Vanderberg?'

'This is English understatement, yeah?'

'You've heard of her?'

'Like I've heard of God.'

I took that as a 'yes'.

'It's just that I need to talk to her and I don't know how to find her.'

'I can give you her agent's number. Yeah, Adie Patman, I think. You'd get her Monday, I guess.'

Putting it aside until Monday wasn't an option. 'It needs to be this weekend. I had an idea that she lives in the Berkshires, Natalie Vanderberg I mean. Is that right?'

'Sounds right. She don't socialize much.'

'You wouldn't have an address?'

'Guess not.'

'I'm sorry, being English, I wouldn't know these things but what *are* the Berkshires?'

'Listen, Milo. You don't need to apologize for being a Brit. All right, you guys invented the slave trade and the opium trade and colonialism and you don't understand about republics and the right to self-determination, but Purcell makes up for a helluva lot.'

Maybe he wasn't in such a hurry after all. 'I'm sorry?' I said.

'There you go again.' He laughed. 'The Berkshires are hills. They're up in Massachusetts. North of New York. A hundred miles. Two-hour drive, maybe.'

'Is it a big area? I could go up and ask around.'

'Sure, if you've got a month or two.' He was indistinct as if his mouth was away from the phone and I could hear rustling noises. 'Easier way would be to go to her concert.'

'What concert?'

'I saw it in the listings. Yup, here she is. Tomorrow night. Eight o'clock. Rotherham. That's right in the Berkshires. Their Fall concert. She's a regular there so I guess you're right, that's got to be her home town or something like that.'

I walked ten blocks to Greenwich Village, because I'd heard of it and I thought if I could find some weed anywhere it would be there. I soon found a bar where I met a guy who had a friend who could get me what I wanted, which had by then escalated from weed to something harder. His friend would meet me round the corner in an alley, out of the way. It was two of his friends who met me and passed over a plastic bag and then, when I opened my wallet, being English and stupid, to get the money, hit me very hard in the eye, then drew out something that I at first took for a toy gun. It didn't occur to me that it was real until I had broken all the rules of New York street robbery and, instead of doing exactly what they said, pushed between them and ran out of the alley into a crowd of people. The crowd was a welcome sight because my brain had now caught up with me and told me this was not London and not a film and therefore they weren't joking. They also weren't coming after me, maybe because of the crowd and maybe because of the two policemen on horses just ahead in the road.

I nearly ran up to them and told them what had happened until I realized first that I would have some explaining to do, and second that I now had in my pocket what might be a bag of talcum powder or might just be the real thing. Looked at that way, apart from a rising, throbbing ache round my eye, I was up on the deal as I'd never even got as far as giving them the money. Wait until I tell Cat about *this*, I thought, but the shock was starting to get me and I flagged down a cab with relief. It's extraordinary how far out of their way New Yorkers will go to avoid noticing that you've got a huge red lump rising all round your eye.

It wasn't talcum powder and I didn't have a syringe so that night I smoked some of it as best I could using the foil from a fast food dish I found in the top of a garbage sack. It wasn't very good stuff but it helped a bit and I felt I'd got away very lightly, all things considered, though my eye had turned purple.

The journey north the next morning was a whole new bundle of experiences superimposed on all the difficulties of hiring a car with only cash and an English driving licence to my name, plus the look of someone who had clearly been in a fight and a half-closed eye which didn't improve my looks or my driving. It was my first time in an automatic, the first time on the other side of the road, the first time in a multi-lane metal flood that drew me in then rushed me past all kinds of banalities of American roadside life, which were not at all banal to me. Everything I glimpsed from the petrol stations to the names on the direction signs gave me a buzz. The rain had gone. To be in a car and heading out into the country was a definite advantage, being on the move.

Beyond Brookfield, the roads got much quieter and smaller and with time on my hands I turned off into a side road that led to the hills. I wanted to get out and walk and get in touch with the bones of this place I had never been to before. That was a cover of sorts, because I suppose I also wanted to put off the moment of coming into Natalie's orbit, the moment when I might be faced with some sort of decision about the next step, about whether to remain simply a spectator or instead to take some more active part in all this.

The lane led me to an autumnal heaven of waterfalls running down through great boulders below a high tree canopy. I saw an unfamiliar black bird with bright red markings and was enthralled. For a long time, I sat on a log, listening to rustlings in the under-growth, hoping to see something else truly American, a chipmunk or a skunk perhaps, but in their absence, just appreciating the odd feeling of being somewhere quite away from the beaten track of my life. For the first time since I'd left London, I felt physically better. The ache in my joints had retreated into the background and my head was clear of the nervous fear which had seemed to be there so often lately.

I killed more time with a cheap and huge lunch in a diner, then drove into Rotherham, a pretty green town with an old-fashioned inn, where I parked the car and walked around. Off the main street was a grand old theatre with the façade of a Greek temple and on a banner strung across the pillars it said, 'Fall Festival. October 6th. Natalie Vanderberg'. A middle-aged woman watched me curiously from inside the foyer as I came up the steps.

'Can I buy a ticket for tonight?' I asked.

'I'm so sorry,' she said, 'there are none left. It's a total sell-out.'

'Oh.'

She looked at my face. 'Have you had an accident?' Maybe this was the difference between New Yorkers and country folk.

'Someone mugged me,' I said.

'Have you come a long way?' Her voice was sympathetic.

'Yes, I have,' I said, 'from Israel and before that from London.'

She was taken aback. 'You didn't come just for this concert?'

'Well, no, but to me it's the most important part of my trip.'

'You must be a big fan of Natalie's.'

I nodded. 'I'm very interested in her but I've never seen her play.'

'Oh, now don't look so sad,' she said. 'I'll see if we can't fix something up. Come back around seven thirty. Ask for me. I'm Joanne.'

I spent the rest of the afternoon wandering around the shops and at about four o'clock I found my idea of the perfect bookshop down a side-street, a barn of a place with side rooms and balconies and, best of all, two large sofas with coffee on a hotplate nearby, where you could browse without anyone trying to speed you into a purchase.

I asked the girl at the desk whether there was a biography of Natalie Vanderberg.

'Should be,' said the girl. She had riveting green eyes in an otherwise ordinary face, so bright that they were all you could see. 'They say there's one being written but they've been saying that for a long time now and we still haven't seen it.'

'She lives round here, doesn't she?'

'Just out of town on the lower valley road. Big gates with stone pillars. All we got on her is the town guide. There's a few lines about her in that. Would you like to see it?'

'Yes please.'

She handed me a small book with a sepia cover showing a photo of Rotherham's main street with horses and a single Model T Ford. 'Sit and have some coffee,' she said. 'Take your time.'

'Thank you, that's very kind.'

'Your face does look sore. Would you like some cream?'

'I'm okay, thanks.'

'I love your accent.'

The coffee was good, rich stuff, and there was a jug of proper milk to go with it. I poured out a mugful and settled down to read. It didn't take very long.

*One of Rotherham's most noted citizens is the world-famous cellist, Natalie Vanderberg, who was born in the Argyll Mansion on Fairfax and returned to build her own house just outside town during the late 1950s. Miss Vanderberg has made a name for herself in performances all over the world. She has the distinction, as described in* No Price Too High *by distinguished Massachusetts historian Hutton Spengler, of having performed while still in her teenage years in front of the King of England.*

The girl with green eyes found me a copy of the Spengler book and I sat back down again, leafing through it while she gave me the occasional smile between dealing with her customers. 'Distinguished' was an over-complimentary word for Hutton Spengler, earned probably more by coming from the same state as by any other quality of excellence. *No Price Too High* was a tired rerun of the story of Edward the Eighth, Wallis Simpson and the abdication, and the opening paragraph made his point of view clear:

*The advantage of vigorous republicanism over decayed, stifling monarchy has never been more clearly shown than in the events of December 1936 when a noble king had the courage to put love before the dry strictures of the British establishment at the cost of his throne. It took an American woman to show him that there could be even more to life than being a king, to rescue him from the English prison cell of royal duty, and that woman was the extraordinary Wallis Simpson.*

Max would have loved it. I had dipped into a few books on the subject since finding the trunk, searching for information on the years at La Cröe, and there wasn't much in this one that couldn't have come straight out of the others except for the personal recollections of a few Americans who had been fringe players. Natalie was one of those Americans.

*It was in February 1935 that Natalie Vanderberg, then just turned nineteen years of age, found herself whisked off on a magic carpet to one of the most glamorous places in all of Europe. Wallis, always skillful when it came to spotting talent, had detected in the fresh-faced girl the spark which would later ignite into the full flame of genius, and*

257

*she knew that Edward would be charmed by the musical skill of the youthful virtuoso. Miss Vanderberg remembers that the beginning of the holiday in Kitzbühl did not go entirely to plan. Mrs Simpson was persuaded to try the unfamiliar sport of skiing for herself and although she tackled it with the determination she always showed in the face of adversity, the conditions were extremely difficult. After several hours of unstinting effort, during which she fell a great number of times, she selflessly decided that the task of teaching her was getting in the way of the enjoyment of others in the party, and turned her mind to indoor activities so as not to monopolize more of their time. It was on the third night of their stay that Miss Vanderberg was called upon to perform in front of the King and his party, and she overcame her nerves to deliver a performance of such exquisite artistry that the King could simply not resist the music and began to conduct her as she played with all the vigor at his command.*

That was all it said about Natalie, but with time to kill and a comfortable chair to kill it in, I leafed through the rest, turning pages at random and scanning down columns until my eye chanced to fall on the words, 'field marshal', so I backtracked to read them. It was a line from a letter written by one of the King's aides. The Duke was very upset, he said, at having no official standing of any kind now that he had abdicated. The quotation had him saying: 'I used to be a field marshal and an admiral of the fleet but now I'm nothing.' I looked for a date and realized that he had written this soon after the abdication, some time in 1936.

I could remember word for word the lines in Max's version of the story of the unveiling of the statue in Cannes, an unveiling which took place a decade later: *'Owen, amongst my other titles I am an admiral of the fleet so it is within my power to command Captain Sir Jeremy . . . By good fortune, it happens that I am also a field marshal . . .'*

Not so, it seemed, if Hutton Spengler was any more to be believed than Max Birkin Owen. It was possible, giving Max the benefit of the doubt, that the Duke had somehow had his rank restored to him later on, but I wasn't convinced that it was wise to give Max that benefit. Without the Duke's powers of promotion in the field, Max's story had no substance and yet I had seen that photograph. Max was a filter through which history passed to emerge much less clear than when it entered. I made some notes from the book, thanked the girl with the green eyes and, on her advice, drove out to the far side of town to book myself into an old-fashioned motel where each room was a separate, white-painted wooden cabin with a small sun-deck outside it.

The rest of that afternoon went on for an absurdly long time. I had a shower, read every word of a local newspaper and tried to watch TV as each minute took an hour to pass. Now that I was so close, I couldn't bear the idea that I might not get in to see Natalie. It would go no further. I would sit there, if Joanne had done her stuff, and listen to music that I neither knew nor understood, but it seemed to me that for someone to develop a reputation like Natalie there must be a great deal of themselves in their playing. If I could see something of that, something that went with what I knew of Natalie's innermost thoughts at the most emotional moment of her life, then that would be enough for me to leave feeling that I had got somewhere. Natalie, it seemed to me, was the finest person I had found in the trunk.

On the dot of half past seven I presented myself at the hall and asked for Joanne, knowing that if there was no ticket I could hardly just go away, but would have to present myself at Natalie's door in the morning and somehow get over that first awful moment of finding a way to tell her how I fitted into her life.

Joanne didn't have a ticket but she had the next best thing.

'I've done the best I can,' she said. 'There's a spare chair by the tech desk. Ivan says if you sit quietly you can use it.'

'Ivan?'

'He does the sound.'

Inside the auditorium it was a proper little theatre, red velvet everywhere and a balcony hanging over the stalls. The sound desk was boxed off on the far side of the balcony, stage left, and the seat was a wooden folding chair but I didn't mind one bit. I leant over and watched as the auditorium filled up with people, and not just older people but what looked like a complete cross-section of Rotherham inhabitants. Ivan was a short, friendly man who came in five minutes after me, stuck out a hand, said, 'Hear you came a long way for this,' then sat down and busied himself with switches and sliders.

There was a programme next to him on the bench. 'May I?' I said, and he nodded.

It was a short list of pieces starting with a Brahms sonata and going on to Bach via some other people I had never heard of. It wasn't all classical. There was a suite from *Porgy and Bess* and there were two pieces, 'Taconic' and 'Rain Dance', that just had Vanderberg in brackets after them, so I presumed she had written them herself.

I hung over the edge of the box, staring towards the wings hoping to catch an early glimpse of her and watching the remaining people streaming in to fill up the seats then, at exactly eight o'clock, for these were clearly punctual people, a tall man in a white tie and tailcoat stepped on to the stage.

'Friends, ladies and gentlemen,' he said, 'it is my pleasure to introduce to you tonight the incomparable, the one and only, our very own star, Miss Natalie Vanderberg,' and there, shockingly abruptly, stepping to life out of her photograph, was Natalie.

It was still the same Natalie. She walked across the stage, not like a star but like a local girl, wryly acknowledging the storm of applause, settling herself in her chair, then bending forward to chat to friends in the front row for a moment before she started. Her face had hardly changed from that childhood-sweetheart photo with Max in their coats. I had worked out that she must be fifty-six or fifty-seven years old, but the years had put no extra flesh on her bones. That striking narrow oval face was still immediately recognizable, and though her hair had been tamed slightly it was still a magnificent tumble of curls, now grey-streaked. I'd never before thought of a woman of that age in terms of attraction but she was still, without doubt, attractive.

'It's nice to see so many friends here,' she said, smiling around her at the audience, and her voice was deeper than I had imagined. That came as a surprise because I didn't even know I had imagined a voice but I realized I had read her letters in my head as if she were speaking them. 'I thought we would start tonight with a Brahms sonata.'

Then she began to play and a silence fell on the hall as if everyone in it realized that what was happening there on the stage was far more than they could ever have expected in that small theatre in that small town. I found I didn't have to know anything about Brahms or about the cello to appreciate that here was someone playing entirely out of a love of the music and a desire to share it, not for self-aggrandisement, profit or reputation. It was faultless but also human, her hands and fingers as much apparent in the notes as the bow and the strings. I looked at her face and saw that she gradually moved away from the stage to somewhere else and that when the piece ended to a moment of silent appreciation followed by a growing swell of applause, it took her a second or two to come back.

Bach came next and Bach had always been an exception to my disengagement from the classics. Bach seems to me to have tapped in to some universal code which goes right to the root of spirituality and is the single best proof that there is something beautiful at the heart of life. Natalie played it as if she were on a direct line from heaven and it made me feel that I had lost something. I thought about my flat and Cat and about what I had been doing to my body with Cat's needles and the soaring music seemed to point a finger of accusation as if asking what right I had to listen to it. At the moment when I felt most unworthy, she lifted her head to the balcony and swept it with a gaze like a searchlight that seemed to fix itself on me so that I had to look away.

She let me off the hook with 'I've Got Plenty of Nothing' from *Porgy and Bess* which went down extremely well with the audience, then she paused, put down her bow and cleared her throat.

'You may have noticed,' she said, 'that in the programme there are two pieces which have my name after them.'

There was a little scatter of applause but she waved her hand for silence. 'This was not my idea,' she said. 'It is true that I sometimes cannot resist the temptation to pick up my pen and begin to compose but I have to say the only real effect is to remind myself just how gifted real composers have to be.' The audience laughed. 'Those pieces were only down in the programme because I once played them for Joanne Patton, who you will all know is our festival director here, and she sneakily put them in without asking me. It just happened however that I was looking through some old scrap books yesterday and I found another piece I wrote a few years ago, so if Joanne doesn't mind I would like to play that one instead.'

She produced a double fold of music sheets, arranged it on the stand in front of her, then looked over the top at the audience. 'If it seems strange that I should need the music for something I wrote, just bear in mind that, until yesterday, it's quite some time since I last saw this.' She picked up her bow again and was about to put it to her cello when she interrupted herself again. 'Oh, I should tell you,' she said, 'I call it "Letters".'

The noise I made prompted Ivan to look at me sharply. I would like to think I would have picked up on the meaning of the piece even without the title, but that's probably pushing the truth a bit too far. There were two alternating parts to it and I wished I knew the musical terms to define them. It started with a busy, loud passage, almost bombastic, with a strong rhythm running through. That ended and a lighter, slower section began with a sweet melody, then she somehow wove into it the first theme so that the two mixed, separated and mixed again but the pace of the loud part, the undeniable rhythm, kept dragging it out of the blend to march by itself.

Then the pace changed. She asked a question with the cello in the voice of the lighter part and the reply came uncertainly in the second, louder voice, its insistent beat slowing and almost faltering. She asked it again, taking some of that rhythm into the lighter part in doing so and this time the reply seemed for a while to take up this new shared form, but gradually its original nature reasserted itself and it slipped back into that busy, relentless formula again. I knew what every part of it meant and as it drew to an end with the two parts taking short turns, dying gradually away into a whisper, I found my eyes pricking with tears as the audience, puzzled but respectful, clapped and Natalie sat in silence.

I didn't pay very close attention to the rest of the music in the concert. I was looking at her face as she played and thinking of her playing in front of the King, the ridiculous King, trying to conduct. Then I started musing on Spengler's view of the whole thing. Wallis Simpson showed Edward there was more to life than being a king. Why had Natalie Vanderberg failed to show Max that there was more to life than tall tales? Would he be sitting in his living death cell now if he had listened to her? I was sure he would not. Natalie exuded life. In her presence, Max would not have grown so old so fast, would not have had his strokes, above all would not have gone on down his blind alley of a life until it all caught up with him and there was no place left to hide but Weston House.

Some time during that last half-hour of the concert, I began to wonder if Natalie knew Max was alive, and from there it was only a short step to dreaming of a happy ending.

# Twenty-three

The concert ended. Natalie played two short encores, received a bouquet from Joanne and walked off smiling into the wings, out of my sight and my life. I sat in my seat while the audience left, regretting it was over. Ivan was between me and the exit, switching things off and tidying up his cue-sheets and I was in no great hurry because I had nowhere to go except back to my motel. When I came out to the stairs leading down from the balcony Joanne was waiting there.

'How was that?' she asked.

'Truly wonderful,' I said. 'Thank you so much for finding me a space.'

'Well, now,' she said, 'I did happen to mention to Natalie that there was someone who'd come all the way from England and she said we must get you in.'

'Would you thank her for me?'

'You could do it yourself. She'd really like to say hello to you. Would you like that?'

Yes I would and no I wouldn't. It was absolutely the best I could have hoped for and it also made my flesh crawl with the dreadful possibilities it opened up. She took my expression for surprised acceptance.

'Come on, then. Come with me and I'll take you backstage,' she said.

So that was it. The decision was taken out of my hands. At the moment when I think I had decided that I had already come as close as good manners would allow, the wheel of fate turned another notch and propelled me into Natalie's presence.

'This is the young man from England, Natalie,' said Joanne, sweeping me into an austere dressing room in which Natalie Vanderberg was putting her cello carefully into its case, protected by a soft cloth.

'I'm very pleased to meet you,' I said, holding out a hand. 'I'm Miles Malan.'

Her hand was dry to the touch. She was different with the music gone, as though it were a gas which held her inflated in a certain curved way. Without it she looked a little older and a shade stiff.

'Well now, Mr Malan,' she said, looking me up and down. 'I'm flattered that you came and I guess I'm puzzled as well.'

'Why puzzled?'

'You could have saved yourself a lot of travelling. I'm playing in London two weeks from now.'

'I didn't know that. I've been in Israel on business and I only heard about the concert when I got to New York.'

'From Israel, huh? Just in time.'

I didn't follow her. 'The concert was wonderful.'

'What did you like best?'

'I love Bach.' That didn't seem quite enough so I blundered on. 'I've never heard that piece played like that before, just a cello and nothing else.'

A mistake, obviously. She raised her eyebrows. 'That's the way he wrote it.'

'Oh, right. What I really loved was "Letters".'

'Well then I'm puzzled all over again. You're a bit of a mystery, Mr Malan, because you didn't *look* like you loved it.'

'I'm sorry?'

'I was looking around the audience while I was playing that. I saw your face. You know it's usually a bad idea to focus on someone's face while you're playing. It can really put you off your stroke.'

'I hope I didn't.'

'You looked like someone had died. I nearly stopped playing right there.'

I remembered that searchlight gaze and what I said next came from pure, unstoppable impulse. 'I found it very moving because I know why you wrote it.'

She laughed. 'Now that is going too far. Nobody knows why I wrote that. I don't even know why I played it. It's just one of those things from way back in my life.'

'I do know, really.'

'Tell me.'

265

'It was about losing someone, wasn't it?'

'Yes, it was, but that's not so clever. A lot of music is about losing someone. You write for comfort.'

'But this was about trying to avoid it.'

'Go on.' She'd stopped laughing.

'The letters – they were offering a compromise, a way to be together, but it didn't work.'

'Well, that's very good,' she said slowly. 'Either that or my composition is much too predictable.' She was frowning a little now.

'I don't want to startle you,' I said gently, 'but I know who he was.'

'So startle me.'

'He was Max Birkin Owen, wasn't he?'

She breathed out in a mirthless snorting laugh and stared at me, then sat down. She didn't say anything at all for some time and I sat down too because it felt wrong to be towering over her. Then she shook her head as if trying to clear it.

'Max Birkin Owen,' she said. 'Out of the blue. Now that raises all kinds of stuff. How could you get from that music of mine to Max? That's so . . . so *weird*. Are you something to do with Max?'

'Sort of.'

'Sort of? I haven't heard from Max in oh, I don't know, twelve, thirteen years and you think you can mumble things like, "Sort of"?'

'I'm sorry, this is quite difficult to explain.'

'I'm sure it is, but you'd better try.'

Before she could go on, the door opened and Joanne put her head round it. 'We're ready whenever you are, Natalie.'

'They're taking me out to eat,' said Natalie.

'I thought she was checking up on you.'

'Yes, that too, but whatever you are, you're not a threat, are you Mr Malan?'

'No, I'm not and please call me Miles.'

'Are you staying in town?'

'Yes I am. The Dover Motel.'

'Living high on the hog, eh?'

'No, not at all, it's . . .'

'Joke.'

'Oh, right.'

She seemed to come to a decision. 'There's not time for this now, whatever it is. Are you still here tomorrow?'

'I can be.'

'Can you come and see me tomorrow morning, say ten o'clock?'

'Yes. I'd like to.'

'You *will* come? I don't think I could bear it if you said what you've just said then vanished.'

'I promise I'll come. How do I find you?'

'Go north out of town,' she said. 'It's the fourth house on the right. A half-mile. Stone gateposts and iron gates, painted white. You have to buzz me from the gate. This is my number if anything goes wrong.'

I don't know what sort of night Natalie had. There was no sign in her appearance the next day that her sleep had been disturbed in any way, but I tossed and turned all night. The mattress was sealed inside a thick plastic cover and the sheet over it made little difference. It was slick and sweaty and there was a cricket trapped inside the casing of the air-conditioner which amplified its chirp like a drum. At two o'clock in the morning, after a lot of door-slamming in the cabin next door, culminating in a car driving off on screeching tyres, I gave it up as a bad job and switched on the light. I got out Max and Natalie's letters and held them in my hand, staring at them; now that I had met Natalie, it felt like a real intrusion. I put them carefully to one side and looked at the other papers I'd brought with me.

There was a bunch of them held together with a rusty paperclip which had left its grooved brown mark on them. Across the top of the first one was a letter heading, 'OC Engineering', in dated, blue lettering with a Maidenhead address and it was signed 'Os'. I was looking for something peaceful and comforting to read. Instead I rediscovered Oswald Chinnery and learnt what it was he had against Max.

Unusually for the contents of the trunk, this bundle of letters was already organized into date order. They were all typed and the first one was dated August 14th, 1956.

Maxie,

We towed the Moretti back here and I got the motor out yesterday. What have you been doing to it? Crank looks very bad. Blower gears stripped. Machining and all will cost at least two hundred and that's if we don't find anything else. Frankly not sure it's worth it. Come down and have a look. I need your decision.

Os.

The next one was December the same year:

Max,

Christmas is coming and I could do with the cash. Sorry to tell you the bank returned the cheque you sent on account, unpaid. In answer to your complaint, I did tell you it was the best we could do and there's no way she will ever run like she used to.

Oswald

Then it was six months later:

Dear Mr Birkin Owen,
*re: Moretti 12-cylinder car:*

With reference to the recent telephone call made by the undersigned in which the above-mentioned vehicle was discussed, may we request that you call at this address at your earliest convenience to settle the question of the outstanding accounts.

You will no doubt appreciate that this matter has been long outstanding and naturally we are anxious to wind up the affair in view of the not inconsiderable charges involved together with the inconvenience of storing your vehicle in what is a productive workshop and not a parking garage. We have to inform you that our total charges to date now amount to £212. 12. 6d for work done and storage of £12. 10. 0.

We feel sure that you will excuse our urging conclusion of this matter at this time.

We are,
Yours faithfully,
pp Oswald Chinnery Engineering,
Mrs Norma Chinnery,
*Director.*

It took Douglas to sort it all out, as a letter dated November 4th 1957 showed.

Max,
Douglas was down here yesterday and has cleared the outstanding matters on your behalf so I am glad to say we can put that behind us. I am taking the necessary steps to transfer ownership of the Moretti to my name and would be glad of any documents you may have in your possession. Duggie mentioned something about a Belgian who says the car really belongs to him. I would not like you to think for a moment that I have done well out of this as it is nowhere near being a proper runner and all it seems likely to do is take up space, but I suppose it is better than nothing. Your brother did mention that you were looking for an investment in the motor trade and I do have an opportunity for a sleeping partner to put some funds into this business as we need a certain amount of new equipment at present. Let me know if you would be interested in discussing this further.
Yours etc.,
Oswald.

You would have thought he would have known better. The next few letters were all about the details of their partnership, such as it was. Max seemed to have got some money from somewhere, but never quite as much as Oswald Chinnery expected and it didn't sound a happy experience for either of them. The letterheading had changed for the last two letters. It now said 'Chinnery Restoration and Race Preparation' in block letters and the address was Farley Heath Garage. October 1960 was the date.

Dear Max,

It was quite a surprise to hear from you again after this time. Now that the final liquidation is over we can, as you say, put that behind us. I have, as you asked, collected the Lister-Jag by trailer from Merstham and given it the once-over.

The clutch is easily fixed. I am surprised it had not happened before as the car was never really intended for road use and from inspection, you must have been slipping it a lot. There are also signs of overheating and if you really want to go on showing off in it round town, you ought to have electric fans fitted.

What bothers me is the state of the chassis, particularly at the front. As we both know all too well it has had a hard life and whoever put it back together for you after the film job wasn't what I would call a top-rate welder. We can do a little bit to strengthen it but it won't be a lasting fix. The only real answer is to strip it right down, cut out several lengths of tube and build it up again properly. I don't think you'll get away with that for less than four hundred, however much we shave the costs.

Let me know what you decide,

Os.

The last one was dated a few days after the Brighton crash and was handwritten.

Max,

If anyone does ask, I will have to say precisely what is true. I welded it for you. I pointed out it was a bodge-up. You didn't want to spend the money so I told you not to go racing it. All right, I won't volunteer anything *unless* they ask, but I'm not up for perjury. To answer your other question, no, I only keep file copies for a year so I don't have the letter from 1960.

Oswald Chinnery

So Chinnery had found himself caught right in the middle of it, and perhaps it was not so surprising after all that he should have developed a fixation about the crash. I thought back to the other car in his workshop, the big old car under the tarpaulin which he'd told me was none of my business. The Moretti? Probably. Chinnery had supped with Max with all too short a spoon and found himself mired in debts, broken promises and pointing fingers. What was he doing in his workshop, trying to put it all back together again with a welding torch?

Above all it made me think hard about Max. Here he was revealed in the most unpleasant light, desperate to cover his trail. He *knew* Chinnery had told him the Lister was dangerous. He *knew* Ginny had died because he had ignored the warning. What sort of man was he that all that had come first? The letters showed it was more important to him to make sure he wasn't blamed than to admit to his brother that Ginny had died because of his mistakes. Against that, I knew what Tiggy would have said. She would have said that Max couldn't live with what had happened, that he had to write it differently in the diary of his life, and before he could do that he had to rub out what was already written there.

None of this made for relaxation. I got angry with Max and glad that Natalie had escaped from life with him. My brain gathered a momentum that kept throwing up random ideas long after I stopped. The only reason I knew I'd eventually gone to sleep at all was the way I woke up at eight feeling very badly rested.

I was at Natalie's gates at ten o'clock. The house had a name, carved in a stone slab, 'The Muse'. She hadn't mentioned that. The gates swung open when I buzzed. The drive curved through a climbing S-bend between high hedges then opened up in front of a long, low wooden house with a wooden deck in front of it protected by overhanging eaves. Natalie was standing on the deck wearing jeans and a shirt. She looked at me curiously as I got out of the car.

'You look terrible,' she said.

'Good morning,' I replied. 'Too much living high on the hog. The Dover Motel doesn't believe in mattresses.'

'My coffee will sort you out. Did you eat breakfast yet?'

'I skipped it. Coffee's fine.'

She looked at me critically. 'You almost qualify as emaciated. Don't skip it too often. I was too polite to ask last night, but does your eye always look like that?'

'No it does not. Some nice guy tried to rob me in New York.'

'If all you got was a punch in the eye, I'd say you were lucky.'

We sat down in her kitchen and she poured coffee for both of us then raised her eyebrows.

'Okay, Mr Surprising Miles Malan,' she said, 'I'm very glad you came. I was beginning to think I must have dreamt you. Now, I suppose you had better take me through all this.'

I had tried to rehearse this but I couldn't remember any of the words I had prepared.

'I want to say something first. Please remember that when I started this whole thing, I didn't know any of you were alive. I didn't think of you as real people.'

'I guess if I knew what you were talking about, it might help. Maybe you shouldn't apologize until you have something to apologize for. Started what whole thing?'

'Well . . . started trying to get to know Max, I suppose. I found a trunk, you see. I bought it in an auction. It was stuffed full of letters and photos and stories.'

'This was Max's trunk?'

'Yes.'

'So how did it get there?'

'They cleared his flat out. It was all meant to be thrown away.'

She stared at the coffee pot, then she shook her head. 'When was this?' she said, and her voice had a tightness in it that made me kick myself as soon as I realized why.

'No, no. He's not dead. I thought he was but he's not.'

She gave a long sigh. 'Miles, you are exhausting. You kill people off who I didn't know were dead and then before I get used to that, you bring them back to life again. Be a little careful here.'

'I'm sorry.'

'Let's take it real slow. Max is alive but you bought his trunk. That's it? That's your entire connection with him and you linked it to me? That's why you're here?' She sounded incredulous. 'You came to America for that?'

'No. There's much more than that. You knew Max's brother, didn't you?'

'Doug. Sorry, Douglas. Sure I did.'

'Well, I was there when his wife got killed and –'

'Doug's *wife* got killed. You mean Ginny? *She's* dead?'

Damn. 1963. It was all over between Max and Natalie by 1963. She looked quite shocked.

'Yes. I'm sorry I forgot you might not know. She was killed in '63.'

'Look, Miles. Please remember I haven't seen Max or any of them since, I don't know, 1960, I guess. You said she got killed, she didn't just die. It was a car, right?'

I told her the bare essentials of the crash.

'And you were how old?' she said.

'Thirteen.'

'Okay, so you saw it happen, then time goes by and you get this trunk, Max's trunk, and you find you've got this connection.'

'That's right.'

'And that's enough to hook you in like this, so you come here and wake up things I thought had gone away for ever?'

'Yes.'

'Any more surprises for me in all of this? Any more people going to die on me or come back to life again?'

'Not like that, no.'

'So just exactly how is Max?'

'He's living in a home in London – a sort of nursing home.' I found I couldn't say old folks' home, not to this lively person, not about someone she had loved. 'He hasn't been well.'

'Where do I come into all this?'

'I read your letters,' I said simply. 'The last few letters you wrote.' I looked at her anxiously, worried that I might see affront or outrage on her face, but she was staring at me as if trying to fathom something deep inside me.

'He kept them all?'

'Yes.'

'All of them? I wonder. People destroy the letters that *really* matter.'

'I don't think so. Not Max.' I had to go in deeper. 'I know what he felt about you. You were so clever. You tried to let him off all his fantasies so that he'd let you come to London. You offered him a way out, didn't you, so that he could turn his back on his . . . exaggerations.' I couldn't use the word 'lie',

273

not to her. 'I didn't know you were both alive when I read them, I'm sorry.'

'Okay,' she said. 'Now you have got something to apologize for. So you read the letters. I take it these would have been *my* letters to him?'

'And his first copy of what he was going to say to you.'

'And from *those* you worked out your theory of what my music was all about last night?'

'Yes. It seemed really clear. The two themes. I know how close you came to saving Max.'

That was too much for her. 'No, you don't. Max was Max, and was always going to be Max. I was kidding myself.'

'That's wrong. Really. You almost got to him.' She still didn't believe me and I thought I could show her. 'Look. I've got the draft of his letter here. The bits he wrote down then crossed out. You can see for yourself. Do you want to read it?'

'This is not the way things work,' she said, but she reached out and took it when I offered it and as I watched her reading it, frowning, I could remember the bits she had never seen before. *If I opted for a touch of romance, you cannot blame me entirely . . . The rest followed from there and has dogged me to this day. I can't, I suppose, just blame circumstances. There is a heady excitement in reinventing one's self . . . You, my dearest, with your admirable common sense, have offered to build me a bridge. So, here is my list, as you request.*

She looked up at me when she'd finished and her eyes were glistening. 'Stupid,' she said, and she could have been talking about him or me or herself. She held it out to me but I didn't want to take it.

'It's yours,' I said. 'He should have sent it to you.'

'But he didn't, so it's not mine. Do you understand? *You* may think he should have sent it but *he* didn't think so. It's not what he wrote. He made a clear decision, Miles. In the end there were things that mattered more to him.'

I shook my head. 'For better or worse, I know a lot about what he thought. You were the one he kept coming back to. Thirty years on and off. You were the one who mattered to him. He fell in love with you in Kitzbühl and he stayed that way.'

She looked down and didn't say anything.

'He's still there,' I said. 'He's in this home near where I live. West London.'

'Have you been to see him?'

'No. I couldn't.' She seemed to need no explanation of that. '*You* could see him, though,' I said, and she lifted her eyes and stared at me. 'You could see him when you go over for your concert. You could see him in two weeks' time.'

'How old are you?' she asked.

'Twenty-four.'

'With all the simplicity of youth. What would be the point?'

'It would make him happy.'

'Would it? How do you know? Max built himself around a skeleton of self-delusion. All I proved was that he couldn't give that up.'

'Why did he do it?'

'How long have you got?'

'Is it that complicated?'

'There's maybe a few bits of it you could call simple.'

'Like what?'

'Like he didn't know he was a nice man and he didn't know that being a nice man was enough. He thought no one would take him seriously if he was "nice". It was glamorous to be a bit bad.'

'He wasn't like that. He was guilty about everything. He wrote all these stories of his because he was guilty.'

'Hey, listen, Miles. I'm the expert on Max, not you. Max was my special subject.'

'I'm sorry.' She didn't say anything. 'Don't you want to see him?'

'That's a big question. I think I have a bigger question for you, Miles Malan.'

'Ask away.'

'Why does this matter so much?'

'I felt . . . well, really sorry for both of you. I thought maybe I could help.'

'No, no, no. This isn't about me and Max. Not really. It's about you, buster. What's gone so wrong with your life that makes you want to come and fix mine?'

'You still wish you'd worked it out between you, don't you? I know that's what your music meant.'

She laughed then. 'Shall I tell you the true irony of all this? The most bizarre aspect of it all?'

'Go on.'

'You've put a lot into this. I understand that. You've made all these connections and you've spun a web that takes in Max and me and you and Ginny and Doug and all the rest. I don't want to tear your web apart because you seem to need it.'

'What do you mean?'

'That music wasn't about Max.'

# Twenty-four

'I don't know that I can tell you Max's story,' said Natalie, 'because I'm not too sure I really know it, even now. I can tell you my story and some of that is Max's story too, and you can make up your mind how it fits in.'

'That sounds good.'

'How long have you got?'

'All day.'

'Ah. Well I only have all morning, but I guess that should be enough. Where shall I begin?'

'At the beginning.'

'I was a sucker for European charm,' Natalie said. 'I should say for European aristocrats, I suppose. I went to Europe at an impressionable age, in my late teens, and suddenly I was in the middle of all these people who didn't have to tell you how much they made in a year or that they were the biggest retailer of aluminum siding in Milwaukee or whatever. They just were what they were, like they had some God-given right to be special.'

'This was in Kitzbühl?'

'Yes, Mr Know-all. This was in Kitzbühl and if you know that then I guess you also know that I was taken there by the very worst woman into whose hands an impressionable teenager should ever fall.'

'Wallis Simpson.'

'She was trying very hard to stop being Wallis Simpson at that time. She'd been Wallis Warfield, then Wallis Spencer, then Simpson. By that time she badly wanted to be Wallis Windsor.' She checked herself for a moment. 'Is this what you want to hear?'

'Oh yes.'

'I was in London, studying cello. This was the end of 1934 so I suppose I was eighteen going on nineteen. My father knew Ernest Simpson. They were both in the shipping business at one time and

I was invited out to dine with them a couple of times. Then Wallis cabled back here to my folks to say she wanted to take me off to give me some continental polish, teach me to ski, how to hold my knife, you know – things like that. Being Wallis, she never asked *me* if I wanted to go. She just decided for me. So I trotted off to Kitzbühl after her, with my bags and my cello case – she was very insistent that I bring the cello – and before I went she told me that there was going to be somebody quite special there, the Prince of Wales, no less. Now, you might say this is twenty-twenty hindsight, but I could tell right then from the way she said it, the way she was curved and tense and watching me hard, that she had him in her sights. Kids aren't stupid. I wasn't very old but I could easily see things that she might have taken more care to hide from people her own age. Would you like some more coffee?'

'Yes, please.'

'Why did I start there? This could take a long time.'

'This is fine. It's fascinating.'

'Well, it does sort of get there in the end. Poor old Ernest didn't come, of course. He knew what Wallis was up to for sure but he wasn't the man to stand up to her. I had to go separately, little me, because Wallis didn't want to nanny me through the journey, she just wanted me to be there at the far end. I went off, all on my own on strange European trains, which was fine through France because I spoke French, but not so fine when I got to the German bits and there was snow blocking the line and I had to go all round by a different way. I've never been so cold and so hungry in my life and it was a huge relief to get there and arrive at this grand, grand hotel where we were staying. I would have been frightened of meeting all these important people, but compared to my journey it seemed quite easy because they spoke English. Now, as for the Prince, it was quite obvious that Wallis was Queen Bee and I just kind of cruised in on her coat-tails.'

'What was he like?'

'Very amused by himself.'

'What do you mean?'

'He had this manic smile and he'd make all these wisecracks but he'd start laughing before he quite got to the end of any of them so you never really found out if they were funny or not. If he hadn't been a prince I guess I would have thought he was a little mad.'

'I read a book in town yesterday. Something by a man called Spengler. He said you played for the Prince.'

'He got it wrong, didn't he? Hutton Spengler, oh yes. He was a terrible man. He came to talk to me four times and he never took notes. Claimed he had a perfect memory but he kept asking the same questions. He didn't listen too good, that man. The book said I played for the King, didn't it?'

'That's right.'

'Of course, he wasn't the King, not then. Hadn't been crowned, hadn't quit. All that was still to come. Wallis made me play. I didn't want to. I knew I still had a lot to learn but it was something to do with giving herself power. She thought she'd seem a bit more queenly if she had a protegée, maybe. She'd probably read somewhere that real nobility had protegées. Art and music didn't come easily to her, she had to work at it. First night there, she insisted they all sat down and listened to me play. I really didn't want to do it.'

'Spengler said Edward started conducting.'

Natalie smiled. 'Oh boy. He got that right anyway. That was when I decided he was mad. I couldn't have been more than four bars in when he jumped up and his arms started going. First I thought he wanted me to stop, then I thought maybe he was having a fit or something. Then in the end I realized what he was doing. He was all out of time but he really thought he was helping. I couldn't look at him because it made me want to giggle and it was kind of off-putting. Then Wallis pulled him down into his seat and hung on to one of his arms but the other arm kept going, up and down, up and down right in front of the face of the guy in the other seat.'

'Was Max there?'

'Not then. No, there were two men from Scotland, Bruce Ogilvy and Andrew something, and this good-looking guy called Dugdale and a few women, plus this nice guy they'd sent up from the British Embassy to keep an eye on the Prince. I'll tell you, they had style, all of them. They were very sure of themselves and *so* charming you would not believe it. I was just a silly teenager who'd only been in London for three or four weeks and before that I'd never been anywhere much outside New York.'

'New York was a pretty stylish place to come from, surely.'

'It was *stylish* if that's the word, or flash, maybe, but it didn't have *class*. Not that effortless, tweed and leather, knowing just what to say, gracious to the lesser man, sort of class.'

'That sounds like snobbishness.'

She shook her head. 'Miles Malan, do you know *nothing* about your own country? It's snobbish when it's done by people who are pretending, because they're scared they might get it wrong so they protect themselves by putting down anyone else who does get it even a little bit wrong. I'm talking about the kind of bred in the bone, bona fide class that takes generations.'

'And you approve of that?'

'Well now, here we are and it's 1973 and you're mister angry young man and I'm some old fossil dinosaur and hell, yes I *liked* it. Okay, I was nineteen and green as they come and they made me feel like the most important woman on earth. After Wallis, that is. Anyway, I never said I'd vote for the feudal system, I just said I was a sucker for it.'

'How did Max come into it?'

'That's a good question. Sideways, I guess, like he usually did. After we'd been there three or four days, this situation began to develop which was kind of getting in the way of everyone enjoying themselves. Wallis wasn't what you would call the physically brave type of person, in fact coward would be a better word. She and I both put on skis for the first time on some really gentle little slope there, and when those skis of hers started to move, you should have heard her yell. She slid maybe two feet and sat down on her backside and that was it. We got her up on her feet again but it took two people to hold her and another one to calm her down and I guess nobody was having much fun. It started off with terrible weather, blizzards and freezing fog but the Prince, he just wanted to go for it and he got pretty bored with all this after five minutes.'

'He was a good skier, wasn't he?'

'The Prince? He was terrible.'

'Really?'

'Hey, Miles. Listen to me. He was a prince. If he thought he was good, everyone else agreed. He could go like hell in a straight line but, oh my gosh, if he had to do anything tough like turning or stopping – bang, that was it.'

'That's not what the books say. They say he was a good sports-man. Skiing, golf, everything.'

'Golf?' She laughed out loud. 'I never saw anyone hit a golf ball such a short way. Every time. A little stiff swing and pop, it would go bouncing off and everyone would say, "Oh *good* shot, sir."' Her plummy English accent was wonderfully, accurately antique.

'So he got cross with Wallis?'

'He wouldn't have dared but he liked her to be masterful not wimpy, so he left us to it. He was being chased all over the slopes by some predatory French women who wanted a slice of the action. Wallis was skidding about and doing the splits and falling over and yelling like it was the end of the world, and then this young English guy comes hurtling down the hill, does one of those real stylish stops right by us and says in this divine voice something like, "I say, can I help at all?"'

'That was Max?'

'Oh yes. Now, knowing Max, I would surmise that he'd been watching for a chance but I didn't guess that at the time and he always denied it later on. Maybe he'd seen the Prince earlier, or maybe he hadn't. Maybe he knew we were in the same party, but I don't think he knew who Wallis was because she was a well-kept secret at the time. Anyway, I was really impressed. Here was this young guy, and he was much nearer my age than anyone else around, and he just told us what to do and talked us right through it so that after a half-hour Wallis was going all of ten feet at a time without stopping and I could get up and down that little slope with no trouble at all. Oh yes, and he had a bit of class too, but he managed not to be so buttoned-up as the others. Next thing, Wallis asked him to come to lunch with us and introduced him to the Prince and all the rest of them like he was her saviour, and then in the afternoon I had him all to myself. My own personal instructor.'

'Where was Wallis?'

She gave me an owlish look. 'I wouldn't have any idea at all. She just faded out of it after lunch. Maybe she was having a rest or something.'

'Tired out after all her exertions?'

'Could be. The Prince must have been tired too. I didn't see him on the slopes either.'

'Oh.'

'Oh indeed. That wasn't the end of it. The next morning Wallis had another go but she was in a real impatient mood. I did up her bindings for her, which was pretty tough because she just would not keep her feet still, and then she saw someone she thought she recognized and lifted up one of her sticks to wave at them and before any of us could do anything at all about it she was moving off real smooth and going faster than she'd ever gone before. Only thing was she was going backwards.' Natalie started to laugh at the memory of it and it was infectious. She got herself under control in the end.

'Oh, dear me. Ogilvy was standing there, yelling, "Fall over, just fall over!" and the other guy, Dugdale, went off on his skis to try and catch her but she went shooting off the piste into this pile of deep snow and turned head over heels so all we could see were her legs sticking up the other side of the pile. Of course, who should show up then but Max, so that was when I really started to think he was keeping a close eye on us, and he helped pull her out of it.'

'Was that the end of her skiing?'

'Oh yes, which of course left the difficult matter of what to do with her all day. There was this problem with Wallis. She was a bird of prey and some of the other men in the party were too handsome for their own good or for the Prince's peace of mind. Okay, she was after him but she might have fitted in one or two more while he wasn't looking and you could catch her looking at Dugdale like a hawk watching a vole. Muggins here got drafted for the first day as chief companion and we drove each other mad because I didn't know how to talk about the kinds of things she liked to talk about.'

'Which were?'

'Who was having who's wife and wasn't the Duchess of thingummy an old bat and what Asprey's had in stock. That sort of rich stuff. She was trying hard to be a Grand Dame. Then Max reappeared when we were having tea and she insisted he joined us which was, I think, exactly what he hoped would happen and after that, there he was, a ready-made companion.'

'But you thought she had designs on him.' Straight away I wished I hadn't said it.

'Did I say so? Have you read my mind? Ah no, I forgot, you did it the sneaky way – you just read my letters.'

I made a face.

'Stop complaining,' she said. 'Who said I have to let you off lightly? You could be put in prison here for doing that. Designs on Max? Well, I thought she had, and then again perhaps she hadn't. Even Wallis would have had to admit he was much too young for her. I always had the feeling with Wallis that whatever she did behind closed doors, and there were a lot of closed doors believe me, it was nothing straightforward.'

I raised my eyebrows.

'I'm serious,' she said. 'Did you ever consider what it took to persuade the future King of England that she was worth more to him than a throne? He had beautiful women falling over him everywhere he went. He could have had any one of them, in fact he did have quite a lot of them and they wouldn't make demands or expect to be out there on the surface. They *knew*, the whole English aristocracy knew that if the Prince wanted a bit of hanky-panky that was part of the game. She changed the rules. Makes you think, don't it. She wasn't even beautiful.'

'Wasn't she?'

'She looks okay in photographs but she had a cruel, hard face in real life. I think it was something about the cruelty. Whatever it was she did to him, he *just* loved it.'

'What are you saying? Sado-masochism?'

'Would I say that? Come to that are *you* allowed to? I mean, you're a British subject. Isn't that sedition or treason or something like that? You could be hung.'

'Hanged.'

'Either way it still kills you.'

'No, it's all right. You're allowed to say anything once they've abdicated, in fact you're expected to. It's the done thing. She didn't try it on with Max?'

'Oh, he was star-struck. He thought she was marvellous, though he never knew for a moment what was going on with the Prince

283

and I didn't like to disillusion him. He would have been scared out of his wits if she'd pulled any moves on him.'

'What did you think of Max, then?'

'Me? Oh, you can guess. He was only four years older than me and he hadn't any of that slickness the others had. They were all so charming but with him you could look into his eyes and know it came up straight from his heart. He was so funny. He had lots of stories. What do you think? I fell head over heels.'

'What did Wallis make of that?'

'I hoped I didn't let it show. I was trying to be terrifically *English* about it.'

'So then? At the end? You just went away and didn't see him again until Antibes?'

That was pushing it a bit too much, or perhaps she was suddenly aware of time passing.

'Look, I could talk about this all day, but I'm getting way off the point here. You want to hear about the music? That piece of mine?'

I nodded.

'Like I said, I was a sucker. I married another glamorous European,' she said, and I bit my tongue in time to stop myself saying I knew. 'He was a count from somewhere in Hungary but he had a German name and all this land and castles and stuff. He was quite like Max to look at and maybe in lots of other ways too. It went wrong pretty quickly.'

'Why?'

'I found I only knew a tiny slice of him, just the bits he had chosen to show me. Not all of those turned out to be true. When he left, I wrote endless letters to him. I tried to tell him he could be whatever he wanted to be so long as he was honest with me – so long as I knew what was real and what wasn't. I wanted him to understand that the things he did that were wrong weren't as bad as the lies he told me to cover them up. That was when I wrote the music.'

'It was like Max all over again, wasn't it?'

'If you say so, Miles. It seems to me that's the way you want it to be.'

'Well, was it?'

'No, as a matter of fact it wasn't. Max never did one single thing that was intended to hurt me. Wolfgang did. History doesn't have to repeat itself exactly for your benefit, you know.'

I shrugged and she perhaps felt the need to meet me halfway.

'He came here, you know.'

'Max did?'

'Yes. I'd bought the site and it had a little shack on it. We stayed a weekend here, just one. He preferred being in town. I had a duplex on the park. He was much happier there. He liked to do the clubs. I told him what sort of house I was going to build and how I wanted it to be cosy. That was what mattered to me. He named it for me.'

'Cosy, like the Mews? Oh, I see.' Suddenly I did. The name on her gates. 'The Muse'.

'Get out of my head. Cosy goes with Mews in my head, not yours.'

'I'm sorry,' I said again.

'You should be.'

'What would you have done if he *had* sent you that letter, the way he first wrote it, before he changed it?'

'How do I know? It's not what happened, Miles. What matters is what did happen, not all the things that nearly did. It's hard enough dealing with the trail you leave through life without worrying about the blind alleys.'

'Would you mind telling me a bit about Ginny?'

'Why?'

'Because I'm still trying to understand the crash.'

'First maybe you'd better tell me about this crash.'

So I told her, in detail, constrained only by the knowledge that she'd known Virginia and loved Max.

'Is that really what this is all about?' she said at the end.

'Yes, I think so.'

'Did you ever talk to anybody about it? When it happened, I mean?'

'Not really.'

'Miles, how do you think knowing about Ginny will help you understand the crash? All I know about the crash is what you've just told me. Like I said, it was after my time, but crashes are crashes. Things break, I don't know. A tyre blows. Someone goes too fast. It's not Shakespeare. It's not like they're fated to die that way, because of the way they are and other people are. This sounds to me like it was an accident, not the ending of *Macbeth*.'

'I don't think that's true.'

She sat back and stared at me hard, and I found I had fooled myself into thinking I knew her very well while I really didn't know her at all. The woman looking at me suddenly seemed capable of getting very angry.

'So you think that this crash was some kind of fate waiting for them because of the people they were?'

'Well, a bit, yes. Ginny liked beating Douglas. Max bought this flashy car and let them drive it when he knew it wasn't safe.'

She shook her head. 'Things *weren't* safe. They came from a time when things weren't safe. Okay, not me. I spent the war back here, but Douglas, he was in all kinds of action – Dunkirk, Tobruk, Italy. Max had to live down the fact that he spent a quiet war, but that wasn't his fault.'

I was a little annoyed. She seemed to be lecturing me. 'You're not going to tell me he got wounded at Narvik?'

'No, why would I say that?' She had clearly never heard that one, so he had spared her some of his wilder inventions. 'He had lung problems, TB then bronchial pneumonia. He was in and out of hospital right through the war.'

'Oh.'

'It wasn't glamorous. He didn't have any good stories to tell. It was hard for a man to look like Max and not be a hero. All this stuff they got up to after the war, being *safe* wasn't a factor. You think Ginny wanted to be *safe*? You want to know what she was like? Her world turned around Douglas. She was clever and pretty and she did the things he did. They knew how to enjoy themselves. She tried to reform Max, then she gave up on him. Still doesn't mean fate killed her.'

I could have argued that. I could have risked telling her about Chinnery and those other letters to see how she would respond. I wasn't sure that would be sensible, and anyway, she was looking at her watch.

'I do have a lunch date today,' she said.

'Oh, I'm sorry.' I got up.

'No, I'm not trying to get rid of you quite yet, though when you get to my age you do need a little time putting on your lunch face.'

'I don't think *you* do.'

'Oh, you cut that out. You English guys. I just wanted you to know my time doesn't go on for ever, just in case there's something else you wanted to know.'

'Do you still . . . well, do you still feel fond of Max?'

'There you go again. Why do you ask a question like that?'

'Because he's all by himself in London and you're coming over in two weeks. Like I said, you could go and see him.'

'Would he welcome that?'

'I think he would.'

'Miles, if it was that easy, I could have gone to see him a long time back.'

'But you *never* saw him in London, did you?'

'He bent heaven and earth to stop me. You must know that. That was why I wrote those letters.'

'But he's got old now, and he's ill. It would be different.'

'You don't give up, do you?'

'Even if you don't, can I come and talk to you again when you're over?'

'Maybe. Give me your address and I'll think about it.' But her smile said she'd be in touch, so I wrote down my phone number and the rest for her.

'You will call me?'

'I said maybe.'

'Please.'

'I might have to, just to check you're eating properly. Miles, you still look terrible. There's nothing wrong with you, is there?'

'No. I'm just naturally thin.'

'Hmm,' she said, and she stood and waved as I drove away.

# Twenty-five

I liked the look of the countryside round Natalie's house. New York, with my money dwindling, held nothing for me but the confinement of a hotel room or the ache all round my eye to remind me of the nervy roulette of the streets. It was therefore easy to decide to stay more or less where I was, spending Sunday afternoon wandering through the woodland trails in the hills which rose behind Rotherham. I climbed on rocks and sat, watching the water churning and sliding down the chaos of the stream-courses as I read those letters yet again, freed from constraint by the fact that I had shared what they said with Natalie. The sheets of old paper rustled and shook a little in the handfuls of light breeze that moved inside the forest's filter and that made the letters seem alive, current, new. I was able now to hear them in Natalie's real voice and see them more clearly in the light of my direct experience of the way she was.

As soon as I left Natalie, I had begun to think of all the other things I really should have asked her about, the Duke and Duchess of Windsor playing out their shadow-life at La Cröe, Max as a soldier, the shady recovery of the big Bugatti and much more. I wanted to cross-check the story of the swimming trunks and the octopus, to find out what she knew of the ceremony for the statue and to see if he had ever talked to her about Sobibor, but I knew that there had been a limit to what I could expect out of that meeting and that I would just have to be patient and hope for another opportunity.

The woods on the hillside were a perfect natural backdrop for thought. The leaves were turning and I could hear the sifting wind, gentle in the high, cathedral canopy, trying their strength and drifting the driest of them down in see-saws to my feet. Water washed my thoughts along in that gentle musing way which takes you into unsuspected creeks and backwaters. The first unexpected realization was that, however I might have looked to Natalie, I felt completely physically well. That showed me by comparison how completely unwell I had been feeling through the last weeks in London, through the surreal interlude in Israel and through New York right up to the point where I had come into these same woods only yesterday. Whatever virus had produced the agues in my bones and the deep ache in my head for so long, I was glad that they were gone and I hoped that their disappearance would survive my re-emergence from the sanctuary of these clean, cool, healing trees.

Reading the letters again left me with a feeling of great warmth for Natalie and I moved on another hundred yards uphill to settle on a boulder above a pool imagining just how it could be if Max, after all these years, looked up from his chair in his prison room and saw her coming to rescue him. It seemed to me that all that had to happen was for her to go to see him and then something good must naturally follow. She could bring him back here to the house that he had named for her to sit in a rocking chair and listen to her music, that cosy life that he must have wanted even though he had turned his back on it. How much better that would be than his incarceration behind the closed windows of Weston House.

It would wipe out their separate pasts if they could be brought to that same, shared endpoint that they could have reached together. If I could only bring that about, I would have done something worthwhile for him. If so, then perhaps the whole story of the trunk, from the first moment of my finding it, had been aimed at this end by some benevolent destiny and was more than just a selfish tale of nosiness.

In the other papers I had brought with me there was one which I had started to read several times on my journey, but in the dried-out atmosphere of the airliners my headaches had got in the way each time. Max's handwriting was unusually flattened out even by the standards of his later writing and it needed a real effort to decipher it, but there in the middle of my soothing woods, clear-eyed, I found in the end that I could read it and what I discovered in it made me wonder. Did Max know that Natalie had married? Natalie presumably had no idea of Max's equally brief experiment with that state and I had not thought it was my business to tell her. They had both married at about the same time, and had stayed married for about the same length of time. What I was reading, I suspected at the start, were Max's reflections when his brief marriage to Laura came to an end.

*These are my thoughts on love, marriage and the advantages of being single, gathered together towards the end of the sixth decade of my life. It is a life whose circumstances have given me a unique vantage point from which to survey the bumpy terrain over which so many of my married friends have spent their lives attempting to travel.*

*I would say that I have led an unselfish life because I have spent it as a single man, never offering any woman more than I knew I could give and never trying to change the way in which any of the women I have loved chose to live themselves . . .*

A single man? An early lie, but then perhaps he really didn't see that brief marriage to Laura as something real.

*I have seen many half-formed couples rush to blend their immaturity together to make one of those three-legged-race pairings, who stumble onwards, growing no wiser. When two people marry it is romantically supposed that something wonderful happens, that they each provide what the other needs so that the whole is greater than the parts. It is my experience that the whole is usually less than the parts. In the worst of cases, both halves stay frozen in immaturity, back to back in life's gun-fight, protecting the weaknesses which living separately would have forced them to address and rectify. Even in the best cases, the give-and-take is uneven so that one may find a golden couple is in fact an alloy, where the quality of one disguises the base metal of the other. It may not be clear until they cease to be a couple, which was which.*

*One cautionary tale is provided by a couple I shall call Tony and Cleo because I still see much of 'Tony' and would not wish to risk wounding him by giving him his correct name.*

*When Tony and Cleo were first hell-bent for the altar, it was generally agreed that it would be hard to find a better-matched pair. Tony was a dashing war hero with fine features, a ready laugh and that British Bulldog utter dependability. Cleo was ravishingly pretty and a thoroughly good sport. Anything he could do, she could do nearly as well, though she was usually wise enough not to do it better. They were, it seemed, a couple made in heaven.*

However, marriage changed many things. Tony's wide circle of friends all liked Cleo but gradually those closest to him noticed a change. Somewhere a clock was now ticking which allowed him so much time spent amongst those friends and no more. On occasions when in the past he would have caroused late into the night, she would now remove him before the final bottles were empty. Even worse, if she were not there, a time would come when he would look in a worried way at his watch and make his excuses. For those of us accustomed to regard him as a central player in our own lives, he was beginning to turn into a furtive ghost.

Such unfamiliar tensions turned into accusations voiced by Cleo, to wedges driven into his male relationships and in the end to ultimatums in which she was fond of quoting him as her joint accuser of those who 'led him astray', to insist that he was behind her in everything she said though usually his own voice was silent.

How this would have ended heaven knows, except that fate intervened. One day, trying to provide by herself to Tony a one-woman substitute for all that easy male competitive camaraderie of which she had begun to deprive him, her foot slipped in what I might for convenience call a mountaineering accident and took her to her death. Poor Tony was left as the half of a whole which was no longer there.

Then there was the case of George, who was married before he was wise, forming a molecule from two infant atoms and laying the seeds of their ultimate destruction in the process. An unacknowledged friction chafed away at their bonds and one day, when another atom came along, calling with a siren voice, he broke free and raced off to form a new compound. Such chemistry releases an unsuspected corrosive heat which leaves no one unscarred. Worse, the errant atom, taking no time to gain wisdom from the whole experience, flies with violent force into its new union and asks us, the onlookers, to go along with the belief that this was the match that was always meant to be. As ever, though, the refugee atom takes the seeds of its undoing with it because it is what it is and has not learnt to be anything else.

When I was young and saw things simply, I was tempted by the intoxication of love to try marriage. War intervened and the uncertainty of survival which goes with membership of an elite regiment made marriage inadvisable. Thus it was that I took my reward for my efforts in that conflict in brief dalliances, at least as pleasurable, I would

*say, to those with whom I shared them as they were to myself. When,
after the war, I chanced to meet again the girl with whom I had been so
in love, I found that she was now a woman. We had both matured and
one might have said the conditions for success appeared to be in place.
We were both beyond that first dangerous age when the chemistry is
the only force that matters and our compound might have lasted.*

*There was a price to pay. To meet my love's demands I would have
had to give up a great deal of my way of life. She wanted me to duck
my head, to live inside a smaller world, to divest myself of much that
made up the life I had long led. Used to a grander way of living, I was
not sure I could sustain that.*

*I had seen, as a close observer, a most notable royal personage
surrender, for love, an enormous prize. I had seen him left only with
love, without the means to give the object of his passion the life and
the fully recognized status that he felt she richly deserved. I had seen
the bitterness that crept into him as a consequence and I had seen the
changes this created in her, for being a duchess in exile is nowhere near
to being a queen at home.*

*I did not want to make the same mistake. I resolved therefore that
I would never make such a decision, for fear of the damage it might
in the end do to my sweet friend, and in consequence of that I have
remained single to this day. I would submit that she and I are the better
for it though the penalty is that one must die alone.*

I turned over the sheet, realized that was the end of it and could
only think, Oh Max, you stupid, stupid man. There could be no
doubt that Tony and Cleo were Douglas and Ginny and it horrified
me that time and tragedy had not dimmed his resentment at having
his brother snatched away by marriage. His post-mortem swipe
at the 'rock climbing' Ginny showed the depth of his bitterness.
What about Laura? When was this written? . . . *towards the end of
the sixth decade in my life . . .* By my maths that made him maybe
fifty-eight, so it was 1970, just three years ago. Before his strokes.
After his marriage. It was the usual edited version of the truth. Did
he truly believe in all those mythical estates of his so that when
Natalie offered to draw a veil over all his past nonsense he actually
thought she was asking him to give up something real? Could he
seriously compare that to Edward VIII giving up his throne?

Could he not even admit to himself that he had tried marriage?

I would have liked to believe that Laura paled into insignificance besides Natalie and that he could not bear to put them both on to the same page, but I suspected that was being too kind. It was more likely that he simply married Laura because she was rich and she came along when he was, as usual, broke.

He should have married Natalie.

A deer wandered into my sight. I was sitting so still that I'd already seen my very first chipmunks but it stayed for only seconds, freezing, then racing off before my less sensitive ear registered the sounds that had scared it. A number of people were approaching, shouting loudly, and without noticing me sitting quietly on my rock they gathered below me to see how much damage they could do to the place. It was a family which Max would definitely have described as three-legged-racers stumbling through life – a bullying father and a mother who took out her anger on her pitiable but also repellent children, who were doing their best to lay off the damage on each other. They careered slowly and noisily through my wood, along the stream beneath my feet with no sign that they knew they were in the countryside at all.

'You wanna go back, you go back!' shouted the father, a round man in a baseball cap. 'You stay that shape, Jess, I don't give a shit.'

His wife turned on their son, who was tearing saplings out of the ground and launching them like spears into the stream.

'Get outa the mud, Jerry!' she screamed. 'I ain't washing your shoes.'

As soon as she turned away, the son pushed his small sister into a bush. They were no advertisement for marriage.

When they sat down directly under my rock, I cleared my throat loudly and the man, a blob under a baseball cap, looked up.

'Hey, Jess!' he bawled as if I wasn't sitting there ten feet away. 'There's a guy up there.'

'Oh yeah,' said his wife.

'You making that noise at me?' the man said.

'No,' I said huskily, 'it's just I've got an infectious lung condition.'

'What's that again?'

'It's a bug. I've got this sickness. Thought I'd better warn you.'

Peace returned quickly when they'd gone, though the deer wisely decided to stay far away. The interruption had broken my train of thought and in the moment before I started thinking in some sort of formal, linguistic way, my mind produced one of those brief abstract pictures which are perhaps the way the brain really handles information. I had a momentary mental glimpse of something like a jigsaw, woven through the trees in front of me, bits and unconnected pieces of ideas and facts and history – successive images of Max's face at all its ages from tousle-haired, teenaged optimist to compromised fifty-year-old, snaking ever downward. Everywhere in it there were huge gaps as the fragments refused to join. In the micro-second before it diminished into the normal, limiting processes of thought, it brought something to me, a little insight into why Max had turned down Natalie's offer. The flimsy structure of his life was held together by his fantasies. Without them, he would not have known who he was. They were the rotting foundations on which he had built himself and from which he derived his sense of himself. It must have been close to a constant state of madness. Perhaps Max *was* being unselfish. He knew, despite Natalie's faith, that he might not be improved by giving all that up.

I also realized at the same time and in a deep, true way that only sounds like a clever paradox when it has to be turned back into incompetent words, how well I knew the essence of him and how huge were the remaining gaps in my knowledge of him.

In the late afternoon I realized that I had work to do, preparing for tomorrow and the sales job for Ephraim which was, after all, paying my bills, so I got back into the car and drove to New York. On the way I finally figured out how to tune the radio and then, with the first news bulletin, I found out what Natalie had meant when she'd said I got out of Israel just in time.

By the time I got back to Manhattan and returned the car, the Yom Kippur War had been churning up the rocks of the Golan Heights and the sands of Sinai for more than twenty-four hours. When I tried to call Ephraim's number from my hotel room, all the lines to Israel were out of action, either due to the war or to the massive overload of worried relations also trying to call.

The meetings on Monday were difficult and the first one set the tone for all the rest. A wiry man was waiting in the lobby when the front desk rang me, on time virtually to the second. I showed him into the tiny meeting room they had laid on for an extra fifty dollars. As if to establish his credentials he was wearing a leather and sheepskin flying jacket and aviator's dark glasses. He'd come all the way from Texas. I showed him the photos of the plane and he brought a magnifying glass out of his bag and went over them, whistling in admiration.

'Yeah,' he said, 'P51H sure enough. Looks original. We're interested. You the owner?'

'No, I'm acting as agent for an associate.'

'So she's in England.'

'No, a foreign country.'

'England is a foreign country.'

I let that one go.

'Okay. We'll want to see it. Where is it?'

'It's in Israel.'

'Shee-it! You're kidding me. In the middle of a war?'

'Well, I don't suppose the war's going to destroy everything that's on the ground, do you?'

'Hey, for all we know there might not be an Israel by this time next week.'

The same thought had occurred to me.

They came, one after the other, and they expressed interest which turned to horror when they found out where the Mustang was, so that after the first three I stopped admitting it was in Israel and simply said it was in a foreign location and that I would tell them where it could be inspected after I had further talks with the owner.

At the end of the day, with half a dozen would-be buyers clamouring for more information and the prospect of by far the biggest commission I had ever made almost in my grasp, I spent another two hours trying to get through to Ephraim and then lay on my bed letting the dark side take over and thinking of the odds stacking up against the deal. For all I knew the Mustang could already be scrap metal. The Egyptians or the Syrians might have overrun the area. My geography of Israel and its neighbours was pretty sketchy; I'd flown in, been taken on a ride for which I might as well have been blindfolded, and left again. I didn't have the slightest clue as to exactly where the plane was and I would certainly never find that old hangar again, so it was all down to the outcome of the war and getting back in touch with Ephraim when he'd finished his flying duties.

If Israel won.

All the progress I'd made with my state of mind and my state of health went out of the window. I couldn't bear to think in any detail of the immediate future and after a while it seemed completely obvious that I should get out the plastic bag, which was still gratifyingly full, and do my best with the foil and matches to make everything go away.

I know now, all these years later from the official accounts of the war, that Ephraim Bar-Lev died during those first twenty-four hours in the cockpit of a Mirage III, though the exact circumstances of his death are a mystery and it may have been due to an engine explosion rather than to the impact of an enemy missile. At the time, I simply packed my bags on Tuesday morning. I looked at the plastic bag and knew it would be sensible to flush it down the lavatory, but you don't do that to your best friend. I put it in my hand baggage but I knew that would just mean I would have second thoughts on the plane, so I committed myself. I took the complimentary plastic bottle of hotel talcum powder, emptied that down the loo and filled it with the skag. Then, for cover, I took all the other complimentary bottles of this and that and put them all together in the bottom of my bag, the one that would go in the plane's hold. I used almost the last of my dollars to settle my hotel bill and as the desk clerk handed me my change, he gave me an envelope with it, a letter addressed to me with American stamps. Preoccupied with finding out how I could get to the airport in time without having to pay for a cab, I assumed it was from one of the warbird people I had seen the day before and put it in my pocket.

The plane was half empty and quite comfortable because I could lift the armrest and sprawl sideways into the seat next to me. It was good to know that there was nothing much to decide about for a few hours, apart from whether I wanted the meals they brought and what I would have to drink, though a nagging worry about the contents of my bag was starting to seep in. I wished I still had the choice. I knew now that I should definitely have flushed it. The penalty, if I was checked, didn't bear thinking about. To distract myself, I plugged in the earphones, flicked my way through the in-flight entertainment channels and by the serendipity of these things heard a mellow, male American voice say, '. . . and that wonderful piece from the pen of Gabriel Fauré is played for us now on the sweet cello of Natalie Vanderberg.'

So, there, leaving the coastline of the United States behind, listening to Natalie's cello, I opened the letter in my pocket to fill the time and keep my fears at bay and found it was from her.

Dear Miles,

I am writing this Sunday evening after an afternoon spent mostly feeling unsettled following your departure, in the hope it will reach you at your hotel before you leave. I was not too sure I had remembered the name of the hotel right, but I called it up and they said that yes, they had an English guy named Malan staying and did I want to be put through? Well, no I didn't because I wasn't sure what it was that I wanted to say and I hope that in a letter it will all come out right.

After I came back from lunch, during which I was so distracted that my friends were quite sure something dreadful must have happened, I played around with feeling resentful for a while to see if that was what lay behind my discomfort, but that wasn't it. I could have felt that way without too much trouble I guess, because can you imagine how *you* would feel if someone turned up with some of the most private letters you had ever written and insisted on going over them with you in detail?

I couldn't make resentment stick because there you were, face to face with me, and it was so very clear that your interest in all this ancient business of ours came from something harmless. I would say it came from something mixed-up maybe, but definitely nothing bad.

Before I tell you one or two things that might help you understand, I need to ask you whether you are really sure all this is good for you? There was a smell of sulfurous decay left hanging in the air after you left. I mean that metaphorically, of course. I had a strong sense that all is not well in your life and that perhaps the energy you are devoting to mine should be better addressed to your own. Forgive me if that seems an intrusion into your life but if it does, then stop being so sensitive and score it off against your own intrusions into mine.

I don't know whether you have looked into a mirror lately but you look pretty terrible. I have seen skeletons looking meatier than you do. You should eat sometimes and maybe sleep sometimes and think longterm, because life's too short for dying. Before you crumple this up and throw it away, I've put in a few bits and pieces at the end which are a bribe to keep you reading, and don't you dare cheat by turning straight to them because I've put a hex on them and if you do that, they won't make any sense at all.

I had an idea this evening that maybe the real thing that keeps you going over all this is some kind of an idea that you and Max are linked up. I don't mean just the crash and I do understand that is a real link to you, though I want to come back to that later if I remember. I mean something else, deeper than that. Maybe you think you are like him? You probably don't know this but you look a bit like him, or at least like he would have if you'd thrown him in a pit and hadn't fed him for a year. You have all that English charm, too.

Let me give you the Natalie Vanderberg free lesson on how to avoid turning into Max Owen.

DON'T: think for a moment that you should be measured by what you own.

DO: find something to do in your life that you really love to do.

DON'T: choose all your friends from people who drink too much (or whatever your generation does), laugh too easily or always make jokes out of the things that really matter.

DO: hit your difficulties head-on instead of tucking them behind the clock hoping they will go away.

DON'T: turn away from friends when they tell you things you don't want to hear. If they *were* friends, you should listen however much it hurts.

DO: keep faith in yourself so that you measure yourself

by your own standards. Never reinvent yourself to fit other people's standards. (In this context, it is a good idea never to join the Guards.)

DON'T: ever inherit enough money to keep you alive without trying.

Okay, lecture over. Here's the bribe that kept you reading.

I never saw Max again after that last letter you have but I did see Douglas. He came here on some business trip and he stayed with me for a night. I guess it was '61? He talked a great deal about Ginny, so I know she was still alive then. He told me Max and Ginny never got along because Max was jealous and he said he wished Max and I had got together because life would have been easier then, as Max would have had nothing to be jealous of. I remember him saying that Max had always seemed to him like a younger, not an older, brother and it was hard to be caught between a wife and a brother. The reason I'm telling you this is because I guess I broke down a little that night and I told him all about how I had tried to give Max a way out.

That made him pretty sad, though he was very British, if you don't mind my saying that, and he didn't take easily to talking about such things. He said he thought it went back to when they were very small. Their father was a fierce old man and their mother, who was much younger, liked to do a lot of things on her own. He said that with a meaningful look, so I am not entirely sure what he meant though I can guess. She left them to themselves a lot. He said they were sent away to boarding school when they were about eight or nine years old and Max kept running away. Once, even, Max stole a master's bicycle late at night and pedalled off into the middle of nowhere. He was found ten miles away by a policeman because the chain had come off and he couldn't put it back on. The teachers didn't understand and he got punished. Doug said he thought that changed him. He said the war had been terrible for Max because he got himself that dose of TB early on and he never got to do anything interesting and Max felt so bad about that that he started making up a lot of stuff. It got so that Doug could not talk to him about what he'd been through himself (and believe me, Douglas was right bang in the middle of the fighting, from beginning to end). Doug said you can't tell what would have happened to Max in combat. You might think it would not have turned out well, but that's when the true hidden core of people comes out to the surface and never goes all the way back in again. Max never had that chance. I think maybe he would have surprised us all.

He said what happened right after the war was the very worst thing for Max, all that fake royal stuff in the South of France. Don't I know it? I'd kind of fallen out with Wallis by that time but I went back there two or three times to keep an eye on Max. It was like watching someone drowning. He was disappearing below the surface of all that pomposity and mannered crap they had going on there. It made me very sad. The Duke and the Duchess were living in a completely unreal world and it was like an infection for him, spreading out the tall stories (that was what he called them) from just war stories to the whole of the rest of his life. By the way, he got pretty much drummed out of the Guards because he got in money trouble then he lost all his soldier friends because he started being 'rather indiscreet' about the Windsors.

I think Doug was telling me all this as some kind of an apology on Max's behalf and right at the end of it, just as I was saying goodbye to him when I'd taken him back to the station, he said, 'Max was never a bad man. He just doesn't know that, so he keeps behaving like one because it's easier.' Sometimes, when I screw my brain up, I think I know what he meant.

Now as for you, Miles, maybe you do see echoes of yourself in Max, but I don't think running around after the past like this is going to do you any good. People are not like they are in books or in movies. Their stories do not have a structure that always makes sense. Ragged things happen to people, chaotic, senseless things, which are not always the unavoidable result of what they are. The crash you saw was one of those chaotic things. You will never tie Max's affairs up in a tidy parcel. If you think you need to do that to make sense of yourself, you are quite wrong, so look to yourself. I think it is important that you stop trying to know Max and start trying to know yourself before this dusty old story gets too deep into you.

I will be in London from October 20th for four or five days. I will be staying at Brown's Hotel and I have your address and number so if you do not contact me then rest assured I shall contact you.

Look after yourself (and that is not an empty instruction),
Natalie.

That gave me plenty to think about. It hurt a great deal to discover that my very first introduction to Max had probably been a tall tale, that he had won my heart with a lie and the motorcycle was only a push-bike, but then I thought about it again. Stripped of the exaggeration, there was a far more touching tale behind it, of a sad little boy who had pedalled off into the night. Didn't I know that feeling? I had done the same, after all. He was punished for it and I wasn't, and then I understood that he dealt with it in the way he had learnt, by readjusting the details and writing down his own version. Perhaps it was, after all, the best way to have met Max.

After a time in which we flew onwards into and out of a shortened night and I dozed, worrying, under a thin blanket, the captain woke us up to tell us the local time in London and inform us it was raining. I had gone to sleep in one reality and woke, muzzy-brained, to the steaming salty bacon smell of an airline breakfast, to entirely another. I was now terrified. Could I find a toilet between the baggage claim and customs? They must watch those, if they exist. What had I been thinking of?

At the end of the line there was my flat and there was Cat and I was not looking forward to going back to either of them, but far worse than that was the prospect of not getting that far. I wondered what the sentence was for smuggling heroin.

Brooding on that, I wondered then if my mother also thought I'd been responsible for the Colonel's death. She'd sold Oakdean with indecent haste and not even told me where she'd gone for a long time after her move to the Channel Islands. I promised myself that if I got through customs I would write her a letter.

# Twenty-six

If I had left myself any way out at Heathrow, I would have taken it, but from the baggage claim to the customs area there is no way out. There's your suitcase, there's you and that's it, a narrowing funnel with fate at the far end of it. I could not believe I could possibly have been so stupid just for the sake of a small bag of powder. It was a moment of realization when I could see myself through the eyes of the outside world, a criminal drug-user, a statistic – not Milo with his reasons and excuses.

It took an age before my bag appeared – enough time to nurse a fantasy that maybe they'd lost it – but then up the ramp it came, sliding out on to the carousel, whose overlapping blades carried it away on a long circuit which would inevitably bring it back round to me. I was in no hurry to face it. This is not my fault, I thought. Where was it exactly that I made a choice in all this? I always needed something, everyone does, but no one filled my need so I had to do it myself and this was what came along. It could just as easily have been alcohol, then no one would have minded if I'd staggered off the plane, boozed to the eyeballs, and sung my way through the green channel. Max would have done that, then happily signed a dodgy deal, bounced a cheque, screwed up a lover and everyone would have said there goes old Max, what a card, eh?

My bag was halfway round, nemesis on a rubber belt.

What right did anyone have to judge me? What chance did I ever have in that bloody, silent, tense house where I wasn't even allowed to know what genes I carried within me? What inheritance did I have from Peter Malan, the wild man, the 'wrong 'un', who fought his hard war? I had his genes, that was all, and how could I be expected to understand what that laid me open to if I was never allowed to know him?

The bag arrived and I picked it up, trying to control the engulfing

302

panic, and as I walked through the green channel, entirely for-getting how a normal person would walk and where they would look, a customs man said, 'Excuse me, sir,' and beckoned me over to his bench.

'Would you mind telling me where you've come from?' he said.

'New York and Israel before that.' My voice did not sound like my voice.

'Business or pleasure?'

'Business. I sell parts for old aircraft.' Stupid. Don't say unneces-sary things.

'Nasty shiner you've got there.'

'I got mugged.'

'You left Israel before the war started, I take it?'

'Yes.' Why did he ask that? Maybe he's just being friendly.

'Would you open the bag?'

He went through it quite fast and the pocket with the hotel shampoos and soaps and the talcum powder bottle were almost the last things he came to. I added another mental guarantee to my list. If I got away with this I would give it up completely. He zipped up the pocket and I felt my knees weaken.

'That's all right, sir,' he said, 'off you go.'

'Thanks,' I said. 'Bye, now.'

Of course, getting away with it changed everything. On the bus from Heathrow to the Cromwell Road, through the grey October drizzle I felt like a master of the universe. I forgot my second promise straight away and modified the first. I would write to my mother. I would demand that she tell me all there was to know about Peter Malan.

I was wet through when I unlocked the door of the flat and I saw at once that it was different. My pictures had gone from the walls and half the furniture had gone, too. The pictures were mine but the furniture had come with the flat. Cat was fast asleep in my bed and I shook her awake.

'What the fucking hell have you done with all the stuff?'

'Wha–? Stop it. Let go.'

'Cat. Wake up. I want to know what's happened to the furniture.'

'Milo! You're back. Have you been in the war?'

'No. Where's it gone?'

'I thought you were dead. You fly off to Israel, then the war starts and there's no sign of you.'

I was amazed she even knew there was a war. Cat didn't listen to news. It must be a big story here to have penetrated to *her* consciousness. I suspected all she was doing was trying to distract my attention.

'I was in New York by that time. Just tell me. Have you sold it all?'

'New York? Wow.'

'I said, have you sold it?'

'Stop banging on about the furniture. I'll tell you later. It's all right. You're all wet. Take that stuff off and come to bed.'

Whatever she had done it had to be bad because she was undoing my shirt too enthusiastically. I was very glad I'd taken the trunk upstairs to Mr Pascal.

'I don't want to come to bed. I want to . . .'

Her hands and mouth found a way of distracting me and this wasn't a version of Cat I'd ever met before, so curiosity overcame distaste and despite myself it was some time before I got back to the point.

'I had to get some stuff,' she said eventually, 'for when you got back. You took all the money.'

'Yeah, that's because it was my money.'

'That's not very nice. Did you get any more from your mate Ephraim?'

I got out of bed and dialled Ephraim's number. This time the phone rang and rang, then just as I was about to put it down a woman's voice answered.

'Hello?' I said. 'This is Milo Malan. Is Ephraim there?'

There was a torrent of what might well have been Hebrew.

'Ephraim,' I said slowly and distinctly. 'Can I talk to Ephraim?'

The voice broke into a sobbing wail and I put the phone down.

Cat looked at me with her eyebrows raised.

'No, I didn't,' I said.

'Do you want a smoke?' she said, and Natalie's face came into my mind. That was there, this was here. A little bit can't do any harm, I thought. One thing led to another.

The next day the flu had come back or maybe it was the dark, dank flat or the bed or something, but I ached everywhere and wished I was back in the Massachusetts woods again. Cat went out to score some more, and I felt jumpy waiting for her to come back so I went up to Mr Pascal and got the trunk.

I took out all the files, all the stuff I had already looked at and sorted out and I put them on one side. Underneath them, there wasn't all that much left to go through. I picked up a letter from a firm of solicitors in the mid-1950s:

Dear Mrs Hutton,
I have now had a word with your husband's solicitors and I am told that he is not prepared under the circumstances to increase his offer to contribute towards your costs beyond the amount he has already offered, viz: fifty guineas. I am further told that if this offer is not accepted in the near future it will be withdrawn. I pass on to you without comment his suggestion that Mr Birkin Owen might care to contribute the balance. The list is making steady progress and the case should soon come on for hearing so we request your instructions in the matter as soon as possible . . .

Then there was a summons for non-payment of a tailor's bill, a receipt for a fine of two pounds ten shillings from a magistrates court, and the old-fashioned brown registration book for a Jaguar XK120 sports roadster. Most of all there were scores more photos, seemingly from the twenties and showing indistinct tiny groups of children on beaches and headlands, and finally there was a piece of pasteboard, the shape and size of a visiting card, on the back of which was written in ink: *Max. Guardroom fracas not well received by the Colonel. Gentlemen do not fight tradesmen. See me before he carpets you. Good luck. Bonzo.*

None of it carried my knowledge one bit further and my attention span, the way my head was feeling, was strictly limited. In the end all there was left in the trunk was the thick yellow wodges of newspaper lining the bottom.

I had come to the end.

\*     \*     \*

A letter came from Tiggy a week later, or maybe it was more than that. Time had started mattering while I was on my trip, forced to think about appointments, flight departures, distances and speed, but now it stopped meaning anything at all and life went back to its familiar ways where I could walk out on the street and never quite know for certain whether the shops would be open.

I'd given up on the furniture. The landlord only came as far as the door when he collected the rent so there was a chance he wouldn't notice for a while yet. Cat had been quite docile, almost affectionate. Maybe I'd surprised her by my trip, or maybe I'd come back different or perhaps it was just that she was using more stuff than usual.

She was dead to the world when the letter came and I opened it and read it, sitting by the window with the paper angled to catch the light.

Dear Miles,

This is a goodbye for now. I've chosen the easy way out of conflict with Mummy and I'm taking myself off for a bit. She's fixed up some cooking for me in Cape Town. Friends from way back. It's meant to be six months working and six months travelling. It will be a relief to get away because she can't leave it all alone. We have the same conversation over and over again and it's always about you. I'm getting pretty fed up with it and I've done my best but you haven't really given me much ammunition to defend you with, have you?

I don't know whether that woman you're living with told you, but I came to see you last week. You weren't there. She said you'd gone to Israel but I don't suppose for a minute that was true.

I do hope you know what you're doing, I'm sure she's got a nice side but she seemed to me to be behaving very oddly and she was very rude to me.

I want to say something to you and I'm sure you'll think it's boring and that Mummy's been getting to me, but this does really come from me. I think I really do understand a

306

lot more about you than you think I do. I know how DULL Sussex seems to you, and how absolutely dreadful all those people like the Hunt Ball crowd are, and if I was a bit braver I might have run off to London and tried lots of new things too. What I want to say is don't be so angry with everything in your old life that you think it's all right to hurt yourself. Isn't there a balance somewhere? I know you don't want to be Miles Drummond any more, but couldn't you be Milo Malan in some way that doesn't seem quite so dangerous? You've got such a lot to offer. There must be a better way. I don't know whether it has struck you but there's old Max in the trunk, turning his back on all the good things in life. Don't do the same.

You're probably scrumpling this up by now, but I wouldn't be saying it if it didn't matter to me. Even if you can't value yourself, try valuing the things you do.

I hope it works out for you, I really do, and I'll send you an address when I get there.

Love, Tiggy.


I'd had enough of lectures. My head was aching badly. I didn't want to throw the letter away and I didn't want to leave it around for Cat to find so I stuffed it in one of the trunk files, then just to prove to myself it hadn't got to me, I got out Cat's new stash of smack, and – ignorant of any of the finer points of the purity of heroin – injected myself with far, far too much.

Instead of the usual rush of peace and pleasure arriving in pumping heart-beats of bliss, it hit me like a rabbit punch. For a few seconds I was aware that I was lying on the floor and that I had lost the power to move my arms and legs. Then I was no longer aware of anything physical at all.

Most of what I experienced in the following forty-eight hours is lost to me. It seems to me that I had a thudding soundtrack, like a slow drum in my head the whole time, but I am told that was probably just my heart-beat. The things I saw all seem to have fitted their movements to that drum so that they marched through the caves of my head on long diagonals, sweeping closer, then vanishing somewhere behind me. Heroin, in normal doses, is meant to abolish fear and worry, but there was plenty of that here, maybe because of the Valoxone they filled me with as an antidote. There was a fear that I was going to die and a deeper fear that I was going to die alone. At the end of it, there was Max – the Max in the David Niven photo, pacing up to me, past me, again and again, clutching bundles of letters, brandishing them in my face as he passed, mumbling at me as he approached then speaking insistently next to my ear just as he disappeared, 'Can you hear me, Miles? Can you hear me?'

I opened my eyes to a room full of tubes and bottles and instruments and the person saying, 'Can you hear me, Miles?' was Natalie, who was sitting by the bed, leaning forward over me.

My mouth was too dry to speak and my throat was horribly painful so I tried to lift up a hand, but that felt uncomfortable too because something was sticking in the back of it.

'You've got a drip there,' said Natalie. 'Don't move. I'll get a nurse to take a look at you.'

The nurse came, followed by a doctor, who asked me strange questions. What my name was, though Natalie must have told them, what month it was, what you got if you added five and four, who was Prime Minister? I didn't want to answer but he wouldn't leave me alone until I did.

When they'd finally finished fussing about with me and I'd been allowed a little water to wet my mouth, we were left alone again.

'Well,' said Natalie, 'aren't you going to ask all the usual questions like where am I and how long have I been here?'

'I've had enough of questions,' I croaked, 'and I know where I am. I'm in hospital. Was I taken ill?'

'Taken ill? You think something happened to you? *You're* what happened to you.' She sounded quite cross. 'If I hadn't come to see you when I did, you wouldn't be here at all. That was the day before yesterday, by the way, and this is St Luke's. Now, I'm doing an afternoon recital so I'll be seeing you later and if you're strong enough then I'm going to tell you exactly what I think of you and your friend and the stupid life you're living.'

My friend? She'd met Cat? I began to put it together. The needle, then falling on the floor. *Natalie* had found me? That felt terrible.

I didn't have much time to myself for the next three hours.

Doctors came back and did things to me and one of them mercifully took the aching tube out of the back of my hand, then a policeman arrived and asked a lot of questions about how long I'd been using hard drugs and who Cat was and where we got the stuff. I was very vague.

'You must know her surname,' he said. 'You're cohabiting.'

I realized with some surprise that I didn't. 'Ask her yourself,' I said.

'We'd like to. Only thing is she's done a runner.'

'Cat's gone?'

'Cleared out. I think your Mrs Vanderberg maybe drove her out.'

After he'd gone a woman with a clipboard came and asked me a million questions about drug usage. That felt like punishment enough. I wanted to howl at them all, to tell them to stop treating me like a junkie. They'd got it completely wrong. I used it sometimes, sure, but I wasn't an addict, for God's sake. Addicts weren't people like me.

By the time Natalie came back in the early evening, the aches were back and I was starting to feel really unwell.

'How's it going?' she said.

'Not great. I haven't been feeling too good for a long time now.'

'That does not surprise me,' she said, 'sticking that stuff into you.'

'It's the other way round. I was feeling ill before. I was just using it to make me feel better.'

'Miles. Let's try and keep ourselves honest here, shall we? You're hooked on that stuff. That's what makes you feel bad.'

I couldn't expect her to understand so I left it. 'What happened when you arrived at the flat?'

'I knocked. Then I knocked some more, then I looked in through the window and I could see you stretched out on the floor so I knocked a whole lot more and I kicked a bit and in the end your friend Cat came out.'

'And then?'

'I said who I was and I asked why you were on the floor and she said you were asleep. She didn't want me to come in but I guess I pushed her out of the way and when I saw the state you were in, I called an ambulance.'

309

'What state was I in?'

'Dead white, blue lips, feeble pulse, barely breathing and the mess around you was unbelievable. The hell you were asleep. She must have known.'

'It was a bad week. What happened with Cat?'

'I guess I found out how much you were worth to her.'

'Oh. You mean she was upset?'

'No, I mean it only cost me a hundred pounds to get rid of her.'

'What?'

'It was a bargain. She started at two hundred but I held out.' Natalie looked at me but I had nothing to say. 'I asked what it would cost for her to go away and never come back,' she went on. 'Like I say, she started at two hundred.'

It hurt my pride a bit, but then I imagined Cat grabbing the money. She'd be back, laughing about it. She'd just wait for Natalie to go away.

Natalie read my thoughts. 'She only got the first fifty. The rest goes to an address she gave me in six months if she keeps to her side of the bargain.'

'What address?'

She shook her head. 'My secret. The police don't get it and nor do you.'

'You're going to a lot of trouble.' I wasn't entirely sure I wanted all this.

'You're a total idiot,' she said. 'You have no idea how much trouble. I did mouth to mouth on you for twenty minutes before the ambulance arrived. I had a concert to prepare and instead I was crouched down on your goddamned floor in all that shit keeping you breathing until they came and put a mask on you.'

'Oh, Natalie, I . . .' The swearwords which had erupted from her shocked me even more than what she was saying.

'I thought you were going to die. I came here with you and they stuck a tube down your throat and put you on a ventilator. Then you stabilized, but when I asked them what the danger was, they said brain damage. Do you know what heroin does when you do that? Do you? Apart from pretending to make things better? Well, do you?'

'No.'

'It slows down your breathing. It drops your blood pressure. It starves your brain of oxygen. Bits of your brain die, Max. They die.'

'I'm not Max.'

'I mean Miles,' she said furiously. 'I know you're not Max. He never touched anything like *that*. Anyway, I stopped that happening, Miles, by the purest chance that I showed up just then. Your Cat wasn't going to do a damn thing for you.'

'Thank you,' I said.

'My decision,' she said wearily. 'If you need a reason, just suppose I couldn't help Max so I'm helping you.'

'Max? Have you been to see him?'

'No, I have not.'

'Are you going to?'

'I think not. That's for another time. It's you I want to talk about. What's going to happen to you?'

'Happen to me? When?'

'When you leave here. When you go out and find another Cat with another syringe.'

'I won't. I'm not addicted to it. It was just a mistake.'

'That's not true.'

'No, really. It is. It was only two or three times. I don't think I . . .'

'It is not true, Miles. You have to believe me. Take a look at your arms. I did. You've got needle tracks all over.'

How could she have got this so wrong? Didn't she know me at all?

'Are you feeling good right now?' she said.

'No. I'm feeling lousy. You see, that's why I was –'

'That's addiction.'

There was a long silence while I grappled with whether I could afford to believe her.

'I have a suggestion to make,' she said.

'Yes?'

'Detox,' she said, 'then rehab.'

I must have looked blank.

'Detoxification and rehabilitation,' she said. 'I've been asking around. There's a place down south. Dorset? Is that right? It's very good. They can take you in tomorrow.'

'Oh, I'll just make sure I don't use it again. I don't need . . .'

'Give me a break, Miles. Take it from me. You need it. You need it bad.'

'Is it National Health?'

'You mean is it on the state? No, it isn't. It's Natalie Health. It's on me.'

'Oh, no. I shouldn't be costing you money. I'm not your responsibility.'

'I'm short on responsibilities. I've got space for you. Just for a while and as long as you show me you're worth it.'

'And will you go to see Max?'

She tutted. 'I've been at your place. I got people to come and clean it up. The landlord showed up along with the ambulance so I had to get some furniture to keep *him* sweet. I was waiting while they cleaned and I took a look through the trunk.'

'What did you find?'

'Strange as it may seem, one of the first things I found was a letter to you written by a very sensible girl called Tiggy.'

'Oh, that.'

'Okay, now supposing I said, hey Miles, I know what's best for you, why don't you go and hitch up with that Tiggy girl?'

'No, that's completely ridic—'

'That's what I'm saying,' she cut in. 'Don't you go telling me what's best for me and Max. Could be the cruellest thing ever, crashing into his life now.'

'You'd do it well.' I couldn't give up my vision of him looking up from his chair and seeing her approaching. 'I'll make you a deal. I'll go to Dorset tomorrow if you'll go to Weston House tomorrow.'

# Twenty-seven

I didn't see Natalie again for two weeks. If I had thought about it at all, I would have assumed she had gone back to America but my head was pretty full of what was happening to me at Tideways. It had once been a Victorian biscuit tycoon's mansion. Now, in its gracious downstairs rooms and conservatories, fragile people recovered from the ravages of the chemical stormtroopers who had recently been violently expelled from the territory of their bodies.

Before you got that far, there was detox. The modern wing at the back of the house was detox and there it was explained to me that my heroin-free trip to Israel had been my first cold turkey, that I'd broken it in New York and that my system had been hit all the harder by the pasting I'd given it back in London. They were sympathetic, but oh so tough, these people who could look into your eyes as if they'd met you a hundred times before but still listen as if you were a brand-new friend.

I'd done it once, they said, so I could do it again and this time there would be help on hand to make sure I understood myself and understood *why* I did it so that I would not make that mistake again.

How was I supposed to know why I did it? I tried to tell them that maybe the answer lay in my inheritance, in the nature of my unknown father. That didn't cut the mustard as an excuse. They told me I had to take responsibility for my own life. They said that, okay, maybe you might inherit something from a parent that gave you a potentially addictive personality, but that was all it was – potential. It was you who took the decisions and unless I realized that, I couldn't hope to make real progress.

They encouraged me to write to my mother and I spent days, when the brain-pain allowed me, trying to form sentences that would make her respond. They didn't tell me that Natalie had been phoning every day but at the end of the detox, when I was

313

pleased with myself for surviving the physical hell of it with only a little recourse to the sham-heroin, the methadone that helped smooth out the very worst of it, then Frank, my main man, put his head round my door and said, 'You've got a visitor.'

'Who is it?'

'Mrs Vanderberg.'

'Natalie?'

'That's her.'

'She's the one who . . .'

He laughed. 'I know who she is. We've talked a great deal, her and me. She's been making sure we're looking after you properly.'

They'd put her in the orangery, which was warm and green and sunny and there was a tray of tea already there.

She stood up when I came in and looked at me with a smile on her face.

'That's a sight for sore eyes,' she said. 'Can this be the same Miles Malan?'

'No,' I said, 'I think it's starting to be a different one.'

She shook her head. 'Not too different, I hope. Don't lose all those good bits.'

'I'm not sure there were any.'

'You stop that right now,' she said. 'You've still got a whole lot of work to do here but I just happen to know that's all about learning to value yourself. People only take responsibility for what they value and what you were doing before was not responsible. You're a lucky guy, Miles. You've got a whole lot to value.'

'Have you been to see Max?'

'I keep my bargains,' she said. 'You've done your bit. I've done mine.'

'Go on.' My pulse, which had been erratic right through detox, racing at random to give the disturbing illusion of panic, began its tricks again now, though for once it had a reason.

'I'll tell you in the car,' she said.

'Where are we going?' The thought of leaving Tideways was terrifying. 'I thought I had two more weeks? I don't think I'm ready for . . .'

'Don't panic,' she said. 'This is just a day-trip. We'll come straight back.'

'Straight back from where?'

'London,' she said. 'You're going to meet Max.'

We were driven to London in a Jaguar with a smart chauffeur.

'What do you think?' she said as we settled in to the seats. 'Pretty swish, yeah? These concert people, they always do me proud in London.'

'Natalie, I promised that photographer woman, Sam Bishop, I wouldn't go and see him.'

'Forget it. That was just your excuse. You tell me what rights Sam Bishop has over Max that I don't have, eh? I never even heard of her.'

We drove on in silence for a mile or two.

'What's the place like inside?' I said.

'It's okay. Good nurses. Kind people, though maybe they're a little familiar with their patients. I'm not too sure Max likes that. He has a big room all to himself with his photographs up on the wall. They take him to the day room where it's warm for him to sit in the daytime and there's music playing in the background. Tacky, I guess, but quiet.' She seemed to be avoiding all the main points.

'What did he say to you?'

'Miles, Max doesn't say too much these days.' She was looking at me as if this news might be more painful to me than to her. 'Three strokes. He's pretty stiff all down one side. Sure, he tries to talk and sometimes it's quite clear but most of the time you can't make it out.'

'But he knew who you were?'

She shook her head. 'I don't know that he did. He was more interested in the nurse and his cocoa. He still likes cocoa. He gave me a little smile like I was some nice joke they were playing on him.'

I only realized then what I had put her through and I reached out and squeezed her hand. She took mine and gripped it.

'He's as happy as he can be,' she said. 'It's no good hoping for more than that. *Sauve qui peut,* as the French would say. I had it in mind that if the place wasn't right I might find him somewhere else, but that would not be kind and Doug still comes up from Wales every month to see him, or so they tell me.'

'So that's it?'

'Yup. Don't finish up like him, Miles.' She closed her eyes for a moment.

'Thank you for going.'

She smiled. 'Now it's your turn,' she said.

'Why do I have to go?'

'Because you need to find a way to give up your obsession with Max so that you have more room to look at yourself.'

'Why will seeing him help me do that?'

'Maybe you'll know that after you see him,' she said. 'I would not want to pre-judge the issue but I think you may suddenly see that he is a separate person, not some vital part of your own life. I hope so, anyway. It's time to put him to rest, Miles, him and Ginny and everything in that damned trunk. You need all your energy for yourself.'

'I think I'm in too deep for that. I know so much about him and yet I don't know nearly enough.'

'You don't give up, do you?' she said, and the rest of the way she just talked about general things, music, London, her concert and so on until we swept up Ladbroke Grove and wound our way through the side-roads to a smooth halt outside Weston House.

A woman with a badge saying 'Ruth Steele, Senior Nursing Sister' met us at the door.

'I've put him in the visits room,' she said, 'so you can have a bit of peace and quiet. Would you like tea or coffee?'

What a moment that was, coming in through the door with my eyes wide open, intent on my first sight of the real Max, awed and nervous and thrilled-sick.

There was just an old man in an armchair in the room, and he looked like Max's grandfather, not like Max. He sat leaning sideways with his head propped against the wing of the chair and his eyes flicked up to us as we came in, then down again, but he moved his head a little and seemed to become slightly agitated.

'Hello Max, it's Natalie,' she said, and waited a second. He looked quickly up at her and a little smile crossed his face. He made a noise. 'I've brought a friend to see you.'

He looked at her again, not at me, and said, 'Is it nice out?' in a slurring voice, then something I couldn't understand. The voice

316

was higher and lighter than I had expected and it turned me inside out. This was not the voice I had heard in my head when I had read Max's written words. I wondered if it was the voice that had got me in through the barrier at Brighton more than a decade earlier. The unexpected voice declared him to be a stranger to me, not a neat match to my mental image.

'It's not at all nice out,' said Natalie. 'You're much better off being warm and cosy in here.'

'Cosy' got me. Cosy was what she had offered him in the mews flat they could have shared. Cosy was what he had turned down and, in turning it down, had set his course for this inevitable place.

Then he twitched his head round to look at me and looked away. Perhaps his muscle control had been affected by the strokes or perhaps he just didn't need to take in the outside world for very long at a time. I hoped he was living in a dream and that his fantasies were still there to console him because I couldn't see that there was anything else on offer in this kind, tedious place of comfortable containment.

'This is Miles,' Natalie said. 'I wanted him to meet you, Max. He's a bit of a fan of yours.'

I don't know why she said that. It sounded all wrong. It could only open up all kinds of upsetting avenues, but she had spent more time with him in this reduced form than I had and I suppose she knew there was no likelihood of sustained conversation.

He tried to hold out a wavering hand. 'Birkin Owen,' he said quite precisely.

I intercepted his hand. It was light and warm and dry and it didn't curl into mine in the way a handshake should, so I held it for a moment as if I was cupping a bird in my palm then gently laid it down on his knee.

'Miles Malan,' I said.

His eyes flicked back to mine and I saw a link established for just a brief second that showed he was still there, deep inside.

'Malan?' he said with surprising vigour. 'You're dead.'

Natalie broke in, 'Oh, come now Max, don't say things like that. Miles has come a long way to see you.'

He waved an impatient hand, rocked his head back and forth and said something quite long and completely indistinct, then he turned his gaze briefly back to mine and said with great clarity and force, 'Malan and bloody Drummond.'

I couldn't say a word. I just stared at him. How could he link the names of Malan and Drummond, my father and my stepfather? How could those two names come from his mouth in the same sentence? Natalie didn't react because I suppose she'd never heard the name Drummond connected to me. There was saliva dribbling from his mouth and she reached forward to mop it with a tissue. I could see that irritated him. He said something, got cross with himself and tried to say it again. I couldn't make it out. I got it the fourth or fifth time because he clearly wasn't going to stop until he got it out.

'The hip flask hero,' was what he was trying so hard to say.

I said it for him: 'The hip flask hero?' in a questioning voice, and he gave a small smile and leant his head back, victorious. I must have made a noise because suddenly Natalie was looking at me with a concerned expression.

As soon as we got back in the car, Natalie was desperate to know what mysterious thing had passed between us and I was equally desperate to sort it out in rational words.

'I saw your face,' she said. 'What did it mean?'

'There's this story Max wrote,' I said. 'It was about smuggling cars back to England. I think you were in it, but the first page wasn't there.' I told her how it went and about the end of it when Major Sharp, who had it in for Max, had caught him red-handed and was about to haul him up before Colonel Ladd. I told her how fate intervened when Max found the naked, drunken Melanie Chester crawling out of Sharp's window.

'I can't remember exactly what happened next,' I said. 'I think Max called Sharp the hip flask hero or was it the other one, Chester?'

'It doesn't mean anything,' said Natalie reassuringly.

'It *does*,' I said. 'He heard my name, Malan, and he said the name Drummond which is the Colonel's name, my stepfather's name – the name I was brought up with for God's sake – then he said "hip flask hero". Of course it means something. The story was about them, about the Colonel and my real father. I *know* the Colonel knew Max somehow.'

'He did?'

'I *told* you. When I was little. He used "Birkin Owen" like a swear-word.'

'Yes,' she said. 'This story about the hip flask hero. Is it at your flat?'

'I suppose so, but I haven't got my key. I left it at Tideways.'

'I have one,' she said.

I knew why she had one when I got there. She hadn't just bought furniture, she'd had it repainted too, as if to remove the stains of the life I had been living there. We went in as the chauffeur waited outside and with the generous light of all the new standard lamps reflecting off bright, white walls I found the manuscript.

'Here we are, listen to this. It starts in mid-sentence . . . *departure was delayed by the after-effects of a night spent well but not wisely. This saw us emerge, blinking, on the streets of Geneva, to get our unlikely convoy under way again. The tank transporters had been too large to bring into the centre of the town* . . . That was you, wasn't it? You were with them that night?'

'Probably.'

I read the rest of the story to her and she laughed at the antics of Private Archer and the incorruptible Brooks, then I came to the bit that was suddenly the only part that really mattered.

*I was immediately hauled up in front of a man I had better call Major Sharp in the light of what subsequently happened. The Major and I were not on good terms. He had a low opinion of me in every way and this was an opinion he had frequently shared with Colonel Ladd. It was quite clear from the look in his eyes that he saw this as my final downfall and to say he was gloating was an understatement. He was a man I had first crossed one night in the Mess when I had referred to him, as I was wont to do, as 'the hip flask hero' without realizing he was standing directly behind me until the hush that instantly fell tipped me off that something was terribly wrong.*

*The Major had come to us accompanied by many stories of bravery, but bitterness had overcome him after an injury prevented him from taking a further active part in the war. Alcohol and anger provided the outlet for his feelings. I could sympathize with the injury and* the enforced rest it had earned him, having suffered the same myself, but I could not sympathize with the rest of it, and we were destined not to get on.

On this occasion the Major informed me with great satisfaction that as soon as Colonel Ladd returned on the morrow, I would be on the carpet in front of him. That is undoubtedly what would have happened but for the extraordinary events of that night.

It happened that the Major's accommodation was almost next to mine and it also happened that for some weeks the Major had been conducting an illicit liaison with the most dangerous woman within miles of the barracks. Melanie Chester, as I shall call her because that has a certain relevance to her physique, was already married to a fellow officer whose credentials as a true hero of several theatres of war were undeniable. It was often said that he was mad rather than just suicidally brave and he and his wife were both very, very fond of a strong drink. In his case, it was the fuel which propelled him to his absurd acts. In her case it was probably the only way she could have any contact with him that made sense.

Somehow the Major had stepped into the middle of this dangerous pair as a third element while Chester was away on active service. The first clear evidence of this arrived fortuitously on my doorstep that very night, when, alerted by the breaking of glass and someone trying to stifle a drunken giggle, I went outside to find Melanie, in the magnificence of totally inebriated nudity, having climbed out of the Major's window while the Major inside was doing his best to haul her back in.

I rose to the occasion, seeing lights coming on elsewhere and also seeing an opportunity to sort out my own little problem. Melanie was hidden in my room with a gag in her mouth and then spirited away to safety by a route that I had used for not dissimilar purposes on many occasions.

Strangely, the entire affair of the tank transporters was forgotten in the cold light of dawn and the Major was himself seen driving a sheeted load out of the camp, following a map I had drawn for him.

'I'm not clear on this,' Natalie said. 'You think this Major Sharp was really Malan, your father?'

'No. Major Sharp was my stepfather, Colonel Drummond,

though I suppose he was only a major at the time. Listen to the last bit. It all becomes clear.'

I read on:

*There was, oddly enough, a postscript to this story. Some years later, walking up the Strand with a friend who had also served with me, I saw the Major, a shadow of his former confident self, walking down the opposite pavement wearing a face that would have curdled milk.*

*'Good heavens,' I said, 'who would have believed it?' And learnt from my friend that, after a highly dubious confrontation in which Chester the gallant hero had managed to shoot himself rather than the Major, probably by mistake, the Major had wound up marrying 'Melanie' out of some misplaced sense of decency and was dedicating his life to the almost impossible task of keeping her off the booze and on the straight and narrow. There was a certain satisfaction in hearing this and reflecting that out of all the tight spots I have ever been in, providence has rarely come to my rescue quite so dramatically.*

'So are you telling me that Chester was Malan?'

'Yes,' I said, with complete certainty.

'So that means Melanie Chester was your *mother*, and the Colonel married her after your father died?'

'After he got shot, yes.'

'Jesus, Miles. I brought you down here to make things simpler. What have I done?'

'What you've done is helped to answer some *real* questions – ones I've wanted answered my whole life.'

Natalie was putting it together in her head. 'So your real father and your stepfather *and* your mother were all pretty wild once.'

I thought of that dry, tight woman and had huge trouble linking her to Melanie Chester. The truth was I had only just realized what the dreadful pun meant, and it felt very distasteful.

'Do you believe him?' asked Natalie.

That was the big question and the big let-out. Disbelieving Max was never more tempting. His story robbed me of the father I wanted. It gave me a hero but a flawed, violent hero. It made the Colonel into a sort of hero, a man who had overcome his own vices and kept my mother in line.

'Yes,' I said. I thought of all those odd, bottled-up moments at Oakdean when the far-off tensions behind closed doors had seemed to press on my ears. I thought of my mother's cut-off life, the absolute absence of alcohol from the house, and I saw for the first time why the Colonel had striven to keep it all so quiet. 'Yes, I do believe it.'

'Did you have any idea that your father died in a shooting incident?'

'No.'

'Write to her, Miles. I think you've earned the right to know.'

'Yes. It's time to face the facts.'

She clapped her hands. 'Bravo! That's what I wanted to hear. I was just going to ask you about that.'

'How do you mean?'

'That was what today was all about. You know what I tried to do with Max? I tried to make him give up his fantasy. That was selfish. He needed it more than he needed me.'

'Natalie. He made a mistake. Look at him now.'

'We can't be sure of that. I think maybe he's still living it all, in there, inside his head and, you know it hurts to say this, but maybe he's better off that way.'

'He can't be.'

'He can be. That's what I'm asking you, Miles. Do you prefer fantasy or truth? Because if you prefer fantasy, I don't want to make the same mistake twice.'

'What does choosing truth involve?'

'Setting aside Max and all his works. Just looking at who you are and where you come from. Taking responsibility for yourself.'

'I think I've already chosen that.'

'I think you have.'

Then, for the rest of the journey back to Dorset, maybe because I was no longer demanding it from her, she told me what *she* had known of Max.

'It was always like a battle,' she said. 'When it was just us, him and me, I could see right through to his soul. He had this way of looking at you that left you feeling you were the only other person in the whole world.'

'That's a good trick.'

'It wasn't a trick. It was real for him while it lasted and it was more than real for me. It was the best thing that ever happened to me.

322

During those times I have never loved anybody more. I thought I knew who he was, then.'

'Only thought?'

'He was promiscuous. Not physically – I think he could be quite faithful for very short periods. He was emotionally promiscuous. He needed to be loved by everybody so he tried to be whatever they most needed. I only knew that when there were other people around. Sharing him was always upsetting because he would turn into some strange chameleon creature. I couldn't keep up with that, especially when I knew he was looking into their eyes, too.'

'You said it was always a battle?'

'I thought I was fighting to save him. I thought that it could only end badly for him if he went on like that. I thought if I could show him I didn't need any of his fantasies to be true then he could throw them off and be cleansed. I was wrong.'

'You don't know that. You only know he didn't do it. You don't know that he *couldn't*. There's a difference.'

'What matters is what happened. I've told you that before, Miles. What matters is the letter he sent me, not the one he didn't send.'

'He didn't know what he missed.'

'Well, that's the worst of it. I think he did know and he still chose to miss it.'

I hadn't heard such sadness in her voice before so I gave her a big hug and she took a minute or two to recover herself.

'I want you to understand one thing,' she said in the end. 'I didn't go to see him for his sake or for mine. I went for you, because that was one way to get you into treatment. I took you there today for your own sake as well. I never expected it to turn out the way it did, but that aside, is he really someone who deserves all that time and emotion you've put into him?'

'I'm glad I did. You can't make me say I'm not.'

'I wouldn't try, but would you at least agree it's time to stop now?'

'Maybe.'

'You're two weeks into rebuilding your life, Miles. You're just starting out. Don't let me push you. Make it a deliberate choice. Don't go rushing it.'

'I don't know where I'm going, Natalie.'

'You will, Miles. By the time you leave here, you'll have an idea and that will be a start. You'll make it.'

'How do you know?'

'I can already see what's there. You just need to stop running away from yourself.'

'What photographs were there?'

'Say again?'

'You said his photographs were hanging in his room. What were they?'

'Still on the trail?'

'I'd just like to know that.'

She thought. 'There was Max skiing and Max driving some car. There was Doug with Ginny. There was Wallis and Max together in the snow at Kitzbühl, things like that.'

'Were you there?'

'Miles, that's for me to know and for you to forget about.'

'Natalie, I'm sorry if this has hurt you.'

'Just make it worth my while,' she said. 'I'm going to keep a close eye on you.'

# Twenty-eight

Smoke climbs into the windless sky from the place where the shingle meets the road. It rises in a thin column from its base where a furnace blazes, consuming something that was precious. From near this spot, a small boy ran away with the devil at his heels, but now a man stands his ground and stares at the fire.

This is the closing of a chapter because last week, in her house in the Berkshires, Natalie Vanderberg came to her end. We had fifteen years of unstinting friendship from that moment when she made me face myself. I was with her for the last month of her life and it was a privilege to help to nurse her through the painful last stages of the illness that was killing her. She appreciated the irony in the fact that it was morphine, respectable sister to that deadly tart heroin, which kept her going and which, when it all got too much, helped her out of it. Until the very last day, she was the same Natalie, wise, sweet and funny.

'Miles,' she said as she took her painkillers, 'if I'd known it was this good, I'd never have tried to stop you.'

We had seen each other at least twice a year and sometimes three or four times in every one of those fifteen years. She was godmother to my first son and best friend to Louisa, my wife, and the whole family had enjoyed wonderful weeks with her at Rotherham in the spring and in the fall. She always called my children her grandchildren. She set me on the road to somewhere in the weeks after I left the big old house in Dorset by using her network of friends to let me try out things, music, museums, archaeology and boat-building. She drove me on to put together the perfect phrases for the letter to my mother, glossing over the most painful points of Max's revelation. It took a long time to get it to the point where I knew it was ready to be sent but finally, after a heart-in-mouth wait of three weeks, it elicited a most surprising reply. When I rang Natalie in America to try to read her that reply, she told me she wanted to read it with me, and by the next morning she had an air ticket waiting for me at Heathrow.

A car took me from JFK to Rotherham and I sat there on the sundeck next to her, with birds singing in the garden, and read her what my mother had written.

Dear Miles,

I cannot say it was a pleasant surprise to receive your letter containing your account of the vile life you have been living or to have to address the strange questions you ask in it. I do not remember anything about this man Birkin Owen other than the fact that your father had no time for him at all. I suspect from what you say in your letter that there may be other allegations that you have omitted to pass on to me. I believe the man Birkin Owen was a liar through and through and therefore, you should disregard his account.

I have found it very hard to forgive the ridiculous affectation by which you have taken the surname of my first husband, Peter Malan. I see no need to spell out any details to you under the circumstances but he was not good to me and it was a merciful release when he died as a result of an ill-considered prank.

You ask me whether I ever had 'problems with alcohol'. I find this high-handed, I must say, considering your own recent history. You know absolutely nothing of the conditions in which we had to live during the war and its aftermath, never knowing for a moment what the future held for us.

Your father, and by that I mean Gordon Drummond who adopted you and *not* Peter Malan, was a great help to me throughout our life together and would have been an equally great help to you, had you allowed him to be instead of repaying his support with a form of behaviour which shocked him to the core.

I have decided to tell you something which no one else on earth knows, in order to bring home to you the full extent of your ingratitude to him. Colonel Drummond was not only your adopted father, he was your real father. He and I formed

326

our first attachment during a very, very bad period in my marriage to Peter Malan, who was a man capable of great cruelty and violence. I did not tell Gordon at the time because of my concern at the likely result of doing so. Later on, in the light of what happened to Malan, it was better that no one should know.

I only tell you this now because I cannot bear to think of you calling yourself by a name which I hate and to which you have no right at all. I do not expect gratitude or understanding from you because you have never shown signs of either of those. I intend to live a peaceful life here and would be glad if you would never again pester me with such a letter.

At the end, when I was wondering if I felt like crying or not, Natalie said soothing things and then looked on, mildly astonished, when I found the feeling in my head wasn't tears but laughter. I shook my head and laughed at the irony of it all and after a while she couldn't help joining in.

'That's a truly maternal letter, Miles,' she said. 'Who could have asked for more sympathy?'

That set us both off again.

'I had a father all the time,' I said, 'and he didn't know and I didn't know and now she's blaming me for not guessing or something.' Then I found I was crying after all.

Now, for the first time with Natalie's death, I feel I really have lost a parent, or perhaps a much older sister. Today I went and stood by my father's gravestone in the Worthing cemetery and wondered if it would have made much difference for me to have known. It might have been just as awkward. There was no way of telling.

I would have liked to try.

What I came to by myself in the end, after all the experiments with life that Natalie made possible, was a discovery that there was something I really wanted to do. It was where she'd started the process off for me, in drug rehab work with teenagers in trouble, and that is where I have spent my years. For the last two years of her life, she helped me plan a new residential centre to let me try out my own ideas using music and art as a key part of the therapy. It is my intention that in our new building, wherever it may be, there will be a quiet, airy room, an orangery, where Natalie's cello music will always be playing. Last week, in her will, she left her entire estate to me, to set up a foundation to bring that dream about and in that will she told me to look for all the other varieties of Miles and of Max.

Tiggy married a comfortable husband. They came to my wedding and she was sweetly nice to Louisa.

And what of Max? He lasted only a few months after Natalie went to see him. She had left her address at Weston House and Douglas wrote to her to tell her the news. He died quietly and there was a cremation with Douglas by himself at the front of the chapel and me at the back. He gave me one puzzled look and probably decided I was a member of the crematorium staff. I don't know if Max felt alone at his end. I hope there were people he knew well enough at Weston House to make it feel otherwise.

When Natalie rang me with the news, she was more concerned with how I would feel.

'Don't go blaming yourself, Miles. You came along at least ten years too late to put us back together again. Anyway, it would have been a blind date. If he didn't know who he really was, how was I meant to?'

I'm not sure I ever got a satisfactory set of bearings on him. The cocked hat he inhabited was always very wide. That's the trouble with bearings. You may think you've got someone pinned down, but all you really ever know for sure is that, looking back the other way, you'll find yourself.

I have hauled out the trunk from time to time, mostly to explain this or that to Louisa, who viewed it with tolerant interest. Max had one last little trick to play, long after I thought I had looked at everything in it a million times and there was nothing more but the newspapers lining it. Nothing more indeed. The newspapers weren't the lining, they were part of the whole dusty archive. They were a mixture of different papers, copies of the English *Weekly Graphic* from the early 1950s as well as various American regional papers from Boston, Detroit, Cleveland and several other cities.

They had one thing in common. In each of them was an episode of *The Love that Rocked a Throne*, billed as 'the enthralling inside story of the abdication and what followed by a close friend and confidante of the Duke and Duchess of Windsor, Grenadier Guards officer, Captain Max Birkin Owen'.

There were revealing differences between the English and the American versions of the same episodes. Secure in the knowledge that he was unlikely to be found out in Milwaukee or Philadelphia, Max made wilder claims about their relationship in those versions than he did in the English press. This was the indiscretion which had gone down badly with the Grenadier Guards.

One paragraph in part seven of the series pulled the rug out from under another of my favourite stories:

*A story that the Duke is still very fond of relating concerns the time when we were involved in the ceremonies around the reinstatement of the statue of Edward VII on the Croisette at Cannes, which had been thrown into the harbour by Italian troops during the war.*

*We had dredged it out and replaced it on its plinth where it belonged and the Duke was to do the honours at the formal unveiling ceremony. The senior naval officer, a four-ringed Captain RN, chose a guard of honour from a submarine flotilla which was visiting Cannes.*

*I arrived ahead of the Duke to see that arrangements for his reception were going according to plan. As I walked towards the guard, the senior naval officer drew up the guard in salute. Because of the 'Guards brass' on my hat, he had mistaken me from a distance for the Duke himself . . .*

Knowing Max, I should never have believed it for a minute and then, knowing Max, perhaps I shouldn't have minded being led up the garden path for a bit of harmless fun.

Now Natalie has gone and the rest of my life begins and, recognizing exactly why she has asked it, I am bowing to the other request she made in her will. Above my head, the column of smoke climbs into the still air from the fire on the shingle, as close to the playground as I can get, as I feed the flames with the last of the papers and the photographs, giving Max's many lives the funeral they deserve.